"Sit down, Emily. We'll have a reunion."

Nick took a noisy slurp from one mug, passed her the other, then flung his left arm across the back of the couch and looked at her. "There. Isn't this nice? Two old friends, renewing their relationship. What could be better?"

"Almost anything," she said drily. "It's two-thirty in the morning and in case you've forgotten, we were never friends. We didn't even know each other."

Nonplussed, Nick wagged his forefinger at her. "Ah, but we might have been—if you hadn't been so standoffish in the old days." His smile widened. "As a matter of fact, I've been wondering for ten years what you'd be like in bed."

MELINDA CROSS would love her readers to believe she was kidnapped as a child by an obscure nomadic tribe and rescued by a dashing adventurer. Actually, though, she is a wonderfully imaginative American writer who is married to a true romantic. Every spring, without fail, when the apple orchard blooms, her husband gathers a blanket, glasses and wine and leads Melinda out to enjoy the fragrant night air. Romantic fantasy? Nonsense, she says. This is the stuff of real life.

Books by Melinda Cross

HARLEQUIN PRESENTS

Don't miss any of our special offers. Write to us at the following address for information on our newest releases.

Harlequin Reader Service
P.O. Box 1397, Buffalo, NY 14240
Canadian address: P.O. Box 603,
Fort Erie, Ont. L2A 5X3

MELINDA CROSS

pulse of the heartland

Harlequin Books

TORONTO • NEW YORK • LONDON
AMSTERDAM • PARIS • SYDNEY • HAMBURG
STOCKHOLM • ATHENS • TOKYO • MILAN

Harlequin Presents first edition July 1991
ISBN 0-373-11375-7

Original hardcover edition published in 1990
by Mills & Boon Limited

PULSE OF THE HEARTLAND

CHAPTER ONE

EMILY could smell the gardenias even before she was halfway down the narrow steps that led from her apartment to the flower shop below. In another week the glossy green plants would be in full bloom, sending their sweet, exotic fragrance all the way up the stairs to perfume her living quarters. It was one of the things she loved most about her little apartment, hot as it had been lately—it always smelled like a garden.

With efficient movements that had become automatic over the years, she unlocked the door at the bottom of the stairs, entered the back workroom, and snatched a green cotton overall from a hook on the wall. It was one more unwelcome garment in the unseasonable May heat, buttoning up the front from knees to neck, but at least it allowed her the freedom of wearing abbreviated shorts and a skimpy tank-top beneath—an outfit that would have raised every brow in the tiny Minnesota farming town of Random, no matter how high the temperature rose. It just wasn't the sort of thing they would expect to see on the body of their sedate, conservative florist. As a matter of fact, there were times when Emily wondered if anyone ever credited her with having a body at all.

She smoothed her closely cut blonde hair back behind her ears, thinking that it was almost time to have it trimmed again. Wispy, frivolous bangs were threatening to brush her pale brows, and frivolity was one thing she simply could not abide, especially when it came to the way she looked. For all of her twenty-seven years, Emily Swenson's appearance had reflected her philosophy and her life—busy, hard-working, and earnest. She kept her hair painfully short to save the minutes a longer length would have required, her clothing simple, and her make-up to a minimum. That any trace of vulnerability managed to survive such a presentation was a credit to her classically feminine features—a small, straight nose, a full, irrepressibly sensual mouth, and large, thickly lashed eyes. Mossy green eyes, 'just about the same colour as the algae on my stock pond', old Martin Tollefson had told her once in a backhanded compliment.

She smiled every time she remembered that, and this morning was no different, but even a smile did little to soften the underlying sternness in her face, a sternness conceived in her farming heritage, and honed by the growing years she'd spent working side by side with her father on the family farm. While other young girls had been giggling at slumber parties and exchanging the baffling secrets of burgeoning femininity, Emily had been tossing hay bales and ploughing fields, developing a decidedly unfeminine musculature. It hadn't been much of a childhood for a young girl—forever trying to match the work output of the sons her parents had never had—but Emily had no regrets. It had made her strong.

Was it attitude that shaped the way you looked, or the other way around? she wondered as she peered into the tiny mirror nailed to the back of the door. Whatever the cause, she had earned the somehow cruel nickname of Earnest Emily way back in school, and, although she hated it, even she had to admit that the label was appropriate. She *was* earnest, and so she *looked* earnest, and if the truth be told there wasn't anything wrong with that. Besides, she remembered with some satisfaction, no one had ever called her that to her face—at least not more than once.

Remembering the old nickname irritated her, and she jerked her head away from the mirror and turned to survey the small room, hands on hips.

Tall, glass-doored coolers lined two walls, and a series of huge wooden work-tables took up the rest of the floor space. The end cooler was literally stuffed with deep purple irises, and it was there that she headed first, removing an enormous armful that she cradled like a baby. Her nose automatically buried itself in the bouquet, searching for a fragrance that she knew refrigeration had already destroyed. It didn't seem right, somehow, that such a beautiful flower should be robbed of its scent; but then it didn't seem right that such a beautiful flower should be associated with sadness, either. And yet that was the way it was in the farming states of America's Midwest—the iris and the gladiolus were traditional funeral flowers, seldom used for any other purpose, because the association with death was so strong.

'And that's too bad,' Emily murmured aloud, almost feeling sorry for the flowers she held, because they were destined to celebrate sorrow, never joy, and that was a poor fate for anything—even a flower.

She shifted the bouquet to one arm and bumped her hip against the swinging door that led to the shop proper. Whenever she could, she preferred to work out here, standing at the long formica counter that ran the length of the back wall, facing the plate-glass windows that looked out on to Random's Main Street. There were dust circles on the windows already, she noticed with a frown, even though she'd just washed them two days earlier.

The shop was an extension of Emily's ordered mind, with cylindrical stands of white plastic for displaying plants and pottery, stark white walls, and crisp green and white tiles on the floor. One's first impression of the shop was cleanliness; the second was coolness—a decided advantage during heat spells like this one.

She laid the irises down on the counter, then went to unlock the front door and flip over the 'open' sign.

Less than ten minutes later the little bell over the door tinkled and Emily glanced up from the spray she was arranging. A tall, raw-boned man entered, whipped a battered straw hat from his head, and approached the counter with that tell-tale shuffle peculiar to farmers in this part of the country. He was as out of place in the shop as any man could have been, in faded blue overalls, heavy boots, and a long-sleeved shirt that made Emily hot just to look at it. A gloriously thick shock of pure white hair topped his head, and his face was as weathered and wrinkled as old leather. Bright blue eyes winked out from the folds of ageing skin around them. 'Morning, Em.'

Emily placed one hand on her chest and feigned surprise. 'Martin Tollefson in a flower shop? I don't believe it!'

He ducked his head with a sheepish grin and turned his hat in his hands. 'Don't think I've been through that door since you opened this place. No need, really. Seemed simpler just to call.'

Emily flashed a brief smile across the counter, then looked back down at her work. Every year Martin ordered a dozen anniversary roses for his wife, but always by phone. 'I heard your whole family is gathering for the celebration this year, Martin.'

'Every one of the kids will be here,' he nodded proudly. 'Bobby and his brood are coming up from Tennessee, Sarah's coming from California, and the twins are flying in from New York. First time in years we'll have all the grandchildren under the roof at one time, and Harriet's just about fit to be tied, she's so excited. Don't know how she'll get through the next couple of weeks, waiting for it.'

'June the fifth, right?'

'Hey,' Martin sounded pleased, 'you remembered.' There was a brief silence, then his boots shuffled self-consciously on the tiled floor. 'I want it to be special this year, Emily.' His voice quivered with a timidity that made her look up curiously. Martin Tollefson was never timid, any more than any other farmer in this township. Certainty, pride, dominance—these were the earmarks of the breed of man who worked this land; timidity was the sole province of their wives.

'Fifty years married to the same woman,' he went on, his expression almost wistful. 'It ought to be special. It still has to be roses, of course. Harriet does love her anniversary roses, but I thought if I gave you enough lead time you might be able to get in some of those tiny ones, so I could put a bunch in every room.'

Emily paused in her work and looked at the old man with something like wonder. Harriet Tollefson was as surely under her husband's thumb as any other farm wife in Random. Relationships were biscuit-cutter duplicates out here…and yet…there was something odd in the old man's voice when he spoke his wife's name. Something undeniably romantic, and very nearly reverent. Extraordinary, she mused. Fifty years, and he still wanted to fill the house with roses for his wife. Maybe the Tollefsons did have something different; something a little more special than all the other farming couples who made up the populace of Random.

'I'll take care of it, Martin,' she said quietly, and something in her gaze made the old seamed face colour from the bottom up, as if they'd just shared something extraordinarily intimate.

'Well,' he hedged, looking around uncomfortably, his gaze finally settling on the spray of irises she was arranging. 'Guess I probably didn't pick the best day to drop in. Looks like you got your hands full.' He nodded down at the flowers. 'Those for Art Simon?'

Emily nodded, her expression properly sombre.

'Well, he was a good man. The town'll miss him. Too bad he had to go so young.'

She had to suppress a smile as Martin turned and left the shop. Art Simon had been a month past his ninety-fifth birthday when he'd died three days ago.

Maybe when she was seventy-eight, as Martin was now, ninety-five would sound young to her, too.

She spent the rest of the morning alone in the shop, putting together the many arrangements that had been ordered for Art's funeral. One by one, vases and sprays and bouquets of irises and gladioli took their place by the front door, waiting for Sam Beckett, the funeral director, to pick them up. She was just tying together the last bunch when the bell over the door jangled for the second time that morning.

'You're early, Sam,' she said without looking up, 'but this is the last one. Ready in a minute.'

There was the soft, muffled squeak of tennis shoes coming to an abrupt stop on the tiles just inside the door, and she knew then that it wasn't Sam. Sam never wore anything but proper shoes.

Emily raised her head with the expression of polite interest she reserved for people she didn't know well, and squinted towards the door. The shadow of a man stood against the backlight of the glass, frozen for a moment in a posture that made her think of a tennis player waiting to receive a serve.

'Can I help you?'

His head tipped at her voice, as if to hear her better. 'Well I'll be damned,' he said after a moment. 'It's you.' There was something familiar about the deep, mellow voice, but she couldn't place it.

'I beg your pardon?'

'It *is* Earnest Emily, isn't it?'

Her face stilled, then she lifted her chin defensively. No one had called her that since those awkward, painful school-days. It irritated her to suddenly hear the nickname again, as if her thoughts of the morning had somehow conjured it up.

'I'm busy,' she said shortly, fussing with the flowers on the counter, completely forgetting that whoever he was he was a potential customer.

'You were always busy, Emily.'

Damn, she knew that voice. She *knew* she did. It snaked across the room like oil on a hot skillet, slick and sure and maddeningly deep, a curious cross between mockery and playfulness . . .

Her head jerked up and her eyes narrowed. 'Nick?'

As if he'd only been waiting to be recognised, he snapped from immobility and approached the counter with that jaunty, confident stride that was so uniquely his; she had never to this day seen one remotely like it. Thank heaven. She'd never liked Nicholas Simon. Not in gradeschool, not in high school, and she probably wouldn't like him as an adult, either. He'd always been in the centre of that high-popularity clique of star athletes and giddy cheerleaders, and even from a distance she'd always thought he exemplified the shallowness of those who worried more about the location of the next party than the harsh realities of life.

And then, of course, there'd been that horrible scene right after the graduation ceremony. Right in front of the whole damn town, on a dare, no less, the most popular boy in school had grabbed the notoriously unapproachable Earnest Emily, and kissed her smack on the mouth. He'd probably forgotten the incident seconds after it had happened, but she still bristled with humiliation every time she recalled it.

She repressed those feelings out of consideration as he bounced towards her, even though she found it irritating that his step could be so light, today of all days. It was *his* grandfather who had died, after all. He could have at least had the decency to temper that cocky walk of his and *try* to look mournful.

In a startlingly neat hop he was perched on the counter, leaning towards her on the rigid brace of his right arm, one corner of his mouth lifted in a smile that seemed to mock the world. If his sudden closeness hadn't been enough to fluster her, his clothing—or lack of it—certainly was.

He wore faded, expensive jeans that lay across his thighs like a second skin, and a tank-top much like the one she was hiding beneath her florist coat—only he wasn't hiding his, or anything else, for that matter.

The powerful shoulders of a fully matured man rose from the slender black straps of the shirt, and, beneath it, the well-defined muscles of his chest pressed their outline into the thin fabric. He was broader, thicker, even taller than she remembered him, and the naked arm braced on the counter looked massive and masculine next to her own.

'Emily, Emily, Emily.' He shook his head slowly, and his thick, light hair echoed the movement a fraction of a beat later, quivering over his brow like the lazy waves of a golden ocean of wheat. There was new breadth to his square jaw, and Emily noted the shadow of a beard that would be several shades darker than his sun-bleached hair.

I'll bet empty-headed females *still* fall all over him, she thought with disdain, feeling wonderfully superior to be above such petty attractions.

As he watched her study him, a network of tiny lines appeared next to eyes the colour of a summer sky, eyes that still glittered with boyish mischief. Such eyes had no business in the face of a mature man, she decided.

'What on earth are you doing back here, Emily?'

'I'm not "back",' she said crisply, intent on letting him know that the exercise of his infamous charm would be lost on her. 'I never left.'

'You're kidding? You stayed in Random, all this time? You didn't go to college?'

'Obviously not.' She concentrated on aligning the flower stems, her lips primly pursed, her eyes narrowed.

'But that's crazy. You could have gone to any college in the country with your grades. Why on earth would you stay hidden away in a place like Random?'

She raised her head with a look of chilling condescension. 'I happen to like Random. It's my home.'

It was a stock answer, of course, and not quite the truth. The truth was, she wasn't sure why she stayed in this little one-horse town, with the lure of a city like Minneapolis less than two hundred miles away. Granted, there had been her mother's illness; but even Emily knew that was just an excuse. She hadn't made a bee-line for the city after the crisis was over, now had she? And that had been nearly nine years ago.

'I know what you mean,' Nick murmured, and she had to concentrate to remember what they'd been talking about. 'I regret leaving Random every time I come back.' He shrugged lightly. 'Don't know what it is, really. The land, maybe; the people, more likely. All those good old-fashioned country values you can't seem to find anywhere else.'

Emily grunted softly as she straightened a folded leaf on a particularly long stem. Country values, indeed. The people who lived here were always touting those, as if they went hand in hand with open fields and country air. 'No fifty per cent divorce rate in Random,' they were fond of saying, and Emily sometimes wondered if they believed broken marriages were a contagious disease of some sort, a city-bred virus that couldn't survive the crop-filled plains. She knew better, of course. If Random and other farm towns like it never saw divorce, it was because the women out here were born and bred to bow down to men, to accept a subservient role, as if that were the way Nature had intended it.

It was typical, she thought, that a man like Nick would see Random, a town filled with obedient women, as paradise.

'If you liked it here that much, why did you leave?' she asked sharply.

He sighed and shrugged, looking around the shop. 'I wanted to be a doctor. Big city practice, big city money, big city life...all the standard dreams, but now that I've got them...' He let the sentence trail away in a sheepish grin. 'Is this shop yours?'

'That's right.'

He stroked his chin thoughtfully with one finger as his jaw jutted forward. 'I suppose that makes sense. You always did love flowers, didn't you?'

She frowned, wondering how he had ever known such a thing.

He saw her expression and smiled. 'The school bus always dropped you off before me. I'd watch out of the back window as we pulled away, and every day during the summer you'd stop in the ditch at the end of your driveway to smell those wild black-eyed Susans, remember?'

Emily blinked at him, astounded that he had ever noticed—that *anyone* had ever noticed.

He chuckled at her astonishment. 'Used to drive me crazy. You were so tough in those days, so hard-nosed; no time for friends, no time for fun...' he paused and shook his head, remembering '... but you always found time to stop and look at those stupid flowers. I couldn't figure it out. It was such a *feminine* thing to do.'

Emily bristled a little. 'And in all other respects I wasn't the least bit feminine, right?'

His smile was almost apologetic. 'There weren't many girls in our class who could toss eighty-pound hay bales as far as a man. And speaking of that, who's doing all the muscle work for your dad, now that you're in business for yourself?'

'I can *still* toss my fair share of hay bales,' she said tightly, thinking that she could probably toss Nick Simon through a plate-glass window, too. 'But he doesn't need much help any more. He cut way back on farming when Mom got sick.'

His eyes were suddenly serious. 'Your mom is sick?'

She looked down at her work and shook her head impatiently. 'Not any more. She had a bout of meningitis the year we graduated——'

'Dear lord,' he whispered. 'Meningitis.'

'But she's all right now. Not as strong as she used to be, but otherwise OK.'

'She must have been laid up for a long time.'

'Over a year.'

He looked off to the side and shook his head. 'I'm sorry, Emily. I didn't know. It must have been a hard time.'

She lifted one shoulder in a dismissive shrug, then glanced up sharply when she heard his chuckle.

'Earnest Emily... still as tough as ever, aren't you?'

'Don't call me that!' she snapped with more vehemence than she had intended, her chin jutting forward like a spear aimed at his face.

'Hey,' he said quietly, raising both hands in surrender. His brows came together in the frown that had created the faint vertical line above his nose. 'Take it easy. It wasn't meant as an insult.' He cocked his head and looked at her for a moment, then added, 'Ever.'

Emily closed her eyes briefly and sighed, then reached beneath the counter for a length of violet florist's paper. She began to wrap the last bouquet of irises, forgetting that their destination didn't require it. 'I didn't mean to snap,' she mumbled down at the flowers. 'I just always hated that name.'

'Then I won't call you that,' he said in that same quiet tone. For some reason, she found an earnest Nick Simon far more disturbing than an ebullient one, but fortunately it wasn't a condition that lasted long. With an abruptness that gave her a start, he hopped down to the floor and faced her across the counter with an impudent grin the years hadn't altered. He certainly didn't look much like a doctor, she thought. Doctors were supposed to be dignified, weren't they? 'We'll start over,' he proclaimed, straightening to his full, considerable height, tipping his head in a mockery of a polite greeting. 'Well, if it isn't Emily Swenson, smartest girl in Random High. How are you, Emily? Nice to see you again. It's been almost ten years, hasn't it?' Suddenly the flip recitation stopped, and his eyes narrowed slightly. 'My God,' he whispered, 'I'd almost forgotten that spectacular figure of yours.'

Emily's eyes widened when she saw he was gazing openly at her bustline, and she felt the sudden, mortifying rush of colour to her face.

His smile was more like a leer, and for a moment she hardly knew how to react. He was mocking her, just as he'd mocked her with that impudent kiss ten years ago, but this time he'd made a mistake. She wasn't the naïve, gullible girl she'd been then. Now she knew how to strike back.

'Too bad you couldn't get back to see your grandfather *before* he died,' she sniped viciously, paying him back for a transgression that was ten years old.

His brows shot up instantly, and, although his smile remained stiffly in place, all the humour seemed to bleed from his eyes, leaving them a much lighter shade of blue. 'My, my,' he drawled. 'Age has certainly sharpened your claws, hasn't it?'

Emily frowned hard and looked down, regretting the cruelty of her words, even if he *had* deserved to hear them. 'I shouldn't have said that,' she muttered sullenly. 'Your relationship with your grandfather was none of my business, and even if——'

'Your hair's a lot shorter.'

While she was still trying to recover from the sudden change of subject, his forearms popped into her field of vision, bracing his weight against the counter, and she found herself staring at them as if she'd never seen a man's arms before. They were deeply tanned, the ridge of muscle running from wrist to elbow frosted with tiny golden hairs.

'I like it, all slicked back like that,' he went on, as if his grandfather's funeral, up-and-coming main attraction, had never been mentioned. 'It's very businesslike; very no-nonsense.' His mouth curved lazily. 'Very masculine. But the body gives you away, Emily. You couldn't hide it then, and you can't hide it now.'

Her lips pressed together like a door slamming shut. He hadn't changed a bit. He was still hustling anything with a pulse, still supremely confident that there wasn't a woman alive who could resist his charms.

'I told you before, Nick,' she said coldly, 'I'm busy. Now, if you want something, fine. If you don't, I suggest you go somewhere and get ready for your grandfather's funeral.'

He remained motionless for a moment, studying her face with quiet amusement, then he pushed away from the counter and straightened. It un-

nerved Emily a little to have to look up to meet his
gaze. 'You have daisies?' he asked.

'Of course I have daisies, but if you're thinking
of the funeral——'

'How many do you have on hand?'

The question caught her off guard. 'Well...I
don't know. I use them for filler, mostly. No one
actually orders *daisies* for anything, especially
around here. The fields are full of them——'

'How many?' he repeated, and for the first time
his voice was firm.

'Five dozen. Maybe six.'

'Good,' he nodded brusquely. 'Wrap them up
and send them over with those sorry things.' His
head jerked towards the mass of deep purple irises
by the door.

She opened her mouth to protest, then checked
his eyes and changed her mind. 'All right. What
shall I put on the card?'

His face shifted instantly to its old mocking
expression. 'Card? Now who on earth, Emily,
would read the card?' Then he turned away and
started towards the door.

Emily watched him go with a disapproving scowl,
thinking how perfectly awful, how disrespectful it
was to order something as gay and common as
daisies for his own grandfather's funeral. Still, when
his hand reached for the doorknob, she felt compelled to call after him. 'Nick?'

He froze, then looked over his shoulder.

'I liked your grandfather,' she said quietly.

'Thank you, Emily. So did I.'

CHAPTER TWO

IN A town of less than five hundred souls, almost everyone was at the very least a nodding acquaintance of everyone else. That was the extent of Emily's knowledge of Nicholas Simon's grandfather—she had known him well enough to exchange a greeting if they met on the street, but that was all. Still, in the long list of all Emily's nodding acquaintances in Random, Art Simon had occupied a special place. Without really knowing him at all, even she had realised that there was something special about the elderly gentleman. There would have to be, she thought wryly, for him to take in and raise an orphaned grandson like Nick.

Sprightly even in his nineties, Art had always been totally self-sufficient, still working a small section of his large farm right up until the day he died—on his tractor, she remembered, thinking that he would have wanted it that way.

In some parts of the country a man his age still working would have been a miracle—in the grain belt of the Midwest it was simply the way things were. A man worked until his last day, because the relationship with the land was something you didn't just turn your back on when you reached the age of sixty-five. It was a part of you, all the way to the grave.

But it wasn't just Art Simon's longevity that had touched the untouchable Emily. 'You're going to be a real beauty one day,' he'd told her at a community picnic when she was twelve and gangling and painfully shy, and even though she'd huffed and blustered, mortified in typical tomboy fashion that her looks had been noticed at all, she had never forgotten the kindness of his words.

She *had* liked him, she thought, as she dressed for the three o'clock funeral—just as she'd told Nick this morning—and then she felt a rush of sadness stronger than she had ever expected, because she wished she had known him better, and now her chance was gone.

Stupid, she derided herself as she pulled on an impossibly hot black dress and slipped into low heels. You barely knew the man, and you're more upset at his passing than his own grandson. The reminder of Nick's callousness made her angry all over again. Big city doctor with big city schedule or not, the least he could have done was spend more time with the old man. Although she'd heard a few times that Nick had visited—on holidays mostly— as far as she knew he had left Random and his grandfather ten years ago, with barely a backward glance.

'Ingrate,' she muttered aloud, beating back the uncomfortable, inexplicable grief for one stranger with contempt for another.

She buttoned her dress up to its high collar, jerked the belt tight, slicked her short light hair sideways up and away from her face, then left the stifling confines of her apartment.

Nick wasn't at the church. Everyone else in Random had come, including her own parents— she could see her father's broad shoulders and her mother's tiny form far ahead in one of the front pews—but Art Simon's only relative was conspicuously absent.

In spite of his apparent nonchalance earlier in the shop, Emily was still shocked by this gross breach of etiquette, this appalling lack of respect for the man who had raised him.

Later, after the last sombre words had been spoken in the town's lonely cemetery, she watched as they piled dozens and dozens of bright white and yellow daisies high over Art Simon's grave-site. They looked impossibly, irreverently gay, and entirely unsuitable in the gathering of black-clad mourners.

'Emily,' her mother's soft murmur came from directly behind her, and Emily's forced smile was automatic as she turned and bent at the waist to kiss her mother's cheek.

Such a tiny, helpless woman, she thought with a sigh, gazing into the green eyes so like her own. Totally subservient to her husband, in a way Emily would never be subservient to any man, by God; and yet so clearly adapted to that kind of existence.

Strong father, acquiescent mother—the standard description for farm-country marriages. Carl and Mary Swenson's roles had been defined long before Emily's birth, and she had decided early which example to follow.

Mary Swenson's brief, terribly debilitating illness had polarised the man-woman positions even further, of course. For the entire year that she had been bedridden, her husband had been fiercely protective, the epitome of masculine strength, coddling and cherishing his wife as if she'd been a helpless doll of some sort. The worst part was that, although the illness made it more visible, that was basically the way they had always related to one another. Emily idolised her father, and felt a tender, protective sort of love for her mother, but she still found the woman's willing submission to male dominance faintly repulsive. *She'd* certainly never fall victim to such archaic role-playing.

'How are you, Emily? You look tired.'

'Maybe just a little. The shop had a lot of orders for today.'

She looks so fragile in black, Emily thought; more like a toy woman than a real one. The green eyes were Mary Swenson's only genetic contribution to her tall, strong, fair-haired daughter. Her own hair was crow-wing black, curved softly around a china-pale face with petite, delicate features and a tiny rosebud mouth.

'You need to get away from the store for a while, dear. Why don't I take over for a week or so——?'

Emily was shaking her head before her mother could finish the sentence. 'Don't be silly. You have your hands full at the farm. Besides, what would I do?'

Her mother's face tightened a little, and something in the green eyes flashed. 'Go to the city. Stay in a ritzy hotel. Shop all day and dance all night. Have a little fun, for a change. Meet some new people...'

'A man, you mean. A nice, strong man who'll marry me and take care of me for the rest of my life.'

Mary looked at her steadily. 'I didn't say that.'

'Not this time,' Emily conceded, remembering all the times she *had* said it. Her mother refused to believe any woman could be happy outside the demanding circle of a man's attention. 'I keep telling you, Mom. I'm not like you. I don't want to be taken care of. And if I ever marry it will be to a man who understands that.'

She sighed and glanced around at the thinning crowd, looking for a way to change the subject. 'Poor Art,' she said finally, an undercurrent of sharp disapproval in her tone. 'His own grandson didn't even come.'

She could feel her mother's gaze on her profile. 'I doubt that Art noticed. Besides, funerals just aren't Nicky's style.'

'"Nicky"?' Emily parodied. 'I didn't know you knew him.'

Her mother turned to look back at the grave and shrugged mildly. 'Art talked about him all the time. I feel I know him.'

Emily's mouth turned down. 'He came into the shop this morning. He actually ordered all those daisies.'

Mary's smile was spontaneous, and not the least bit disapproving. Disgruntled that her mother found neither the daisies nor Nick's absence disturbing, Emily turned away and pretended an interest in the clusters of people who were finally moving away towards their cars. She caught sight of her father out on the road, leaning against the dusty side of his pick-up truck, waiting impatiently for his wife. He raised a long arm when he caught Emily's eye, signalling that he wanted to leave. Occasionally death intruded on the placid existence of Random's farming residents, but it never stopped life for long.

'Father wants you,' she said sullenly, knowing that those three words would always produce an immediate obedient response. Carl Swenson beckoned, his wife followed. Always.

'I suppose,' Mary sighed, turning to give her daughter a quick hug before she left. 'You know your father. An hour away from the fields is too much. Don't forget. You're coming out for dinner on Friday.'

'Six o'clock,' Emily promised, then watched her mother walk away towards the man who controlled her life—the man who *was* her life. Never, never, never, she vowed, would she let herself become so humiliatingly enslaved to a man. If that kind of subservience was the price one paid for love, then she didn't want any part of it.

She sighed and pushed her hands back through her short-cropped hair, wondering for the millionth time if perhaps she shouldn't move to the city, where the old-fashioned, sharp divisions between men and women had died an ignominious death long ago.

Suddenly just being in the town's peaceful, tree-shaded cemetery made her feel trapped, and she strode briskly across the dried, clipped grass to her car. Her low heels sank into the sod, as if the place itself was a malign presence that wanted to keep her there forever.

'Ehh-mih-lee! Oh, Ehh-mih-lee!'

Her eyes flew open, and for a moment she lay paralysed in the total blackness of her bedroom, her palms pressed tight against her chest, wondering what had shattered her sleep so abruptly. She heard the gentle whisper of the curtains at the open window, the muted tick of her bedside clock, and, off in the distance, the barking of a dog. Other than that, nothing.

She released the breath she'd been holding and closed her eyes.

'Ehh-mih-lee!'

This time she shot out of bed, her heart pounding, and stood next to it with her green eyes wide and frightened. When the sound was repeated yet again, she recognised it as a human voice, and her whole body sagged in relief. In the next second it straightened with indignation. Kids, probably, caterwauling beneath her window on a dare.

Her face tight with irritation, she padded across the room towards the window, the wooden floor deliciously cool beneath her bare feet. She draped the curtain in front of the thin cotton nightie that barely hung to her thighs, and peered out and down.

'You!' Her lips formed the word almost inaudibly as she saw Nicholas Simon a full storey below, his head tipped back on his shoulders to look up, a lop-sided grin showing the white of his teeth in the darkness.

'Emily! Hi!' he bellowed delightedly when he saw her, and she clamped a forefinger to her lips.

'What are you doing?' she hissed down at him. 'Do you want to wake the whole town?'

His head started to shake in a slow roll, the foolish grin still in place, and Emily's eyes narrowed suspiciously. Now she could see that his wide-legged stance was not pure arrogance; it was an attempt to counter unsteadiness.

'Get away from here!' she whispered. 'Go home!'

'Nope.' His head was still shaking, throwing his hair back and forth across his brow. 'I came to pay a visit. I came to see my old schoolmate, Earnest Emily, and I'm not leaving until I do.'

Her lips pursed in consternation. 'You're drunk,' she accused him, but that only prompted an even broader grin.

'Could be, could be. But, drunk or not, I'm going to stand down here and shout until you let me in!' His voice grew louder and louder with every word, and Emily jerked back from the window in alarm. He really *was* going to wake the whole town.

'What do you want?'

'I told you. I just came to pay a visit. It's a courtesy call.' The word 'courtesy' was the first he had stumbled over, and to Emily that seemed incredibly appropriate. 'Not very hospitable, are you, Earnest Emily? Least you could do is invite an old friend in for coffee. 'Specially one in my condition. You wouldn't want me to *drive home drunk, would you*?'

'All right, all right!' she hissed, panicking because he was shouting so loudly. 'Just a minute!'

She snatched her short cotton robe from the chair in the corner, shrugged into it, jerked the belt tight around her waist, and opened her bedroom door so hard that it slammed against the wall.

She muttered continually under her breath as she stomped through her dark apartment, down the narrow wooden stairs, then through the workroom to the door that opened on to the back alley. Who did he think he was, bellowing outside her window in the dead of night, and, come to think of it, why was she letting him in?

The last question stopped her with her hand frozen on the deadbolt.

'Emily?' It wasn't a shout, but it was loud enough.

She snapped the bolt back and jerked open the door. He was standing directly on the other side, still wearing that foolish grin, his fingers jammed into the pockets of his jeans, rounding his shoulders under the same black tank-top he'd been wearing that morning. 'Be quiet and get in here!' she whispered viciously.

'Why, thank you kindly, Emily,' he said, walking past her into the dark workroom. 'Nice of you to ask.'

She locked the door behind him and, without a second glance in his direction, stomped back towards the stairs. 'You want coffee?' she shot irritably over her shoulder. 'Fine. I'll make coffee. It's obvious that you could use some.'

She heard his unsteady step behind her as she mounted the stairs, and then his mumbled, 'S'dark in here. Light a candle, for God's sake.'

She flipped the light switch at the top of the stairs, then spun round and glared down at him, hands on hips.

'Wow!' he gasped involuntarily, staring up at her with his blue eyes impossibly wide. He nearly fell down the stairs backwards as he grasped for the railing. 'You can see clear through that damn thing.'

Emily's face went white as she realised what backlighting would do to the thin cotton robe and nightie. She swallowed once, then darted away from his line of sight, into the bedroom, leaving him to find his way for himself. In a panic that was totally unlike her, she shed her nightclothes and scrambled into the first clothes she laid her hands on—the old jeans and baggy white shirt she wore on cleaning days.

He was slumped on her couch when she came out, looking straight at her across the room, smiling.

'I liked the other outfit better,' he said carefully, enunciating each word with exaggerated precision. His hair was tousled in a blond tangle over his forehead, and his eyes were at half-mast, but something she saw in them made Emily wonder—just for a moment—if he was really as drunk as he pretended to be. When he blinked—not really a blink at all; more like a sagging of his eyelids—she dismissed the suspicion instantly. He was drunk, all right. Irresponsibly, irrefutably drunk.

'I'll make the coffee,' she said sharply, turning away from him with a look of disgust.

She stayed in the kitchen the whole ten minutes it took for the coffee-maker to finish, half hoping that he'd have passed out when she emerged, so she wouldn't have to talk to him.

Oh, hell, what are you wishing for? she asked herself suddenly, clapping a hand to her mouth. Wouldn't that look just dandy, Nicholas Simon spending the night? Passed out or not, you know perfectly well what the people in this town would think if they found out.

Now frantic that what she had wished for might come true, she hurried to fill two mugs and bumped the swinging door between the kitchen and living-room with her hip.

'Oh.' She stopped dead on the other side. He was still slouched on the couch—actually, it looked more like he'd been *propped* there—but, for all his limp helplessness, he had apparently managed to walk to the wall switch, turn off the overhead light, and switch on a small table-lamp instead. It cast a warm golden circle on just the right side of his head, but the rest of the room was in shadow.

'Oh,' he mimicked, white teeth flashing. 'Oh, what? Did you think I'd have gone?'

'No,' she said coldly, walking over and stiff-arming the mug towards him. 'I thought you'd have passed out.'

He chuckled deep in his throat, and, with a swiftness that shouldn't have been possible in view of his condition, snatched both mugs from her hands and tipped his head to the space next to him on the couch. 'Sit down, Emily. We'll have a reunion.'

She eyed the space warily, not wanting to sit that close to him, but not wanting him to think he could make her uncomfortable, either. She sat in the opposite corner of the couch, her legs tucked under her, twisted to face him.

He took a noisy slurp from one mug, passed her the other, then flung his left arm across the back of the couch and looked at her. 'There. Isn't this nice? Two old friends, renewing their relationship. What could be better?'

She eyed his hand warily. It was much too close to her shoulder. 'Almost anything,' she said drily. 'It's two-thirty in the morning, and, in case you've forgotten, we were never friends. We didn't even know each other.'

Nonplussed, he wagged his forefinger at her. 'Ah, but we might have been. As a matter of fact, we might have been a lot more, if you hadn't been so stand-offish in the old days.' His smile seemed to slide across his face. 'I've been wondering for over ten years what you'd be like in bed.'

Emily couldn't help herself. Her mouth fell open and her eyes flew wide.

Nick laughed out loud at her expression. 'Oh, come on, Emily. Don't try to tell me you find the idea offensive.'

'I find everything about you offensive!' she snapped. 'And I always did!'

There was something sly, something absolutely sober about his smile. 'You know what, Emily?' he asked very, very softly. 'I don't believe you. I don't believe you ever found me offensive at all.'

Emily pressed her lips into a tight line and said nothing. There was nothing she could say that would make a dent in conceit like that. When his gaze and the silence became intolerable, she said, 'Finish your coffee and get out of here.'

He spread his fingers across his chest and affected a wounded expression. 'Just like that? You're going to throw me out in the cold?'

She closed her eyes and turned her head away. 'Just like that.'

When he didn't move after a few seconds, she glanced sideways and found him gazing around the apartment with a bemused expression, completely ignoring her instruction to leave. 'You've got a lot of plants up here,' he murmured, his eyes travelling from the pot-hugging succulents to the towering figs, from the exotic bird-of-paradise to the lowly philodendrons.

'I'm a florist, remember?' she retorted.

He nodded absently.

'Listen, Nick, I don't know why you came here tonight, but it's late, and I want you to leave.'

'You said that before.'

'And I'm going to keep saying it, until you go home.'

He rolled his head to look at her. 'There's nobody there.'

Emily's brows and lips twitched uncertainly, but in the end she refused to let him play on her sympathies. 'So call some of your old schoolfriends. A lot of them still live around here.'

'I didn't want to be with any of them,' he shrugged. 'I wanted to be here, with you.'

'Why?' she demanded.

He shook his head helplessly. 'Damned if I know. I must be out of my mind. But still, it feels right. I like it here.'

'But I don't like *you* here.'

He arched one brow and grinned. 'You will.'

Thoroughly exasperated, she moved to jump up from the couch, but before her feet hit the floor his left hand shot out to close around her upper arm, and he jerked her towards him, pulling her off balance. Caught totally by surprise, she fell sideways on his chest, gasping at the impact. Before she could even digest what had happened, let alone react to it, he had her by the shoulders and had pulled her up until her face was level with his.

'Remember graduation night, Emily?' he said, and his eyes were so close to hers that she couldn't bring them into focus. 'I think it's high time we tried that again, don't you?'

Just as she opened her mouth to fire back a vicious retort, his lips came down hard on hers.

If it hadn't been so unexpected, such an outright shock, she would have exploded away from him in a surge of indignation that would have obliterated all her senses. But for just a fraction of a second she was so stunned by his actions that she froze, just as she had on graduation day, and she was fated to pay dearly for that.

In that brief second of her immobility, the bruising, grinding pressure of his mouth stilled abruptly, almost as if he was as stunned as she was. When his chest hitched beneath her, she became shockingly aware of the blossoming tenderness of her breasts, and the awareness itself horrified her.

'Let *go*,' she tried to say, but the words were lost against his mouth and only the movement of her lips registered. In an immediate response, his hands slid from her shoulders down to her waist, encircling it with a quivering restraint that made her back arch involuntarily.

Even while one part of her mind was recording outrage at what he was doing, another part was recording a volley of unfamiliar stimuli—the strength and breadth of the hands at her waist, the hardness of his mouth, the sandpaper rasp of his jaw against the delicate skin of her face. When she felt her body automatically respond with an accelerated pulse and a strange tingling sensation that began in her breasts and spread quickly downwards, she twisted her mouth from his and gasped, 'Stop!' flattening her hands against his chest, pushing away. With barely a pause, his hands jerked on her back, pulling her against him again. He shuddered visibly when her breasts flattened against him, then blinked in surprise when she pushed away again, her hands curled into fists this time.

'What are you doing, Em?' he breathed, somehow managing to sound innocent in spite of the hoarseness of his voice.

'What are *you* doing?' she countered sharply, trying to twist away. Just when she thought she was close to managing it, his hands shot around to grab her wrists and tug them against his chest.

'You know damn well what I'm doing. The same thing you are. What we should have done ten years ago.'

'No!' She was struggling in earnest now, her face contorted with the effort, and there was one terrifying moment when she was completely aware of his massive size, of his strength, and all that that implied. 'You're drunk!' she cried out, as if that were some sort of magic talisman that would stop him.

All it did was make him laugh. 'That's right. I'm drunk. I can't be held responsible. What's your excuse?' His hands were on her back again, pulling her so sharply against him that the air left her lungs in a rush, but he'd made a mistake. He'd let her hands go, and the right one swung back in an instinctive defence, then crashed into his cheek with a resounding slap.

His arms fell from her back instantly, and for a moment his expression was dumbfounded. While

Emily watched wide-eyed, holding her breath, afraid to move now that she finally could, he reached up with one hand and rubbed his cheek. It made a rasping sound against his whiskers that seemed somehow deafening in the quiet apartment.

Slowly, warily, her eyes never leaving his, Emily reached back with her left hand, grabbed the couch cushion behind her, and pulled away. His head turned to follow her progress like a snake matching every movement of its prey, and at the last moment, just as she jumped to her feet, he snatched out at her.

He really was drunk, she realised then, because his reflexes were slow. He only managed to catch the hem of her blouse in his fingers, but a row of buttons strained and popped and flew across the room under the force of his tug. Emily was left standing over him, looking down with horrified dismay at where her blouse hung open, snagged over one shoulder, nearly baring her right breast. She snatched the blouse from his unprotesting fingers and turned her back to cover herself.

'You bastard!' she managed to choke out furiously, spitting the words over her shoulder. 'I want you out of here. I want you out of here right now! I don't care where you go, or how you get there, *but I want you out!*'

She spun back to face him on the last word, her face screwed into a red mask of humiliated fury... and then she caught her breath, blinked in disbelief, and finally remembered to close her sagging jaw.

Nicholas had finally passed out.

CHAPTER THREE

EMILY lay rigidly on her back in bed, her eyes squeezed shut, alert for any sound from the living-room for fear that Nick would...what? Wake up and storm into her bedroom and attack her? If she'd been so worried about something like that, why had she let him in in the first place? Why had she sat right next to him? Why had she waited so long to slap him?

She slammed the door on her thoughts, unable to face them for the moment.

It had been absolutely impossible to waken him. She'd whispered, then demanded, then almost shouted that he wake up, and when that hadn't worked she'd prodded gingerly at his shoulder with one finger, ready to leap backwards in an instant. Finally, totally frustrated, she'd sagged into a chair facing the couch, her chin propped miserably in her hands as she watched him sleep. She didn't dare call anyone to take him home; how would she explain his being there at three o'clock in the morning, and who would she call anyway?

'Bastard,' she'd hissed again at the sleeping figure, but there had been no venom in her tone. He hadn't looked like a bastard, slumped in one corner of the couch, blond hair tumbling over his brow, the strong lines of his face softened in sleep. He'd looked strangely defenceless, vulnerable in spite of his size, and it was when she felt that first peculiar tug at her heart that she'd jumped up from the chair and stormed into her bedroom, hoping he'd wake up miserable and aching and cramped.

Maybe you should have covered him with something, she thought now as she lay in bed. It isn't *that* warm, with the windows wide open, and that tank-top of his is so thin that you can almost see right through it to his chest...

She groaned aloud and rolled over and buried her head in the pillow. Everything would be better in the morning. It had to be. Who knew? She might get lucky. Maybe he was so drunk that he wouldn't remember what had happened here tonight; that she had actually—just for a second, mind you— kissed him *back*. Maybe, it there was any justice in the world, he'd remember the slap and forget the kiss, and she'd never have to face that smug grin of his, look into his eyes and see that knowing, mocking look...

Her pillow absorbed a long sigh of despair. And maybe there would be an earthquake during the night, and the whole town would be swallowed up in a deep pit. There seemed to be as much chance of one thing happening as the other.

Nick had gone when she woke up and peered out into the living-room, and only a slight indentation on the couch cushions convinced her that he had ever been there at all.

He got up and left before sunrise, she told herself hopefully as she stepped into the shower, and no one will ever find out he was here. He certainly wouldn't advertise it—what reputed ladies' man wanted it known that he was rebuffed by the resident old maid? She lathered her short hair, frowning when she remembered that Nick had called her cut masculine.

The early morning air wafting through the window was brutally dry, promising another blistering day. As sick as she was of the standard garb of shorts, she pulled a fresh white pair from a drawer and stepped into them, then tugged on a clean white tank-top. As she stood in front of the dresser mirror, brushing her damp hair back from her face, her eyes wandered to the generous swell of her breasts beneath the cotton material. The brush stopped in mid-stroke and she blushed.

She'd never paid much attention to her body since that first fearful wonder of puberty; she'd certainly never given a second thought to forgoing a bra in heat like this, not with the green overall concealing her shape so thoroughly. But, overall or not, this morning was different—*she* was different—more aware of her body than she had been in...ten years.

With an irritated sigh, she turned away from the mirror and rummaged in her drawer for a bra.

Less than half an hour later she was downstairs, glass cleaner in one hand, cloth in the other, busily polishing every flat surface in the showroom.

She always opened the shop a full hour before most people had finished their breakfast, using the quiet time to perform the daily cleaning that had become ritual. A place for everything, everything in its place, and, above all, everything gleaming.

The long formica counter-top had always been her nemesis, so worn from years of service that the lustre was gone. Still she polished it diligently every day, trying to buff back to life a shine that had died years before. She was standing in front of the counter, her back to the door, rubbing vigorously when the bell jingled the arrival of her first customer.

'Good morning, Em.'

She shot upright at his deep voice, then forced herself to bend back to her work without looking around. The heat of colour rose to her face, and she tried to will it away. He was even more arrogant than she'd thought, coming here on the heels of last night's fiasco. Unless he'd come to apologise, of course. She considered the possibility for a fraction of a second, then dismissed it. More likely he'd come to gloat. If he remembered anything at all.

'Don't tell me you're going to ignore a man who just spent the night with you, Emily.'

The cloth in her right hand moved in faster, smaller circles and she gritted her teeth.

As he came up to stand at her left, the first thing she was aware of was the faint scent of soap, and then, beneath that, a more elusive fragrance. It's his scent, she thought, frowning down at the formica. What you're smelling is the very distinctive scent of one particular man, identifying it as one animal identifies another. That she was capable of such a thing astonished her, horrified her, and she rubbed even harder, her lower lip caught between her teeth.

'You work too hard, Emily.'

She flinched when he leaned on the counter, his hands laced together, his right forearm right next to her left. Out of the corner of her eye she could see that he was staring at the back wall, not even looking at her. She inched away until there was a wide space between their arms. Without commenting, almost absently, he mimicked her move until his forearm was pressed against hers again.

This is stupid, she told herself, trying to rub the pattern right off the speckled white formica, pretending not to notice him. He can chase me right off the edge of the counter if we keep this up.

Suddenly the fingers of his left hand were on her arm, and the circular motion of the cloth stopped dead.

'Look, Em,' he murmured, and reluctantly, knowing it was a mistake, she risked a quick glance at his profile.

He was wearing a white short-sleeved shirt, open to expose a tanned throat, and he looked impossibly cool and crisp, as if heat never affected him. His head was bent, shiny blond wisps dangling from his forehead, and he was staring raptly at their two forearms, lying side by side. She followed his gaze.

'It's amazing, isn't it?' he went on in a deep, soft, hypnotic murmur. With every word he spoke, his breath puffed against the skin of her arm, snapping the tiny, almost invisible blonde hairs there to attention. 'The difference between man and woman, so obvious, so simple on the surface, and yet so profound.' His fingers trailed delicately from her inner elbow down to her wrist, making the hair on the back of her neck stand up. She told her arm to jerk away, but it just lay there, obstinately refusing to obey.

'Look at it, Em. Look at the difference.'

The command was entirely unnecessary. She was so mesmerised by his voice, so helplessly caught up in what he was saying, that she had forgotten to breathe. She stared down at where his broad, muscular forearm pressed against her much slimmer one; where his wide wrist mocked the delicate bones of her own; where the power of his splayed hand suggested that hers could be crushed in its grip. Her skin tingled where his crisp blond hairs brushed against it, and she exhaled quietly.

'It's a good difference, Emily. A natural one. It's nothing to be afraid of.'

'I'm not afraid.'

'Oh, yes, you are,' he murmured, still looking down at their arms lying side by side. 'You were afraid the first time I kissed you ten years ago, and you were afraid again last night.'

She caught her breath silently and held it.

'Are you afraid every time a man kisses you, Emily? Or just me?'

'I'm not afraid!' The words tumbled out in a rush as she jerked her arm off the counter and backed away from him. He turned towards her, showing the left side of his face for the first time. 'Oh, lord!' she whispered.

It wasn't much of a black eye, as far as black eyes went. As a matter of fact, the red and purple discoloration didn't surround the eye at all. It was off to one side, towards the temple, barely touching the outside corner. Still, it was brilliantly visible, and to Emily it looked like an accusing finger, pointed directly at her.

'Did I do that?' she asked in a small voice.

He smiled briefly. 'You've got a mean right hook, Emily, but not that mean. This wound,' he reached up to touch the spot, wincing, 'was self-inflicted.

It was dark when I left this morning. I walked into a wall on my way out.'

Her relief was so great that she allowed herself a little smile—not only because she wasn't responsible for his injury, but also because he'd left her apartment when it was still dark. No one ever had to know.

As if her smile had been an invitation, he reached over to brush her cheek with the backs of his curled fingers.

She scowled and backed away from his hand.

He took a step towards her, touched her cheek again. This time she reached up and plucked his hand away from her face. 'Stop that.'

One of his brows quirked. 'You didn't seem to mind when I touched you last night. Not until you remembered you were supposed to.'

His hand went right back up to her cheek, and she slapped it down angrily. 'You were drunk last night!' she retorted, as if his drunkenness somehow explained her behaviour.

He laughed out loud at the twisted reasoning, then jammed his fingers into the front pockets of his jeans and looked down at the tops of his tennis shoes. 'Yes, Emily. I certainly was. About as drunk as I've ever been in my life.'

She wrinkled her nose primly, folded her arms across her chest, and waited for a long moment. 'Well,' she said finally, 'aren't you going to apologise?'

He turned his head slowly and met her eyes head-on, and for some reason Emily felt as if she'd been punched in the stomach. 'The only thing I'll apologise for is passing out. Everything else was forgivable. That wasn't. And it won't happen again.'

Her laugh was supposed to sound disdainful, but it came out a little weak. 'It most certainly won't, because that's the last time you'll ever see the inside of my apartment...' she began, but then he tipped his head back, just a little, and looked down at her through narrowed lids, his eyes suddenly a darker blue. She didn't quite understand why the rest of her sentence trailed away into nothingness—maybe it had something to do with the way he was looking at her... almost as if he wasn't looking *at* her at all, but into some secret place inside that even she hadn't known existed. It was a compelling gaze, a commanding one, and the sheer force of it took her by surprise.

'I didn't expect it, either,' he murmured, barely moving his lips, his gaze so brilliantly fixed on hers that it felt like a physical connection. 'But last night was just the beginning, Emily. It isn't going to end there. My goodness, your eyes are green, the colour of spring.'

She blinked once, frozen by his expression, her thoughts short-circuiting crazily. No, she remembered suddenly; that's not right. Algae. That's the colour of my eyes. Like the algae on Martin's livestock pond.

Somehow the everyday nature of that thought slashed through her dreamlike state and brought her sharply to her senses. He was seducing her. And she was just standing there, letting it happen.

A muscle twitched its warning just beneath her right eye, but apparently Nick hadn't noticed.

'You're beautiful, you know.' He took both her hands and brought them up to his chest. 'And tonight you're going to feel beautiful. I promise.'

She focused on the corner of his mouth that was curved upwards, wondering why she'd never noticed that slight indentation there, just to the left of his lips. He must smile like that often, she thought, with just one side of his mouth. That was the mark of a cynic, wasn't it? A person perpetually amused by the gullibility of others?

'Really?' she said, her voice suddenly flat and cold.

'Really. You'll see. Trust me, Em.'

His pretence at earnestness would have been comical, if his motives hadn't been so obvious, so juvenile, so despicable. She jerked her hands down, out of his grasp, back to her sides, and the suddenness of the gesture startled him. He actually seemed to recoil from whatever it was he saw in her face, and Emily liked that.

'You tell me I'm beautiful and I hop into bed, is that how it goes?' she asked sarcastically. She felt ten feet tall, infinitely superior, magnificently haughty.

Unfortunately, after that one second of startled confusion, he actually seemed amused by her posturing. The tiny lines around his eyes had deepened, and he was wearing that stupid, one-sided grin of his. 'Something like that,' he replied steadily.

She clenched her jaw and glared at him.

His smile broadened a little. 'You will, you know. Eventually, you will, Emily. I can wait.'

She pulled in a huge breath that would have fuelled a thousand words, then closed her lips on it when the bell over the shop door jingled.

'Hello, Emily dear.'

Oh, lord. Mrs Hoeffer. Ancient, lilac-scented, blue-haired Mrs Hoeffer, in for the Tuesday bouquet for her bridge luncheon. As dear a soul as lived in this town, and as garrulous a soul as lived in the whole damn state.

Emily jerked her head like a marionette wearing a painted smile. 'Good morning, Mrs Hoeffer. How are you? Lovely day, isn't it? I have your flowers all ready for you in the cooler. You know Nick Simon, don't you? Art's grandson? Why don't you two have a little chat while I get your order? It'll take just a minute.'

She dashed back into the workroom, straight to the tiny mirror, and peered worriedly at her face. Except it wasn't her face. It belonged to some other woman. Some stupid, flustered woman with unnaturally bright eyes and terribly flushed cheeks... flushed? They were downright scarlet.

She blew air out through her cheeks, took several deep, calming breaths, then looked warily into the mirror again. There. That was a little better; a little less colourful, anyway. She held the cooler door open longer than necessary, letting the chill air finish what the deep breathing had started, then she breezed back into the showroom with a bright smile that sagged when there was no one to see it.

Nick and Mrs Hoeffer were huddled by the front window, his arm over her plump shoulders while she giggled like a schoolgirl.

'Oh, *Nicky*!' she tittered, slapping his hand playfully. 'You haven't changed a bit!'

You can say that again, Emily thought bitterly. He's still incorrigible. With a vicious jab, she punched the total button on the cash register and the little bell rang.

'Oh! Emily, dear!' Mrs Hoeffer turned around, and Emily would have bet her life that the woman hadn't blushed like that in sixty years. He'd probably propositioned her, too. 'Back so soon? I've just been having the nicest talk with Nicky here...' Suddenly she looked from one to the other, almost mischievously, then she covered her mouth and giggled again. 'I really must be going now.'

Emily smiled uncertainly as Mrs Hoeffer bustled to the counter, paid for the bouquet, snatched her cone-shaped package and hurried towards the door. At the last moment she turned around and smiled one of those smiles old people bestowed on favoured grandchildren. 'I'm very, very happy for you, Emily dear,' she said, 'and I won't tell a *soul* about the black eye, I promise!' Then she bounced out of the door, fairly bursting with whatever information she had just promised not to tell. She waggled her fingers merrily as she passed the big front window on her way down the street.

Slowly, slowly, Emily's head turned towards Nick, her eyes narrowed in suspicion. He was leaning back against the door-frame, grinning at her, his legs crossed at the ankles, his arms folded across his chest.

'What was she talking about?'

He shrugged innocently.

'*What*?' she repeated, green eyes flashing.

He pushed away from the door and walked back to lean towards her over the counter. 'Did you know Mrs Hoeffer used to bake cookies for me?'

'No, I didn't know Mrs Hoeffer used to bake cookies for you,' she repeated impatiently. 'So what's that got to do with anything?'

'Well, every week she'd bake three dozen cookies and make her husband drive her out to the farm so she could deliver them. Guess she thought I'd die of a cookie shortage or something, living out there alone with Grandpa.'

'Fascinating. Is this story going anywhere?'

He shook his head, disappointed. 'Every story goes somewhere, Emily. They're all worth hearing, you know.'

She sighed, exasperated, but he pretended not to notice.

'This story, for instance, establishes background. Mrs Hoeffer and I are old friends, and in the way of old friends we were just catching up on the news. I asked her if the bursitis in her shoulder was responding to medication——'

Emily frowned. 'Mrs Hoeffer has bursitis?'

'And she asked me where I got this.' He grinned and pointed to the bruise. 'I told her you slapped me.'

'*What?*' she breathed, grabbing the edge of the counter so hard that all the colour bled from her fingertips. 'You told her *I* did that?'

'Of course not. That would have been a lie.'

'But you just said——'

'I said that she asked where I got the bruise, and, in a totally unrelated thought, I chose that particular moment to make mention of the fact that you slapped me. That's all.'

'That's *all*?' she shouted. 'But you *know* what she'll think! And if you really know Mrs Hoeffer, you also know that within the next thirty minutes everyone in town will be thinking exactly the same thing!' She slammed her mouth closed furiously. Of course he knew. Look at that grin. Look at those eyes. 'Fine!' she snapped viciously. 'You want the whole town to think I decked you? Well, that's just fine with me. Should put a well-deserved crack in that old Casanova reputation of yours, and, in addition to that, it makes my position abundantly clear!'

'Maybe,' he said lazily. 'Then again, maybe not. You see, I explained that it was a late-night lovers' quarrel in your apartment, just before we went to bed.'

'Oh, hell,' she mouthed, face falling.

'Well, it was the truth, right? It did happen in your apartment, it was late at night, and afterwards we both went to bed. You certainly can't blame me if Mrs Hoeffer reads more into it than what I said.'

Emily didn't know whether to scream or cry, so she just stood there, mute, while the options played havoc with her expression. Nick's smile was gentle, almost sympathetic.

'Well, I've got some things that need doing this morning.' He pushed away from the counter and lifted his arms over his head in a mighty stretch. A casual, indifferent stretch, as if he'd done absolutely nothing wrong. 'I'll be back at about noon to take you to lunch. Is Alfred's Café as good as it used to be?'

For a moment, Emily's voice was lost in the open cavern of her mouth. Finally she managed to croak, 'Why are you doing this?'

He cocked his head a bit, almost as if the question surprised him. 'You're a big girl, Emily. You figure it out.'

She ground her teeth together so hard that it hurt.

'Look at it this way.' He grinned devilishly. 'Your standing in the community will sky-rocket, once they've all heard you're sleeping with me.'

Emily gaped, hardly able to believe that one man could support an ego of that size, even while she was listening to the evidence of it.

Nick just chuckled and walked to the door, then turned back towards her in an afterthought. 'It's really too hot for a bra, Emily, don't you think?' he asked casually.

And then, while her mouth and her eyes were still forming three enormous circles, he went out of the door.

CHAPTER FOUR

NOT a single customer passed through the shop door before noon, and still it was the most harrowing morning of Emily's life. She spent most of the time wandering aimlessly through the displays, touching a leaf here, a flower there, as if she could find some sort of reassurance in the static plant life; some sort of guarantee that the world was still right-side-up and the past twenty-four hours had only been a bad dream.

Why was he doing this to her? Why would he deliberately set out to compromise her reputation? Simply because she'd slapped him?

'You're a big girl, Emily. You figure it out.' His words echoed like a challenge in her mind.

At mid-morning she glanced at the clock and thought that, if Mrs Hoeffer was up to her usual standard, by this time everyone in town would believe that she was sleeping with Nick Simon. Good lord. If it weren't so embarrassing, so maddening, it would be almost laughable. Sleeping with someone? She'd barely been kissed in all of her twenty-seven years, and, almost without exception, those men who had risked it had slunk away nursing a bruised ego.

Except Nick, of course, proud owner of the most inflated ego of all. So inflated, in fact, that when he'd finally been rejected last night—probably for the first time in his life—he'd absolutely refused to accept it...

Her thoughts slammed to a halt. Of course. Of *course*. All this time she'd been looking for some deep, profound motive in a man who probably hadn't had a deep, profound thought in his life. Her slap hadn't hurt him, but her rejection had been an unacceptable affront. He might have left Random years ago, but you didn't leave behind the standards a place like this seared into your mind—standards that dictated that men commanded, and women obeyed. She had had the audacity to ignore that basic principle, and Nick was out to teach her a lesson.

Once she'd figured it out, she could hardly wait for his return, for another shot at putting him in his place. If Nick Simon wanted to play power games, he'd chosen the wrong adversary.

He was back at the shop just as the noon siren set every dog in town howling. He sauntered in with the slick confidence of a man who had never confronted an indifferent woman, and inside, at least, Emily smiled to see it. The bigger they are...she thought smugly.

It was a little disconcerting when he totally ignored her carefully rehearsed, barbed refusal to have even another conversation with him, let alone a public lunch. It was more disconcerting when he followed her out on to the street, actually grabbing at her arm, laughing at her futile attempts to shake him off. She turned on him then, actually shouting, slapping at his hands when they reached for her, finally concluding in a furious, red-faced bellow that she wouldn't have lunch with him if he were the last man on earth with a sandwich and she were starving to death.

She'd known, of course, that every ear on Main Street was attuned to the confrontation—public quarrels were a novel occurrence in the quiet little town—but that didn't bother her. Let them all hear how she really felt about him, and Mrs Hoeffer's tale would die a rapid, painless death.

But somehow it didn't work that way. When her tirade finally ended, she looked smugly at the faces watching from up and down the block, and suddenly felt as if she were in a bad performance of *The Taming of the Shrew*. They were all smiling. Every one. Dammit, they were almost beaming.

So it was that by suppertime that night every soul in Random knew that quiet, conservative, some might even say prim Emily Swenson was having a tempestuous love-affair with that charming Nicky Simon. So tempestuous, in fact, that they'd had an ear-splitting shouting match right on Main Street at high noon, in front of God and everybody. Who would have guessed, they whispered among themselves, that the heat of such passion had been buried in their own stiff-necked Emily all these years, just waiting for the right man to bring it to a boil?

No one said that directly to her, of course, but she had a steady stream of suspicious customers that afternoon, people who'd never bought a flower in their lives. 'Just browsing,' they said, sauntering around the shop with guilty little smiles, sneaking peeks at her as if she were some exotic animal they'd just found living in their midst.

That night Emily locked her door and slammed her windows and pulled all the shades, then waited, trembling, for Nick Simon to start caterwauling under her bedroom window again. He'd sworn to do just that if she continued to rebuff him, and she was ready, a full bucket of ice water stationed right next to the window.

By midnight the ice had melted, the water was tepid, and Emily felt as if she'd been run through the wringers of an old washing-machine three or four times. Defeated, exhausted from hours of tension, she went to bed in the stifling heat of the closed apartment—still wearing her bra.

There was a long bright red convertible parked directly in front of the shop when she opened for business the next morning. It had blazing white leather seats and a frivolous, feathery thing attached to the radio aerial. It was an insolent-looking car, too bright, too garish for the drab, dusty Main Street of drought-plagued Random—precisely the kind of car she'd expect Nicholas Simon to own.

She took one timid step out on to the pavement, peering this way and that to make sure she wasn't observed trying to get a closer look.

Main Street was as still as the early morning heat hanging over the town. The pavements were empty, the store-fronts dark, the street deserted. If they'd had a traffic light in town, she would have been able to hear it blinking. She took two more steps towards the car.

'Morning!' He popped out of the doorway of the hardware store next door, startling her so badly that she had to stifle a scream.

For a moment, she couldn't find her voice. The hand that had flown automatically to her chest recorded the frightened pounding of her heart through her green florist's coat, the sleeveless blouse, and the bra underneath.

'Sorry,' he grinned sheepishly, stepping out to the middle of the pavement. 'I didn't mean to scare you.'

'I'll bet,' she said acidly, then fixed him with a cold glare. He was wearing a light blue T-shirt that matched his eyes, with short sleeves straining over the smooth rise of tanned biceps. At least it was a more decent covering than the tank-top he'd worn on that first day, but, as if to counter the extra material on top, he'd traded his jeans for a pair of abbreviated white running shorts. Her eyes dropped involuntarily to long, ridged thighs and the angular musculature of a runner's calves.

'You like my legs?' he asked happily, following her gaze, turning on the toes of his tennis shoes in a comical preen.

'Oh, stop it!' she hissed, jerking her eyes up to the relatively harmless sweep of blond over his brow, then back to the car. 'This thing is yours, I take it?'

He strolled over to the car, patted the bonnet affectionately, then leaned back against it with his arms braced to either side. The thin cloth of his shirt clung to stomach muscles that rippled with the gesture. 'This "thing" happens to be a '66 Chevy Malibu—a classic. Pretty, isn't she?'

Emily scowled at the chauvinistic propensity to ascribe the female gender to possessions. '*She* is taking up two parking spaces,' she said frigidly.

'Now, now.' He moved to push away from the car, but when she scrambled back two panicked steps he froze, then leaned back again. 'Oh-oh. You're angry, aren't you? I was afraid you might be, when I didn't show up last night after I promised, but I just couldn't get away from——'

'Move the car.'

He was silent for a beat. 'Move the car?'

'Move the car,' she repeated.

Sunlight bounced off his head when he shook it. 'Can't.'

'What do you mean, you can't? Why?'

'Well, the truth is it's awfully dusty out at the farm. All those dirt roads, and all those ploughed fields drying up, you know. There's no garage, and the barn is just stuffed with old machinery. No room for the Chevy in there. So I decided I'd just leave my car in town and use Grandpa's old truck to get around instead.'

'You think you're going to just *leave* this here, right in front of my shop?'

'Seemed like a good place to me,' he shrugged innocently.

'It's *not* a good place! It's an *awful* place! You leave this car here all the time and everyone's going to think...'

He smiled at her, waiting patiently for her to finish.

'I'll call the sheriff,' she finally threatened, her face red.

'Well, you can do that, of course, but I already asked him if there was any law against leaving the car parked outside your place all night, and you know what he said? Nothing. He didn't say a thing. Just winked at me.'

Emily clenched her jaw against the whirlpool of helpless rage threatening to explode inside her head. 'Leave me alone!' she finally shouted.

She spun on her heel and stormed back into the shop, but he was right behind her. As she reached the counter he grabbed her left wrist and jerked her around and against him with hardly any effort at all.

'You don't want me to leave you alone, Emily.'

Just as he started to bend his head towards hers, her free arm flew up and back and started a power swing towards his face. In a blur of motion his hand shot up and grabbed her wrist, then he slammed both her arms down and held them pressed against her sides. As she glared up at him, her face twisted with the frustrated effort to free herself, she saw a dark, controlled anger tighten his features, and caught her breath. He didn't even look like Nick Simon any more. There was no happy indifference in that rigid expression; no happy-go-lucky charm.

'Once, Emily,' he warned her. 'I let you get away with that once, but that's your limit. Don't raise your hand to me again.'

It was partly the change seriousness wrought in his face that made her gape with amazement, and it was partly uncertainty. She knew how to deal with a cocksure, insolent Nick Simon; she had no idea how to manage the man who stood before her now.

Like a mindless automaton, she let herself be backed against the counter, her wrists still pinned at her sides, the position of her arms throwing her chest out. She felt her hands open and her fingers press against the rough wood base as he walked into her, bent his head, then froze for a moment, his mouth a fraction of an inch from hers. He held her with his eyes and his hands while the full length of his body—were men's bodies all so hard?—pushed tight against hers, forcing a soft gasp from her throat. His breath was warm, then hot as it broke against her chin, and a few strands of his hair brushed across her eyebrow like tiny filaments charged with electricity.

'Do you always have to force yourself on women?' she managed to hiss at him.

'This is force?' he asked wryly, and then, as if to counter the brute strength with which he held her, his lips plucked delicately at hers, so soft, so warmly gentle, that for a moment she forgot she was at war. It seemed almost innocent, this kissing—just a harmless, wonderfully natural thing that flooded your senses with such a sense of well-being that there couldn't possibly be anything wrong with it.

Helplessly, Emily's lips softened and moved in a response that was pure instinct, since she had no experience to engineer it.

He pulled away a fraction of an inch, just enough to move his lips in a whisper that she felt more than she heard. 'And this?' His tongue swept over her lips and she went rigid. 'Is this force, too?' His tongue found the corner of her mouth, ran along the inside of her upper lip to the other corner, and then, heaven help her, she shuddered against him, her body saying things her mind would never permit her to utter.

Feeling it, apparently stunned by it, Nick sucked in a quick, hard gasp that was an explosion of sound in the quiet shop, and then everything suddenly shifted into high speed.

His mouth moved desperately, hungrily, tongue probing between the seam of her lips, his breathing as hard and fast as the heart she felt beating against her breast. Was it hers? Or his? For an instant, all the mysteries of the universe seemed to hinge on that particular riddle, but her mind refused to address it. It was far too busy concentrating on the more urgent problem of simply remembering how to breathe.

At last Nick pulled his lips from hers to draw air in through his mouth, letting his forehead rest momentarily against hers. 'Hot,' he breathed, his eyes closed. 'So damn hot. I knew it. Everyone else thought I was crazy, but even ten years ago I knew I could do this to you.'

She went suddenly stiff, pressing the small of her back against the counter. She jerked her head to one side. 'Do *what* to me?' She made her voice cold. 'Pin me down and force yourself on me? A gorilla could do that much.'

The words sounded wonderful, even her tone was the perfect combination of revulsion and disdain; the problem was that, even as she was speaking them, there was this peculiar red-hot pool of feeling deep in the pit of her stomach which she couldn't seem to turn off. In some way it seemed connected to his hands on her wrist, the pressure of his body against hers. If he would just move away, surely it would go with him?

As if he'd heard her thoughts, he backed away a step and released her wrists, holding his palms up with a dark, confident smile—look, Ma, no hands.

Emily caught her lower lip between her teeth. The feeling was still there. Maybe it was connected to his eyes, too. She started to move away, but his hands dropped to the counter on either side of her, trapping her. 'I might have forced you to stand still, Emily,' he said smoothly, 'but I didn't force anything else. You wanted it as much as I did.'

She swallowed once, pressed her lips together in determination, then ducked beneath his arms and skittered away to put the counter between them. Once safely on the other side, she raised her eyes defiantly.

He hadn't moved. He was still standing with his arms braced on the counter, blue eyes intense with a heat that flared deep beneath the surface expression of amusement. 'Come here, Emily,' he said quietly, but for some reason she had the impression that he had shouted.

She stood there without moving, her fingers pressing hard against the sides of her thighs.

'Come here.' He said it again, and the words coursed through her body like an electric current, and finally, with something like horror, she realised that she wanted to obey. Oh, lord—to *obey*.

The connection between them snapped in that instant, and she let her eyes fall closed briefly as she released a long sigh of relief. She was free again.

'What are you doing, Emily?' he asked quietly, not moving, sensing that something had changed.

'I'm not "doing" anything, Nick. I already did it. I walked away from you, just as I did on graduation night, just as I did in my apartment, just as I'll continue to do every time you touch me.'

The indentation between his brows deepened, and Emily felt a cold surge of satisfaction. At least she'd managed to wipe that cocky grin off his face. But not for long. It reappeared almost instantly.

'Have you noticed, Emily, that it takes you a little longer each time? And eventually you're not going to be able to walk away at all.'

'Don't bet on it,' she said icily, and his brows crashed down over the blue chips of his eyes.

'Is that a challenge?'

Emily's smile was placid, chilling. 'That's a promise, and don't take it so personally, Nick. I'm just not interested.'

His eyes narrowed and a muscle in his jaw clamped down hard. 'The hell you aren't.'

She raised her brows and made herself shrug, the picture of nonchalance.

His long arm flashed over the counter before she realised what was happening, and his fingers pressed white circles into the flesh of her forearm. 'The hell you aren't,' he repeated in a menacing tone, but there was the first trace of uncertainty in it as well, and absolutely no humour.

Their eyes locked in a silent battle of wills, and she was holding her own brilliantly, glaring at him with just the right measure of contempt, when his thumb began to move on her arm. She held his gaze, kept her expression stiff, but even she could feel something flash in her eyes—something hot and vibrant that she hadn't wanted him to see. His gaze had been fixed on her face, watching for something, alert for every nuance of her expression. When she'd felt that single, uncontrollable flash, his face had relaxed instantly, his mouth had curled in a satisfied smile, and he'd released her arm. Within the space of a second, he was the old, disturbingly confident Nick again.

Emily's brows twitched, and she caught herself just before it turned into a full-fledged frown of uncertainty. 'I'd like you to leave now.'

He laughed out loud, propped his elbows on the counter and dropped his chin into his hands, gazing at her with a lazy, sceptical smile. 'I'll just bet you would, Emily. Did I tell you I loved your hair?'

She dropped her head and brushed furiously at the front of her green florist's coat.

'Do that again,' he murmured, and she looked up to find him gazing boldly at her bustline.

She spun until her back was to him, her fists knotted, her nostrils flaring.

'You have a striking face, you know.' His voice floated over her shoulder. 'Those high cheekbones, that marvellous brow...long hair would be an insult to a face like that. A distraction.'

'I'm letting it grow!' she snapped with childish spite.

'I'll just cut it off again when you're sleeping, some night when you're so exhausted from love-making that you won't even wake up.'

Emily swallowed and felt a shudder pass through her body.

'What are you really afraid of, Em?' he asked softly from behind her.

She let her eyes fall closed in despair, then took a short, hitching breath and turned to face him. 'I'm not afraid of anything,' she said calmly. 'I told you, I'm just not interested.'

He dropped his hands to the counter and looked right at her. 'It's going to be a fight to the finish with you, isn't it?' There was a little smile playing at the corners of his mouth. 'But you know what? It's going to be worth it. In the end, when we finally go to bed together, it's going to be absolutely spectacular.'

CHAPTER FIVE

BEGINNING with the very next day, Nicholas became Emily's shadow, trailing her through the shop, peering over her shoulder with pretended interest in what she was doing, occasionally falling into silence when they were alone, but always making a great show of amiable chatter for the benefit of any customer who came in. He seemed oblivious to her outraged protests, and gradually they lessened in intensity, simply because they were pointless.

'Shouldn't you be getting back to that big city practice of yours?' she finally asked in exasperation after nearly tripping over him.

'Not yet. I'm on leave.'

'What about your patients? What if one of them needs you?'

'I work in a clinic, Emily, with a lot of other doctors. My patients are being very well taken care of. Besides, I needed this time more than they needed me.'

Her face tightened with disapproval. 'A *real* doctor wouldn't desert the people who depend on him.'

He looked at her with a gentle, somewhat surprised smile, as if she had just stated some profound, universal truth he hadn't expected her to grasp. 'You're absolutely right about that, Emily.'

By the second day he'd taken to touching her casually—a hand on her arm in passing, a pat on the head whenever he thought he could get away with it. Shrugging off such harmless physical contact became tedious with repetition, almost ridiculous, and if she were truly as indifferent as she was pretending she'd just ignore it, wouldn't she? So she did. There were a couple of satisfying moments when she caught him watching her with a puzzled frown, no doubt wondering why his campaign of torment wasn't producing the expected reaction. At those times the temptation to smile was strong, but she fought it.

Whatever else Nicholas Simon was, he had a bulldog's persistence. He followed her to the grocery, up and down the aisles and through the check-out; to the hardware store; even on an aimless, silent walk through the town. And yet, as closely as he trailed her during the day, he had never again shown up at her apartment at night. It was such a glaring inconsistency that Emily almost wanted to ask him why, but cold silence was her only defence against him, so she stifled her curiosity.

Of course every resident in Random believed he spent every night with her, thanks to the constant presence of that outlandish car on the street out front. Emily seethed inside whenever she met someone's knowing leer or slyly arched brow, but after a series of flustered denials, each met with much tongue-clucking scepticism, she gave up. She didn't know what lies he was spreading, but apparently they were effective. The townspeople clung to the Nick-and-Emily fabrication like ageing children reluctant to give up a belief in Santa Claus. They *wanted* to believe she was sleeping with Nick

Simon. They *wanted* to believe their dead little town was hosting the romance of the century, and finally she said to hell with them all. They'd been duped by a master, and they deserved the shame-faced guilt that would come eventually, when they learned the truth.

On Friday he broke the pattern of his constant presence by popping in and out of the shop, sometimes gone for as long as an hour. Emily struggled to relish the privacy—the first she'd had since he'd begun this ridiculous shadowing crusade—but the odd thing was that she caught herself listening for the bell over the door whenever he left, waiting for his return. Especially this time. It was almost four o'clock, and he'd been gone since two. The silence in the shop was like that pregnant, terrifying silence before a storm, when you huddled in the basement and wondered what form it would take, when it would arrive, and whether or not you would survive it.

'Hi, Em.' Nick's head poked through the door and her feet nearly left the floor. 'Thought I'd let you know I have some things to do. Won't be back for the rest of the day.'

She made a tight little prune-face and ignored him.

'Will you miss me?'

She couldn't resist one sarcastic lash. 'Desperately.'

He grinned, closed the door behind him, then immediately opened it again, just far enough to poke his head around the edge. 'For Pete's sake, Emily, you could fry an egg on the pavement today. Take

that silly bra off before you go out to your parents',
at least.'

She was deep into a thoroughly satisfying scowl
before she thought to wonder how he knew she was
having dinner with her parents.

Carl Swenson's farm lay three miles west of town,
right off the two-lane tar road that formed
Random's Main Street. It wasn't the prettiest land
in the area, with barely a tree to interrupt the flow
of cropland, but it boasted some of the richest loam
on the northern border of America's breadbasket.
As desolate as it appeared for most of the year, at
harvest time it was spectacularly beautiful—an
endless sea of golden wheat and corn-filled plain
marching off to the horizon—and the people who
knew the land could even see its beauty in spring,
when the rich black-brown colour of freshly turned
soil promised a future bounty.

But this year was different. The normally plentiful April rains had veered to the south, again and
again, and the landscape looked starved and pale.
The ploughed and planted fields were dangerously
dry, seeds lying dormant and lifeless, topsoil
blowing away with the slightest breeze.

The land looked bleached, Emily thought as her
car sped westward to her parents' farm. Three more
weeks, her father had said; if they didn't get rain
by then, the whole year's crop would be lost.

She sighed as she turned the car on to a lane that
bisected the drying field on her right. The driveway
was typically Midwestern—a long dirt track as
straight as the thoughts of a farmer, heading right
for the big red barn at the back without so much

as a pause at the two-storey white farmhouse. It seemed to say that the barn was the only worthy destination for any visitor, but Emily stopped her car right next to the house and climbed the steps to the back porch.

The oversized, cluttered kitchen was fragrant with the aroma of beef, onions, potatoes and carrots all roasting in a pan together. Her mother looked up from the sink in surprise, her dripping hands suspended over the soapy water.

'Well, hello, dear. I didn't expect you so soon.' She was wearing a peach dress that flattered her complexion and complemented her dark hair, but it was long-sleeved and cinched tightly at the waist, and had to be uncomfortable in this heat.

Emily walked over and kissed her lightly on the cheek. 'I closed the shop early today, Mom. I must have known you were making pot roast. What are you doing in that hot dress on a day like today? You should be in shorts and a halter.'

'Your father loves this dress,' she replied with a smile that spoke of secrets.

Emily shook her head, thinking that her mother would wear feed sacks, if that was what Carl Swenson wanted.

'Grab a cup, dear. We'll have some coffee before it's time to make the salad.' She looked at Emily, her brows raised expectantly. 'So!' she said, grabbing a towel to dry her hands while that 'so' hung in the air. It was the traditional beginning of all the serious talks they'd ever had, a verbal gunshot that warned the listener that her next words, no matter how innocent they seemed, were important. 'That Nicky has certainly grown into a handsome young man, hasn't he?'

Emily could have sworn that the air in the kitchen had suddenly become electrified. 'Nicky?' she asked innocently, easing herself into a chair at the round wooden table.

'Nicky Simon, of course.' Her mother smiled as she sat down.

You old fox, Emily thought, careful to keep her expression blank. You've heard the talk, and, if I know you, you're hoping it's all true. 'When did you see him?'

'Oh, I ran into him somewhere,' her mother replied vaguely, looking around as if she'd never seen her own kitchen before.

'Really? Where?'

Her mother turned her head and looked at Emily, eyes wide with feigned innocence. 'What, dear?'

'I asked where you ran into Nick Simon, Mother.'

'Oh. Well, here, actually.'

'*Here?* Nick was out *here*?'

Her mother shrugged with a guilty little smile.

Emily leaned back in her chair and narrowed her eyes. 'OK, Mom. Let's have it. What on earth was Nick Simon doing out here?'

'He was just paying a call, dear. A *social* call. Being neighbourly, you might say.'

'He's not your neighbour,' Emily pointed out. 'His grandfather's farm is on the other side of town.'

Her mother looked straight into her eyes. 'We're all neighbours in a town this size, Emily. You know that.'

'Baloney,' Emily muttered. It was as profane a word as was ever spoken in this house. 'Nick Simon isn't neighbourly, and he doesn't pay social calls unless he thinks he can get something out of it.'

'Oh?' Mary's brows lifted blithely. 'The way I hear it, he pays quite a few social calls on you, dear.'

Emily scowled, exasperated. 'Forget what you heard, Mother. None of it is true. It's all a lie, all part of some bizarre plan of his—to drive me crazy, I think.' She sighed, thoroughly frustrated, because that had sounded preposterous even to her.

She leaned across the table and spoke earnestly. 'The truth is that he came howling under my window on the night of his grandfather's funeral, drunk as a lord, threatening to wake the town if I didn't let him in. So I did. I let him in, I made him some coffee...then he passed out on the couch. That's *all* that happened. He's just having the time of his life letting the town think there was a whole lot more to it.'

'I see.' Her mother sighed sympathetically, but it was clear that the sympathy was meant for Nick. 'He took Art's death very hard, didn't he? It was nice that he had you to come to for comfort.'

Emily rolled her eyes. 'He wasn't looking for comfort,' she said firmly.

Mary pulled absently at a strand of her hair, but there was a warning in her normally placid green eyes. 'Are you really so sure about that? He was absolutely devoted to his grandfather, you know.'

Emily made a sound of impatience and turned her head.

'He never missed a month; not in ten years,' Mary went on, musing. 'Art was so proud of that. Third weekend of every month, just like clockwork, Nicky would come home. It had to be hard for him, especially during those years when he was working and going to school.'

Emily looked back at her mother, a frown building behind her eyes. 'He came home once a month?' she murmured. 'But I never saw him...'

'He came to visit Art, not the town,' Mary smiled, then she cocked her head, reconsidering what she'd said. 'Then again, maybe they were one and the same, as far as Nick was concerned.'

Emily's teeth tugged at her lower lip, and her frown was full-blown. 'I didn't know that,' she mumbled, a little disturbed to learn that Nick had been a devoted grandson after all. Somehow it just didn't mesh with the image she had of him.

'Wouldn't it be nice,' Mary asked with sudden brightness, 'if Nick decided to stay on in Random?'

Emily just stared at her, inexplicably terrified by the prospect of such a thing happening. 'He isn't considering that, is he?' she whispered.

Mary shrugged, then her expression softened, and she reached across the table to pat her daughter's hand. This time, Emily knew that the sympathy she saw in those china-doll features was for her, as if she were in some way defective, a poor creature you just had to feel sorry for, because there was some essential part missing.

CHAPTER SIX

NICK was slouched in the front seat of his convertible when Emily opened the shop door the next morning. His head was flung back on the headrest, his eyes were closed, and his jaw was shadowed with the unshaven stubble of his beard. He didn't move at the sound of the door opening, and he didn't move when she clicked it shut behind her.

He's awake, she told herself. He just wants you to think he isn't, so he can pop up and scare you to death.

Lips pursed, she ignored him and started to sweep the pavement, banging the wooden top of the broom more often than necessary on the cement, making as much noise as possible.

Even with the sun barely over the horizon, it was already intolerably hot, and she paused halfway through the chore to wipe her forearm across her brow. Ever so warily, she peered at him from under the cover of her arm, fully expecting to see him upright, one arm flung over the seat back, grinning at her impudently.

He was in precisely the same position, eyes still closed, and the steady rise and fall of his chest marked the unmistakable condition of deep sleep. Random seemed even more quiet than usual; so quiet that she could hear the muted rustle of a single dried leaf skittering across the cement somewhere far up the street.

She jumped at the sharp crack of a door slamming on one of the back streets, shattering the silence, but Nick didn't move.

Emily lowered her arm slowly and looked at him directly, frowning. Her gaze was so intent that she was certain he would somehow sense it and snap upright with a mocking grin—'Caught you, Emily! Caught you looking!'—but after a few seconds of tension it became obvious that that wasn't going to happen, and she relaxed a little, leaning on the broom.

She was going to be nice to Nick today. In spite of everything he'd done to her personally, she was going to make an honest effort to be nice. Ever since her mother had told her how close the two Simon men had been, she'd felt guilty for that awful thing she'd said the first day—the thing about Nick not getting to see his grandfather before he'd died. The words had been cruel enough even without knowing Nick had loved the old man; now the memory of saying them made her cringe. She had to purge the guilt somehow. Maybe she could pretend absolutely nothing had happened between them; that they were meeting for the first time after a ten-year hiatus. She'd ask him how he'd been, what he was doing, where he was living—all the things you were supposed to ask in the polite, controlled conversation of a first meeting.

It would have troubled her greatly to know just how long she stood there looking at him, as motionless as he was, but time seemed to have stopped in the early morning stillness, and she wasn't aware of its passing. Had anyone been around to see it, they might have marvelled at how much Random's

Main Street looked like a still photograph this Saturday, with a single red car at its deserted kerb, the figure of a man slumped inside, the statue of a woman positioned on the pavement close by.

Emily had never dared examine Nick this closely, for fear of being caught at it, and she found the opportunity almost exhilarating—as if she were a smug child performing mischief with absolutely no fear of discovery. The feeling actually made her smile a little, and the smile made her almost beautiful.

He was dressed as casually—as thoughtlessly, really—as he always was, in a plain white T-shirt and faded jeans. His clothes were obviously clean, the T-shirt so white that it was almost blinding, and his hair glittered in the morning sun as if it had just been washed. But his jaw was dark with a day-old beard, and Emily wondered why he would shower and change into fresh clothing, but forget to shave.

Her mouth quirked impatiently to one side. Riddles had always annoyed her. She didn't like unanswered questions, insoluble puzzles. It offended her sense of order.

He stirred slightly in the seat, shifting the position of his pelvis to one side, but even that didn't awaken him. It was strange enough that she'd found him in the car this morning, instead of waiting to pop out at her from some hiding-place, but it was stranger still to find him so deeply asleep. Obviously, he'd had a very hard, very late night.

And then it all came together in her mind, and her face tightened a little. Of course. Just because he loved his grandfather, it didn't automatically make him a saint, any more than becoming a doctor had graced him with dignity. Her eyes narrowed as she focused on the car, coated with dust from one of the dirt roads he'd pretended to avoid so assiduously. He'd probably been out all night, perhaps drinking again as he had that first night; perhaps even looking for 'comfort', as her mother had so naïvely put it, from some other woman. *That* was why he hadn't come back to her apartment again; he'd probably found more tractable company somewhere else... like at Crooked Corners over in the next county, a tavern notorious for loud bands and willing women and a few upstairs rooms decent people never talked about.

She scowled at the thought, experiencing the flash of an unfamiliar feeling she didn't care to analyse too closely. Quite without intention, she found herself wondering what kind of woman he'd spent the night with, what she'd looked like, and then she blew air sharply out of her nose, disgusted by her own curiosity.

His head rolled slowly towards her, and he opened his eyes. They were bloodshot, she noticed, hoping that he had a brutal hangover. By now the bruise on his temple had faded to a sickly greenish-yellow, and she wondered how he had explained *that* to whomever he was spending his nights with.

'Well,' he drawled, his mouth curving in a sleepy smile. 'Can't think of anything I'd rather see first thing in the morning.'

She banged the head of the broom on the pavement, raising a cloud of dust. 'It looks as if you certainly had a good time last night,' she said snidely, turning her head away as if she couldn't bear to look at him.

After a moment he said, 'I see you've decided to exchange silence for sarcasm. It's going to take me a while to decide which is worse.' He chuckled softly when she began to push the broom furiously across a patch of pavement she'd already swept. 'And in answer to your question——'

'I didn't ask a question.'

'And in answer to the question you didn't actually ask, but wanted to...' she could hear the smile in his voice '...I did indeed have a good time last night. One of those rare, rare times that make everything else worth while.'

Her eyes flashed as she banged the broom on the pavement again, then she spun round and stomped into the shop, slamming the door behind her. Whatever he'd done last night was obviously bad enough, without throwing it up in her face, actually *bragging* about it!

Her sandals clattered angrily as she stormed around the counter to fling the broom through the curtained doorway that led to the back room. Lord, her face felt red, and she knew damn well she was ruining everything, letting her outrage show so clearly, but she couldn't seem to control it.

She'd managed to take several deep, calming breaths before Nick got into the shop and over to the counter, but her face was still flushed, and it reddened even further when she saw the amusement in his expression.

'Goodness, Em, you're just as jealous as hell, aren't you?' he grinned, legs spread, thumbs jammed in the front pockets of his jeans.

'In your dreams!' she snapped, glaring at him.

His grin broadened. 'You have every reason to be jealous, of course. I *did* spend last night with a woman—a naked woman...'

Emily blanched, shocked that even he could be so blunt.

'And my one and only regret is that you weren't there with us.'

Her mouth dropped open in disbelief.

'Let me tell you about it, Em——'

'I don't believe it!' she whispered, stunned. 'You're perverted.'

He tried to hold it in, but finally gave up and laughed out loud. 'No, Emily, whatever else you may think I am, I am definitely not a pervert. Even by your rather narrow standards. Let me tell you about last night——'

'No,' she whispered. 'For heaven's sake, no. What kind of a person do you think I am? I don't want to hear this. I *won't* hear this——'

'The naked woman was pregnant,' he inserted quickly.

'*What?*' Sheer horror was clearly imprinted all over Emily's face, and Nick doubled over the counter, burying his face in his hands, laughing helplessly.

'Emily, Emily,' he gasped. 'She was having a baby. I just happened to be in the right place at the right time, and I helped her deliver it.'

Emily blinked at him, felt her chest jerk in a hitched breath. 'Oh.'

Nick pushed himself up from the counter and dragged his hands over his face, as if he could wipe away the smile that kept cropping up again. 'I was checking out the facilities at Fairfax Hospital when

Tommy Hendricks and his wife came in—remember Tommy Hendricks? A tall, skinny guy in our class? Anyway, his wife was in the last stages of labour and the doctor on call hadn't arrived yet, so I lent a hand.'

All she could do was stare at him, even though she knew she must look every bit as foolish as she felt.

'It's what doctors *do*, you know,' he smiled. 'What *I* do.'

Of course she knew that. But she hadn't really pictured it before. Nick Simon, actually practising medicine? Delivering babies? Saving lives?

He sighed distractedly and pushed the fingers of one hand deep into his hair. 'I think you could see birth a million times and still never get over the wonder of it,' he said softly. 'But it's even more incredible when it's someone you know; someone you've known all your life. I never felt that before.'

The wail of the town siren interrupted the first peaceful moment they'd had in days, starting as a low growl, rising steadily in volume and pitch as it climbed to full, ear-splitting power.

Emily's and Nick's heads both jerked simultaneously towards the front window, their faces wiped clean of any expression except worry. Their bodies were similarly tensed, ready. You didn't grow up in the American Midwest without learning early to listen and heed the warning howl of a siren, particularly during the hot, dry months, when its terrifying sound usually meant one of two things, both equally ominous.

Nick was already out of the door, running into the middle of the street, by the time Emily had circumvented the counter. She followed him as fast as she could, her green coat flapping open at her knees. Doors opened up and down the block as other early risers instinctively ran outside to circle the horizon with their eyes.

'Wildfire or tornado?' someone hollered from down the street.

'Don't know yet!' someone else called out an answer.

Even though the street that was deserted just a moment before was gradually filling with people, it was still eerily silent. As if they were mindless robots obeying some universal command from an unseen master, they all turned in slow circles where they stood, shading their eyes with their hands, scanning the sky for either smoke or storm clouds.

'No clouds,' Emily murmured, squinting up at the bleached blue canopy like everyone else. 'It can't be a tornado.'

'No smoke, either,' Nick replied. 'Maybe it's just a small house fire, too far away to see.'

'There!' Herman Belson, owner of the Random Hardware, was twenty yards further down the street, his pudgy finger pointing south between two buildings.

Like a wave rolling on to a beach, the growing crowd surged towards him, all craning their necks to peer at the slice of sky that showed between the buildings. Emily and Nick were in the centre of the flow, caught in the press of people like the nucleus of a cell. There were at least fifty of them jammed there together, sharing a tiny space on the otherwise empty street, and Emily caught herself marvelling that they had all appeared so quickly from the dark, blank-faced shops and the few second-storey apartments. Somehow she hadn't thought that that many made their homes right on Main Street, just as she did.

'Five miles,' Herman said certainly, staring at the white haze of smoke at the horizon line. 'Mebbe more.'

There was a collective sigh of relief, and Emily could almost feel the subtle relaxation of all the tense bodies around her.

'But it's a big one,' Herman added ominously.

Like a single organism, all heads turned at the sound of the big door on the fire station, one block behind Main Street, rolling up on its massive hinges.

'Looks to be clear over in Fairfax Township,' an elderly male voice came from somewhere behind Emily. 'They must have called our boys for help.'

The undulating wail of the Random Volunteer Fire Department's truck siren pierced the morning air, confirming the statement. A few seconds later the truck's red nose poked around the corner and aimed for the crowd. Like a piece of paper ripped on the dotted line, the crowd parted into two neat halves to give the truck clearance.

'What is it!' Herman called to one of the men standing on the truck's running board, trying to shrug into his gear and hang on at the same time.

'Big swamp fire over by Fairfax!' he called out as they passed. 'Every rig in the county's been called to help! See you all in about two days, if we're lucky!' His voice faded away as the truck picked up speed.

'Another one,' someone muttered, and a grumble rolled through the crowd like the irritated sound of a very large animal.

'Over ten thousand acres gone to fire already,' another voice grumbled. 'Whole damn state's going to burn down if we don't get rain soon.'

A dozen deep-throated assents rumbled through the crowd, and there was something disturbing in the sound. Emily frowned, looking around at the faces she'd known all her life, but had never seen quite this long before. Not that the farmers of Random had never known hard times—the average crop year was never perfect, usually leaning a little to one side of either too wet or too dry—but not since the dust-bowl days of the '30s had the conditions been this extreme, and many of the people here were now facing total devastation. Sometimes that was all it took to wipe out a farm that had been in the same family for generations—one horrendously bad year. It didn't happen often in this part of the country—perhaps once every fifty years—but when it did farming operations tumbled like wobbly dominoes on a board.

'We've gotta have rain!' Wilbur Lindberg shouted, as if there were someone within hearing distance who had rain to give, and was withholding it out of spite. 'I've got three hundred acres of seed blowing away with the topsoil, and my life savings with it!'

Four hundred! Six hundred! Eight hundred! The cries came furiously, as if they were all trying to outdo each other with the size of their potential losses.

Inside, Emily hurt for all of them; all of the people here, and the hundreds of others on farms scattered throughout the county and the state. They were her people, these grim, stalwart farmers whose very lives depended on the fickle whims of the weather; and now their lives were being threatened by circumstances they couldn't control.

In the best of years they still had to battle brush fires, tornadoes, drought, winterkill—and still they persevered. Uneducated, uncultured, unsophisticated, the residents of Random and a thousand Midwestern towns like it were all that—but there was something noble about them, too. Something wonderfully courageous that always made Emily proud to be among their number. But now they were hurting, and there was nothing anybody could do about it.

'I can't remember it ever being this bad,' Nick said into her ear, looking around at the disgruntled faces, catching pieces of a dozen muttered exchanges that were growing louder and louder with the frustration that had been building for months.

'It's never been this bad,' Emily replied dully. 'Not in our lifetime, anyway. A lot of these people are going to lose their farms if we don't get rain soon.' She sighed, as frustrated as everyone else on the street, thinking of her father.

It didn't seem fair that an entire way of life could hinge on something as fickle, something as incidental to the rest of the world as a single rain shower. She wondered how the other segments of the country's population—construction workers, factory workers, doctors, lawyers, teachers—would survive if *their* careers and livelihoods depended on something as unreliable as the weather. They wouldn't, she decided with a grim nod. It took a special kind of courage—or madness—to live with that kind of a shadow over your head.

She felt Nick's warm, dry hand grasp hers at her side, and, perhaps because the despair in the street was almost tangible, the pressure of his fingers was comforting, and she didn't pull away.

'How long since Random's had a rain dance?'

She looked up at him with disbelief. 'You've got to be kidding? I can't even remember the last one. We haven't had a really good crop year here in almost a decade. What's to celebrate?'

His fingers tightened on her hand and he smiled down at her. 'The best parties are never celebrations—ever been to a wake?'

Emily's face hardened and she jerked her hand away. 'You don't party when you're looking disaster right in the eye!' she hissed irritably, looking around quickly to make sure she hadn't been overheard.

'I do.'

'Well you're not one of us!' she said sharply. 'Not any more!'

His head flinched back a little, eyes narrowed as if to ward off a blow. 'A little fun never hurt anyone,' he said carefully, 'and sometimes it even helps; makes waiting out the bad times easier.'

'And sometimes things are so bad that nothing helps,' she said flatly. 'A good time may be a cure-all in the city, but not out here. You've been away too long, Nick.'

After a moment she had to fight the urge to fidget, his gaze made her so uncomfortable.

'I think a good old-fashioned rain dance is just
what this town needs, Emily,' he said finally. 'Let's
suggest it. You and me. We'll organise it together,
get the people——'

Her brows shot up at the idea of being associated
with anything so frivolous. 'Don't be ridiculous,'
she said, then turned on her heel and started to
make her way hurriedly back to her shop.

The crowd had separated into smaller groups,
each deeply involved in their own private conversations, each face as dour as the next. Not exactly
a gathering primed for dancing in the street, Emily
thought with satisfaction. Rain dance, indeed!

She knew the history as well as any farm
daughter—the street dance had once been as much
a part of Midwestern tradition as silos were a part
of the landscape. In Random, back when they had
still had them, they had always been called rain
dances. As far back as pioneer days settlers had
held dances in the street, simply because in those
days no town had had a building large enough to
host its entire population. Because they were held
outside, and therefore limited to the hot, dry
summer months when rain was infrequent, the irony
of calling them rain dances had apparently ap-
pealed to the town's founders, and the label had
lasted for generations. But enthusiasm for any celebration had waned with the crop yields during the
past decade, and, as far as Emily knew, there hadn't
been a street dance in the whole county in years.

And this certainly isn't the summer to resurrect
the custom, she thought. Who wanted to dance
when crops were dying in the fields and hogs were

convulsing in the heat and wildfires were gobbling up huge tracts of the land they lived on?

Sighing, Emily retreated to the workroom at the rear of the store and began the laborious monthly task of scrubbing out the coolers. If there was one saving grace to the morning, it was that Nick hadn't followed her in from the street.

It was almost a full half-hour before the sporadic shouts from outside became loud enough to attract her attention. Curious, she dropped her scrubbing brush in the bucket, wiped her hands on a rag, and passed through the shop to the front door.

The people who had gathered on the street in response to the siren were just now dispersing, *en masse*, oddly enough, instead of in little groups. It looked as if they were all headed for Alfred's Café.

'Guess what, Emily!' Herman Belson called over his shoulder when he caught sight of her. 'We're going to have a rain dance! How about that?'

Emily blinked in disbelief, almost as surprised by the smiles on those previously sullen faces as she was by the preposterous announcement. Finally she lifted her hand in a feeble wave because Herman seemed to expect it, then stared after all of them as they walked away.

She was still standing there, frozen in her doorway, when she heard the sound of a pebble scraping under someone's shoe. Her eyes lifted to the chemist's across the street, seeking motion, seeing none. Finally they focused on Nick, standing directly opposite her, nearly invisible because he was so motionless. He was leaning against a lamppost, hands stuffed in his jeans pockets, his mouth curved in a quiet, mocking smile.

'Got a date for the dance, Emily?' he called out clearly.

CHAPTER SEVEN

THE days grew hotter. Even though it was still May, the lawns in town took on the brown, crisp look of late August, and tree branches drooped towards the ground, as if scanning the dried soil for a drop of moisture. Cattle huddled in barren pastures, tails busily swishing at the early onslaught of summer flies, and Random Creek slowed to a sluggish trickle.

Emily saw all this, and more; but apparently she was the only one. The rest of the town was so caught up in a totally childish frenzy, anticipating that damned street dance, that they barely noticed the earth drying up under their feet. Fools.

She'd stayed in her apartment all day Sunday, sprawled on the floor in front of a fan, trying to concentrate on the shop books. She'd been continually interrupted by phone-calls that excitedly relayed the news of an unprecedented Sunday night town meeting to make plans for the dance. After dark the steady rumble of cars and trucks rolling up to the town hall had filtered in through the open window, and she'd had to turn her television on loud to drown out the noise of mass foolishness.

At least the silly project had distracted Nick enough to give her a little relief from his torment. As a matter of fact, it seemed that he was the only one in town who *hadn't* called her, and Sunday had passed without a sign of him.

But he was waiting outside when she opened the shop on Monday morning, his hair in a boyish tangle, his eyes glinting with mischief. He had sheets of poster-board tucked under one arm, a packet of markers clutched in his hand. 'Signs for the dance,' he explained, his bare arm brushing against her as he pushed his way into the shop. She closed the door and stomped after him, protesting all the way.

'If you think I'm going to make posters for that stupid dance——'

He stopped suddenly and turned, and she brought herself up with a jerk just before she ran right into his chest.

'Of course not. But your shop is the perfect place to do it. God knows the floor is as clean as anyone else's kitchen table, and there's enough room to spread this stuff around. It's what you get for being so compulsively tidy, Emily. When I told them at the meeting I was sure you wouldn't mind——'

'You told them *what*?'

'The town voted unanimously to make your store dance headquarters.' One side of his mouth lifted in a suggestive smirk. 'Of course, we won't be alone much for the next few days, and you'll have to try to keep your hands off me...'

If a customer hadn't chosen precisely that moment to appear, she would have thrown him out on his ear right then, or so she told herself. But that first customer turned into a steady stream of people popping in and out as the day wore on, and it was no longer a question of kicking Nick out of the shop—she'd have to kick out the whole damn town. At one time or another, almost everyone she knew was sprawled over a piece of poster-board on her green and white floor, diligently lettering under Nick's supervision while she looked on with an owlish glare.

By Tuesday the shop was a shambles, display benches shoved against the wall, poster-board and pens scattered all over the floor, stacks of leaflets teetering in precarious piles on the counter. The bell over the door jingled constantly as people came and went, there was the persistent drone of a dozen conversations going on at once, and order had become chaos. Although Nick was a constant presence, they'd barely exchanged a word. She'd had to satisfy herself with a few well-timed malevolent looks, but he'd only laughed. Emily's composure was as crumpled as the discarded wads of paper cluttering her shop floor.

On Wednesday, she came downstairs a full hour earlier than usual, hoping for a little peace, just a little time to try to straighten the showroom. She looked around at the mess and sighed helplessly, not knowing where to start. For two days now she hadn't been able to perform the morning cleaning ritual, the place was so cluttered, and today, apparently, would be no exception.

'Damn you anyway, Nick Simon,' she muttered, but there was no real feeling in her tone. He'd robbed her of her reputation, her privacy, and now even her shop; and anger seemed so feeble against such a list of transgressions that it was suddenly pointless. To hell with it. To hell with *him*. All this would be over soon enough; today, in fact.

She jumped at the sound of tapping on the door window, then sighed in resignation. If she didn't let him in, he'd probably just jump through the plate-glass window.

'You're down early,' he grinned as he brushed by her on the way inside. He was wearing snug jeans and a white dress-shirt that clearly belonged under an expensive suit jacket. The sleeves were rolled halfway up his browned forearms, and for some reason Emily found that more disquieting than the revealing T-shirts and tank-tops he favoured in the heat.

She covered her uneasiness by sniping at him. 'If I come down any later than this, I have to stand in line to get into my own shop.'

He stopped halfway towards the counter and frowned at her over his shoulder. 'The past two days have really been tough on you, haven't they, Emily?' he asked quietly. For once, there was no mockery in his voice. 'I guess I never thought about it before, but all this activity must be a nightmare for someone who loves order as much as you do. I don't suppose it's doing much for your business, either.'

Emily was about to accept the commiseration as her due when she frowned suddenly, remembering the receipts from the last two days. Her sanity might be at risk, but sales had sky-rocketed with all the extra traffic. She looked down and brushed prissily at the front of her green coat. 'Well,' she admitted grudgingly, 'business hasn't really been *that* bad...'

His face broke into an immediate smile. 'Great. Glad to hear it, because you'll probably be getting a lot more traffic through here between now and the dance.'

Her eyes jerked up sharply. 'You said today was the last day you'd be working in here. You *promised*.'

'And I keep my promises,' he was quick to say. 'But . . .' he left the sentence unfinished, and turned to walk rapidly to the counter.

'But *what*?' she demanded, hurrying after him.

His forearms were braced on the formica as he stared at the back wall.

'Ni-ick . . .' she drew his name out into a two-syllable warning, and he handed her a sheet of paper without looking at her.

'What's this?' she mumbled suspiciously, frowning down at it.

'Just the leaflet advertising the dance,' he said innocently, but he still wouldn't look at her. 'It's going all over the county this afternoon.'

She sighed impatiently and scanned the sheet, then flapped it at him. 'So? What's this got to do with me?'

'Read the bottom line.'

She grimaced and found the large print at the bottom, then began to read aloud. '"All proceeds to benefit the Random Fire Department. Tickets can be purchased at" . . . *what*? "Tickets can be purchased at the" . . . "the Random Flower Shop?" What *is* this?'

Finally he looked at her. Sheepishly. And then he shrugged. 'You had the ideal location. You're right in the middle of the block.'

'Dammit, Nick, you can't do this! I'm running a business here, not a ticket booth for your stupid dance! You erase that right now!'

'Can't.'

'What do you mean, you can't? You *can*, and you'd *better*.'

'Wouldn't make any difference if I did. We've already got a hundred posters out that say the same thing.' He moved quickly to grab the leaflet from her hands, sensing that she was about to rip it down the middle.

Her hands snatched at empty air, then fell to her sides and clenched into fists. She felt her face reddening, her whole body starting to tremble. A hundred posters...

'I won't do it,' she whispered, trying so hard to keep from screaming that she overcompensated. Her voice was barely audible. 'First you donate my shop—*my* shop—for this...this...art project, and now you've got me selling tickets! What's next? Am I singing with the band, too?'

He smiled with delighted surprise. 'To tell you the truth, I never thought of that. Can you sing, Emily?'

She blew a frustrated blast of air out of her cheeks and clenched her fists even tighter to keep from punching him on the nose.

'Oh, come on, Em.' He reached out to touch her face and she jerked her head to the side. 'A little community involvement will do you good. It's probably just what you need to bring you out of your shell——'

'I'm not in a shell! And I don't need you to tell me what I need!'

'Of course you do,' he replied, completely un-ruffled. 'You need me for that, and a whole lot more.'

She just stared at him, her mouth open, her eyes wide. It just didn't seem possible that any one man was capable of that much conceit. She hitched in a furious breath, and forced herself to speak in a steady, controlled monotone. 'What I need is for you to go back where you came from,' she said quietly. 'To leave me and my business and my town alone. The happiest day of my life will be the day I see the last of you.'

He looked at her for a moment, and, although for days she'd wanted nothing more than to wipe that cocky smile off his face, now that she'd finally managed to do it she wasn't quite as satisfied as she'd thought she would be.

He stared straight at her for the longest time, then he cocked his head, apparently searching for something in her face. She kept her eyes focused and narrow, her mouth in a rigid line, but he must have imagined he saw something other than the chill she was trying so hard to project, because his cheeks suddenly dimpled in a knowing smile.

'You're going to miss me when I go, Emily.' He said it like a prophecy. 'You're going to lie up there on your back in your little old-maid bed, and you're going to wish I were there, with my hands all over you.'

Emily gasped audibly, the size of the breath caught in her throat threatening to choke her.

Nick's smile just broadened, then he rolled the leaflet into a tube and walked towards the door.

She closed her eyes and breathed deeply after the door closed behind him. She had to stop letting him see how much he disturbed her. That was the obvious reason for his behaviour, of course. He was like a little boy, taking perverted pleasure from saying things just for their shock value. The trick was to ignore him, like any other pest, then maybe he'd leave her alone.

She was still breathing hard. Suddenly she became conscious of her breasts pushing up the light green fabric as they rose and fell, and she frowned hard and willed them to stop. 'You're going to wish I were there, with my hands all over you...'

Her eyes fell closed in a motion that was more despair than outrage, and she tried to concentrate on the blessed silence of her little shop while she still had it. Lord, she mused, it's so peaceful when he's not around. So restful. That's all I want. Just a little peace.

She sagged against the counter, her lips trying for a smile, but after a few seconds the smile faltered a little as the first silence she'd experienced in days began to irritate her. A few seconds more, and she began to frown, then drum her fingers on the counter-top.

Had the shop ever been this quiet?

She jerked her head around at the jangle of the little bell over the door, then felt something very close to relief when a knot of chattering people came in. Without realising it, she smiled.

By ten o'clock the shop was crowded with a dozen people hunched over the counter, crouched on the floor, all labouring over the last of the posters. There was an undercurrent of chatter, frequent giggles, and, occasionally, uproarious laughter as some preposterous comment made the rounds.

After that first impulsive smile of greeting, Emily remembered to frown disapprovingly at the nonsense going on around her. Almost everyone here certainly had something better to do—something more productive than huddling over a poster like a child with a new box of crayons. What was Mr Tollefson doing off the farm, his gnarled old hand clutching a marker instead of the gear lever on a tractor? And wasn't this the day Mrs Hoeffer's bridge group met for needlework? And yet here they were, a collection of fussy old ladies apparently having the time of their lives, if their giggling was any measure. Even young John Clauson and his wife had stolen a few hours from their dairy farm to come in, and they were as hard-working and reclusive a pair as lived in the township.

As the morning wore on, her disapproval gave way to resigned tolerance. Let them fritter away their valuable time on such frivolous pursuits. It wasn't her concern. She, at least, was bent earnestly over the shop books; she, at least, was accomplishing something worthwhile. 'The only sane person left in the whole town,' she muttered down at her ledger.

'What did you say, Emily?' Mrs Hoeffer piped up.

Emily's head jerked up and she forced a businesslike smile. 'Oh, nothing. Just talking to myself.'

'Well, come on, dear. Try your hand at this.'

Emily's smile weakened when she saw the piece of blank poster-board Mrs Hoeffer was holding

towards her. She stared at it as if it were a poisonous snake, ready to strike. "Uh...no...I don't think
so...'

'Oh, come on. It's *fun*.'

Her smile twitched nervously, and she felt an odd
fluttering in her stomach. Suddenly someone shoved
a blue marker into her hand, and every muscle in
her body tensed. Permitting this craziness in her
shop was one thing; participating in it was something else altogether—something no one would have
expected of her a few days ago.

'Here you go, Emily.' John Clauson and his wife
were pushing their materials to one side, making
an empty space between them on the floor. They
both looked up at her with expectant smiles. Did
they actually think she was going to get down there
and colour and giggle with the rest of them? What
was wrong with these people? Didn't they remember who she was?

At noon, a large shadow blocked the light from
the door and everyone looked up from their work.
The silhouette of Nick's form looked massive,
wrenchingly masculine, standing there with his legs
spread and arm muscles bulging under the weight
of the crate he carried. 'I've got two dozen ham-
burgers, a mess of fries, and a case of pop in here,
if anyone's interested,' he said, and there was a
chorus of hungry voices. 'Where's Emily?' His
glance scanned the shop, passing right over her.

'Here.' Her hand shot up automatically, then
froze in mid-air when she realised what she must
look like. The rising temperature had made her
discard the green overall over an hour ago, and now
she sat cross-legged on the floor in only shorts and

a sleeveless blouse, a half-finished poster propped on her lap.

Nick's blue eyes found her voice, passed on without a pause, then snapped back in a double take. She looked away quickly, smoothing the short blonde hair behind her ears as if that would somehow make her appearance more dignified.

'Emily?' His voice pulled at her eyes. The colour deepened in her already flushed cheeks as his eyes wandered down her bare arms to her legs, then lifted slowly to her face again.

A smudge of dirt made an angle of his cheekbone, strands of his own blond hair clung damply to his brow, and his white shirt hung open, revealing an avenue of tanned chest and stomach that made Emily's hand whiten around the marker it held.

He pulled his eyes away reluctantly, passed out food and drink to everyone else first, then hunkered down next to her and pushed the box of food between them. His smile was mischievous, but his eyes were strangely intense when they locked on to hers.

'Who the hell are you?' his voice rumbled in a tease too low to be overheard by the others.

She frowned and grabbed a can of pop from the box. Ignore him, she reminded herself. Just pretend he doesn't exist.

'Certainly not Earnest Emily,' he goaded her. 'That woman would never crawl around on a dirty floor and show *that* much leg, let alone help make posters for a stupid town dance.'

She tried not to blush at the reference to her legs; tried even harder not to bristle at the sarcasm in his tone. 'The sooner the posters get finished, the sooner I'll have my shop back,' she said in defence of her behaviour.

He grinned, somehow making fun of her explanation without saying a word. She sniffed and looked away, and the next thing she knew he'd dropped from his crouch to sit cross-legged right next to her, his jeans-clad knee pressed against her bare one. She sidled a little to the left, and he followed.

'Stop that!' she hissed out of the side of her mouth.

His knee pushed more insistently against hers, and now she felt the tickling brush of his shirt-sleeve against her arm as he leaned towards her.

Ignore him, ignore him, she reminded herself firmly, so intent on her concentration that she missed his head bending towards her ear. His breath fluttered like the wings of a moth against the sensitive skin of her neck, raising goose-bumps. 'You have beautiful legs,' he whispered. 'I'd like to kiss them.'

Emily twisted her head away, blushing so hard that her eyes almost started to water.

'You keep leaning towards John like that, and he's going to think you're coming on to him.'

She jerked her eyes to the left, saw John Clauson's arm a fraction of an inch from her shoulder, and jerked herself straight, bumping Nick in the process.

'Not so rough, Em!' he said loudly, and someone behind her tittered.

She glared straight ahead at nothing, gritting her teeth so tightly together that her jaw ached. I'll kill him, she thought calmly. I'll just have to kill him. That's all there is to it.

Somehow she found the presence of mind to reach for a hamburger, unwrap it, and take a bite that tasted like sawdust. She could feel him watching her from the side, but steadfastly refused to look at him, pretending great interest in the tasteless food she was trying to force down.

Finally, out of the corner of her eye, she saw his legs unfold and tuck beneath him as he rose. At the last minute, he bent to whisper, 'Be careful, Emily. It's starting to look suspiciously as if you're having a good time. A thing like that could destroy your image.'

Before her lips could form the first word of a retort she hadn't even composed yet, he was clapping his hands for attention. 'OK, people. You've got two more hours before school lets out, then we'll have a gang of kids to distribute all this artwork. Finish as many as you can.'

She cringed visibly when his hand ruffled the short hair on the top of her head with a casualness that implied he did it often.

'I'll see *you* later,' he added, just before walking away.

There wasn't a person in the shop who didn't draw the obvious conclusion from that remark, and as Emily saw all the conspiratorial grins on all those faces she wondered if it were actually possible for someone to die of embarrassment.

'You two are so cute,' Kathy Clauson chuckled, stabbing a French fry into her mouth.

Emily looked over at her, dumbfounded. How could these people be so blind? Couldn't they see what was really going on here?

It was the first time she really understood how much her image had changed since Nick's arrival. As far as these people were concerned, she was no longer the earnest, solitary, rather uninteresting town florist. In their imaginations, at least, she was now a fascinating half of a wildly romantic twosome, an object of curiosity and gossip and wistful speculation. *That* was why they'd been so certain she would join in the silly poster brigade. They didn't think of her as Earnest Emily any more. They thought she was the woman whom Nick Simon had made up.

She looked around at all the friendly faces smiling at her, and realised that this, at last, was her chance to set the record straight. She could tell them the truth right now: that the only night Nick had spent in her apartment, he'd spent passed out on the couch; that there wasn't a shred of truth to the fantasy relationship he'd let the whole town believe they were having; that she was not having some stormy affair; that, in fact, she was the same old steady, quiet, slightly prudish Emily Swenson she'd always been . . .

She looked down briefly, sighed with determination, then stood up and faced her audience. Tell them, she told herself. Tell them right now.

'Well,' she said after a moment of stomach-rolling anticipation, and then for some reason her mouth refused to form the words her brain was dictating. She just stood there with everyone staring at her, paragraphs forming in her mind while her lips remained mute. *Tell them!* her thoughts shrieked inside her head. Or for the rest of your life they're going to think you're someone you're not, someone you've never been, and could never hope to be. You don't want *that* to happen, do you?

The words popped out like a cork under pressure. 'If two hours are all we've got,' she said, 'we'd better get back to work.'

CHAPTER EIGHT

NICK came back to the shop in the late afternoon, followed by a caravan of wildly diverse vehicles—old, unpainted pick-up trucks, flashy hot rods, and even a few classic convertibles, every bit as flamboyant as his own. Each vehicle was crammed with exuberant high-school students who spilled out on to the pavement and then into the flower shop, and the noise level swelled with their animated chatter.

Emily was behind the counter when they came in, helping Mr Tollefson stack the completed posters. She looked up and frowned at the sudden, alien infusion of youthful energy into her normally staid environment.

'All right, kids!' Nick called out over the noise, and if it hadn't been for his physical maturity he would have been indistinguishable from the students. The way he moved, the enthusiasm in his voice, everything about him seemed terribly young at that moment, and the students seemed to sense that. They gathered around him like groupies. 'You've all got your assignments! Grab your posters and leaflets and start your routes. Remember, the more people we pull from other townships, the more money for Random's Fire Department!'

Emily's shoulders lifted in a heavy sigh as she watched the kids bustle around like revving engines, excess energy and high spirits exaggerating every move, and suddenly she felt older than she had in a long time. The old line about never being that young, even when she was that young, kept running through her mind, and soon she found herself resenting the students, and resenting Nick, too, because he seemed every bit as young as they did.

Her mouth tightened as she watched the girls cluster around him, more than one pausing to touch his arm, to ask a wide-eyed question, to bat a long-lashed eye. A particularly winsome brunette tossed her long hair so that it brushed Nick's shoulder, and Emily absently reached up to touch her own closely cropped blonde hair, frowning.

He just loves this, she thought, her features hardening as she watched him respond to the girls. When one of them grabbed his hands and babbled something in excitement, he actually gave her a quick hug, laughing at whatever she'd said.

Everyone was too busy to notice Emily standing there quietly, her expression flattening, her posture growing more rigid and aloof by the minute.

Gradually the shop began to clear as students filtered out to begin their delivery routes, and poster-makers were finally free to go home and attend to other chores. Eventually Emily and Nick were the only ones left: she still behind the counter, he standing in the middle of the shop, watching her. She glanced at him briefly, saw that his open shirt clung damply to his body in the heat, that the gold of his hair had been dulled by blowing dust.

'I'm proud of you, Emily. You actually loosened up a little today. Got down there on the floor with the natives and did something absolutely useless, just because it felt good.'

She made a face, then dropped her eyes and pretended to study an old cash-register receipt someone had left on the counter.

'Alone at last,' he said quietly.

Emily pursed her lips without looking up.

'There's no reason for you to be jealous of a bunch of high-school girls, you know.'

Her head jerked up and her face flooded with colour. 'Don't flatter yourself.'

'I'm not. You are.'

She made a disgusted face and started clearing the day's debris off the counter.

'Not that I'm objecting, mind you,' he said with a chuckle, approaching the counter and resting his arms on it. She didn't have to look at him to know he was smiling. She could hear it in his voice. 'I like it when you're jealous. You can shoot daggers all the way across a room with those green eyes of yours.'

Emily grabbed a rag and started polishing furious circles on the formica. 'You've got an imagination to match your ego,' she said icily. 'I couldn't care less what you do, or with whom.'

His hand shot down to cover hers, and she froze, the rag still clutched in her hand, her hand clutched in his. 'Oh, you care all right,' he said quietly. 'You're just not ready to admit it yet. Maybe not even to yourself.'

Emily frowned down at her hand, wondering why it hadn't jerked away as she'd told it to. It looked small and pale and helpless, trapped beneath the broad, darker span of his. For a moment she forgot herself, and was mesmerised by the sharply defined lines of his tendons, tracking from wrist to knuckles.

'You know,' he murmured, 'your mouth drives me crazy.'

Shocked by the intimate quality of his voice, her eyes snapped up and collided with his. Almost instinctively, she sucked her lips inwards.

'Oh, Em...' he chuckled deep in his throat '...when you finally let go, it's going to blow me away.'

She took a shallow, shaky breath, then remembered to pull her hand from beneath his and look away. Not the least bit discouraged, he hopped sideways on to the counter and smiled down at her over his right shoulder. 'It was your mouth that got to me in the first place, you know, all the way back in high school.'

Emily started polishing circles again, her eyes riveted to her rag.

'You were always so damn prim and proper, collars buttoned up to your chin, face pursed up like a prune, as defensive as hell—that keep-away look you wore all the time was like a blast of cold air from a freezer...' He paused and sighed. 'But sometimes—not often, but sometimes—the look slipped. Like in Mr Barker's history class. You just loved that class, didn't you?'

She glanced up suspiciously, wondering how he knew that—it was the second time he'd surprised her by knowing things she hadn't thought anyone knew. She realised too late that she shouldn't have looked up at all. Once her eyes met his, she couldn't seem to pull them away...

'And whenever you got really involved in what old Barker was saying... well, your eyes would go soft and that mouth...' he took a quick breath '...that mouth of yours would just...unfold. Like a flower.' His gaze shifted downwards to her lips, the blue of his eyes seemed to grow darker, and his voice became husky. 'Just like now.'

She was staring at him, her lips unconsciously parted, her eyes growing wider by the second. She couldn't remember when she'd breathed last. As she watched, his nostrils flared slightly, and his tongue passed over his lower lip.

'There's a softness in you, Emily. There always has been. You just knock yourself out trying to hide it, but little hints of it keep rising to the surface—like when you stopped to smell the black-eyed Susans every day—and when I kissed you for the very first time.' His eyes fell closed at the memory, and his head tipped slightly to one side, as if the memory itself were still just a little beyond belief. His voice dropped even lower. 'It was like... being burned.' He opened his eyes and looked deeply into hers. 'I've kissed a lot of women since then, Em, but it never felt the same. I didn't think it ever would again—I thought it was just one of those moments in your past that your memory distorts all out of proportion. Then I saw you again that first day I was in town, and I had to find out; I had to find out for sure. And that night in your apartment... I did.'

Emily was sure that if she stood there for one second longer, trapped by the blue fire in his eyes and hypnotised by his voice, she would simply burst into flame. She blinked, snapped her mouth closed, then dropped quickly to her knees behind the counter and pretended to start straightening the shelves.

Almost before she could register the motion, he'd swung his legs over and was standing with his legs spread next to where she knelt. Instantly she was at a disadvantage, on her knees before him like a supplicant; but at the very moment when the muscles in her legs tightened to rise he said clearly from above her, 'Get up, Emily,' and that made rising just an obedient response to his command. No way was she going to do that.

'Maybe you're right.' He dropped to his knees suddenly, facing her. 'This is better. No one passing by can see us if we're down here.'

Now she could get up. But just as she reached for the top of the counter, he grabbed her wrists and turned her on her knees, then pulled her so sharply against him that her teeth clicked together.

With as much disdain as her position would allow, she raised her eyes slowly and said, 'Are you going to try the forceful man bit *again*?'

Amazingly, he just laughed, pulling at her wrists until her fingers were forced open to splay across his chest. 'If you like,' he smiled, flattening his hands over hers. 'Feel that, Emily?'

Her eyes flashed, but of course she did. The hard, steady beat of his heart pumped against her palms. 'Feel what?' She arched one brow, but the effect was lost when her voice cracked.

'My heart,' he whispered, 'beating as fast as yours.'

His eyes dropped immediately to her throat, and she realised with something like horror that he was staring at the pulse-point there; that no matter how chilling her tone, how contemptuous her expression, that pulse in the hollow of her throat was going to give her away if she couldn't manage to control it.

He leaned into her slightly, until they were pressed tightly together from knee to shoulder, with only the fold of her arms between them. She felt the hard ridge of his thighs against hers, watched his brows twitch and his eyes flicker, and then saw the delicate flare of his nostrils and the slight tightening of the skin beneath his eyes.

Oh, please don't let that be happening to my face, she thought frantically. Please don't let it be that obvious.

'Feel it,' he commanded hoarsely, his voice deadly serious now. His head rolled back slightly; his eyes impaled hers through narrowed lids.

Her pulse leaped, forcing her green eyes wide, and her breath caught silently in her throat. Sit down, she told her body. Sit back on your heels, away from him; but the moment she tried, his hands released her wrists and clutched at her lower back, pulling her into him. Fingers kneaded at either side of her spine, making it arch, then crawled upwards, sealing her torso to his, inch by inch.

When his fingers threaded through her short hair and his palms covered her ears, she heard the waves of an ocean she had never seen pounding on a distant shore. When his thumbs prodded her chin upwards, she felt the pulse of his breath like a hot tropical breeze.

'Don't,' she breathed, but his mouth came down firmly on her parted lips, absorbing the word and the protest right out of existence.

There were too many sensations, racing from millions of nerve-endings across a baffling, complex circuitry that went absolutely haywire in her brain. For separate flashes of time, certain signals stood out from the rest, so intensely clear that they demanded total attention—like right *now*—the sound of his breath breaking against her cheek; and, in the next instant, the slick warmth of his tongue searching for hers; and in the next the unmistakable hardness grinding into her hips, making her breath catch and her head feel incredibly heavy.

Without any warning at all, his hands dropped to grip her upper arms, and his face buried itself beneath her chin, tongue working at the hollow of her throat, then trailing downwards into the opening of her blouse. She felt his teeth graze her skin as he bit down on one side of her blouse and jerked his head to the side. She barely heard the tiny clatter of buttons skittering across the floor over the harsh sound of his breathing, and even if the thought that he had ruined yet another blouse had registered, it wouldn't have made any difference, because now he was kissing the swollen rise of her breast, and now his tongue was whisking beneath the lace top of her bra, and now he was tugging urgently at the strap... and then his mouth closed over the tip of her bared breast and she fell into him helplessly, feeling the tug of his lips pull something hot and seething all the way up from her stomach.

He groaned once against her flesh, then raised his head and looked right into her eyes. His mouth was open, his lips wet, and he pulled in air with a rasping sound. His eyes looked black. He filled his hand with her breast, and when he pressed against it lightly her eyes slammed shut and a tiny sound crawled up from her throat.

'Come on, Em. We're going upstairs,' he growled. 'Right now.'

And there it was again. The masculine command, demanding feminine obedience; the most loathsome thing imaginable, to become subservient to another, to let the desires of the body rule the logic of the mind; but oh, she wanted to go.

Nick reached up and ran his finger over her lips until they parted helplessly. '*Now*, Emily,' he said in a stranger's voice, and a shudder passed through her body, evidence of her last futile struggle in a war she knew she had lost.

'Hey, Nick!' The shout and the bell over the door shattered the silence simultaneously, and they both froze behind the counter, staring at each other with wide-flown eyes. 'Hey Nick! You in here?'

Emily slammed her hand over her mouth so she wouldn't cry out. It felt like the bottom of her stomach had fallen to the floor.

It was Herman from the hardware store next door, and any second now he was going to stomp across the floor and peer over the counter and see her cringing here half-naked...

The vision was so horrifying she couldn't imagine its ending; the fear of discovery was so great that she didn't dare move, even to cover herself. For one miserable moment, she thought she was going to lose control entirely and just burst into tears.

Nick frowned hard at her, then suddenly called out, 'I'm here!' and popped upright from behind the counter. One of his hands pressed down firmly on top of her head, and his right foot nudged her hip, forcing her into the cubby-hole right beneath the cash register.

Even in her quiet panic, she had enough presence of mind to be surprised by his actions. After all his efforts to convince the town that she was having a scandalous affair with him, now that it was close to being the truth he was actually trying to spare her the embarrassment. Something about that just didn't make sense, but she was too distraught to dwell on it.

'Herman!' she heard him say from above her, and it seemed impossible that Herman wouldn't notice the thick breathiness of his voice and know precisely what had been going on. 'I'm just putting some of this stuff away for Emily. What's up?'

He was stacking something on the counter, making enough noise to cover her movements. She pressed even deeper into her hiding-place, tugging her bra up and her blouse closed.

'Nothing, really,' Herman replied. 'Where is Emily?'

'Oh, she went upstairs a little while ago...' his voice became lighter, conveying a message only she would understand '...to change her blouse, I think.'

She rolled her eyes and reached out to pinch his leg, then jerked her hand back, aghast at what she'd been about to do. It was such a ... *playful* gesture, so incredibly out of character that Nick would probably have fainted dead away from shock, then Herman would have had to rush behind the counter to pick him up, then he'd have seen staid old Emily folded into a ball with her blouse hanging open, and then *he* would have fainted dead away...

She squeezed her eyes shut and suppressed an insane giggle. A moment ago she'd been ready to burst into tears of humiliation. Now, with the danger of imminent discovery over, the whole situation seemed suddenly hilarious. Here she was, stuffy old Emily Swenson—*half-naked*, stuffy old Emily Swenson, she amended—jammed into a cramped hiding-place like a high-school girl trying not to get caught in the boys' locker-room. She didn't know which was worse: that she'd got herself into such a situation in the first place, or that she was actually beginning to enjoy it.

She clamped a hand over her mouth, feeling devilish and young and terribly adventurous—and then, suddenly, a little sad, because she was twenty-seven years old and she'd never felt those things before.

'Well, I really stopped by to catch you before you left town, Nick,' Herman said. 'Just wanted to say goodbye.'

Slowly, ever so slowly, the words penetrated Emily's brain, and the whole world seemed to grind to a halt. Her hand fell away from her mouth, and her smile faded.

'Oh.' Nick's voice sounded lame. 'You didn't have to do that, Herman. Nice of you, though.'

'Well, wish you didn't have to go. Lord knows you'll be missed. Any idea when you'll be coming back?'

Emily held her breath while Nick cleared his throat. 'Not really, Herman. Nothing definite.'

For a moment, the floor seemed to shift slightly under her, and she felt dizzy. He's leaving. He's leaving Random, and his last act was going to be the promised seduction of the town spinster. He was going to take me upstairs and ... and all the time he was planning that, he knew that he was leaving. Her lower lip almost disappeared and she had to remind herself to blink.

Of course he's leaving, some rational part of her mind muttered. What did you think? That he'd pop back into town after a ten-year absence and put down roots? That this vacation would simply go on forever? He had to go back to his real life eventually. You knew that. You just ... forgot.

A long splinter was pulling away from the wood divider, right at Emily's eye-level. She focused on it, reached for it absently, and started to work it away from the wood. Herman and Nick were exchanging small talk above her, but their voices receded to a distant drone. A cramp was threatening to seize her right calf, but the sensation was recorded in such a remote corner of her brain that she hardly noticed it. She was too intent on the splinter. Nothing else in the world existed, except that single fragment of wood; and nothing seemed quite as important as removing it.

'Emily?'

She snapped to awareness and bumped her head on the shelf above her. Nick's crouching form was a peripheral shadow on her left, and she turned her head slowly to look at it. He was smiling. Dammit, he was smiling.

'You can come out now. He's gone.'

She looked down at the tangle of her legs with a glazed, stupid expression, as if she couldn't imagine how they'd got there; then absently forced her numbed muscles to unfold. She emerged from the cubby-hole on hands and knees, and that seemed horribly appropriate.

'Here. Let me help you up.'

She ignored his hand and pulled herself up by the counter-top, then remained standing there, facing the front of the store. She stared at the door as if she could already see him walking through it, and spoke without looking at him. 'You're leaving,' she said dully.

'Not for an hour,' he leaned to whisper playfully in her ear. She was too numb to pull away. 'We've got an hour.'

The sheer callousness of his response left her stunned. Her head turned slowly until their eyes met. His were intensely blue, sparkling with anticipation; hers were a chilling, flat green.

She kept trying to tell herself how lucky she was. She'd been totally out of control, her body responding without the direction of her mind, and Herman's interruption was all that had saved her from becoming exactly what her mother was—what she had sworn she would never be—a woman commanded by a man, ruled by a man, controlled by a man.

The realisation of how close she had come made her shudder. How horrible it was to learn after all these years that strength of will was just an illusion; that locked somewhere within her body was an automatic weakness, just waiting to betray her the moment a man pushed the right buttons. She hadn't lost control—she'd almost *given* it away, to a man who would have been watching the clock, no less, counting off the minutes of a single hour.

'Emily?' He was looking at her strangely, trying to read the expressionless mask she wore.

'You're very good, Nick,' she said calmly, looking up at him. 'I underestimated you.'

He went perfectly still, his eyes riveted on her face.

'I was actually going to go to bed with you,' she continued, her voice so devoid of emotion that it sounded mechanised.

Nick watched her carefully for a moment, his eyes suddenly wary. 'There's nothing wrong with that, Emily,' he finally said, very softly. 'When two people——'

'Everything's wrong with that, Nick, because the reasons were all wrong. I didn't plan it, I didn't think about it, I just . . .' she could barely force out the words '. . . lost control.' When she raised her eyes, she looked beaten, defeated. 'I didn't even know that could happen to women,' she added in the pathetic voice of a bewildered child.

Slowly, as if he were afraid she would bolt at the slightest movement, he reached up and took her shoulders in his hands. 'But, Emily, that's the best part——'

'No!' she whispered, her eyes a little wild.

His fingers tightened on her shoulders, but only slightly. 'It's part of giving, Emily.' He bent at the knees to peer directly into her eyes. 'Part of relating. You lose a little control when someone gets close, but it's worth it.'

'No,' she whispered, shaking her head slowly. 'I don't want that. Ever.'

'Em . . .' he frowned so hard that the line over his nose looked etched there '. . . you've been in control all your life. It's all you've ever had. Let it go. You're running out of time.'

In the space of a single blink, her eyes hardened. 'Am I, Nick? Is my hour almost up?'

His lips tightened in exasperation. 'That's not what I meant, and you know it,' he said, a little more sharply than he had intended. 'Dammit, Emily!' He dropped his hands from her shoulders and looked down at them, frustrated. 'Ask me to stay,' he said quietly, still looking down. 'That's all you have to do. Just ask me to stay.'

Her brow twitched a little. It sounded like such a simple, harmless thing, just asking him to stay... but it wasn't simple, and it wasn't harmless. As long as he was around, she was at constant risk. All he had to do was touch her, look at her, and she'd be back behind the counter again, ready to subjugate her will to his, ready to move when he called and follow where he led, because he had that power over her, that power she didn't understand and couldn't fight, and she would only be safe if he just left.

'I don't want you to stay,' she said firmly, her voice suddenly back at full strength.

Every nuance of expression bled from his face as he stared at her, and in the sudden silence the echo of her words hung in the air like a death knell.

He stared at her for a very long time, and as she watched his eyes seemed to empty of colour until they were a pale, glassy, doll-like blue. Finally he sighed and ran one hand back through his hair, leaving darker tracks in the sun-bleached blond.

She couldn't really remember his turning away, stepping through the clutter of discarded posters and papers on his way to the door. One minute he was standing in front of her, and the next, it seemed, he was all the way across the room with his hand on the knob, half turned to look back at her.

His right arm was knotted with the force of his grip, and a dark slice of chest and stomach showed between the parted halves of his shirt. His face was in shadow, but his hair caught all the light coming in through the door, and it looked like a crown of white fire. Oddly enough, Emily knew even then that this was the way she would remember him— not laughing, teasing, blue eyes alight with mockery and mischief, but like this: half in shadow, blond hair flaming with an unearthly light, and silent.

'You're going to miss me, Em,' he said quietly.

She felt her lips tighten convulsively as the door closed behind him. The latch fell into its notch with a faint click, but the sound reverberated in her mind like the slamming of a prison-cell door.

CHAPTER NINE

HE'S gone.

It was the very first thought in Emily's mind when she woke the morning after Nick left town, and for a moment it paralysed her. As long as she was trapped in that netherworld between sleep and full wakefulness, that place where feelings ruled before the mind kicked into gear, she felt the full, brutal weight of desolation bearing down. Thankfully, the moment passed quickly, and her orderly mind pushed ridiculous notions like actually missing Nick Simon back into the shadows where they belonged. Why should she miss him, after all? Did you miss a toothache? An itchy cast on a broken arm? And that was all he was, really, just one of those constant, inescapable irritations in life that left a strange emptiness when you were finally free of them.

She made her bed, started the coffee, showered and started to dress, grumbling automatically as she tugged on the straps of the confining bra. The second strap was halfway up her arm when her hand jerked to a stop, and she remembered that she wouldn't have to wear the hated thing any more. There wouldn't be anyone to notice.

She tried to smile as she shoved it back into the drawer, then saw in the mirror that the smile looked fake. Irritated by her own reaction, she snatched a lipstick and started to put it on. She'd dragged the coral gloss halfway across her lower lip when she remembered what Nick had said about her mouth, and her lip trembled. Furious, she flung the tube down without finishing and grabbed her hairbrush to slick her short blonde strands in place with vicious, impatient strokes. 'I like your hair like that,' his voice rumbled from the back of her mind, and the brush clattered to the floor as she stood rigidly in front of the mirror, her eyes slammed shut—eyes he thought looked like spring, she remembered involuntarily. Dammit! Wasn't there *anything* in her life that wouldn't remind her of him?

She poured coffee—just as she'd poured coffee for him that night he'd shown up drunk; she fluffed the cushions on the couch—the couch where she had first felt his mouth on hers; and finally, desperate to escape, she literally ran down the narrow steps to the workroom, through the door to the shop proper, and came face to face with a flood of memories—so many memories, from such a short span of time.

She walked the length of the counter as if in a trance, trailing her fingers on the cool formica, remembering the times he had hopped up to sit there, the way his forearms had looked braced on its edge, the unspeakable things she had felt crouched behind it before Herman had come in...

Her eyes lifted slowly to the door, and she imagined she could see him there still, standing with his hand on the knob, his shadowed gaze touching her all the way across the room...

Her eyes fell closed briefly, then opened again to focus on that place outside where the flashy red convertible had become a fixture, as much a part of Main Street as Nick Simon had become a part of her life. As she stared at the empty space, she felt a sharp, almost physical pain in her chest.

'You'll miss me, Em,' he'd warned her, and oh, it wasn't fair that she did. She hadn't even *liked* him, really. He was too flip, too sure of himself, and, above all, too...controlling. Good heavens. He'd only been in town a couple of weeks, and in that time he'd managed to turn the whole place upside-down, and her along with it. How could you possibly like a man like that? And—an even more frightening question—how could she have felt the things she had for such a man? They had names for women like that, didn't they?

A shudder passed through her as her body remembered the things her mind was trying to forget. Thank heavens he was gone, she tried to tell herself. We're all better off.

She clung to that thought all day Thursday and Friday, while the drought tightened its grip on the country's breadbasket. Think about the drought, she commanded herself whenever thoughts of Nick popped into her mind. And lord knew the drought should have been enough to occupy anyone's thoughts.

For the rest of the week the sun beat down on the Midwestern plains, burning the topsoil into dust, bleaching the colour from trees and grass, baking the tops of stones that poked through the alarmingly shallow waters of every creek and pond. Grass and marsh fires raged throughout the state, fish began to die in the too-warm waters of their once icy lakes, and the worried eyes of every farmer searched the maddeningly empty sky for the clouds that would mean salvation.

Except in Random. Oddly enough, the farmers there didn't seem to notice. Right in the middle of the worst drought in state history, the residents forgot the fires and their dying crops and the cattle stuck in mud wallows and the hogs convulsing in the heat; the only topic on anyone's lips was the Saturday night street dance.

It wasn't just heedlessness, Emily finally decided. It was a defence mechanism. For once, reality's picture was simply too grim to contemplate for long, and the dance was everyone's escape.

They came into her shop in droves to buy tickets, and inevitably they stopped to chat with their neighbours about who was coming, what they would wear, and whether the terrible heat would persist into the night and ruin the dancing. There was something terribly sad about their pervasive gaiety, Emily thought, perhaps because it was destined to be so fleeting.

By the end of Saturday night the dance would be over, and minds would be forced to return to serious matters—deadly serious matters upon which lives and lifestyles turned.

You were right, Nick, Emily thought as she watched them laugh and chatter and forget for a time that catastrophe was waiting in the wings. They needed this. They needed to forget, if only for a little while. How selfish I was not to see that.

Added to the torment of her introspection was the uncanny perception of a select few, like Mrs Hoeffer.

'I don't believe I've ever seen you so down in the mouth, Emily, dear,' she'd chirped, peering sympathetically over the counter on Friday. 'You must miss Nicky terribly.'

That particular sentiment had been repeated a number of times, and Emily had been so startled by the directness of it that she had never been able to manage a reply. So. They all knew he was gone, and they were all busy feeling sorry for poor Emily. It was bad enough to have to admit to herself that his absence left a hole in her life; it was far worse to realise she was the object of everyone's pity.

By late Saturday afternoon, hundreds of hands working together had transformed a full block of Main Street into a huge, open-air ballroom. Sawdust covered the faded tar and dozens of milk cartons stuffed with wild flowers lined the pavements. Strings of tiny lights criss-crossed the street overhead, waiting for darkness to turn them into a canopy of electric stars. A makeshift bandstand had been erected in front of Herman's hardware store, and even stodgy old Albert had turned his restaurant into a pavement café, with every table moved outside.

Everyone had gone home to supper and chores before returning for the dance, and, when Emily ventured out on to the pavement before closing the shop, the street was deserted.

She sagged to the kerb in front of her shop, exhausted, and looked up and down the empty street. It was strangely quiet after the bustle of the day, and in its emptiness the town looked rather sad—like an abandoned carnival. She closed her eyes and drew the sweet, woody smell of sawdust into her lungs, wondering if it would sound as marvellous as it smelled when hundreds of dancing feet scuffed over it. It was something she would never know, because she had no intention of leaving her apartment that night.

'Looks good, doesn't it?' Mr Tollefson said suddenly from the silence behind her, making her jump.

'Martin!' She smiled over her shoulder at the tall elderly man—one of the few genuine smiles she'd worn this day. 'Shouldn't you be at home, helping Harriet get ready for the anniversary picnic tomorrow?'

He nodded solemnly, but his blue eyes twinkled from a web of laugh-lines years in the making. 'With a house full of kids and grandkids, she's got more bodies in that house than she knows what to do with right now. Thought I'd drive in and take a peek at the town before it gets all cluttered up with bodies tonight. And I wanted to thank you, too, for taking time out to deliver the roses personal today. I know how busy you've been.'

Emily's smile was wistful, remembering the look on Harriet's face when she'd taken the roses out to their farm over the lunch-hour. 'It was my pleasure, Martin. I'll bring the table arrangements out first thing in the morning. I thought they'd keep better in the shop coolers in this weather.'

Martin nodded. 'Appreciate that, Emily. Sincerely.' He pocketed his big hands in his overalls and rocked back on his heels, musing with a satisfied expression, 'The whole family together under one roof, the anniversary picnic tomorrow, and now this dance, to start it all off... almost feels like the whole town is celebrating our fifty years right along with us. Life surely can be good, can't it?'

Emily blinked up at him, managed a feeble smile, then jerked her head to look down at her tennis shoes, half-buried in the sawdust, and pressed her lips together.

A frown flickered across Martin's features, then he folded his long body into impossible angles to sit next to her on the kerb. He leaned forwards with his arms draped across his knees, his head tipped sideways to study her profile.

'Does loving Nick hurt that bad?' he asked softly, and she jerked her head to stare at him with dismayed astonishment. It was a thought she hadn't even articulated to herself, and thoughts like that were private—secret—not a matter for public discussion, and certainly not with someone she barely spoke to more than once a year.

Martin watched her thoughts track across her face, and an old pattern of lines deepened around his mouth when he smiled. 'Oh, I know it's none of my business, but I'm an old man, you know. You can't expect an old man to keep his mouth shut when he should.'

Emily blinked and pressed her lips even tighter together. 'I don't even *like* Nick Simon.'

His shock of white hair bobbed when he chuckled. 'Now, Emily, I'm not so old that I can't remember what lovesickness looks like on a girl's face.' He watched her lips purse in distaste, and then quiver, just a little. Lord, but she was Carl Swenson's daughter—locked up tighter than a drum. 'There's no shame in loving, child,' he said gently. ''Specially not a man like Nick. Never did know a woman who could resist that rascal once he set his mind to it.'

'Well, somehow I managed,' Emily mumbled, watching her toe dig a hole into the sawdust. 'And now he's gone. So that's that.' She jumped abruptly to her feet, brushing her hands against the front of her green overall.

As Martin peered up at her, he saw the trouble in those fine green eyes of hers, that kind of deep-down weariness that came from holding people at arm's length for too long. Sure as sunshine in July, she was hurting; and just as sure, she'd be too proud to admit it. He decided not to press the point.

'Well,' he said, pushing his hands against his knees and rising to face her, 'I sure would take it kindly if you'd save an old man a dance tonight.'

She looked down at where her fingers were twining together. 'Truth is, I don't know how to dance, Martin. I've never done it before.'

His eyes almost disappeared in a frown. Good lord. The girl must be looking thirty right in the eye, and she'd never danced before? 'Then you'll need an experienced teacher,' he said with a definite bob of his head. 'And no one's been waltzing more years than I have.'

'Actually...' Emily looked around aimlessly, biting her lip '...I wasn't even planning on coming tonight...'

'But that was before you knew you'd have a chance to dance with me, right?' His grin was impossibly infectious.

She hesitated a moment, then shook her head with a resigned smile. 'Right,' she conceded.

'Good. Now you be down here when this shindig starts, or Harriet and I will be at your door, I can promise you that. And Emily,' he put his huge, gnarled hands on her shoulders and smiled down at her like a benevolent grandfather, 'a girl should wear her prettiest dress to her first dance.' He grinned and winked at her, then turned and ambled away, whistling like a young man.

Emily stared after him with a baffled frown, feeling a little bit as if she'd been run over by one of those shiny metal milk trucks that tracked in and out of Martin's farmyard. He saw too much, that old man, and, without knowing her at all, he knew her too well.

She shook her head and went back inside, feeling strangely exposed, terribly vulnerable—but, now that she thought about it, a lot better than she had felt in days. Someone had looked beneath the surface, had seen the cracks in the strong façade she preserved so diligently—and it hadn't been as bad as she'd thought.

The muted twang of an electric guitar floated in through the open window as the band warmed up while Emily was still soaking in a cool bath. She'd argued with herself for the past two hours, deciding one minute she absolutely would not go down to that ridiculous dance, then deciding the next that she would. She'd been back and forth a dozen different times, until she'd finally realised that, if she didn't show up, Martin and Harriet Tollefson probably *would* come upstairs and drag her down. The certainty of that should have made her feel threatened, indignant—who were they to interfere in her life like that?—but, for some reason, it just made her feel ... welcome.

With a resigned sigh she drained the tub, wrapped a towel around her dripping body, and padded barefoot into the bedroom. She grimaced at the pile of white eyelet cotton draped across her bed. She'd bought the dress on one of her rare trips to Minneapolis two years ago, and hadn't even cut the tags off yet.

You were in Minneapolis, her thoughts skittered away. You were in Nick's city that day, maybe within a few blocks of where he works or lives or walks, and you weren't even aware of it. She frowned immediately, distressed that he kept popping into her mind, and forced herself to concentrate on the dress.

It was a preposterously feminine thing, with a scooped neck and full, gauzy sleeves, cinched at the waist and exploding beneath into a puffy, cloudlike circle of fabric. She still didn't know what had prompted her to buy it—lord knew she had no call for such a dress in her life—and the truth was, she'd just snatched it off the rack without ever trying it on. She'd probably look like a perfect idiot in this pile of fluff, she thought as she slipped it over her head, jamming her arms impatiently into the sleeves; and if she did, she'd just tug on a pair of old jeans and——

She caught a glimpse of her reflection in the mirror, and her thoughts stopped dead and her expression froze. Like creatures with wills of their own, her hands rose in slow motion to press together beneath her chin. 'Oh,' she whispered, blinking at the mirror; and then, after what seemed like a very long time, she reached with a shaky hand for the make-up she hardly ever used.

Darkness was kind to Random, painting soft shadows on the squarish, straightforward architecture of a town that had better things to do than beautify its buildings. Most of the decorations were hidden by the press of hundreds of bodies, but the canopy of lights twinkled overhead, transforming this drab street into a fairyland, for at least one night.

It's our coming-out party, Emily thought wryly, wandering through the crowd in her white dress and low-heeled shoes. Mine and the town's. We're both decked out in all our finery, a couple of Cinderellas for a few magic hours, dressed to hide the plainness beneath.

Wouldn't Nick be surprised if he could see us now? she mused.

On impulse, she'd flicked her hair forward instead of slicking it back behind her ears, and let the wispy fringe sweep down to her brows. In a way, she'd been creating a disguise—an *alter ego* completely dissociated from the sedate woman who ran the Random flower shop. It was all right that this new person was frivolous enough to own a dress like this and wear eye make-up and little button earrings and go dancing in the street, because she didn't have anything to do with the real Emily at all.

She felt comfortable for her first few minutes in the crowd, almost smug in her marvellous disguise as she greeted the people she knew and marvelled at how many she didn't. But then she began to notice the quality and duration of their unabashed stares, and her confidence faltered.

Too much eyeshadow, she worried, remembering how intensely green her eyes had looked in the mirror. Or maybe the lipstick is too bright, or maybe my mascara is running down my cheeks and I've got a horn growing out of my forehead.

With every step she took down the pavement, a new pair of eyes brushed over her, then jerked back to look again. At first she just smiled and nodded politely, pretending it didn't bother her at all; but after a time she began to feel as if she were some sort of alien species, walking a gauntlet so the locals could stare with gape-mouthed wonder at the oddity. Her head dropped and she scowled at the pavement, wishing she were back in the security of her empty apartment where no one could see and secretly laugh at the spectacle of Emily Swenson pretending to be something she wasn't. She was just about to duck into the flower shop and flee upstairs when the sound of the band's first chord exploded over the murmur of the crowd and shattered the night air.

Traditionally, every dance in the farming towns of the Midwest began with a rousing polka, and this one was no exception. Emily paused to watch the first farmer tug his plump, blushing wife out on to the sawdust, and wondered how long they would be out there alone, moving in awkward, embarrassed circles before a few others moved tentatively to join them.

It took about two seconds.

Emily blinked hard at the throng of laughing couples spilling immediately out on to the street.

For the most part, the first wave looked like an invasion of the elderly—white-haired men with sunburned bald spots and eyes permanently squinted from years in the sun, rosy-cheeked wives who looked better suited to needlepoint and vegetable gardening than cavorting on a makeshift dance-floor. Stiff new overalls and crisply starched shirts spilled into the street with Paisley dresses and sturdy block-heeled shoes, and they all danced. Lord, how they danced, as if they hadn't a care in the world; as if they were all happily caught in those precious years before the young come to realise that life is hard and the world is a sobering place.

Emily gaped at the sight of people she'd always thought of as old and stooped swirling with a grace and fluidity of motion that seemed gay and almost choreographed. Spinning skirts and bobbing grey-haired heads mocked the infirmities of age with the abandon of youthful spirit, and Emily found it hard to believe that these sprightly figures were the same ones who had bounced on tractor seats for years, and now spent most evenings on porch rocking-chairs.

The town should never have stopped having these dances, she caught herself thinking. It was almost as if Random had gone to sleep, as if the spark of life had mysteriously abandoned the town, leaving it old and lifeless and without spirit. The description she'd formed in her mind made her frown, because it was too close to a description of herself.

This was her first introduction to the playful side of all the stalwart people she had known since her youth; the first confirmation of that old myth that

farmers loved two things almost to distraction—
the land, and the dance.

She saw her own bemused expression reflected
on the faces of teenage bystanders who, like Emily,
had never seen their parents and grandparents kick
up their heels, and then someone began to clap in
time, and the street rocked with the sound of hands
coming together to music that seemed to match the
beat of her heart.

Before long the young people joined in, spinning
in awkward imitation of the practised moves of their
elders, too impatient to wait for the rock and roll
the band would play later. As Emily watched the
melding of generations, she forgot that she had once
thought the idea of a dance silly, and wondered why
the custom had died, why it had taken a man from
the city to bring it to life again.

Look at those faces, she thought, her toe unconsciously tapping the beat. Not a troubled frown
among them, not a single furrowed brow, and as
long as this night lasts there *is* no drought, no
hardship, no misery. Almost unwittingly, her hands
moved to keep time and her lips curved in a smile.

He should be here, she thought suddenly, and
her hands slowed, then stopped, and her smile
faded. The truth was that Nick had given this night
to these people, and, no matter how badly things
had ended up between them, it was too bad he
couldn't have stayed long enough to see the measure
of joy he'd left behind.

Her shoulders slumped with the force of her sigh,
and for a moment she stood staring sadly at the
dancers, wondering how much the gaiety on the

street would have been multiplied with the catalyst of Nick's irrepressible personality.

'I don't think I ever saw anyone look so miserable in my life. What's the matter, Emily? Can't you stand watching other people have a good time?' a voice said behind her, and her hand flew to her chest to see if her heart had really stopped, or if it had only felt that way. There wasn't another voice quite like that in the world.

She didn't really hear the words or the sarcastic delivery, only the voice, and for once in her life she never thought to hide what she was feeling, to put on the rigid mask of indifferent stoicism she had worn for so long. She just spun to face him with her breath caught in her throat and her heart in her eyes, because he'd come back, and she didn't care why, and she didn't care for how long, she just ...

The joy fell away when she looked up into the hard, expressionless face. For brief moments in the past two weeks she had seen his grin fade and the blue eyes grow serious, but never had she seen him look so coldly indifferent.

There was no light of mischief in the blue eyes, no hint of amusement in the grim line of his mouth; and for perhaps the first time she noticed that his jaw was capable of a stubborn thrust, that the angles of his face could look harsh and unforgiving when he chose.

Her lips quivered slightly, straining for a smile, but there was something wrong about smiling at a face like that. It would be like smiling at a funeral. Her hands moved to rub at her arms, as if she were chilled. 'You came back,' she murmured stupidly.

He didn't say anything, and the longer the silence between them lasted, the more nervous she became. She finally found the courage to look up at him again, but his expression was so solemn that it was like looking into the face of a stranger. 'You look . . . different,' she said.

He raised one brow. 'So do you.'

He was staring at her with chilling directness, and she dropped her eyes and pressed her lips together, horribly aware of how foolish she must look in this ridiculous dress and hairstyle, with all that whorish make-up.

She frowned and plucked at the front of her skirt. There was a loose thread there, right in the fold; she didn't know how she could have missed it when she was cutting off the tags . . .

Even over the sound of the music and the crowd, she could hear his long sigh, as if he were letting something go. 'Do you want to dance with me, Emily?'

Her eyes shot up, horrified at the prospect of stumbling around through the sawdust to the fast, frantic rhythm of the polka. 'No!'

His head moved in a silent, humourless chuckle. 'I didn't think you did.' And then he turned his back and strode quickly away before she could explain.

She stood there with a dismayed expression, wanting desperately to call out, 'Wait!' but somehow unable to force out that single syllable— that one word that would acknowledge all the yearning, all the need, all that dreadfully human weakness that she had managed to lock inside for so long.

'Go after him, dear.'

Emily turned to see her mother standing next to her, her smile gentle, her eyes soft and incredibly wise.

CHAPTER TEN

'GO AFTER him,' her mother had said, and Emily's mind had immediately flashed back to when Nick had told her, 'Just ask me to stay.' Such simple phrases, both; but so hard, so damned hard to execute. How did you erase a lifetime of thinking a certain way, and just jump into a new personality as if it were a new pair of jeans? And did she really want to? Was she ready to give up her prized independence with the utterance of a single sentence, or with the blatant pursuit of a man who by his own admission wanted nothing more than an hour of pleasure?

'Your heart's all over your face,' her mother persisted. 'Go and tell him, Emily. Go and tell him how you feel.'

Lord, it wasn't just Martin Tollefson who could see the truth. It was her mother, too; and Mrs Hoeffer, and probably everyone else in the town. The mask hadn't just slipped; it had shattered into a million irretrievable pieces, and if she didn't correct that soon she'd be an object of pity for the rest of her life.

With a concentrated effort, she immediately donned an artificially bright, couldn't-care-less expression. Seeing it, recognising the stubborn, prideful look she'd seen on her husband's face a thousand times, her mother sighed and walked away, and Emily closed her eyes briefly in relief.

If there was a woman Nick *didn't* dance with that night, it wasn't for lack of trying. Every time Emily saw him he was swirling a new partner in his arms, each one gazing up at him more raptly than the last.

She'd clamped down hard on that first awful impulse to flee to the solitude of her apartment, to wallow there in self-pity and might-have-beens. But with each new woman that Nick swept into his arms it became easier to stay at the dance; she was determined to show him he couldn't hurt her—that she couldn't be hurt, full stop—because she just didn't care.

As the night wore on, maintaining the pretence of nonchalance became more and more of a strain. She strolled along the pavement, initiating conversations with startled people who had never known Emily Swenson to be so sociable; but, whatever the subject matter, it was never interesting enough to keep her eyes from straying back to the street, back to the one fair head that was taller than most of the others. She tried to concentrate on the other dancers—Martin and Harriet Tollefson in a vigorous, foot-stomping csárdás; Mrs Hoeffer blushing and tittering as an elegant-looking man from the next township waltzed her around—but inevitably her gaze would shift and sharpen on Nick and his current partner.

At one point her mother tugged her father out on to the street, and that, at least, was novelty enough to capture and hold her attention for the duration of the complex dance they executed. Afterwards her mother joined her while her father went to fetch soft drinks, and this time Emily's smile was genuine. 'You two looked like a couple of kids out there,' she told her.

Mary Swenson laughed modestly and fanned her flushed face with one hand. 'We haven't danced in years,' she mused happily. 'It's how I first fell in love with your father, you know. At a barn dance. He just swooped in on me from out of nowhere, a complete stranger, swept me out on to the floor...' She raised her eyes and exhaled with a smile, remembering. 'He never said a single word during that whole dance, but by the time it was over I knew I wanted to feel what I'd felt in his arms for the rest of my life.' She looked up at her tall, lovely daughter a little sheepishly. 'Those were pretty disgraceful feelings for a woman in those days,' she admitted wryly, 'and I was ashamed of them for a long time. It took years before I understood that the physical and the mental things were all connected. My body knew your father was the right man instantly. It took my mind a little longer.'

Emily just blinked at her in astonishment.

'Oh, dear.' Mary tried to suppress a little smile. 'Your old mother's shocked you, hasn't she?'

Emily licked her lips and swallowed, uncomfortable at sharing this extraordinarily intimate view of her mother's feelings for her father.

'When you look at Nick,' her mother continued softly, 'I can see myself, thirty years ago, in your face. I think Nick must make you feel the way your father made me feel, and oh, Emily, if he can do that, don't let him get away.'

Emily took a deep breath and scowled. 'I don't want to feel that way, Mother. It's——'

'Demeaning?' her mother interrupted with a wry smile. 'Don't look so surprised, dear. I know that's the way you've always thought of me—some poor, downtrodden, weak-willed woman, bowing to her husband's whims all the time.' She shook her head and chuckled. 'What you never understood, Emily, is that subservience isn't an external condition. It's a state of mind. It only exists in here.' She tapped one finger to her head. 'I give to your father because it makes *me* happy, not him. Loving isn't a selfless thing, you know—a sacrifice only weak people make—it's really the most selfish act of all, and sometimes, I think, the most courageous.'

Mary smiled gently at her daughter's troubled expression, then looked back to the dancers. 'Look at that Nick,' she murmured. 'Who could blame you for falling in love with a man like that?'

A little stunned by the depth of her mother's philosophising, Emily forgot to deny loving Nick, and shifted her gaze to the street. Her gaze hardened and her mouth compressed at the sight of Nick's arms around a particularly voluptuous redhead.

'Handsome, isn't he?'

'If you like the type,' Emily replied, her voice sullen, and her mother just smiled.

It was amazing, really, that a man with such a powerful physique could move so gracefully, so effortlessly, lending an almost formal elegance to a street covered with sawdust and filled with farmers.

He was wearing a white shirt over snug, faded jeans, and every time his legs moved the delineation of long, hard musculature rose against the fabric. Broad, tanned forearms poked out of the rolled-up sleeves, looking massive and powerful as they tightened around the woman's waspish waist. She was saying something to him now, and his teeth flashed whitely in a slow, lazy smile.

'He certainly seems to be *her* type,' Emily's mother pointed out.

Emily's eyes narrowed in irritation. Just then the music stopped, and the band leader announced a full set of waltzes.

'Emily!'

She followed the voice to see Martin Tollefson lumbering towards her, his hand outstretched.

'Come on, darlin'.' He tucked her hand in the crook of his elbow and led her out on to the street. 'Harriet's just about tuckered out, and it's time for your first lesson.'

If she could have done it unobtrusively, Emily would have dragged her heels, pulling against Martin's grip, and steadfastly refused to go out there and make a fool of herself. But at the last minute she caught Nick's eyes on her, so she just smiled bravely and let Martin lead her away to her doom.

Through the clenched teeth of her smile she admitted the truth. Martin seemed to know everything there was to know about her already; what was one more weakness? 'I don't know how to do this, Martin,' she confided in a shaky whisper. 'I'm going to make a fool of myself, and everybody's looking at me. They're going to laugh.'

Martin stopped in front of the bandstand and turned her gently, nestling her in the perfect cradle of a gentlemanly embrace. 'Of course they're all looking at you,' he whispered back with a smile, blue eyes twinkling. 'You look like a fairy princess tonight, and you're breaking hearts all around.'

She was so stunned at the sheer impossibility of what he said that she barely noticed when the music started, was hardly aware of her feet automatically following his in a slow, elegant pattern that felt somehow like floating.

'That's it.' He nodded down at her with approval. 'I'll dance, you come along for the ride. Feels good, doesn't it?'

'Yes,' she agreed, amazed.

So this was dancing, she marvelled as they turned in wonderful, graceful arcs that made the lights overhead blur in streaks across the night sky. She could feel the swirl of her skirt spinning away from her legs, the soft rush of warm air against her cheeks, the strange weightlessness of her limbs.

Martin guided her with the gentle pressure of his hand on her back, the smallest tug of the hand that held hers, and just when she was beginning to feel that she could dance like this forever he stopped abruptly and, with a gracious nod, relinquished her hand to a tall, dark man who had tapped him on the shoulder.

Before Emily had a chance to protest, she was swirled away from Martin in the arms of a stranger, but he had a pleasant smile and warm brown eyes, and his hands and feet were every bit as expert as Martin's had been, and Emily found herself laughing for the sheer pleasure of it.

She danced every waltz in the set: two in a row with the man with warm brown eyes, one with Herman, who surprised her by moving his bulk with considerable agility, one with an angry-looking

black-haired man whose eyes drilled hers with such
intensity that he almost frightened her, and the last
with Martin again, who teased her about being
fickle, she changed partners so often.

'I didn't realise there were this many men in the
county,' she laughed breathlessly, trying to sneak
a peek over his shoulder at where Nick was dancing
with the redhead—again. 'I feel like Cinderella at
her first ball.'

Martin turned her smoothly—almost inten-
tionally, it seemed—until she couldn't see Nick and
was forced to look up into his own kindly face.
'You having trouble keeping your eye on the prince,
Cinderella?' he asked with a gentle smile.

An indignant denial sprang to her lips, then died
there, and she dropped her eyes. Fortunately, the
set ended and Harriet reclaimed him before he could
say anything else.

Emily joined her parents during the break, trying
not to notice Nick and the redhead at one of the
beer booths, standing so closely together that light
couldn't find a space between them. At one point
the woman reached up to slip long-nailed fingers
into his hair, then pulled his head down to whisper
in his ear. Her nails were painted a vibrant red, and
from a distance they looked like drops of blood
against the lightness of his hair. He laughed at
whatever she said, then his eyes met Emily's over
the redhead's shoulder, narrowed slightly, and his
smile faded. She looked away quickly, but not
quickly enough. The next time she glanced casually
in his direction, he was leaning back against the
booth, his elbows propped on the ledge, smiling
insolently at her. You can't take your eyes off me,

his expression seemed to say, and from that moment on she determined to do precisely that.

For the rest of the evening she was witty, she was gay, and, above all, she was gregarious, dancing whenever she was asked, flirting awkwardly with every man who took her into his arms, because flirting was as novel an experience as dancing, and Emily hadn't perfected the art yet. Still, the disguise she had hoped for at the beginning of the evening was complete, and so comfortable, in fact, that she began to wonder if it was really a disguise at all. Maybe this gay, laughing, exceedingly feminine persona had been lurking inside all along, somewhere deep beneath the years of stern features and plain clothes.

Emily felt Nick's eyes on her more than once, and, although she made a point not to seek him out in the crowd, there were times when he passed into her line of sight as they danced with their respective partners. Those moments left flashing images burned into her mind—his broad hand splayed across another woman's back, the line of his jaw shadowing his neck, the damp tumble of darkening blond spilling over his brow.

She'd just finished perhaps her fifth dance with the man with the brown eyes when she felt a hot, rough hand come down on her shoulder from behind.

'You don't mind, do you?' Nick said to the man, and, although his mouth smiled, something in his eyes stated clearly that his question was not a request.

Before the man had had a chance to declare whether he minded or not, Nick had turned Emily to face him, and his hand pressed hot and wide across the small of her back. Although it felt as if it were burning through the thin cotton fabric of her dress, his hand didn't jerk her towards him; the pressure was light, implying strength rather than executing it, and somehow that was more powerful a force.

'Emily.'

He didn't have to say any more than that. She knew what he wanted. Her eyes lifted slowly to his, then flinched slightly, as if they had encountered a brief flash of blinding light. While his eyes held hers in a smouldering blue gaze, his left hand found her right shoulder, slid slowly down her arm to her hand, then twined its fingers through hers.

'The last songs of the night are always slow dances.' His voice was a faint rumble of deep-throated thunder, and his breath stirred the hair on her forehead. 'They're supposed to cool us down...' his mouth curved in a deadly smile '...or heat us up, as the case may be.'

She felt the muscles of her neck straining as she looked up at him.

'Put your hand on my shoulder, Emily.'

Her hand moved to obey him with a will of its own, and when the music started her legs moved as well, following his lead, although she couldn't remember telling them to do that.

He didn't dance like anyone else. As a matter of fact, whatever it was they were doing didn't feel like dancing at all. There was no sensation of gliding or flying, no lifting of the spirit to soar free. It was something much more primitive than that, something that bordered on eroticism. Surely the band was playing a song? Surely there must be a melody? But if there was, Emily couldn't hear it. She could barely hear anything. Her consciousness was fixed on the throbbing beat of the drum, the strident, demanding rhythm that pumped like the heart of a huge animal.

Their bodies never touched, save for the contact-points of their hands, and yet never had Emily been so physically aware of him. She didn't have to look to see that his shirt clung damply to the rippling muscles of his stomach; she *knew*. She didn't have to see the hand on her back to know how dark his skin would appear against her dress. Somehow these things were evident in his eyes; eyes that seemed to bore into hers, screaming silently something beyond articulation, something meant only to be felt, and never spoken aloud.

She had read somewhere that dance was the most stimulating foreplay of all, and now she believed it. Blind and deaf and mindless, her body followed the movements of his with a surety and trust that was pure instinct, and in one stunning flash of revelation she understood that the dance was a microcosm of life itself, the way Nature had intended it to be. The man led, and the woman followed; the man protected, and the woman trusted, and, as abhorrent as such a concept might have been in twentieth-century conversation, in the dance, at least, it was still the essence of desire.

She wanted to be closer. Her eyelids fluttered at the thought of the power of the arm at her waist, and she wanted to feel that power pulling her towards him. Unconsciously her body moved towards his, and unobtrusively, but unmistakably, he kept her at arm's length. But his eyes shot sparks of blue, as if they had suddenly caught fire.

'Don't,' he warned her, and the hoarseness of his voice made her catch her breath audibly. He winced at the sound, then gritted his teeth and drew their locked hands up to rest on his chest.

It was just a little thing; a natural position for dancers. Emily had seen a dozen couples doing the same, but she had never imagined that it would feel like this.

His chest was rock-solid under her hand, and the wonder of the sensation made her spread her fingers and press her palm against him. Muscles jerked under her touch, and it was like holding her hand on a furnace that got hotter and hotter without burning, a furnace that expanded and contracted, faster and faster, as the beat of something that lived inside pounded against her flesh.

Her lips parted unconsciously, and she saw his gaze lash at her mouth like a whip that struck and retracted quickly.

'Emily...' He sucked her name in through his teeth, and the hand on her back jerked convulsively. For a full four steps of a dance she was no longer aware of performing, he kept his eyes closed. They were hard with determination when he opened them again.

'Who was the man you were dancing with?' he demanded in a low growl.

She frowned, mis-stepped for the first time, and struggled to make the awesome shift from sensory input to lucid thought. Had she danced with another man? Yes, of course she had ... Martin, and then the brown-eyed man . . . what had he said his name was?

'Michael,' she remembered suddenly. 'Michael, from Dakota County. . .' Why did he want to know this?

His brows raised slightly, and his eyes looked suddenly icy as they raked her face. 'Don't dance with him again,' he warned her. 'He's more than you bargained for.' And then in a blatantly sensual gesture he took his hand from her back and circled her bare neck, pressing his thumb ever so slightly into the pulse in the hollow of her throat. Her heartbeat quickened, and she couldn't seem to catch her breath.

'I won't come to you again, Emily,' he said in a low tone, his eyes fixed on hers. 'You'll have to come to me.'

Dazed, she watched him walk purposefully away through the crowd of dancers, a little surprised to find that his shoulder was no longer beneath her fingers. It was only then that she realised the song was over.

'Last dance!' the bandleader called through the microphone, and before she had completely regained her senses, the black-haired man whose eyes had disturbed her was at her side, lifting her hand in his, circling her waist with his arm.

He had never uttered a word the first and only time they had danced together, and he said nothing now, just swept her close and began to move languorously to the plaintive melody of the last song. Something about the way he looked at her made her want to pull away, but she caught a glimpse of Michael moving in her direction and changed her mind. She smiled apologetically at the kind brown eyes, puzzled that Nick would warn her about dancing with him again, but none the less compelled to heed his warning. He was a man, after all, and she was totally without experience. He would know about such things. But why had he left her at all? Why hadn't he stayed to dance the last dance with her?

In a sudden, uncomfortable tug, she was swirled around until she could see Nick lounging against the beer booth, watching her intently. For some unaccountable reason, his eyes looked murderous. Just before the black-haired man spun her away, Nick raised a glass of beer towards her in an insolent, angry salute, then tipped it to his mouth.

She frowned in confusion as she was swirled away through the crowd, so baffled by his attitude that she didn't notice the tension in the arm tightening around her waist.

A few seconds later her apparently skilled partner bumped them into another couple, and he jerked her against his chest to pull her out of the way. She gasped at the surprising impact, then laughed nervously.

The next time she saw Nick, he had both hands on the redhead's waist and the woman was flattened against his body, her hips gyrating slowly in a motion that made Emily blush just to see it. His cheek was pressed to the side of that wild red hair, but his eyes were fixed on Emily, demanding that she look, and see, and understand what was going on.

The colour brightened in her face and her green eyes flashed, and when the black-haired man felt her tense he pulled her even closer, until his belt buckle pressed into the soft flesh of her stomach. She shot a hard, brittle smile at Nick, and she didn't pull away.

CHAPTER ELEVEN

ALTHOUGH the out-of-towners slipped into the darkness almost before the last chord had faded away, the people of Random lingered, clearly reluctant to see the evening end. They milled about in the street and on the pavements, chatting with friends and neighbours, almost comical in their common desire not to go home just yet.

But the magic was gone for Emily. The moment Nick had walked away from her the night had become old and tired, and she felt like a wilting flower drooping on its stem. Cinderella, indeed, she thought miserably. At least Cinderella had had enough sense to leave the ball before the spell had worn off. She, on the other hand, had stayed too long, until she was physically exhausted and emotionally drained, and, to make matters worse, she imagined she could still feel the clammy imprint of the black-haired man's hand on her back. All she wanted now was to be up in her apartment, out of her dress and shoes and under the stinging pellets of a cool shower.

She was close to the row of food and drink booths, ready to make good her escape, when Nick caught her eye.

He was standing in front of the beer booth again, just a few yards away. The redhead was still at his side, gazing up at him with blatant sensuality.

Emily felt her face grow hot, and snapped her gaze back to Nick in what she hoped was a glance of disdain. The moment their eyes met, the noise seemed to fade into the background, and the press of bodies around her seemed to vanish, and the only thing Emily could be sure really existed was the invisible thread that connected blue eyes to green.

She felt her heart thud against the wall of her chest as their gazes met and seemed to melt together; and then, with brutal intention and a grin that was almost malicious, he raised his arm and draped it around the redhead's shoulders.

Emily blinked once, her face blank, then turned sharply on her heel and walked away. She made her way through the noisy crowd to the pavement, then, simply because she was headed in that direction and couldn't seem to stop, she walked all the way around the block to the dark alley that ran behind her shop, instead of entering through the front door.

The sounds from the street were muted back here, lending a surreal sense of isolation. There was life and laughter and light just half a block away, but here, in the narrow, shadowed alley, Emily was alone. In a way, it seemed like a frozen moment from all the years of her life. People had always been there, just a short distance away, and yet by her own choice she had always been alone. It had never bothered her before. The pride of independence, the haughty sense of superiority that came from knowing you didn't need anyone—those things had always been enough to sustain her. But suddenly they weren't any more, and she didn't know how to deal with the despair.

She walked with her head down, her hands clenched behind her back, her dress and shoes the only spots of light in the black passageway.

By the time she was halfway to her back door she could hear the crowd beginning to dissipate. Truck and car doors slammed shut and engines rumbled to life, and the night was filled with sporadic calls of farewell. When she paused at her back door and fumbled in her pocket for the key, the town was already settling into its customary silence.

'Dammit, where *is* it?' she muttered, digging furiously into the one deep pocket that seemed to plunge all the way down to the hem of her dress. She stretched the mouth of the pocket wide and peered into its depths, but away from the Main Street lights she could barely see her hands, let alone the glint of silver deep in a shadowed pocket.

'Let me help you,' a deep voice rasped suddenly from behind her, and her heart jumped into her throat as she spun around, green eyes wide. 'Sorry.' But the voice didn't sound sorry. It sounded smug. 'Didn't mean to scare you.'

Emily's pulse fluttered at the sinister shadows painting holes on his face. His eyes looked black in their deep hollows, and she scrambled backwards without thinking until her spine pressed against the door. 'What…what are you doing back here?' she whispered, her voice as breathless as if she'd just run a mile. It was the black-haired man, the man with disturbing eyes and a face she had thought looked angry.

He didn't reply, but in the darkness, just before his hands snatched out to imprison her wrists, she saw the white flash of his teeth.

'Don't!' she tried to scream, but it came out as a whimper she could barely hear herself, and before she could say anything else his mouth was grinding against hers and the full weight of his body had fallen against her, pinning her to the door.

Every muscle in her body froze instantly into immobility. It wasn't happening. This simply wasn't happening. She would just stand here perfectly still and hold her breath and pretend that she wasn't being mauled, and soon this man would simply vaporise into thin air, like the bad dream he really was.

The delusion lasted for the space of a second, then her thoughts raced screaming through her mind, stirring all her frozen muscles to action. With a mighty thrust born of panic she used her body like a whip, flinging him backwards and away, and opened her mouth to scream for help.

The scream died in her throat when she saw the bewildered tip of his head, his unsteadiness as he stumbled backwards and spread his legs quickly to keep from falling.

'Wha...?' he mumbled in drunken confusion. She smelled the malty odour of beer on his breath, and heard a baffled apology in his tone when he spoke. Harmless—her mind registered the thought as she released a shaky sigh of relief. 'Hey lady, take it easy.' He raised his palms defensively. 'You don' wanna play, just say no. Don' have to tell me twice, no sir...'

All the air whooshed out of him as something dark and huge exploded into his side and knocked him a full three feet down the alleyway before he fell to the ground.

Emily jumped back in alarm and flattened herself against the door, and it was only when she saw the black-haired man jerked to his feet like an empty sack and slammed against the brick side of the building that she realised the huge dark shape had been Nick.

'No!' she cried out as she saw his fist draw back and hesitate before driving towards the man's face. 'Stop it, Nick!' He jerked his head towards her, and the illumination of a street light a block away reflected in the whites of his eyes. 'No.' She shook her head rapidly until it felt as if her brains were rattling inside her skull. 'He's drunk. He didn't mean any harm . . . he was just leaving.'

Nick's eyes disappeared in the darkness as they narrowed, but his fist quivered in the light as he held it in check. He glared at Emily, then jerked his head to look at the bleary, startled eyes of the man he held pinned against the wall.

'Nick,' Emily said quietly, her heart pounding in her chest.

His fist lowered ever so slowly, but both hands remained clenched at his sides and he hunched towards the man in a threatening posture. 'Get the hell out of here,' he said in a low, shaky voice, and the man demonstrated that he didn't indeed need to be told anything twice. He scrambled sideways away from Nick, his back against the wall, his posture defensive until he was out of range. Then he turned and staggered away down the alley, muttering under his breath. Long after he'd disappeared into the darkness, they could hear the desperate stumbling of his shoes against the tar, and then, at last, it was perfectly quiet.

Emily was still pressed back against the door, more shaken by the extraordinary sight of perpetually pleasant Nick turned violent than she had been by the man's unexpected assault. Her legs felt like columns of jelly, with only her locked knees keeping her from crumbling to the ground in a heap.

Nick hadn't moved, hadn't even turned his head towards her. 'I told you to stay away from him,' his voice lashed out at her.

She closed her eyes and pressed her lips together hard, suddenly on the defensive. 'You told me to stay away from Michael, not him!'

There was complete silence for a moment as his head rolled slowly to face her. 'I don't know who the hell Michael is, but that was the creep I was warning you about. He didn't take his eyes off you all night, and an idiot could have seen what he had in mind.' He hesitated, then his shoulders rose and fell in a silent sigh. 'He didn't hurt you, did he?' he asked gruffly.

Emily smiled bitterly in the dark. How ironic, she thought. In all of her twenty-seven years, she'd been kissed by two men, and now the only one who had the power to hurt her—who *had* hurt her—was standing here worrying that the other one had.

'No,' she said quietly. 'He didn't hurt me.'

Nick cocked his head, listening to something different in her voice, then walked to stand within a few inches of her.

She could see his features now—the heat-dampened strands of blond clinging to his forehead; the worried tilt of his brows; the masculine cut of his mouth. 'Are you sure you're OK, Em?' He brushed the backs of his curled fingers against her cheek in a heartbreakingly tender gesture.

She nodded silently, her eyes falling closed at his touch.

Oh, lord forgive her, it was all she wanted right now, just to feel his touch on her skin; *his* touch, she realised with a start, and no other. For reasons she didn't understand, it was through him that she felt connected to the rest of the world, as if he were the only gateway to a place she had never been. She needed that connection desperately, and if that need was a damning weakness, then let her be damned. Is that what love is? she wondered absently. Is it really a gut feeling—an instinctive sense of rightness that overrides everything your rational mind decrees?

'Come on, Em, let's get you upstairs.'

She nodded mutely, then turned for the door. The key that had been so elusive just moments before seemed to leap from her pocket into her hand, and she inserted it into the lock. She heard him close the alleyway door firmly behind them, then heard his steps follow her carefully through the darkened workroom, up the black, narrow stairway, and then all she could hear was the anticipatory pounding of her heart.

It wasn't exactly the way she'd pictured it, in those rare moments when she'd ever imagined herself with a man at all. No flowers, no courtship, no heartfelt declarations of love . . . no date for the spring prom, she added with a wry smile. Her chance at those things was long past, and this was what was left. A long walk up a dark stairway, a silent man behind her who had never promised anything more than that with him she would feel like a woman.

And that, she realised, was the most staggering promise of all. It was enough.

At the top of the stairs she turned to face him without turning on the lights. He was little more than a larger, denser shadow in a room of shadows.

'I think I'll have a little wine,' she said, and she didn't know if she said it because she'd heard it in a film, or read it in a book, or if she really needed the time and the numbing relaxation that drinking a glass of wine might offer.

'Good idea.'

The light from the refrigerator painted an eerie yellow stripe across the kitchen floor. It was all the light she needed to find two glasses and fill them from the bottle of white wine lying on its side next to the milk cartons.

Her hand shook a little as she poured, and she wondered if she would ever look back on this night with regret. He would not tell her he loved her— he had never pretended that—and now she was quietly surprised to understand how very unimportant that was. Love was not a bargaining tool, and it couldn't be withheld until you were certain of an equal return. It was just something you gave. Unconditionally. And, surprisingly, there was a sense of pride in being able to do that; in finding the courage to give love without a guarantee that you would get it back.

She carried the wine back into the dark living-room, her hands now so steady that the liquid barely moved in the glasses.

'Nick?'

She stopped just inside the doorway, sensing a new sort of quiet in the dark apartment. 'Nick?'

Nothing.

Emily didn't move for what seemed a very long time, and then very slowly, as if she paid for each motion with excruciating pain, she walked to the coffee-table, set down the glasses, then turned on the lamp by the couch. The tiny click of the switch almost covered the sound of the alley door closing downstairs. Almost, but not quite.

CHAPTER TWELVE

EMILY stopped the motion of the old wooden rocking-chair and leaned forward a bit, squinting out of her bedroom window. Yes, it *was* getting lighter out there. It really was. Just a little.

For the first time in hours, she permitted herself a brief glance at the clock over next to her bed. Five o'clock. Thank heaven. The night was nearly over.

She leaned back against the hard wooden spindles and began to rock again, pushing the floor with her bare toes. She was clad only in a loose T-shirt and panties, but even those clung damply to her skin in the heat that even darkness hadn't been able to relieve. The white dress lay in a crumpled heap next to the chair.

Too late, too late, too late—it was the litany she had rocked to for all the hours since she had found Nick gone. She had learned so much in the past twenty-four hours—about Nick, about her mother and father, about joy, about love; and mostly, about herself—and yet all the knowledge had come too late.

There was a strange quality to the lightening sky outside her window, and her brows twitched as she stared at it.

Finally she pressed her hands against the rocker arms and pushed wearily to her feet, her mind too numb to register the wispy clouds that filtered the light of dawn.

'Emily!' Her mother smiled and frowned all at the same time. She was always happy to see her daughter, of course; but an unannounced visit at noon on a Sunday was absolutely unprecedented. Something had to be wrong.

'Hi, Mom.' Emily smiled tentatively through the screen of the back door, and Mary hurried to open it.

'Well, for heaven's sake, come in, child. Surely you don't have to wait for an invitation to walk into this kitchen? Sit down while I pour you some coffee. Is something wrong at the store? Don't tell me those coolers have gone on the fritz again, not in this heat! Your father's in the barn, of course, but if you need him——'

'Mom.' Emily caught her hand just as she was about to bustle away to the stove, and held her still. 'Relax. There's nothing wrong. I just wanted to see you, that's all.'

Mary smiled uncertainly, searching her daughter's face, trying to pin-point what it was that made her look so different today. Her hair, maybe. The short, fair strands were in total disarray, as if she'd just rubbed it dry with a towel and forgotten to comb it. In a way, it was a charmingly disordered look—but disorder, charming or not, had never been Emily's style. Nor had cut-off jeans and a baggy T-shirt that looked as it had been slept in, but she was wearing them, too.

Emily was examining her just as intently, as if she'd never seen her before. It was such a thorough inspection that Mary actually blushed as the green eyes so like her own flicked busily over her face, down the soft blue dress and crisp white apron, then back up to her face again.

For a moment it was so quiet that Mary became keenly aware of the rasp of grasshoppers out in the field, a sound so much a part of life on the Midwestern plains that she was rarely conscious of it.

'Emily.' She took her daughter's hand lightly in her own. 'What is it?'

Emily tried to shrug, tried to smile, but somehow couldn't quite manage either gesture.

'He stopped by this morning,' her mother said quietly, as if the half-smile and half-shrug had been explanation enough. 'To say goodbye.'

Emily looked down at the floor. There didn't seem to be anything to say, but her fingers tightened on her mother's hand, and she swallowed visibly.

Every muscle in Mary's face tensed as she searched her daughter's face. 'He'll be at the Tollefsons' all afternoon. He promised Martin he'd stay long enough for the anniversary party.' She hesitated for a moment, then squeezed her daughter's hand urgently. 'For goodness' sake, Emily, go and find him. Tell him,' she repeated her advice of the night before.

Emily released a prolonged sigh and looked up. 'I don't have to tell him. He knows already. He's known all along, I think. And still, he walked away.'

Mary's fine dark brows twitched in uncertainty.

Emily swallowed again and blinked rapidly and reached for her mother's other hand.

It was a perfectly astonishing thing, really, how a mother's arms could wrap around a fully grown woman and still manage to feel every bit as comforting as they had to a small child. For so many years, Emily had prided herself on not needing such comfort—strong people didn't, after all—but even if she had, the last place she would have expected to find it was here, in the arms of a woman she'd always loved, but secretly disdained for what she saw as weakness. Her father's arms would be strong—not her mother's—and yet here it was, a different kind of strength that went much deeper than size or demeanour, flowing into her, then back into her mother, then back to her again, completing a circle.

Carl Swenson finished his morning chores and came up to the house, pulled open the back screen door, looked inside, then stopped in his tracks. In that first instant when his wife's and his daughter's faces turned towards him, he thought it might be a wise thing for him to go right back to the barn and stay there until the world was right-side-up again. In the right-side-up world Emily never popped in unexpectedly, and she sure as hell never cried. As a matter of fact, he couldn't remember ever seeing her cry, not since he'd told her when she was a tyke that crying never solved anything but being tough often did. Damn him, anyway, for burdening his own daughter with a pioneer philosophy and a stubborn set of mind that made almost any task possible—except loving. That was the hard one.

But from the look of Emily's eyes—all red and swollen and misty—she'd been doing some crying now, and a lot of it, too, if he was any judge. His glance touched his wife, and he decided that they must have made weeping a major league sport. Mary's eyes were all misty, too.

He looked long and hard at his daughter's face and felt a lump form in his throat. 'You two are sure a sight,' he said gruffly, thinking that he had never seen either one of them look quite so beautiful before.

'You're letting every fly in the county in, Carl,' Mary admonished him gently.

He let the screen door slam shut behind him, and his Adam's apple moved up, then down in his sunburned throat. 'Clouds coming in,' he said.

'Oh, thank God,' Mary murmured, jumping up from the table at the one and only announcement monumental enough to distract her from her daughter's abrupt, tardy, painful leap into womanhood. The three of them nearly jammed together in the doorway as they rushed to the back porch.

Above them, the sky was a blue-white layer of gauze, but just to the west, the tall domes of black-bellied thunderheads were rolling towards them.

Mary stood with one hand braced on the porch railing, the other shading her eyes as she looked westward. 'Rain,' she murmured, with the same reverence as if she had murmured, 'Life.'

Emily looked out over the barren field behind the barn, where corn seeds were buried in a death-trap of thirst a few inches beneath the surface. How ironic, she thought, that the rain would come the very day that Nick would leave, as if Nature wanted to balance the departure of one with the arrival of the other.

'Let's hope that's all it is,' Carl said worriedly, pulling the collar of his chambray shirt away from his neck.

The heat seemed worse than ever, lying over the land like a blanket on a corpse. The air was still; breathless.

'Listen,' Mary whispered, and they all held their breath. 'The grasshoppers have stopped.'

Emily's eyes—the greenest things for miles around—passed over the parched landscape. There was nothing quite as ominous as the Midwestern plains gone completely silent. 'The quiet before the storm' was a phrase that this land owned, and, if the depth of this particular quiet was any measure, the storm that was coming was a big one.

'Could be hail,' Carl said thoughtfully, turning to Emily. 'Best get back and protect those big windows.'

Emily nodded absently. Like every other store-front on Main Street that had lost an expensive piece of plate glass to hail, the flower shop boasted slatted wooden blinds on outside rollers. It had been a long, long time since she'd seen them all pulled down and fastened against a coming storm.

She sighed, then turned to her mother and gave her a warm, heartfelt hug. 'You two keep your eyes on the sky, and don't forget to turn on the radio,' she reminded them. When she would have pulled away, Mary's hands lingered on her shoulders and she looked her straight in the eye.

'You might think about dropping in at the Tollefsons',' she said. 'Just to wish them happy anniversary. And if you see Nick out there, you could tell him goodbye again for me.'

Emily tried to smile at her transparency, but she couldn't quite pull it off. 'I took the rest of the flower arrangements out to the Tollefsons' early this morning, Mom. I wished them happy anniversary then.' She went down the steps and began walking rapidly towards her car before her mother could say anything else, her arm lifted in a parting wave. 'Remember the radio!' she called just before she slammed the car door and started the engine.

'Damn!' Mary muttered fervently from the porch, watching the car pull out of the drive.

Carl's eyes widened at the very first curse he had ever heard pass his wife's lips.

CHAPTER THIRTEEN

EMILY switched on the car radio before she was even out of the driveway, but the gesture was born of habit more than concern. A hundred thunderstorms marched across Minnesota every spring and summer, each one a potential threat, but part of the price you paid for reaping the bounty of the plains was learning to live with the violence of Nature.

The trees that flourished in this part of country did so because they could withstand the nearly gale-force winds that were a part of every season, and the same could be said of the people, too. Nowhere in the world was the technology of storm warning more advanced—the new weather radars detected wind velocities from miles away, and could spot tornadoes almost before they began to form. That didn't stop a storm from doing its damage, of course, but it did give the people in its path the time they needed to head for the storm shelters.

Emily had her own cosy nook in the basement under the flower shop, stocked with torches and blankets and a battery-operated radio. In an average year, the warning sirens sent her down there a half a dozen times or more, and if today was to be one of those times, so be it.

The radio crackled with static as she turned the dial. Finally she found the station that broadcast weather twenty-four hours a day.

'...massive storm front moving across the plains,' the announcer was saying in a matter-of-fact tone. 'Heavy rains, golf-ball sized hail, and damaging winds have been reported in Nebraska, Kansas and Iowa. Conditions are right for the formation of tornadoes, so leave that dial right where it is, folks, and keep your eyes on the skies.'

Emily smiled a little to hear the flip, familiar warning, and then she sensed the darkness of a huge truck closing in behind her, glanced at her rear-view mirror, and her smile vanished.

'Oh, my lord,' she murmured aloud, green eyes wide, because it wasn't a truck.

She jerked her head over her shoulder to confirm what she saw, then jerked it back and squinted at Random, shimmering in the white heat of sunlight less than a mile ahead. And there *was* sunlight ahead of her, parching the fields, flashing blindingly off the metal road signs ... but behind her the world was black and terrifying.

'Too fast,' she whispered, a little knot of worry forming in her stomach because those clouds had been miles away back at the farm, but now they were nearly on top of her, and she'd been travelling at sixty miles an hour. Her eyes darted to the radio when she realised that it had suddenly gone dead, and her right hand scrambled for the dial. She found the Minneapolis stations, all broadcasting warnings of the coming storm, but the local station she'd been listening to had simply vanished from the air—the station situated in a little town thirty miles to the west, she remembered, biting down on her lower lip.

She glanced over her shoulder once again, the knot in her stomach growing larger now, and her foot jammed the accelerator to the floor even before her head had turned completely around to face the front again.

There was a wall of cloud racing up behind her with terrifying speed, and it stretched as far as she could see in either direction and thousands and thousands of feet up into the sky, where it topped out in fluffy white cottonballs. It was pitch-black and perfectly flat on the bottom, skimming close to the ground, leaving only a narrow swatch of grey between it and the horizon. Any two-year-old knew that this was the type of cloud that could, and usually did spawn tornadoes, and if Emily knew one thing, she knew she didn't want to be on the highway in a car if one should suddenly spiral down.

She was going so fast by the time she reached the outskirts of the town that she had to stand on the brakes to bring the car down to a safe speed. There were a few people standing in the middle of the sawdust and clutter left from last night's dance, all facing west, watching the sky.

She pulled up to the kerb at an angle, killed the engine, then jumped from the car, her breath quickening.

The very air around her was eerie, tinged with a sickly greenish hue that made her palms sweat. Worse than that was the deathly stillness, strangely foreboding with the black cloud racing towards them. The sounds of life were strangely absent— no dogs barking, no birds chirping, not so much as the rustle of a single leaf.

As she glanced around the scattered observers for a familiar face, Emily thought that she could actually hear them all breathing, the world was so quiet.

'Herman.' She walked up to stand next to him and spoke softly. 'See anything?'

He stared intently westward, then raised one arm and pointed. 'A little wisp dangling down, over there...see it?'

Emily followed a line from his finger and saw a thready appendage of white trailing from the cloud. It was the beginning. 'Maybe it'll go back up,' she whispered, staring at it.

'Maybe,' Herman allowed, but his feet shuffled in the sawdust, and Emily heard the sounds of other feet doing the same thing, and knew they were all preparing to sprint for cover. 'One touched down, you know. Blew the Haverford radio tower all to hell.'

Emily pursed her lips, her eyes still fastened on that harmless-looking tail of white. So that was what had happened to the radio station.

'Cloud sucked it back up, though,' Herman went on in a subdued voice. 'The National Weather Service said nothing else is showing on the radar, but I don't like the looks of that little thing, do you?'

Emily opened her mouth to answer, but in the time it took for her lips to part a million other white threads shot down from the wall cloud to join those first few trail-blazers, and even from this distance they could see the tail begin to twist.

'Lord almighty, that was fast!' Herman whispered, or maybe he'd been yelling and it only sounded like a whisper, because suddenly there was a blast of sound that resembled a freight train bearing down at full speed. Within seconds, the town sirens wailed in sympathy.

Watching the massive wall cloud give birth to a tornado was spellbinding, and Emily stood rooted to the spot by morbid fascination. It was the unstoppable majesty of Nature delivering a child of incomparable destruction, and there was almost as much beauty in it as there was terror.

With horrifying speed, the twister fattened and spread where it joined the cloud, then skewered down to stab at the ground. A spiral of brownish-black climbed the white column like a barber's pole and Emily knew that the colour represented soil and trees and pieces of buildings and whatever else the tornado had sucked in with its first deadly kiss with the earth. Whipping like a snake, it raged towards downtown Random, and within seconds of that first ear-splitting blast of noise the wind hit Main Street like the smack of a giant fist.

It flung Emily backwards, plastering her skirt to her body, driving flying sawdust into her eyes and nose and mouth.

A meaty hand snatched at her arm, tightened around it, and hauled her towards the hardware store. Unprotesting, she let Herman drag her into the store, then rush her down the centre aisle towards the basement steps. Halfway down it occurred to her that she'd forgotten to lower the wooden blinds in front of the shop windows, but there was no question of going back outside now.

'Don't think it'll hit here,' Herman hollered over the noise that sounded like an advancing army even from inside the building, 'but it never hurts to be too careful.' He pulled a battery-powered lantern out of the dark and turned it on, then gestured towards a couple of old tattered chairs in the far corner. 'The ceiling's reinforced with concrete over there. That's where we'll wait it out.'

Emily nodded, breathless, and picked her way over to the chairs.

It was too noisy to talk for nearly five minutes, and then it was so suddenly quiet that it was hard to imagine there had even been a storm. Herman and Emily both stared up at the ceiling in silence, then glanced at each other sheepishly, like two Chicken Littles who had run for cover with no reason.

'Must have hopped clean over the town, but for a minute there it sure looked like we were going to get it,' Herman remarked, trying to justify two adults' cowering in a basement.

'It sure did,' Emily agreed with a nervous laugh. 'I never saw one that close before.'

Upstairs they found the hardware store in perfect order, quiet except for a heavy rain splattering against the windows. Outside, debris from the street dance was plastered wetly against buildings and cars, and the pavement had been swept clean of its dusty carpet of sawdust, testament to the force of the wind that had passed through. There would be branches down and scattered shingles throughout the town, and the electricity might be out for hours, but as far as Emily could see up and down the street there had been no serious damage. The colour of the world had returned to the normal dreary grey of any thunderstorm, and the store windows across the street showed other faces peering out, just like theirs.

She and Herman stood in front of the window, as still as two mannequins, watching the blessed rain pelt down.

'It was worth a scare, to get this rain,' Herman mused finally.

'Amen to that,' Emily replied.

'Still, it's too bad it couldn't have waited a few hours. Must have put a damper on the Tollefsons' picnic.' Herman shoved his hands in the pockets of his baggy trousers and rocked back and forth on his heels, studying Emily's profile out of the corner of his eye. 'You planning on going out there?'

She shook her head, still staring out at the rain.

'Nick's there, you know.'

'So I heard.'

For a time there was nothing but the sound of the rain outside, then Herman sighed dramatically. 'Says he's leaving town for good tonight.'

Emily pursed her lips and said nothing.

'Thought you might be going out there to say your goodbyes before he left.'

Emily shot a glance to her left, but Herman was still rocking, staring innocently out of the window.

'The town sure will miss him. Almost everyone wishes he'd stick around, make his home here again.'

Emily blew a sharp breath out through her nose. 'Then "almost everyone" should ask him to stay,' she said irritably.

Herman nodded sagely. 'Almost everyone has.' He let that sink in for a moment, then added,

'Except you.' He turned his head sideways to look at her, his face genuinely puzzled.

Emily just took a deep breath and ignored him.

Eventually, Herman turned back to look out of the window. The rain was slowing to one of those steady drizzles that promised to last for a long time. Suddenly his head jerked backwards in surprise as a muddy brown pick-up roared out of nowhere and screeched to a halt in front of the store, its blunt nose pointing straight towards them, rocking with the force of its stop.

Fred Larson's truck, Emily's mind recorded automatically.

A whipcord-lean man popped out of the driver's door and stood on the running-board, rain dripping from the brim of his straw hat, one hand cupped around his mouth as he yelled frantically, 'We need help out here!'

By the time Herman and Emily reached the door and yanked it open, Fred was leaning on the truck horn, filling the town with a steady, raucous blare that was somehow more frightening than the sirens had been. All up and down Main Street people were popping out of the doors of Sunday-quiet shops, running through the rain to where the pick-up had stopped, its noisy engine still racing.

'We been hit!' Fred cried, and Emily's heart seemed to plummet to her stomach. 'Touch down at the Tollefsons',' he panted, panic shortening his breath, 'and the place is damn near levelled!'

'Oh, dear lord!' was the fearful exclamation that raced through the mind of every person within earshot, and for a brief instant they all froze where they stood. That instant was a lifetime for Emily as names flashed through her thoughts with the blinding glare of a neon rollcall.

Martin. Harriet. Their children and their grandchildren.

And Nick. Oh, yes. Let's not forget about Nick.

'Anybody hurt?' Herman demanded, giving voice to the question they all wanted answered.

Fred was already clambering back into the truck, ready to race away. 'They're all trapped in the storm cellar,' he hollered through the window, 'but the house collapsed on top of 'em, and we gotta dig through.' His eyes closed briefly, as if he'd just remembered something. 'Except for one guy,' he added tightly. 'Don't know how bad he is, but there was a godawful lot of blood. Old Art Simon's boy—what's his name?'

The world seemed to go perfectly still and Emily's lips formed the name silently. Nick. His name was Nick.

'Oh, Jesus,' Herman mumbled under his breath, his eyes sagging closed for a heartbeat.

'Come on, everybody!' Fred banged the top of his truck in frustrated impatience, and the sound seemed to galvanise everyone into action. A few scrambled into the back of the pick-up, a few more inside, and the rest ran for their own vehicles.

Emily couldn't remember racing for her car. All she knew was that one minute she was standing next to Herman mouthing Nick's name, and the next she was behind the wheel, a rain-wet hand fumbling at the ignition, her heart pounding so hard it felt as if it would burst through her chest. Herman jumped in the passenger side just as her hand hit the gear lever and slammed it into gear.

'Call the sheriff!' he bellowed out of the window to someone, and then Emily's foot found the accelerator and the car leaped forward in a screeching take-off eastward out of town.

'Turn on the windscreen wipers, Emily,' Herman said with amazing calm, reaching for his seat-belt, his eyes squinting through the rivulets of water running down the glass.

Her left hand scrambled over the buttons on the dash-board while her right clutched the steering-wheel of the speeding car in a death-grip. White showed all around the green of her eyes as she stared straight ahead. 'I-can't-find-it-Herman-I-can't-find-it.' The words ran into one another desperately, breathlessly, and then Herman's hand reached over behind the steering-wheel and pulled a button, and rubber blades swept two fans shapes on to the windscreen.

The wipers thumped frantically on high speed, barely keeping up with the force of the rain. Emily's palms were sweating, and her hands felt slick on the wheel.

You shouldn't be driving, she told herself mindlessly, even as her foot pressed harder on the accelerator. You've never driven this fast in your life and there's water on the road and there could be trees down ahead and you'll never be able to stop in time and your hands keep slipping off the wheel and——

'Emily.' Herman's quiet voice shattered her thoughts. 'Slow down a little. The turn-off's just ahead.'

She lifted her foot obediently, then jerked her eyes left for just a second. Even through the rain, she could see the emptiness of a ploughed field stretching towards the horizon. 'No, not yet. You can always see the barn from the road, it's so damn big; you can see that big red barn from half a mile away, and that's when you turn——'

'Slow down, Emily,' Herman repeated in a solemn voice. 'We won't be able to see the barn.' He was leaning forwards against the strap of his seat-belt, frowning out of her side window. 'It's gone.'

The car fishtailed on the slick road when she hit the brakes, barely managed to turn on to the Tollefsons' dirt road, and it was then that they saw the first evidence that the twister had indeed touched down.

They sped past what looked like a pile of kindling stacked by a madman, and Emily remembered that only this morning it had been a thick grove of young birch. Further down the washboard road, hundred-year-old pines lay on the ground like enormous arrows, pointing the way the storm had gone, showing their plate-bottom root clusters to the road. And where there had been no trees to jerk up or topple, the tornado had cleared a quarter-mile-wide path by ripping up the earth itself and leaving the clay subsoil exposed to the rain. The path led directly to the Tollefsons' farm.

'I can't see the place,' Emily murmured, her lips strangely numb, her eyes wild.

'Wait till we round the curve,' Herman tried to reassure her, but his voice was shaky, too. 'You can never see the house till you round the curve.'

But there was no house.

Emily spun into the long driveway, mud flying from her car's back wheels, and only just managed to veer the car around the feathery top of a doomed cottonwood lying on its side. Before they were halfway up to where the house had been, her expression had become glazed. The extent of the destruction was simply too much for her mind to absorb.

Off to the left, the once massive hay barn that held ten thousand bales in a good year had been flattened like a collapsed house of cards.

Less than twenty feet away, the smaller dairy barn stood pristine and undamaged, spared by the fickle nature of a storm that hopped helter-skelter over the earth, raising hell itself in one square foot and leaving the next untouched.

But the house looked as if it had exploded from the inside, and its pieces were scattered as far as the eye could see. All that was left was a pile of rubble heaped over the foundation. Perversely, Harriet Tollefson's grandfather clock stood in the centre of the destruction that had once been their living-room, as staid and dignified as ever.

Emily and Herman leaped from the car just as the brown pick-up led a caravan of vehicles into the driveway.

'This way!' Herman cried, his stout legs pumping towards the remains of the house, the rain plastering wisps of hair to his balding crown.

A lone man was tearing through the rubble on the far side, trying to clear a path to the outside storm-cellar doors. He was incredibly tall and looked like a younger version of Martin himself— a son, perhaps, or maybe even a grandson. With her heart in her throat and the rain flattening her hair to her skull, Emily raced after Herman, passed him, and reached the man first.

'Where's Nick?' she screamed, grabbing his arm and jerking him upright with a strength that belied the difference in their sizes.

Panic-stricken blue eyes blinked in confusion and his hands clenched and unclenched as if they were still pulling at the clutter of debris at his feet. 'I gotta get them out!' he yelled suddenly, coming to his senses, jerking away to tear at the rubble again.

'But where's Nick?' she shrieked at the top of her lungs. 'Fred said he was hurt!' But then the people from the town dived into the wreckage and pushed her aside. A hand grabbed her shoulder from behind, trying to turn her, and she pulled away furiously, but the grip was too tight and now the hand was dragging her back, further away from the only man who might know what she had to know, what her life suddenly depended on knowing, and with a rush of rage-fuelled adrenalin she spun with her eyes wild and her hands raised to shove the man aside, and then she froze.

'I'm all right, Em,' he said softly.

His hair was soaking wet, with blond strands glued to his forehead, dripping water on to the shelf of his lashes and down over cheeks that were pale beneath the tan. An ugly gash skittered over the full length of his right brow, oozing bright red blood that the rain kept trying to wash away; but his eyes were bluer than ever and his mouth quirked in a half-smile.

'It bled a lot,' he said, following her eyes to his forehead. 'Head wounds always do.'

Her lips turned inwards as her body wondered what to do with all the adrenalin rushing through her veins, then she covered her face with her hands and simply burst into tears.

'Em,' her name came out in a stunned rush of air as he reached out with both arms and drew her close, and she buried her head in his shoulder and let the tears come. She heard his soft chuckle in her ear. 'You're blowing it, Em,' he murmured. 'You know what people are going to think, if they see you crying on my shoulder like this...'

But Emily just kept crying, clinging to his upper arms, because people weren't going to think anything they didn't know already. They *all* knew, it seemed. She was the only one who hadn't.

For a moment that was over too soon, because it was where he wanted to be and what he wanted to be doing more than anything in the world, Nick stood there holding her in the rain. Then he took her shoulders in his hands, pushed her gently away and crouched a little to look directly into her eyes. 'Dammit, Emily,' he said tenderly, 'you've got a lousy sense of timing. We have to dig those people out.'

His hands left her shoulders so abruptly that she nearly fell, and it was as if his hands had kept her from remembering anything but how close she'd come to losing him. Standing there alone, she suddenly remembered Martin, Harriet, all the children. She spun and moved quickly to follow him to where Herman was straining to lift a ceiling joist from the debris over the storm-cellar doors.

'Dam-*mit*!' Herman cried. 'It's too heavy. We need the tractor!'

Oh, lord, Emily thought as she eyed the beam in dismay. It was as thick as a man's body and a full ten feet protruded from the pile of splintered lumber and brick.

'The tractor's buried under the hay barn,' Nick shouted over the rain. 'But we don't need it; not with all these hands.' He approached the centre of the beam, bent to a squat, then slid his arms beneath it up to the elbow. He looked up at the circle of faces around him with that maddening grin of his. 'Well, come on, people. Let's get this thing out of the way.'

Every face in the circle, including Emily's, gaped at him as if he'd lost his mind.

'Nick.' Herman laid a hand on his shoulder. 'There's no way in hell we can move that thing. It's just too damn big. We'll have Fred run over to his place and bring back his tractor.'

Nick was still smiling, but Emily saw something flash in his eyes; something bright and hard and almost frightening. 'I'm not so sure we want to wait that long, Herman,' he said with forced calm. 'Not without knowing if anyone down there is hurt.'

Emily looked worriedly at the dreadful paleness of his face, the too-bright eyes, and moved quickly to crouch next to him. 'It's too big, Nick,' she whispered earnestly. 'You can't move it.'

His grin only broadened. 'Not alone, I can't. None of us can do anything very well alone, Em. Haven't you figured that out yet?'

And then he bent to the task, his head twisted to one side, his eyes screwed shut, white teeth grinding as the muscles in his arms bulged and snapped. There was something decidedly pathetic about Nick straining down there all by himself while the rest of them looked on, all resigned to the futility of it . . . but in a way, hopeless or not, his effort was a rebuke to those who wouldn't even try, and Emily actually caught herself smiling, wondering if there was anything in the world quite as unwilling to admit defeat, quite as insanely stubborn, as the son—or the daughter—of a Midwestern farmer.

Without another word, she slipped her own arms under the beam, and felt the prickle of splinters slicing into her flesh.

His eyes opened long enough to see her face straining next to his, and a defiant blue gaze met a defiant green one as they tackled their very first common enemy.

'Oh, hell,' Herman muttered, dropping to Nick's other side, and then everyone stooped to the task and the beam was cradled in a row of arms, and the sound of perfectly synchronised grunts and gasps drowned out the sound of the rain. A little time later a new sound chimed in—the agonised screeching of wood scraping across metal and concrete and glass as a small group of people defied all the laws of physics, and, working together, moved an enormous length of timber where it didn't want to go.

CHAPTER FOURTEEN

FOR the rest of her life Emily would carry one pictorial memory of the day the tornado hit the Tollefsons' farm—a single image so sharply etched that it crowded all the others from her mind. She would forget the dulling shock at her first sight of the destruction; she would even forget the rousing cheer when the storm doors were finally uncovered and Martin and his whole family stepped out of the cellar like a parade of phoenixes rising from the ashes—but she would remember forever what she had seen in Nick Simon during the fifteen minutes between the two events. Grim determination, a singularity of purpose, and an enormous strength of spirit—the dark, powerful forces that lived beneath the mischievous eyes and the cocky grin—things she had never seen before.

He'd worked like a madman after the beam had been pushed to one side, his blue eyes narrowed against the driving rain and his jaw grimly set, the muscles of his back and arms bulging and straining as he heaved two-by-fours and concrete blocks and pieces of furniture aside as if they were weightless. He'd been wearing the familiar black tank-top, and it had clung to his torso when he'd twisted, and sagged with its weight of moisture when he'd straightened. Sometimes his face reddened and the cords of his neck stood out sharply with effort, and sometimes, when he pressed his hands to his waist and bowed backwards for a moment, his features relaxed.

But always there was the aura of absolute invincibility about him, the sense that he was not, and perhaps had never been, a man who would surrender to circumstance, but rather, a man whose heart and spirit were every bit as strong as his body.

As she worked beside him, her vision blurring from rain and sweat, her hands scraped raw and her muscles screaming, Emily glanced at him occasionally and thought she saw ghostly images of other men—her father, stone-faced and tight-lipped as he rushed to bring the hay in before a storm; Nick's own grandfather, tall and wiry and defiant, right up to the day of his death. This land made men like that, and for the first time she realised that Nick was one of them, that he had always been one of them.

Accommodations for the entire Tollefson clan were quickly arranged, with the rescuers nearly coming to blows over who would have the privilege of putting them up. There would be a barn-raising here in the next week, Emily thought; and soon after that, a house-raising, too.

While Fred Larson waited patiently in his truck, Harriet next to him, sheltered from the rain, Martin lingered to look back on the devastation that had been his farm such a short time before. Emily and Nick stood next to him.

'It's a real mess, isn't it?' Martin clucked, shaking his head, and for a moment Emily thought she might burst into tears again, the scene around them was so awful, so hopeless. 'But by heaven,' Martin went on, his old face lifting in an incredible grin, 'isn't this just the dandiest rain you ever did see? The corn should fairly leap out of the ground after this one.' He sighed happily, and Emily's impulse to cry was gone immediately. Martin didn't need it. 'The family's OK, even the cattle are OK, and the rest...' He shrugged lightly, dismissing the importance of anything else. He looked down at Emily at his side, then reached over to chuck her under the chin. 'As I told you, Em, life can be so good sometimes, can't it?'

Emily shook her head a little and smiled up at him. 'You're crazy, Martin, you know that?'

He nodded soberly, then winked at her. 'Man would have to be, to be in this line of work.' Then he joined his wife in Fred's truck, and the old pickup backed gingerly out of the muddy drive.

'He's an amazing man,' Nick said quietly as they both watched the truck pull away.

'He's a farmer.' Emily shrugged, still smiling, loving Martin Tollefson and all the men like him so hard that it hurt. She swallowed hard, then glanced over at Nick. 'You're bleeding again.'

He reached up wearily with two fingers to touch his forehead, then shrugged when they came away red.

'Maybe I should take you to the hospital.'

'I'm a doctor, remember?' he sighed. 'And it's a clean cut. One stitch, maybe two. I'll take care of it when I get home.' He looked right into her eyes, and she noticed how pale he had become, how unutterably weary the old cocky grin seemed when he tried to put it in place.

'Come on,' she said brusquely, grabbing his arm and leading him to her car. 'Home is exactly where you're going.'

'Yes, ma'am.'

By the time she pulled the car to a stop beneath the ancient cottonwoods that sheltered his grandfather's driveway, Nick was sound asleep in the passenger seat. His head was rolled towards her, and she just sat there for a moment, looking at him, reluctant to move.

Already his rain-soaked hair was drying to a blond fluff over his forehead, nearly obscuring his brows. It needs trimming, she found herself thinking. I could do that. Her hand reached automatically to smooth it back, then jerked away when his eyes fluttered open. The sky will be that colour, she thought, just as soon as these clouds pass. A pure, glistening, crystalline blue.

The rain had finally stopped, and the only sound was the car engine ticking as it cooled, and the steady drip of water from freshly washed leaves.

'Well,' he sighed, straightening in the seat and looking around. 'I could use some help with this cut. Will you come in?'

She nodded, unsmiling, and reached for the doorknob, then hesitated, her eyes focused on the house. 'I don't believe it,' she whispered, dumbfounded.

It was an enormous white frame farmhouse, like a hundred others dotting the countryside, except for one thing. Barring a four-foot wide staircase that led up to the front porch, the entire building was surrounded by a broad flower-bed necklace of daisies. White daisies, yellow daisies, even pink daisies; hundreds of them, perhaps thousands, crammed together around the house like a magic circle.

Nick followed her gaze and smiled. 'My grandmother planted those beds, years ago,' he said. 'Grandpa said she loved daisies more than anything except him. He used to spend hours taking care of these flowers. I think they connected him to her somehow, even after she was gone.'

Emily nodded numbly as she followed Nick into the house, remembering the bright pile of daisies heaped on Art Simon's grave-site. It didn't surprise her, then, to find the interior of Art Simon's house almost painfully neat, yet somehow crowded with the presence of a wife who had died nearly a quarter of a century before.

As they passed through the living-room on the way to the kitchen, Nick gestured at a sideboard that held dozens of framed photographs of his grandmother. 'The shrine,' he explained with a fond shrug. 'She was never really gone, as far as he was concerned.'

They were all the same, Emily thought as she followed Nick through the house. Martin, filling his home with roses for his wife, after fifty years together; her father, so devastated at nearly losing her mother a decade ago that he still couldn't speak of that time aloud; and now Art Simon, preserving a memory a quarter of a century old with a living tribute he'd tended every day. All strong, commanding men, all seemingly dominant over retiring, complacent wives—and yet their lives revolved around their women, began and ended with their women, and in truth no one person controlled another. Love controlled them all.

Nick turned in the kitchen doorway to face her, and Emily had to stop quickly to avoid running into his chest. 'I'm going to shower, clean this cut, then stitch it up now,' he said.

'I thought you wanted me to help.'

He stared at her for a moment, his face expressionless. 'I lied.' And then without a word he left the room, and Emily knew he was leaving her the option of slipping away gracefully, without any awkward explanations.

She was sitting at the scarred wooden table when he came out, fresh coffee in the pot, a mug steaming in her hands. She looked up when he paused in the doorway and stared at him.

He wore fresh jeans and a clean white T-shirt. His hair was damp and tangled, pushed up and away from the two neat black stiches over his brow. The area around the cut was rapidly turning an angry purple colour, making the rest of his face appear pale and his eyes shockingly blue.

'You're still here,' he said softly, hunching his shoulders and leaning sideways against the doorjamb.

She looked straight at him, her face expressionless, saying everything she wanted to say in a single word. 'Yes.'

He hadn't been moving, but it still seemed that he had suddenly jerked to a halt. 'Em...' he began, then he frowned hard at her, clamped his mouth closed, and walked over to stand behind her chair.

She couldn't see him, but she didn't have to. She imagined what he looked like, standing tall and broad behind her, a powerful, muscular figure that dwarfed hers, wearing an expression that rendered all that power useless, that brought them to the same level.

His hands covered her shoulders almost completely, they were so large; and even while she felt the strength of those hands she felt the love that tempered that strength and made his touch gentle, almost reverent.

She felt the brush of his lips against the top of her head, then pressed her cheek into the palm cupped to receive it, her eyes falling closed. They remained like that for a long moment while he stroked her short hair with one hand and cradled her face with the other. Then slowly, inevitably, his hands moved back to her shoulders, then crept downwards until his fingers rested on the rise of her breasts. He pressed lightly into the yielding flesh, and she heard his breath catch, and imagined his eyes slamming shut. She felt the trembling of his hands through the thin cloth of her shirt, and let her head fall back to rest against his stomach. Muscles jumped and tensed where her head pressed against him, and, almost reflexively, his hands slid quickly down over her breasts to flatten against her ribcage, pulling her back against the wooden spindles of the chair.

'You left me last night,' she said quietly, and his hands stilled.

After a moment of complete silence, he spoke. 'Because you didn't ask me to stay.'

Emily took a deep, shaky breath, then added in a whisper, 'And today you're leaving Random, for good.'

His fingers tightened almost imperceptibly across her ribs, and then he said it again. 'Because you didn't ask me to stay.'

'Everyone else did.'

'I know. But you didn't.'

Her lips felt almost liquid as they moved into a smile, and for the first time she finally understood the enormous power of submission. 'Stay, Nick,' she whispered, a little surprised because the words hadn't been so hard to say after all. 'Please stay.'

Above her head, where she couldn't see it, Nick's eyes fell closed and his face tightened. He didn't move for what seemed like a very long time, then he bent his head next to hers and his rasping whisper felt like a hot wind against her neck.

'Is that what you want, Em?'

She nodded weakly, her eyes closed.

'For how long?'

'For as long as you want me,' she whispered back, and then she smiled, because it sounded like such a subservient thing to say, and yet it wasn't subservient at all, because she knew he wanted her forever. Just as her mother knew, and Harriet Tollefson, and Nick's grandmother... and all the other strong, country women who built marriages that would last a lifetime and beyond, because they weren't afraid to be women, or afraid to let their men be men.

'I'll want you forever.' He said it aloud, not realising that he didn't have to, and then he took a deep breath, removed his hands from her, and walked back to the doorway.

Emily turned in her chair to see him standing there, his jaw clenched, his blue eyes on her steadily.

'Come with me, Em,' he said quietly, as if this one last gesture had to be made. When he raised his hand towards her, it quivered slightly.

Because old habits died hard, and because there was a lingering trace of rebellious independence in her soul, she didn't immediately leap from her chair and rush into his arms. As a matter of fact, she rose very slowly, sedately enough so that the old Emily would have been proud of her, and then she walked towards the man who had called her.

It was a simple thing—just moving one foot forward, then the other, then the first again—but somehow it felt like dancing.

This August, don't miss an exclusive
two-in-one collection of earlier love stories

MAN
WITH A PAST

TRUE COLORS

by one of today's hottest
romance authors,

Jayne Ann Krentz

Now, two of Jayne Ann Krentz's most loved books are
available together in this special edition that new and
longtime fans will want to add to their bookshelves.

Let Jayne Ann Krentz capture your hearts with the love
stories, MAN WITH A PAST and TRUE COLORS.

And in October, watch for the second two-in-one
collection by Barbara Delinsky!

Available wherever Harlequin books are sold.

Praise for *The Red Tent*

Los Angeles Times Bestseller
The Washington Post Bestseller
San Francisco Chronicle Bestseller
USA Today Bestseller
Entertainment Weekly Top Ten Bestseller

"In *The Red Tent,* women handed down wisdom through storytelling inside the red tent. Today's women's gatherings, including book groups, serve the same purposes. And what are they talking about? *The Red Tent.* In that way, this book is a red tent. And women are passing it on." —*The Washington Post*

"Achingly earnest." —*Newsweek*

"A compelling story told by a writer who knows what she is doing." —*Fort Worth Star-Telegram*

"Diamant succeeds admirably in depicting the lives of women in the age that engendered our civilization and our most enduring values." —*Publishers Weekly*

"Although Anita Diamant is best known for her nonfiction work, in this fresh, new way of retelling Bible stories, she just may have opened up a whole new world for herself and us, too." —*Cleveland Jewish News*

"Here is a book of celebration. . . . This is a book to share with a friend c_____ y groups . . . or just keep it c_____ tstand for any

time you need to remind yourself of the simpler truths."
—*San Antonio Express-News*

"Startling in its originality, *The Red Tent* fairly sings its moral message of love and honor."
—*Pittsburgh Post-Gazette*

"A remarkable combination of historical research, biblical story, and sheer talent. Very absorbing."
—*The Tab*

"Anita Diamant has constructed a full-bodied novel."
—*Hadassah* magazine

"I couldn't put it down."   —*Detroit Free Press*

"The most absorbing aspect of *The Red Tent* is the way Diamant gives form, context, and a new perspective to important incidents in the Bible.... Diamant's version of Dinah's life is poetic and powerful, well worth reading."
—*Colorado Springs Independent*

"Richly imagined and vividly told, *The Red Tent* offers a glimpse into the lives of women whose voices were silenced in the texts of their time."
—*The Philadelphia Inquirer*

"Cubits beyond most Women-of-the-Bible sagas in sweep and vigor . . . Stirring scenery and a narrative of force and color."   —*Kirkus Reviews*

ALSO BY ANITA DIAMANT

Fiction

Good Harbor

The Last Days of Dogtown

Nonfiction

The New Jewish Wedding

How to Be a Jewish Parent: A Practical Handbook for Family Life
(with Karen Kushner)

Living a Jewish Life: Jewish Traditions, Customs, and
Values for Today's Families (with Howard Cooper)

Bible Baby Names: Spiritual Choices from Judeo-Christian Tradition

Choosing a Jewish Life: A Handbook for People Converting
to Judaism and for Their Family and Friends

Saying Kaddish: How to Comfort the Dying,
Bury the Dead, and Mourn as a Jew

Pitching My Tent: On Marriage, Motherhood,
Friendship, and Other Leaps of Faith

The New Jewish Baby Book: Names, Ceremonies, and Customs—
A Guide for Today's Families

THE RED TENT

ANITA DIAMANT

St. Martin's Paperbacks

This is a work of fiction. Although loosely based on stories found in the Bible, the events and characters described here are products of the author's imagination.

THE RED TENT

Copyright © 1997 by Anita Diamant.

All rights reserved.

For information address St. Martin's Press, 175 Fifth Avenue, New York, NY 10010.

Library of Congress Catalog Card Number: 97-16825

ISBN: 978-1-250-06799-9

Printed in the United States of America

Picador trade paperback edition / January 1997
St. Martin's Paperbacks edition / December 2014

St. Martin's Paperbacks are published by St. Martin's Press, 175 Fifth Avenue, New York, NY 10010.

10 9 8 7 6 5 4 3 2 1

FOR EMILIA, MY DAUGHTER

GENERATIONS

FIRST GENERATIONS

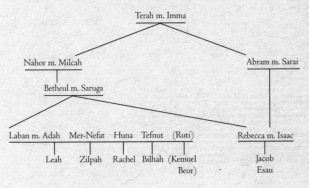

Terah m. Imma

Nahor m. Milcah — Abram m. Sarai

Betheul m. Saruga

Laban m. Adah   Mer-Nefat   Huna   Tefnut   (Ruti) — Rebecca m. Isaac

Leah   Zilpah   Rachel   Bilhah   (Kemuel   Jacob
Beor)   Esau

THE CHILDREN OF JACOB

Jacob m. Leah	m. Zilpah	m. Rachel	m. Bilhah
Reuben	Gad	Joseph	Dan
Simon	Asher	Benjamin	
Levi			
Judah			
Zebulun			
Naphtali			
Issachar			
Dinah			

THE CHILDREN OF ESAU

Esau m. Adath	m. Basemath	m. Oholibama
Eliphaz	Reuel	Jeush
Edva	Tabea	Jalam
Libbe		Korah
Amat		Iti

DINAH IN EGYPT

Paser m. Nebbetany

Re-nefer m. Hamor — Nakht-re m. Herya

Shalem m. Dinah m. Benia

Re-mose

PROLOGUE

We have been lost to each other for so long. My name means nothing to you. My memory is dust.

This is not your fault, or mine. The chain connecting mother to daughter was broken and the word passed to the keeping of men, who had no way of knowing. That is why I became a footnote, my story a brief detour between the well-known history of my father, Jacob, and the celebrated chronicle of Joseph, my brother. On those rare occasions when I was remembered, it was as a victim. Near the beginning of your holy book, there is a passage that seems to say I was raped and continues with the bloody tale of how my honor was avenged.

It's a wonder that any mother ever called a daughter Dinah again. But some did. Maybe you guessed that there was more to me than the voiceless cipher in the text. Maybe you heard it in the music of my name: the first vowel high and clear, as when a mother calls to her child at dusk; the second sound soft, for whispering secrets on pillows. Dee-nah.

No one recalled my skill as a midwife, or the songs I sang, or the bread I baked for my insatiable brothers. Nothing remained except a few mangled details about those weeks in Shechem.

There was far more to tell. Had I been asked to speak of it, I would have begun with the story of the generation that raised me, which is the only place to begin. If you want to understand any woman you must first ask about her mother and then listen carefully. Stories about food show a strong connection. Wistful silences demonstrate unfinished business. The more a daughter knows the details of her mother's life—without flinching or whining—the stronger the daughter.

Of course, this is more complicated for me because I had four mothers, each of them scolding, teaching, and cherishing something different about me, giving me different gifts, cursing me with different fears. Leah gave me birth and her splendid arrogance. Rachel showed me where to place the midwife's bricks and how to fix my hair. Zilpah made me think. Bilhah listened. No two of my mothers seasoned her stew the same way. No two of them spoke to my father in the same tone of voice—nor he to them. And you should know that my mothers were sisters as well, La-ban's daughters by different wives, though my grandfather never acknowledged Zilpah and Bilhah; that would have cost him two more dowries, and he was a stingy pig.

Like any sisters who live together and share a husband, my mother and aunties spun a sticky web of loyalties and grudges. They traded secrets like bracelets, and these were handed down to me, the only surviving girl. They told me things I was too young to hear. They held my face between their hands and made me swear to remember.

My mothers were proud to give my father so many sons. Sons were a woman's pride and her measure. But the birth of one boy after another was not an unalloyed source of joy in the women's tents. My father boasted about his noisy tribe, and the women loved my brothers, but they longed for daughters, too, and complained among themselves about the maleness of Jacob's seed.

Daughters eased their mothers' burdens—helping with the spinning, the grinding of grain, and the endless task of looking after baby boys, who were forever peeing into the corners of the tents, no matter what you told them.

But the other reason women wanted daughters was to keep their memories alive. Sons did not hear their mothers' stories after weaning. So I was the one. My mother and my mother-aunties told me endless stories about themselves. No matter what their hands were doing—holding babies, cooking, spinning, weaving—they filled my ears.

In the ruddy shade of the red tent, the menstrual tent, they ran their fingers through my curls, repeating the escapades of their youths, the sagas of their childbirths. Their stories were like offerings of hope and strength poured out before the Queen of Heaven, only these gifts were not for any god or goddess—but for me.

I can still feel how my mothers loved me. I have

cherished their love always. It sustained me. It kept me alive. Even after I left them, and even now, so long after their deaths, I am comforted by their memory.

I carried my mothers' tales into the next generation, but the stories of my life were forbidden to me, and that silence nearly killed the heart in me. I did not die but lived long enough for other stories to fill up my days and nights. I watched babies open their eyes upon a new world. I found cause for laughter and gratitude. I was loved.

And now you come to me—women with hands and feet as soft as a queen's, with more cooking pots than you need, so safe in child-bed and so free with your tongues. You come hungry for the story that was lost. You crave words to fill the great silence that swallowed me, and my mothers, and my grandmothers before them.

I wish I had more to tell of my grandmothers. It is terrible how much has been forgotten, which is why, I suppose, remembering seems a holy thing.

I am so grateful that you have come. I will pour out everything inside me so you may leave this table satisfied and fortified. Blessings on your eyes. Blessings on your children. Blessings on the ground beneath you. My heart is a ladle of sweet water, brimming over.

Selah.

PART ONE

MY MOTHERS' STORIES

CHAPTER ONE

Their stories began with the day that my father appeared. Rachel came running into camp, knees flying, bellowing like a calf separated from its mother. But before anyone could scold her for acting like a wild boy, she launched into a breathless yarn about a stranger at the well, her words spilling out like water into sand.

A wild man without sandals. Matted hair. Dirty face. He kissed her on the mouth, a cousin, son of their aunt, who had watered sheep and goats for her and told off the ruffians at the well.

"What are you babbling?" demanded her father, Laban. "Who is come to the well? Who attends him? How many bags does he carry?"

"He is going to marry me," said Rachel matter-of-factly, once she had caught her breath. "He says I am for him and that he would marry me tomorrow, if he could. He's coming to ask you."

Leah scowled at this announcement. "Marry you?" she said, crossing her arms and throwing back her shoulders. "You won't be marriageable for another year," said the older girl, who, though only a few years older than Rachel, already acted as head woman of her father's small holdings. The fourteen-year-old mistress of Laban's house liked to take a haughty, maternal tone with her sister. "What's all this? And how did he come to kiss you?" This was a terrible breach of custom—even if he was a cousin and even though Rachel was young enough to be treated as a child.

Rachel stuck out her lower lip in a pout that would have been childlike only a few hours earlier. Something had happened since she opened her eyes that morning, when the most pressing matter on her mind had been to find the place where Leah hid her honey. Leah, that donkey, would never share it with her, but hoarded it for guests, giving tastes to pathetic little Bilhah and no one else.

All Rachel could think of now was the shaggy stranger whose eyes had met hers with a shock of recognition that had rattled her to the bone.

Rachel knew what Leah meant, but the fact that she had not yet begun to bleed meant nothing to her now. And her cheeks burned.

"What's this?" said Leah, suddenly amused. "She is smitten. Look at her," she said. "Have you ever seen the girl blush before?"

"What did he do to you?" asked Laban, growling like a dog who senses an intruder near his herd. He clenched his fists and beetled his brow and turned his full attention to Rachel, the daughter he had never once hit, the daughter whom he rarely looked at full in the face. She had frightened him from her birth—a tearing, violent entry that had killed her mother. When the baby finally emerged, the women were shocked to see that it was such a small one—a girl at that—who had caused so many days of trouble, costing her mother so much blood and finally her life.

Rachel's presence was powerful as the moon, and just as beautiful. Nobody could deny her beauty. Even as a child who worshiped my own mother's face, I knew that Leah's beauty paled before her younger sister's, a knowledge that always made me feel like a traitor. Still, denying it would have been like denying the sun's warmth.

Rachel's beauty was rare and arresting. Her brown hair shaded to bronze, and her skin was golden, honeyed, perfect. In that amber setting, her eyes were surprisingly dark, not merely dark brown but black as polished obsidian or the depth of a well. Although she was small-boned and, even when she was with child, small-breasted, she had muscular hands and a husky voice that seemed to belong to a much larger woman.

I once heard two shepherds arguing over which was Rachel's best feature, a game I, too, had played. For me, the most wonderful detail of Rachel's perfection was her cheeks, which were high and tight on her face, like figs. When I was a baby, I used to reach for them, trying to pluck the fruit that appeared when she smiled. When I realized there was no having them, I licked her instead, hoping for a taste. This made my beautiful aunt laugh, from deep in her belly. She loved me better than all her nephews put together—or so she said as she wove my hair into the elaborate braids for which my own mother's hands lacked patience or time.

It is almost impossible to exaggerate the dimensions of Rachel's beauty. Even as a baby, she was a jewel upon whatever hip bore her from place to place, an ornament, a rare pleasure—the black-eyed child with golden hair. Her nickname was Tuki, which means "sweetness."

All the women shared in Rachel's care after her mother, Huna, died. Huna was a skilled midwife known for her throaty laugh and much mourned by the women. No one grumbled about tending to Huna's motherless daughter, and even the men, for whom babies held as little fascination as cooking stones, would stoop to run a callused hand across her remarkable cheek. They would rise, smelling their fingers and shaking their heads.

Rachel smelled like water. Really! Wherever my aunt walked, there was the scent of fresh water. It was an impossible smell, green and delightful and in those dusty hills the smell of life and wealth. Indeed, for many years Laban's well was the only reason his family hadn't starved.

There were hopes, early on, that Rachel would be a water witch, one who could find hidden wells and underground streams. She did not fulfill that hope, but somehow the aroma of sweet water clung to her skin and lodged in her robes. Whenever one of the babies went missing, more often than not the little stinker would be found fast asleep on her blankets, sucking his thumb.

No wonder Jacob was enchanted at the well. The other men had grown accustomed to Rachel's looks and even to her startling perfume, but to Jacob she must have seemed an apparition. He looked directly into her eyes and was overcome. When he kissed her, Jacob cried out with a voice of a man who lies with his wife. The sound woke Rachel out of her childhood.

There was barely time to hear Rachel describe their meeting before Jacob himself appeared. He walked up to Laban, and Rachel watched her father take his measure.

Laban noticed his empty hands first, but he also saw that the stranger's tunic and cloak were made of fine stuff, his water skin was well crafted, his knife hilt was carved of polished bone. Jacob stood directly before Laban and, dropping his head, proclaimed himself. "Uncle, I am the son of Rebecca, your sister, the daughter of Nahor and Milcah, as you are their son. My mother has sent me to you, my brother has chased me to you, my father has banished me to you. I will tell you the whole story when I am not so dirty and weary. I seek your hospitality, which is famous in the land."

Rachel opened her mouth to speak, but Leah yanked her sister's arm and shot her a warning glance; not even Rachel's youth would excuse a girl speaking out when men were addressing one another. Rachel kicked at the ground and thought poisonous thoughts about her sister, the bossy old crow, the cross-eyed goat.

Jacob's words about Laban's famous hospitality were a courteous lie, for Laban was anything but pleased by the appearance of this nephew. Not much caused the old man pleasure, and hungry strangers were unwanted surprises. Still, there was nothing to be done; he had to honor the claim of a kinsman, and there was no denying the connection between them. Jacob knew the names and Laban recognized his sister's face on the man standing before him.

"You are welcome," Laban said, without smiling or returning his nephew's salute. As he turned to walk away, Laban pointed his thumb at Leah, assigning her the task of seeing to this nuisance. My mother nodded and turned to face the first grown man who did not look away when confronted by the sight of her eyes.

Leah's vision was perfect. According to one of the more ridiculous fables embroidered around my family's history, she ruined her eyes by crying a river of tears over the prospect of marrying my uncle Esau. If you believe that, you might also be interested in purchasing a magical toad that will make all who look upon you swoon with love.

But my mother's eyes were not weak, or sick, or rheumy. The truth is, her eyes made others weak and most people looked away rather than face them—one blue as lapis, the other green as Egyptian grass.

When she was born, the midwife cried out that a witch had been brought forth and should be drowned before she could bring a curse on the family. But my grandmother Adah slapped the stupid woman and cursed her tongue. "Show me my daughter," said Adah, in a voice so loud and proud even the men outside could hear her. Adah named her beloved last-born Leah, which means "mistress," and she wept a prayer that this child would live, for she had buried seven sons and daughters.

There were plenty who remained convinced that the

baby was a devil. For some reason, Laban, who was the most superstitious soul you can imagine (spitting and bowing whenever he turned to the left, howling at every lunar eclipse), refused to hear suggestions that Leah be left outside to die in the night air. He swore some mild oath about the femaleness of this child, but apart from that, Laban ignored his daughter and never mentioned her distinction. Then again, the women suspected the old man could not see color at all.

Leah's eyes never faded in color—as some of the women predicted and hoped—but became brighter in their difference and even more pronounced in their strangeness when her lashes failed to grow. Although she blinked like everyone else, the reflex was nearly invisible, so it seemed that Leah never closed her eyes. Even her most loving glance felt a bit like the stare of a snake, and few could stand to look her straight in the eye. Those who could were rewarded with kisses and laughter and bread wet with honey.

Jacob met Leah's eyes straight on, and for this she warmed to him instantly. In fact, Leah had already taken note of Jacob on account of his height. She was half a head taller than most of the men she had ever seen, and she dismissed them all because of it. She knew this was not fair. Surely there were good men among those whose heads reached only to her nose. But the thought of lying with anyone whose legs were shorter and weaker than her own disgusted her. Not that anyone had asked for her. She knew they all called her Lizard and Evil-Eye, and worse.

Her distaste for short men had been confirmed by a dream in which a tall man had whispered to her. She couldn't recall his words, but they had warmed her thighs and woken her. When she saw Jacob, she remembered the dream and her strange eyes widened.

Jacob noticed Leah with favor, too. Although he was still ringing from his encounter with Rachel, he could not ignore the sight of Leah.

She was not only tall but shapely and strong. She was blessed with full, high breasts and muscular calves that showed to good advantage in robes that somehow never stayed closed at the hem. She had forearms like a young man's, but her walk was that of a woman with promising hips.

Leah had dreamed once of a pomegranate split open to reveal eight red seeds. Zilpah said the dream meant she would have eight healthy children, and my mother knew those words to be true the way she knew how to make bread and beer.

Leah's scent was no mystery. She smelled of the yeast she handled daily, brewing and baking. She reeked of bread and comfort, and—it seemed to Jacob—of sex. He stared at this giantess, and his mouth watered. As far as I know, he never said a word about her eyes.

My aunt Zilpah, Laban's second-born, said that she remembered everything that ever happened to her. She laid claim to memories of her own birth, and even of days in her mother's womb. She swore she could remember her mother's death in the red tent, where she sickened within days after Zilpah arrived in the world, feet first. Leah scoffed at these claims, though not to her sister's face, for Zilpah was the only one who could cause my mother to hold her tongue about anything.

Zilpah's memory of Jacob's arrival is nothing like Rachel's or Leah's, but then Zilpah had little use for men, whom she described as hairy, crude, and half human. Women needed men to make babies and to move heavy objects, but otherwise she didn't understand their purpose, much less appreciate their charms. She loved her sons passionately until they grew beards, but after that could barely bring herself to look at them.

When I was old enough to ask what it was like on the day that my father arrived, she said that the presence of El hovered over him, which is why he was worthy of notice. Zilpah told me that El was the god of thunder, high places, and awful sacrifice. El could demand that a father cut off his son—cast him out into the desert, or slaughter him outright. This was a hard, strange god, alien and cold, but, she conceded, a consort powerful enough for the Queen of Heaven, whom she loved in every shape and name.

Zilpah talked about gods and goddesses almost more than she spoke about people. I found this tiresome at times, but she used words in the most wonderful ways, and I loved her stories about Ninhursag, the great mother, and Enlil, the first father. She made up grandiose hymns in which real people met with the deities and together they danced to the sound of flutes and cymbals, singing them in a high, thin voice to the accompaniment of a small clay drum.

From the age of her first blood, Zilpah thought of herself as a kind of priestess, the keeper of the mysteries of the red tent, the daughter of Asherah, the sister-Siduri who counsels women. It was a foolish idea, as only priests served the goddesses of the great city temples, while the priestesses served gods. Besides, Zilpah had none of the oracle's gifts. She lacked the talent for herbs, and could not prophesy or conjure or read goat entrails. Leah's eight-seeded pomegranate was the only dream she ever interpreted correctly.

Zilpah was Laban's daughter by a slave named Mer-Nefat, who had been purchased from an Egyptian trader in the days when Laban still had means. According to Adah, Zilpah's mother was slender, raven-haired, and so quiet it was easy to forget she had the power of speech, a trait her daughter did not inherit.

Zilpah was only a few months younger than Leah, and after Zilpah's mother died, Adah gave them suck together. They were playmates as babies, close and loving friends as children, tending the flocks together, gathering berries, making up songs, laughing. Apart from Adah, they needed no one else in the world.

Zilpah was almost as tall as Leah, but thinner and less robust in the chest and legs. Dark-haired and olive-skinned, Leah and Zilpah resembled their father and shared the family nose, not unlike Jacob's—a regal hawk's beak that seemed to grow longer when they smiled. Leah and Zilpah both talked with their hands, thumb and forefinger pressed together in emphatic ovals. When the sun made them squint, identical lines appeared around the corners of their eyes.

But where Leah's hair was curly, Zilpah's black mane was straight, and she wore it to her waist. It was her best feature, and my aunt hated to cover it. Headdresses caused her head to pound, she said, putting a hand to her cheek with silly drama. Even as a child I was permitted to laugh at her. These headaches were the reason she gave for keeping so much inside the women's tents. She did not join the rest of us to bask in the spring-time sun or find the breeze on a hot night. But when the moon was young—slender and shy, barely making herself known in the sky—Zilpah walked around the camp, swinging her long hair, clapping her hands, offering songs to encourage the moon's return.

When Jacob arrived, Bilhah was a child of eight, and she remembered nothing of the day. "She was proba-bly up in a tree somewhere, sucking on her fingers and counting the clouds," said Leah, repeating the only thing that was remembered of Bilhah's early years.

Bilhah was the family orphan. The last daughter born of Laban's seed, she was the child of a slave named Tefnut—a tiny black woman who ran off one night when Bilhah was old enough to know she had been abandoned. "She never got over that hurt," said Zilpah with great gentleness, for Zilpah respected pain.

Bilhah was alone among them. It's not just that she was the youngest and that there were three other sis-ters to share the work. Bilhah was a sad child and it was easier to leave her alone. She rarely smiled and hardly spoke. Not even my grandmother Adah, who adored little girls and gathered motherless Zilpah to her inner circle and doted upon Rachel, could warm to this strange, lonely bird, who never grew taller than a boy of ten years, and whose skin was the color of dark amber.

Bilhah was not beautiful like Rachel, or capable like Leah, or quick like Zilpah. She was tiny, dark, and silent. Adah was exasperated by her hair, which was springy as moss and refused to obey her hands. Compared to the two other motherless girls, Bilhah was neglected dreadfully.

Left to herself, she climbed trees and seemed to dream. From her perch, she studied the world, the patterns in the sky, the habits of animals and birds. She came to know the flocks as individuals, giving each animal a secret name to match its personality. One evening, she came in from the fields and whispered to Adah that a black dwarf she-goat was ready to give birth to twins. It was nowhere near the season for goats to bear, and that particular animal had been barren for four seasons. Adah shook her head at Bilhah's nonsense and shooed her away.

The next day, Laban brought news of a strange event in the flocks, with a precise retelling of the little girl's prediction. Adah turned to the girl and apologized. "Bilhah sees clearly," said Adah to the other daughters, who turned to stare at this unseen sister and noticed, for the first time, the kindness in her black eyes.

If you took the time to look, you could see right away that Bilhah was good. She was good the way milk is good, the way rain is good. Bilhah watched the skies and the animals, and she watched her family, too. From the dark corners of the tents, she saw Leah hide her mortification when people stared. Bilhah noticed Rachel's fear of the dark and Zilpah's insomnia. Bilhah knew that Laban was every bit as mean-spirited as he was stupid.

Bilhah says her first clear memory of Jacob is from the day his first child was born. It was a boy—Reuben—and of course Jacob was delighted. He took his new son in his arms and danced the baby around and around outside the red tent.

"He was so gentle with the boy," Bilhah said. "He would not let Adah take Reuben away from him, even when the little one began to wail.

"He called his son perfect and a miracle in the world. I stood beside him and together Jacob and I worshiped the baby. We counted his fingers and stroked the soft crown of his head. We delighted in him and in each other's joy," Bilhah said. "That is when I met Jacob, your father."

Jacob arrived late in the afternoon in the week of a full moon, ate a simple meal of barley bread and olives, and fell into an exhausted sleep that lasted through most of the next day. Leah was mortified by the simplicity of the food they had offered him at first, so the next day she set out to produce a feast seen only at the great festivals.

"I suffered over that meal like nothing else I had ever cooked," said Leah, telling me the story during dull, hot afternoons while we rocked the narrow-necked jars, straining the water from goat curd.

"The father of my children was in the house, I was sure of it. I could see he was smitten by Rachel, whose beauty I saw as if for the first time. Still, he looked at me without flinching, and so I hoped.

"I slaughtered a kid, an unblemished male, as though it were a sacrifice to the gods. I beat the millet until it was as soft as a cloud. I reached deep into the pouches where I kept my most precious spices and used the last of my dried pomegranate. I pounded, chopped, and scraped in a frenzy, believing that he would understand what I was offering him.

"Nobody helped me with the cooking, not that I would have permitted anyone else to touch the lamb or the bread, or even the barley water. I wouldn't let my own mother pour water into a pot," she said and giggled.

I loved this story and asked to hear it again and again. Leah was always reliable and deliberate, and far too steady to be giddy. And yet as she recounted her first meal for Jacob, she was a foolish, weepy girl.

"I was an idiot," she said. "I burned the first bread and burst into tears. I even sacrificed a bit of the next loaf so that Jacob might fancy me. Just as we do when we bake the cakes for the Queen of Heaven on the seventh day, I broke off a piece of dough, kissed it, and offered it to the fire as an offering of hope that the man would claim me.

"Don't ever tell Zilpah about this or I'll never hear the end of it," said Leah, in a mock-conspiratorial whisper. "And of course, if Laban, your grandfather, had any idea of how much food I put together for a beggar who showed up without so much as a jug of oil as a gift, he would have flogged me. But I gave the old man enough strong beer that he made no comment.

"Or maybe he made no mention of my extravagance because he knew he'd be lucky with this kinsman. Maybe he guessed he had discovered a son-in-law who would require little by way of a dowry. It was hard to know what the old man knew or didn't know. He was like an ox, your grandfather."

"Like a post," I said.

"Like a cooking stone," said my mother.

"Like a goat turd," I said.

My mother shook her finger at me as though I were a naughty child, but then she laughed out loud, for raking Laban over the coals was great sport among his daughters.

I can still recite her menu. Lamb flavored with coriander, marinated in sour goat milk and a pomegranate sauce for dipping. Two kinds of bread: flat barley and raised wheat. Quince compote, and figs stewed with mulberries, fresh dates. Olives, of course. And to drink, a choice of sweet wine, three different beers, and barley water.

Jacob was so exhausted he nearly missed the meal that Leah brought forth with so much passion. Zilpah had a terrible time waking him and finally had to pour water on his neck, which startled him so badly that he swung out with his arms and knocked her to the ground, where she hissed like a cat.

Zilpah was not at all happy about this Jacob. She could see that his presence had changed things between the sisters and would weaken her bond to Leah. He offended her because he was so much more attractive than the other men they saw, foul-mouthed shepherds and the occasional trader who looked at the sisters as though they were a pack of ewes.

Jacob was well spoken and fair of face. And when he met Leah's gaze, Zilpah understood that their lives would never be the same. She was heartsick and angry and helpless to stop the change, though she tried.

When Jacob finally awoke and came to sit at Laban's right outside his tent, he ate well. Leah remembered his every bite. "He dipped into the lamb stew over and over again, and had three helpings of bread. I saw that he liked sweets, and that he preferred the honeyed brew to the bitter-flavored drink that Laban gulped down. I knew how to please his mouth, I thought. I will know how to please the rest of him."

This line would always get my other mothers shrieking and slapping their thighs, for although she was a practical woman, Leah was also the lewdest of her sisters.

"And then, after all that work, after all that eating, what do you think happened?" Leah asked, as though I didn't know the answer as well as I knew the little crescent-shaped scar above the joint on her right thumb.

"Jacob grew ill, that's what happened. He vomited every morsel. He threw up until he was weak and whimpering. He cried out to El, and Ishtar, and Marduk, and his blessed mother, to save him from his agonies or let him die.

"Zilpah, the brat, she sneaked into his tent to see how he fared and reported back to me, making it sound even worse than it was. She told me that he was whiter than the full moon, that he barked like a dog and spewed up frogs and snakes.

"I was mortified—and terrified, too. What if he died from my cooking? Or, just as bad, what if he recovered and blamed me for his misery?

"When no one else showed any ill effect from the meal, I knew it wasn't the food. But then, fool that I was, I started worrying that my touch was hateful to him. Or maybe I had done wrong with the bread offering, given not in homage to a god or goddess, but as an attempt at magic.

"I got religious again and poured the last of the good wine out in the name of Anath the healer. That was on the third night of his suffering, and he was healed by the next morning." At this she always shook her head and sighed. "Not a very auspicious beginning for such fruitful lovers, was it?"

Jacob made a quick recovery and stayed on, week after week, until it seemed he had always been there. He took charge of the scrawny herds so Rachel no longer had to follow the animals, a job that had fallen to her in the absence of brothers.

My grandfather laid the blame for the state of his herds and his dwindling wealth upon the fact that all his sons had died at birth or in infancy, leaving him nothing but daughters. He gave no thought to his own sloth, believing that only a son would turn his luck around. He consulted the local priests, who told him to sacrifice his best rams and a bull so that the gods might give him a boy-child. He had lain with his wives and concubines in the fields, as an old midwife suggested, and all he had gotten for that effort was an itchy backside and bruises on his knees. By the time Jacob arrived, Laban had given up his hope of a son—or of any improvement in his life.

He expected nothing from Adah, who was past childbearing and sick. His other three women had died or run off, and he couldn't afford the few coins for a homely slave girl, much less the price of a new bride. So he slept alone, except for the nights he found his way up the hills to bother the flocks, like some horny little boy. Rachel said that among the shepherds, my grandfather's lust was legendary. "The ewes run like gazelles when Laban walks up the hill," they hooted.

His daughters despised him for a hundred reasons, and I knew them all. Zilpah told me that when she was a few months away from her first blood and the task fell to her of taking my grandfather his midday meal, he reached up and put his thumb and forefinger around her nipple, squeezing it as though she were a she-goat.

Leah, too, said Laban had put his hand under her robes, but when she told Adah, my grandmother had beaten Laban with a pestle until he bled. She broke the horns off his favorite household god, and when she threatened to curse him with boils and impotence, he swore never to touch his daughters again and made restitution. He bought gold bangles for Adah and all of his daughters—even Zilpah and Bilhah, which was the only time he acknowledged them as kin. And he brought home a beautiful asherah—a tall pillar, nearly as big as Bilhah—made by the finest potter he could find. The women placed her up on the bamah, the high place, where sacrifices were offered. The goddess's face was especially lovely, with almond eyes and an open smile. When we poured wine over her in the dark of each new moon, it seemed to us her mouth broadened even farther in pleasure.

But that was some years before Jacob came, when Laban still had a few bondsmen working for him, and their wives and children filled the camp with cooking smells and laughter. By the time my father arrived, there was only one sick wife and four daughters.

While Laban was glad enough of Jacob's presence, the two men disliked each other heartily. Although different as a raven and a donkey, they were bound by blood and soon by business.

Jacob, it turned out, was a willing worker with a talent for animals—especially dogs. He turned Laban's three useless mongrels into fine shepherds. He whistled and the dogs raced to his side. He clapped and they would run in circles and get the sheep to move after him. He yodeled and they stood guard with such ferocity that Laban's flocks never again saw harm from a fox or jackal. And if there were poachers, they ran off rather than face the bared teeth of that fierce little pack.

Jacob's dogs were soon the envy of other men, who offered to buy them. Instead, he traded a day's work for the stud of the male cur with cunning wolfish eyes. When the smallest of our bitches bore the wolf-dog's litter, Jacob trained her puppies and traded four of the five for what seemed a mountain of treasure, which he quickly converted to gifts that proved how well he had come to understand Laban's daughters.

He took Rachel to the well where they had met and gave her the blue lapis ring she wore until her death. He sought out Leah where she was combing wool and, without a word, handed her three finely hammered gold bangles. To Zilpah he gave a small votive vessel in the shape of Anath, which poured libations through the nipples. He laid a bag of salt at Adah's swollen feet. He even remembered Bilhah with a tiny amphora of honey.

Laban complained that his nephew should have

turned over the profit from the puppies directly to him, since the mother was his goods. But the old man was mollified by a bag of coins, with which he ran to the village and brought back Ruti. Poor thing.

Within a year, Jacob became the overseer of Laban's domain. With his dogs, Jacob led the flocks so the lambs fed on the gentle grass, the sheep grazed on patches of juicy herbs, and the full-grown rams rummaged through the tough weeds. The flocks did so well that at the next shearing Jacob had to hire two boys to finish the work before the rains came. Rachel joined Leah, Zilpah, and Bilhah in the garden, where they enlarged the wheat patch.

Jacob made Laban agree to sacrifice two fat lambs and a kid to the god of his father, as thanks for the bounty. Leah baked raised cakes from the precious stock of wheat for the sacrifice, too, which was carried out as Jacob directed. In the manner of his fathers, he burned entire loaves and all the choice parts of the animals rather than a few portions. The women muttered among themselves at the waste.

It was a year of change for my family. The flocks multiplied, and the grain flourished, and there was a marriage in the offing. For within a month of his arrival, Jacob asked Laban about Rachel's bride price, as she had said he would that very first day. Since it was clear that his nephew had no means or property, Laban thought he could get the man cheap, and made a magnanimous show of offering his daughter for a mere seven years' service.

Jacob laughed at the idea. "Seven years? We are

talking about a girl here, not a throne. In seven years' time, she might be dead. I might be dead. And most likely of all, you could be dead, old man."

"I will give you seven months," Jacob said. "And for the dowry, I'll take half your miserable herd."

Laban jumped to his feet and called Jacob a thief. "You are your mother's son, all right," he raged. "You think the world owes you anything? Don't get too proud with me, you afterbirth, or I'll send you back to your brother's long knife."

Zilpah, the best spy among them, reported on the argument, telling how they haggled back and forth over my aunt's value, about how Laban stormed out and Jacob spat. Finally, they agreed on a year's service for a bride price. As to dowry, Laban pleaded poverty. "I have so little, my son," he said, suddenly the loving patriarch. "And she is such a treasure."

Jacob could not accept a bride without a dowry. That would have made Rachel a concubine and him a fool for paying with a year of his life for a girl who had only a grindstone, a spindle, and the clothes on her back to her name. So Laban threw Bilhah into the bargain, giving Rachel status as a dowered wife, and Jacob the possibility of a concubine in time.

"Also you must give me a tenth of the lambs and kids born to the flocks while I stand guard over them for you during my year of service," Jacob said.

At that, Laban cursed Jacob's seed and stormed away. It was a week before the men finished their negotiations, a week in which Rachel wept and carried on like a baby, while Leah said little and served nothing but cold millet porridge, food for mourners.

When they worked out the final terms, Laban went to Adah, so she could start planning the wedding. But Adah said no—"We are not barbarians who give children to wed."

Rachel could not even be promised, she told her husband. The girl might look ready to marry, but she was still unripe, having not yet bled. My grandmother claimed that Anath would curse the garden if Laban dared break this law and that she herself would find the strength to take a pestle to her husband's head again.

But threats were unnecessary. Laban saw the advantage in this delay and went immediately to Jacob with the news he would have to wait until the girl was ready before they could plan a date for the marriage.

Jacob accepted the situation. What else could he do? Furious, Rachel yelled at Adah, who cuffed her and told her to take her temper elsewhere. Rachel, in turn, slapped Bilhah, cursed at Zilpah, and snarled at Leah. She even kicked dust at Jacob's feet, calling him a liar and a coward before bursting into pretty tears on his neck.

She began to nurse dark fears about the future. She would never bleed, never marry Jacob, never bear sons. Suddenly, the small, high breasts of which she had been so proud seemed puny to her. Perhaps she was a freak, a hermaphrodite like the gross idol in her father's tent, the one with a tree stalk between its legs and teats like a cow.

So Rachel tried to rush her season. Before the next new moon, she baked cakes of offering to the Queen of Heaven, something she had never done before, and slept a whole night with her belly pressed up against the base of the asherah. But the moon waned and grew round again, while Rachel's thighs remained dry. She walked into the village by herself to ask the midwife, Inna, for help and was given an infusion of ugly nettles that grew in a nearby wadi. But again the new moon came and again Rachel remained a child.

As the following moon waned, Rachel crushed bitter berries and called her older sisters to see the stain on her blanket. But the juice was purple, and Leah and Zilpah laughed at the seeds on her thighs.

The next month, Rachel hid in her tent, and did not even slip away once to find Jacob.

Finally, in the ninth month after Jacob's arrival, Rachel bled her first blood, and cried with relief. Adah, Leah, and Zilpah sang the piercing, throaty song that announces births, deaths, and women's ripening. As the sun set on the new moon when all the women commenced bleeding, they rubbed henna on Rachel's fingernails and on the soles of her feet. Her eyelids were painted yellow, and they slid every bangle, gem, and jewel that could be found onto her fingers, toes, ankles, and wrists. They covered her head with the finest embroidery and led her into the red tent. They sang songs for the goddesses; for Innana and the Lady Asherah of the Sea. They spoke of Elath, the mother of the seventy gods, including Anath in that number, Anath the nursemaid, defender of mothers.

They sang:

"Whose fairness is like Anath's fairness
Whose beauty like Astarte's beauty?

Astarte is now in your womb,
You bear the power of Elath."

The women sang all the welcoming songs to her while Rachel ate date honey and fine wheat-flour cake, made in the three-cornered shape of woman's sex. She drank as much sweet wine as she could hold. Adah rubbed Rachel's arms and legs, back and abdomen with aromatic oils until she was nearly asleep. By the time they carried her out into the field where she married the earth, Rachel was stupid with pleasure and wine. She did not remember how her legs came to be caked with earth and crusted with blood and smiled in her sleep.

She was full of joy and anticipation, lazing in the tent for the three days, collecting the precious fluid in a bronze bowl—for the first-moon blood of a virgin was a powerful libation for the garden. During those hours, she was more relaxed and generous than anyone could remember her.

As soon as the women rose from their monthly rites, Rachel demanded that the wedding date be set. None of her foot-stamping could move Adah to change the custom of waiting seven months from first blood. So it was arranged, and although Jacob had already worked a year for Laban, the contract was sealed and the next seven months were Laban's too.

CHAPTER TWO

Those were not easy months. Rachel was imperious, Leah sighed like a cow in labor, Zilpah sulked. Only Bilhah seemed untouched by the turmoil, spinning and weaving, pulling weeds from the garden, and tending Adah's fire, which was always lit now, to comfort her chilled bones.

Rachel spent as much time with Jacob as she dared, slipping away from the garden and the loom to find her beloved alone in the hills. Adah was too ill to keep her from such wild behavior, and Rachel refused to obey Leah, who had lost some of her status now that the younger sister was to become bride and mother first.

Those days in the fields with Jacob were Rachel's delight. "He would look at me with wonder," said my beautiful aunt, "his fingers in my hair. He made me stand in shade and then in the sun to see the different light play across my cheek. He wept at my beauty. He sang the songs of his family, and told me about the beauty of his mother."

Rachel said, "Jacob made up stories about how beautiful our sons would be, too. Golden boys, like me, he said. Perfect boys, who would be princes and kings.

"I know what they all thought—my sisters and the shepherds—but we never touched. Well, only once. He held me to his chest, but then he began trembling and pushed me away. After that, he kept his distance.

"Which was fine with me. He smelled, you know. Much better than most of the men. But still, the smell of goat and of man was overpowering. I would run home and bury my nose in coriander."

Rachel boasted that she was the first to hear the story of Jacob's family. He was the younger of the twin boys, making him his mother's heir. He was the prettier one, the clever one. Rebecca told her husband, Isaac, that Jacob was sickly in order to keep him at the breast for a year after she weaned the brother.

Giving birth to the twins nearly killed Rebecca, who bled so much there was nothing left to sustain another life inside her. When she realized she would have no daughters, she began whispering her stories to Jacob.

Rebecca told Jacob that Esau's blessing was rightly his, for why else had Innana made him the finer of the two? And besides, in her family, it was the mother's right to decide the heir. Isaac himself was the second-born son. Left to Abram, Ishmael would have been patriarch, but Sarai had claimed her rights and named Isaac instead. It was she who sent Isaac to seek a bride from among her family, as was the custom from the oldest days.

Even so, Jacob loved Esau and hated to do him any kind of harm. He feared that the god of Isaac his father and Abram his grandfather would punish him for following his mother's words. He was haunted by a dream that woke him in terror, a dream in which he was utterly destroyed.

Rachel stroked his cheek and told him that his fears were groundless. "I told him that had he not followed his mother's bidding, he would never have found me, and surely the god of Isaac who loved Rebecca smiled upon the love of Jacob for Rachel.

"This cheered him," she said. "He told me that I gladdened his heart like a sunrise. He said such pretty things."

While Jacob spoke sweetly to Rachel, Leah suffered. She lost weight and neglected her hair, though never her duties. The camp was always well run, clean, provisioned, and busy. The spinning never ceased, the garden flourished, and the herbs were plentiful enough to be traded in the village for new lamps.

Jacob noticed these things. He saw what Leah did and learned that it was she who had maintained order during the lean years while Laban moped. The old man was completely worthless when Jacob had a question about whether the black-bearded trader from Aleppo was trustworthy, or which of the boys to hire at shearing time. Leah was the one to ask about the flock; which ewes had borne in the previous year, which goats were the offspring of the black sire and which of the dappled. Rachel, who had worked among the animals, could not tell one beast from another, but Leah remembered what she saw, and everything that Bilhah said.

Jacob approached Leah with the same deference he

showed to Adah, for after all, they were kinswomen. But he approached her far more often than necessary, or so it seemed to Zilpah.

Jacob found a new question for the eldest daughter every day. Where should he pasture the kids in the spring? Had she any extra honey to barter for a likely-looking ewe? Was she ready for the sacrifice of the barley harvest? He was always thirsty for the beer she brewed from wonderful recipes her mother had learned from an Egyptian trader.

Leah answered Jacob's questions and poured his drink with her eyes averted, her head nearly tucked into her chest, like a nesting bird. It was painful for her to look at him. And yet, every morning when she opened her eyes her first thought was of him. Would he come to speak to her again that day? Did he notice how her hand trembled when she filled his cup?

Zilpah could not bear to be anywhere near them together. "It was like being near rutting he-goats," she said. "And they were so polite. They almost bent over not to see each other, lest they fall on top of each other like dogs in heat."

Leah tried to ignore the desire of her own body and Rachel was unaware of anything but the preparations for her wedding, but Zilpah saw lust everywhere she looked. To her, the whole world suddenly seemed damp with longing.

Leah tossed and turned at night, and Zilpah had seen Jacob in the fields, leaning against a tree, his hands working his sex until he slumped over in relief. For a month before the wedding, Jacob stopped dreaming of battle or of his parents and brother. Instead, he spent his nights sleepwalking with each of the four sisters. He drank at the waters of a stream and found himself in Rachel's lap. He lifted a huge boulder to find Leah naked under it. He ran from the awful thing that chased him, and fell exhausted into the arms of Bilhah, who had begun to grow the shape of a woman. He rescued Zilpah from the acacia tree, untangling her long hair from the branches where she was caught. He woke up every morning, sweating, his sex aroused. He would roll off his blanket and squirm on the ground until he could stand without embarrassment.

Zilpah watched as the triangle of Jacob, Rachel, and Leah grew into a wedge she could use. For as much as she loved Leah, Zilpah had never cared for the lovely Rachel. (That's what Zilpah always called her—"Ah, and here comes the lovely Rachel," she would say, vinegar in her voice.) She knew there wasn't much she could do to stop Jacob from becoming the family patriarch, and indeed she was as impatient for children as everyone else. Still, she wanted to make this river flow in a direction of her choosing. Zilpah also wished to make the lovely Rachel suffer just a little.

Zilpah suspected that Rachel feared her wedding night, and encouraged her to confess every worry. The older girl sighed and shook her head in sympathy as Rachel revealed how little she knew about the mechanics of sex. She had no expectation of pleasure— only of pain. So Zilpah told her nervous sister that the shepherds spoke of Jacob's sex as a freak of nature. "Twice the size of that of any normal man," she whispered, demonstrating an impossible length between her hands. Zilpah took Rachel up to the highest pasture and showed her the boys having their way with the ewes, who bleated pitifully and bled. The older sister commiserated with the trembling girl, whispering, "Poor thing," as she stroked Rachel's hair. "Poor female thing."

And that was why, on the day of the wedding, Rachel panicked. Jacob's chaste adoration had been pleasant, but now he would demand everything of her and there would be no way to refuse. Her stomach rebelled and she retched. She pulled out handfuls of hair. She ran her fingernails down her cheeks until she drew blood. She begged her sisters to save her.

"Rachel wept as we tried to dress her for the banquet," Leah said. "She cried, claiming she was unready and unwell and too small for her husband. She even tried that trick with the crushed berries, lifting her skirt and whining that Jacob would kill her if he found moon blood in the nuptial bed. I told her to stop behaving like a child, for she wore a woman's belt."

But Rachel wailed and fell on her knees and begged her sister to take her place under the bridal veil. "Zilpah says you will do it," she cried.

"I was struck dumb," Leah remembered. "For of course, Zilpah was right. I had not permitted myself to imagine such a thing—that it might be me with him that night. I could barely admit it to myself, much less to my sister, who was not so lovely at that moment, her eyes red from crying, her cheeks streaked with blood and berry juice.

"First I said no. He would know at once, for no veil could hide the difference in our height. He would refuse to have me, and then I would be damaged goods, unmarriageable, and nothing to be done but sell me for a slave.

"But all the while I protested, my heart pounded its own yes. Rachel asked me to do what I wanted more than anything in life. So even as I argued, I agreed."

Adah was too ill to help dress the bride that morning, so Zilpah took charge of the plot, rubbing Leah's hands and feet with henna, drawing the kohl around her eyes, covering her with baubles. Rachel sat in a corner, hugged her knees to her chest, and shivered as Leah prepared for what was meant to be her wedding night.

"I was happier than I had ever been," said Leah. "But I was also filled with dread. What if he turned away from me in disgust? What if he ran out of the tent and shamed me forever? But something in me believed that he would embrace me."

It was a simple banquet with few guests. Two flute-players from the village came and went quickly; one of the shepherds brought a gift offering of oil, which he left as soon as he had filled his belly. Laban was drunk from the start, his hand under poor Ruti's dress. He stumbled over his own feet when he led Leah to Jacob's side. The bride, crouched low under her veil, circled the groom three times in one direction, three times in the other. Zilpah served the meal.

"I thought the day would never end," Leah said. "I could not be seen through my veil, nor could I see out clearly, but how could Jacob not know it was me? I waited in misery for him to expose me, to jump up and claim he had been swindled. But he did not. He sat beside me, close enough for me to feel the warmth of his thigh against mine. He ate lamb and bread, and drank both wine and beer, though not enough to make him sleepy or stupid.

"Finally, Jacob stood and helped me to my feet. He led me to the tent where we would spend our seven days, with Laban following, hooting and wishing us sons," Leah remembered.

"Jacob did not move toward me until it had fallen silent outside. Then he removed my veil. It was a beautiful garment, embroidered with many colors and worn by generations of brides who had lived through a hundred wedding nights filled with pleasure, violence, fear, delight, disappointment. I shuddered, wondering which destiny would be mine.

"It was not fully dark inside the tent. He saw my face and showed no surprise. He was breathing heavily. He took off the rest of my clothes, removing first the mantle from my shoulders, untying my girdle, and then helping me as I stepped out of my robes. I was naked before him. My mother told me my husband would only lift up my robes and enter me still wearing his. But I was uncovered, and then, in a moment, so was he, his sex pointing at me. It looked like a faceless asherah! This was such a hilarious idea, I might have laughed out loud had I been able to breathe.

"But I was afraid. I sank to the blanket, and he moved quickly to my side. He stroked my hands and he touched my cheek, and then he was on top of me. I was afraid. But I remembered my mother's counsel, and opened my hands and my feet, and listened to the sound of my breath instead of his.

"Jacob was good to me. He was slow to enter me

the first time, but he finished so quickly I barely had time to calm down before he fell still and heavy upon me, like a dead man, for what seemed like hours. Then his hands came to life. They wandered over my face, through my hair, and then, oh, on my breasts and belly, to my legs and my sex, which he explored with the lightest touch. It was the touch of a mother tracing the inner ear of her newborn child, a feeling so sweet I smiled. He looked at my pleasure, and nodded. We both laughed." And then Jacob spoke tenderly to his first wife.

"My own father rarely addressed me and seemed to prefer my brother's company," he whispered. "But once, while we were traveling, we passed a tent where a man was beating a woman—wife, concubine, or slave we had no way of knowing.

"Isaac, my father, sighed and told me that he had never taken any woman to his bed but my mother, even though she had only given him two sons early in their marriage. Rebecca had welcomed him with tenderness and passion when they first were married because as her groom he treated her as though she were the Queen of Heaven and he her consort. Their coupling was the coupling of the sea and the sky, of the rain and the parched earth. Of night and day, wind and water.

"Their nights were filled with stars and sighs as they played the part of goddess and god. Their touches engendered a thousand dreams. They slept in each other's arms every night, except when it was her time for the red tent, or when she gave suck to her sons.

"That was my father's teaching about husbands and wives," said Jacob my father to Leah my mother on their first night together. And then he wept over the loss of his father's love.

Leah wept out of sympathy for her husband, and also out of relief and joy at her good fortune. She knew that her own mother had cried on her wedding night, too, but those had been tears of despair, for Laban had been a boor from the beginning.

Leah kissed her husband. He kissed her. They embraced again and again. And even on that first night, when she was tender from being opened by a man, Leah responded to his touch. She liked the smell of him and the feel of his beard on her skin. When he entered her, she flexed her legs and her sex with a kind of strength that surprised her and delighted him. When Jacob cried out in his final pleasure, she was flooded by a sense of her own power. And when she followed her breathing, she discovered her pleasure, an opening and a fullness that made her sigh, and purr, and then sleep as she hadn't slept since she was a child. He called her Innana. She called him Baal, brother-lover of Ishtar.

They were left alone the full seven days and seven nights. Food was set out for them at dawn and at dusk, and they ate with the ravenous hunger of lovers. By the end of the week, they had made love in every hour of the day and night. They were certain they had invented a thousand new methods for giving and taking pleasure. They had slept in each other's arms. They laughed like children at Laban's stupidity, and at Zilpah's strange ways. But they did not speak of Rachel.

It was a golden week, every day sweeter but every day sadder, too. There would never be another time when Leah and Jacob could wander in each other's memories or lounge during daylight in each other's arms. These were the only meals they would ever share, talking and finding in each other kindred spirits for business and family politics.

They decided that Jacob would emerge from the week feigning anger. He would go to Laban and say, "I have been duped. I was given strong wine and you gave me the harridan Leah rather than my beloved Rachel. My labor for Rachel was repaid with a swindle, for which I demand restitution. And although I spent these seven days and seven nights with your eldest girl as my duty required, I do not consider her my wife until you make me a dowry in her name, and until Rachel is also mine."

And that is precisely what Jacob said when he left the tent. "I will take the maiden Zilpah as dowry for Leah, just as Bilhah will be dowry for Rachel. I will take another tenth of your herd for relieving you of your ill-favored daughter. And to be fair, I will work for you another seven months, as the bride-price for Leah.

"These are my terms."

Jacob made this speech before everyone in camp on the day he and Leah emerged from their seclusion. Leah kept her eyes on the ground as her husband recited the words they had rehearsed the night before, naked, sweating each other's sweat. She pretended to cry while twisting her mouth to keep from laughing.

As Jacob proclaimed himself, Adah nodded assent. Zilpah turned white at the mention of her name. Laban, who had spent the week drunk in honor of his daughter's marriage, was so stupefied he could barely sputter a protest before throwing up his hands, cursing the lot of them, and returning to the dark of his tent.

Rachel spat at Jacob's feet and stormed off. By the end of the nuptial week, she had come to regret her panic. She had lost forever her position as first wife, and then she had heard the sounds from the bridal tent— laughter and muffled cries of pleasure. Rachel had poured out her sorrow to Bilhah, who took her to see two dogs mating, and two sheep, none of whom seemed to suffer in the act. Rachel went to the village and told Inna what had happened. Inna told her tales of passion and pleasure, and took Rachel inside her hut and showed her how to unlock the secrets of her own body.

When Jacob found Rachel at their accustomed tree, she cursed him soundly, calling him a thief and a bastard, a devil and a pig who inserted himself into sheep and goats and dogs. She accused him of not loving her. She shrieked that he must have known it was Leah, even when she was veiled, sitting beside him at the wedding feast. He could have stopped it. Why hadn't he? She cried bitterly.

When her tears were spent, Jacob held her to his chest until it seemed she was asleep, and told her that she was the moon's own daughter, luminous, radiant, and perfect. That his love for her was worshipful. That he felt only duty toward Leah, who was a mere shadow of Rachel's light. That she, only Rachel, would be the bride of his heart, his first wife, first love. Such pretty treason.

So it happened that the day before the next full moon

there was a second wedding feast, even simpler than the first. And Rachel took her turn in the tent with Jacob.

I do not know much about that week, for Rachel never spoke of it. No tears were heard coming from the nuptial tent of Jacob and Rachel, which was a good sign. No one overheard laughter either. When the week was over, Rachel crept to the red tent before dawn, where she slept until the following morning.

At the first new moon after Leah's bridal week, there was no blood between her legs. But she kept this news to herself. Amid the hurried preparations for Rachel's wedding, it was easy enough to conceal the fact that she did not really need to change her place on the straw or use a rag between her legs when she moved around.

Two days after Rachel entered the nuptial tent with Jacob, Leah went to her mother and put Adah's dry hand on her young belly. The older woman hugged her daughter. "I did not think I would live to see a grandchild," she said to Leah, smiling and crying at once. "Beloved girl, daughter mine."

Leah said she kept quiet about her pregnancy to protect Rachel's happiness. Her status as head wife would be assured with the birth of a son, and she knew from the first that she was carrying a boy. But Rachel was furious when she learned that Leah was with child. She thought her sister had kept the news from her as part of a complicated plot to shame her, to assure her own role as first wife, as a way to cause Jacob to abandon her.

Rachel's accusations could be heard from as far away

as the well, which was a good distance from the tent where she bellowed. She accused Leah of asking Zilpah to help cheat her of her rightful place. She insinuated that Leah was pregnant not by Jacob, but by a hare-lipped, half-witted shepherd who loitered at the well. "You jealous bitch," Rachel screamed. "You evil-eyed lummox, you only wish Jacob loved you as he loves me, but he never will. I am the one. I am his heart. You are a brood mare. You pathetic cow."

Leah held her tongue until Rachel was finished. Then she calmly called her sister an ass and slapped her face hard, first on one cheek and then on the other. They did not speak a word to each other for months.

I suppose it only natural to assume that Leah was always jealous of Rachel. And it was true that Leah did not sing or smile much during Jacob's week with Rachel. Indeed, over the years, whenever my father took my beautiful aunt to his bed, my mother kept her head bent over her work, which grew as her sons increased and as Jacob's labors yielded more wool to be woven.

But Leah was not jealous in the way of silly girls in love songs, who die of longing. There was no bile in Leah's sadness when Jacob lay with his other wives. Indeed, she delighted in all his sons and had most of them at her own breast at one time or another. She could depend upon Jacob to call for her once or twice in a month, for talk about the herds and for an extra cup of sweet beer. On those nights she knew they would sleep together, her arms locked around his waist, and the next morning her family would bask in her smile and enjoy something good to eat.

But I am rushing my story. For it took years before Leah and Rachel finally learned how to share a husband, and at first they were like dogs, circling and growling and giving each other wide berth as they explored the boundary between them.

Even so, at first it seemed a kind of parity would prevail, because at the next new moon, Rachel, too, found she had no use for the rags or the hay. Both sisters were pregnant. The barley crop was enormous. The shepherds slapped Jacob on the back and joked about his potency. The gods were smiling.

But just as Leah's belly began to swell against her tunic, Rachel started to bleed. Early one morning, nearly three months after her wedding, she woke the whole camp with her cries. Leah and Zilpah rushed to her side, and found her sobbing, wrapped in a bloody blanket. No one could comfort her. She would not let Adah sit with her. She would not permit Jacob to see her. For a week, she huddled in a corner of the red tent, where she ate little and slept a dreamless, feverish sleep.

Leah forgave Rachel her nasty words and grieved for her. She tried to tempt her with her favorite sweets, but Rachel spat at the food and at Leah, who seemed to grow bigger and rounder every day, and as beautiful as she had ever been.

"It was so unfair. So sad," said Bilhah, who finally got Rachel to eat a few olives and coaxed her out of the stained, stiff blanket. Bilhah was the one who walked to the village where Inna lived, to see if the midwife had some potion that might rouse her sister from her half-death. Inna herself came back and spent hours with Rachel, washing her, feeding her tiny bits of bread dipped in honey, coaxing her to take sips of an aromatic red mead. Inna whispered secret words of comfort and hope into Rachel's ear. She told her that bearing children would not be easy for her, but foretold that someday Rachel would bear beautiful sons who would shine like stars and assure her memory. Inna promised to put all her skills to work to help Rachel conceive again, but only if she would do exactly what the midwife told her to do.

That is why, when Leah in her sixth month sought her sister's blessing, Rachel put her hands on Leah's belly and caressed the life there. Rachel cried in her sister's arms, kissed Adah's hands, and asked Zilpah to comb her hair. She took Bilhah aside, embraced her, and thanked her for bringing Inna. It was the first time Rachel had thanked anyone for anything.

The next morning, Leah and Rachel, side by side, walked out of the darkness of the red tent and back into the light of the world, where Jacob stood. Rachel said he wept when he saw them together, but Leah said that he smiled.

"Leah's first birth was not especially difficult," said Rachel. By the time she told me the story of Reuben's arrival, my aunt had seen hundreds of babies born. And though Rachel would forget where she put her spindle the moment she put it down, she remembered the details of every birth she ever witnessed.

She told me that even though Leah's travail began before sunset and did not end until daylight, it was a straight path. His head was down and her hips were

wide enough. Still, the heat of that summer night in the
red tent was stifling, and none of the sisters had ever
seen a birth. Truly Leah suffered most because of her
sisters' fear.

It began slowly in the afternoon, with small, grabbing pains in her back. Leah smiled after each little sei-
zure, glad to be started, eager to be admitted to the
sisterhood of mothers. Confident that her body, so broad
and big, would fulfill its purpose, she sang in the early
stages. Children's songs, ballads, lullabies.

But as the night wore on, and the moon rose in the
sky and then started to sink, there were no more smiles
or songs. Each contraction took Leah up and wrung her
out, like a bit of cloth, and left her panting and fearful of
the next pain. Adah held her hand. Zilpah muttered
prayers to Anath. "I was of no use at all," Rachel remembered. "I wandered in and out of the tent, eaten up
by jealousy. But as the hours came and went, each one
harder than the last, my envy waned and I was horrified
by the pain I saw on Leah, the strong one, the invincible
ox who was on the ground trembling and wide-eyed. I
was terrified by the thought that I might have been in
her place, that I might yet be. And I'm sure that the
very same thoughts made Zilpah and Bilhah shudder
and keep silence while our sister labored."

Bilhah finally realized that they needed more help
than Adah could provide, and she went to fetch Inna,
who arrived at daybreak. By that time, Leah was whimpering like a dog. When Inna arrived, she put her hands
on Leah's belly and then reached up inside her. She
made her lie on her side, and rubbed her back and thighs
with a mint-scented oil. Inna smiled into Leah's face

and said, "The baby is nearly at the door." And while she emptied her kit, she bade the women gather around to help their sister bring the baby.

"It was the first time I'd seen a midwife's kit," Rachel said. "The knife, the string, reeds for suction, amphorae of cumin, hyssop, and mint oil. Inna put her two bricks on the ground and told Leah she would stand on them soon. She moved me and Zilpah on either side to lend support when Leah squatted over a bed of clean straw. Zilpah and I became Leah's chair, with our arms around her shoulders and beneath her thighs. 'You lucky girl,' Inna said to Leah, who by then did not feel the least bit lucky. 'Look at the royal throne of sisters you have.'"

Inna talked and talked, banishing the frightened silence that had made a wall around Leah. Inna asked Adah about her aches and pains, and teased Zilpah about the tangled mat of her hair. But whenever a contraction came, Inna had words for Leah only. She praised her, reassured her, told her, "Good, good, good, my girl. Good, good, good." Soon, all of the women in the tent joined her in repeating "Good, good, good," clucking like a clutch of doves.

Inna began to massage the skin around Leah's bottom, which was swollen out of shape. She rubbed with stronger and stronger motions as the pains came closer and closer. And then she put Rachel's hand on Leah's belly and showed her how to press downward, gently but firmly, when the time came. She told Leah not to push, not to push, until Leah bellowed curses.

Rachel said, "I saw that baby come into the world as I had seen nothing before in my life. Clearly. Without a thought to myself. I thought of my own mother who had seen this so many times, whose hands had guided so many souls into the world, but who died giving me life.

"But I had no time to be sorry for myself, because suddenly a strange red bubble emerged from between Leah's legs and then, almost immediately, a flood of bloody water washed down her thighs."

Leah tried to stand, terrified, but Inna told her not to take her feet off the bricks. This was good, she said. He was coming.

Leah pushed, her face red, her eyes bulging, blue and green, glittering. Her legs were trembling as though they would buckle at any moment, and it took all of Zilpah's and Rachel's strength to hold her. Then Inna told Bilhah to take Rachel's place so she could catch the baby; perhaps the birth blood would rouse Rachel's womb to fill again, too. And so Rachel washed in the river of life.

Leah roared and delivered her son. He was so big it took both Inna and Rachel to catch him, and he started to cry even before they raised up his head. No need for the reeds to clear out this baby's nose and mouth. They all laughed, tears streaming down their faces, panting from the effort of Leah's birth.

They passed the baby around the tent, wiping him and kissing him, praising his limbs, his torso, his head, his little sex. They all talked at the same time, making more noise than any six women can make. Jacob cried out to the women to tell him the news. "You are a father," said Inna. "Go away. We will send for you soon and then you will see your son, your firstborn, when we have finished." They heard Jacob shout with joy, and call out the news to Laban and Ruti, and his barking dogs, and the clouds in the sky.

The afterbirth fell out of Leah, who was nearly asleep with exhaustion. Inna made her drink and eat before she rested, and put the baby to Leah's breast, where he nursed. Mother and son slept, and the sisters covered them. Adah watched, a grandmother's smile lingering even after she dozed off. Inna wrapped the placenta in an old rag and they buried it that night, in the eastern corner of the bamah, as befits a firstborn son.

A few hours later when Leah awoke she named the baby Reuben. It was a joyful shout of a name, a name that fairly dared evil spirits to do him any harm. But Leah had no fears for her strapping boy. Jacob was sent for and greeted his son with great tenderness.

As Jacob walked away from his first meeting with his son, his happiness seemed to evaporate. His head sank to his chest as he contemplated what had to be done next. According to the custom of his family, the boy had to be circumcised, and there was no one to do it but him. Jacob would not let Laban touch the baby, much less take a knife to him. He knew of no other man in the village or nearby hills who knew how, much less why he would do this to his firstborn son. It would have to be him.

Jacob had seen his father cut the foreskins from his bondsmen's baby boys, and he had not looked away or even winced when it was done. But he had never done this himself, nor, he now realized, had he watched carefully enough how his father had dressed the wound.

And, of course, he had never cared so much for any baby in his life.

It had to be done, though, and he began the preparations, which Zilpah watched and reported to Leah, who was sick at the prospect of having her baby, her prize, put on the altar of the bamah and mutilated. For that's what she considered it. The flap of skin on the penis meant nothing to her. Indeed, now that she had seen the look of an uncircumcised man, she preferred the look of Jacob's sex—exposed, clean, audacious even—to the tiny shroud her son wore on his member, which was the source of many silly and crude jokes in the red tent. Once, Leah threatened to take a bit of charred wood and draw a face upon Reuben's sex, so that when Jacob retracted the foreskin, he would drop his knife in wonder. The women rolled around on the mats, holding their sides, laughing about the tender equipment that men carried between their legs.

But after a few days, the joking stopped, and Leah cried so long and so hard over the boy at her breast that the dark curls on his head were salted with tears. Still, she did not object to the custom of her husband's father. Jacob had survived this, she told her sisters again and again, mostly to reassure herself. Isaac had been circumcised, and Abram before him. Nevertheless, the thought of her baby in pain and in danger made the new mother tremble, and the realization that Jacob had no experience at the task put her in a frenzy of worry.

Zilpah watched and saw that Jacob was not at ease about the ritual either. Every night, he sat on the bamah with his knife and sharpened it on the altar. From sunset till moonrise three nights running, until the edge was perfect, he honed and polished the blade until it could cut a hair from his head with the slightest motion of his wrist. He asked Adah to make small bandages, woven of new wool taken from the first shearing of the firstborn lamb of the season. He sent word to Leah, inquiring whether she had any of the midwife's unguents to aid in healing.

On the seventh night after Reuben's birth, Jacob sat up, silently watching the sky, until sunrise. He poured libations and sang to the god of his fathers. He poured libations over the asherah, too, and opened his hands before her. Zilpah watched all of this and afterward stopped referring to Jacob as "that new man" and began to call him by his name.

At dawn of the eighth day after his son's birth, Jacob killed a kid and burned it on the altar. He washed his hands, rubbing them red with straw, as though he had handled a corpse. And then he walked to the red tent and asked that the women give him Reuben, the son of Leah.

He called for Laban to follow him, and the two men walked alone to the bamah, where Jacob undressed the baby, whose eyes were open, and placed him on the altar. Jacob sighed a loud, long sigh as he stripped the boy, and then he signaled Laban to grab the baby's legs. At this, Reuben began to wail. Jacob took the knife in his hands and knotted his brow.

"There were tears in his eyes," said Zilpah. "He took the baby's sex in his hands and pulled the skin up tightly, holding it between the two long fingers of his left hand.

With his right hand, he cut, with a quick, sure stroke, as though it was an old custom of his, as though he knew what he was doing," she said.

Reuben howled, and Jacob dropped the knife. Quickly, he bound the wound with Adah's bandage, and swaddled the baby, badly, the way men do. He carried his son back to the women, whispering into Reuben's perfect ear words that no one else could hear.

The red tent, which had been quiet during the baby's absence, now burst into activity. Leah dressed the wound with the cumin oil that Inna had left for her own birth wounds. Adah swaddled Reuben properly and gave him back to his mother, where he took her breast with relief and then slept.

The baby healed quickly, as did Leah during her first month as a new mother inside the shelter of the red tent. She was pampered by her sisters, who barely let her feet touch the earth. Jacob came by every day, carrying freshly dressed birds for her meals. Through the hairy wall of the tent they relayed the news of their days with a tenderness that warmed those who overheard them.

Adah beamed that whole month and saw her daughter step out of the red tent restored and rested. She delighted in her grandson's first yawns and sneezes and was the first to notice Reuben lift his head. Adah held the baby whenever Leah would put him down, and the joy of him lifted years from her face and the pain from her bones. But the illness that had wasted her strength could not be cured by even the greatest joy. And one morning she did not rise from her blanket.

Adah was the only mother any of the sisters had known, and they put ashes in their hair and honored her. Leah washed Adah's face and hands. Zilpah combed her hair smooth. Rachel dressed her in the finest tunic they owned, and Bilhah placed Adah's few rings and bangles on the withered wrists, neck, and fingers. Together, they crossed her arms and bent her knees so that she looked like a sleeping child. They whispered wishes into her ears so she could carry them to the other side of the light, where the spirits of her ancestors would greet her soul, which could now rest in the dust of the earth and suffer no more.

They wrapped her in a shroud of unbleached wool lined with sweet-smelling herbs and buried her amid the roots of the big tree where the women often gathered to watch the moon rise.

Jacob dug the grave while Laban stood and watched, ashes on his head to honor his first wife. With Adah, Laban buried his youth, his strength, and perhaps some forgotten better self. He threw the first handful of dirt, then turned and walked away before the four sisters finished tucking her in with earth, flowers, and loud lamentation.

Two months after Adah died, Bilhah entered the red tent. With Adah gone and no other elder to take the part, Leah, nursing her son, became the welcoming mother. She greeted the acolyte and taught her how to manage the flow of blood, how to rejoice in the dark of the moon, how to join her body's cycle with the repetition of life.

The wheel had turned. And even though Laban retained title as head of the clan, Jacob's time as patriarch had begun. My mothers, too, began numbering their days with the wisdom of women.

There followed many good years. The rains came in season, and the well water was sweet and abundant. The land was spared pestilence, and there was peace among the surrounding tribes. The herds prospered so that Jacob could no longer manage the work alone and he contracted with Shibtu, the third son of a local shepherd, as a seven-year bondsman. And then he hired Nomir, who brought a wife, Zibatu, and there was a new face in the red tent.

The family's good fortune and increasing wealth were not entirely the result of Jacob's skill, nor could it all be attributed to the will of the gods. My mothers' labors accounted for much of it. While sheep and goats are a sign of wealth, their full value is realized only in the husbandry of women. Leah's cheeses never soured, and when the rust attacked wheat or millet, she saw to it that the afflicted stems were picked clean to protect the rest of the crop. Zilpah and Bilhah wove the wool from Jacob's growing flocks into patterns of black, white, and saffron that lured traders and brought new wealth.

This was also the time of great fertility among the women. Many babies were born, and most survived. Leah wore the mantle of the great mother, seemingly always pregnant or nursing. Two years after Reuben's birth, she bore a second son, Simon. Levi was born only eighteen months later. Leah miscarried after that, but within another year her sorrow was forgotten in the joy of her fourth son, Judah.

Those brothers, so close in age, were a tribe unto themselves. Reuben, always the heaviest and tallest, was gentle with the younger ones. Simon was a demon—handsome and smug, demanding and rude—but forgiven everything for his dimples. Levi was a meek mouse and Simon's slave. Judah was a quiet boy, affectionate toward everyone. He was much fairer than his brothers, and Jacob told Leah that he resembled his own brother, Esau.

While Leah was carrying Simon, Laban's Ruti showed a big belly, too, and bore a boy, Kemuel, who was followed a year later by Beor. The old man doted on his slope-browed sons, who played rough-and-tumble with Leah's boys at first, but then invented a secret language, which locked them into a narrow world of their own making. Laban thought this demonstrated his sons' superiority, but the rest of the family saw it as proof of their stunted nature and limited prospects.

The happy noise of children surrounded them, but the blessing of generation was not equally distributed. Rachel miscarried again and again. After the bloody flood washed away her hopes a fourth time, she sickened with a fever that drove her out of her mind for three days and nights. This frightened her sisters so badly they insisted she stop trying to conceive and persuaded her to drink the infusion of fennel seed that seals the womb, at least until she had regained weight and strength. Rachel, exhausted, agreed.

But she could not rest long amid the clamor of her sister's sons. Although she no longer hated Leah with the full force of the past, Rachel could not smile at her sister while her own body remained fruitless. She was often away from the family's tents, seeking the counsel of Inna, who had a seemingly endless list of concoctions and strategies to open her womb.

Rachel tried every remedy, every potion, every rumored cure. She wore only red and yellow—the colors of life's blood and the talisman for healthy menstruation. She slept with her belly against trees said to be sacred to local goddesses. Whenever she saw running water, she lay down in it, hoping for the life of the river to inspire life within her. She swallowed a tincture made with bee pollen until her tongue was coated yellow and she peed a saffron river. She dined upon snake—the animal that gives birth to itself, year after year.

Of course, when anyone, adult or child, found a mandrake—the root that looks so much like an aroused husband—it would be brought to Rachel and handed over with a wink and a prayer. Reuben once found an especially large one, and brought it to his auntie with the pride of a lion hunter. But mandrakes did nothing for Rachel's womb.

During her quest for a child of her own, Rachel assisted Inna and became her apprentice. She learned what to do when the baby presented itself feet first, and what to do when the baby came too fast and the mother's flesh tore and festered. She learned how to keep a stillborn's mother from giving up her spirit in despair. And how, when a mother died, to cut open the womb and save the child within.

Rachel brought her sisters stories that made them weep, and sigh, and wonder. Of a mother who died and a father who sold the infant before her body was cold. Of a man who swooned at the death of a beloved wife. Of a woman who cried blood for her dead child. She told of potions that worked a miracle upon one woman and seemed to kill another, of an armless monster left out to die in the night air, of blood that carried off and blood that healed.

There were triumphant stories, too, of healthy twins, of a baby born blue, the cord wrapped tight around its neck, brought to life by Inna, who sucked the death from the little one's nostrils with a river reed. Sometimes Rachel made her sisters laugh with imitations of women who roared like lions and others who held their breath and fainted rather than make a peep.

Rachel became their link to the larger world. Along with tales of life and death, Rachel brought back new herbs for seasoning vegetables, recipes for unguents that healed wounds, and ever stranger remedies for her barrenness, all of which failed.

Often, Rachel returned bearing a bracelet, a bowl, or a skein of wool—tokens of gratitude for her generosity at childbed. The imperious beauty became a tenderhearted healer in the service of mothers. She wept at every birth, the easy, happy ones as well as the ones that ended with keening and whimpering. She wept with Ruti and even with Leah.

When it came time for Zibatu to stand on the midwife's bricks, Rachel alone—without Inna—led her through the ordeal, tied off the cord, and flushed with pleasure when she held "her" first, the baby that conferred upon her the title of midwife. Leah cooked her a feast that night, and Zilpah poured out salt and wine before her, in recognition of her new status as a servant of women in the name of Anath, the healer.

As time passed, more bondsmen came to live and work for Jacob, and with them came women who bore children and lost children. Zibatu gave birth to Nasi, but then lost her second child, a girl who came two months before her time. Iltani bore twin girls who thrived, though she died of fever before her daughters knew their mother's face. Lamassi gave birth to a son, Zinri, but her daughter was left out to die because she had the harelip.

In the red tent we knew that death was the shadow of birth, the price women pay for the honor of giving life. Thus, our sorrow was measured.

After Judah's birth, Leah grew tired. She, who had always risen the earliest and retired last, who seemed most content when doing two things at once (stirring a pot while nursing, or grinding grain as she oversaw the spinning), began to stagger in the afternoons and see shadows where there were none. Inna advised her to leave off bearing for a while, and brought her fennel seeds and also showed her how to fashion a pessary out of beeswax.

So Leah rested. She rejoiced in the sturdiness of her sons, and stopped every day to caress them and play their game of smooth stones. She baked honey-eyed cake as she used to, and planned a new garden where herbs would attract more bees to nearby hives. She slept soundly at night and rose in peace every morning.

Leah remembered her fallow years as a time of great contentment. She held the fu of every day in her hands, numbering the sweetness of children, the pleasure of work. She gave thanks for the fennel seeds and the wisdom to use them. Her cake never tasted sweeter than it did that year, and she responded to Jacob's body with more ardor than she had felt for years.

When she spoke of that time, Leah said, "The flavor of gratitude is like the nectar of the hive."

After two years, she put away the fennel seeds and pessary and conceived another son, whom she bore easily and named Zebulun, by which Leah meant "exalt," because with his birth, Leah exalted in her body's ability to heal and to give life once more. She adored the new baby nearly as much as her firstborn. And when she handed her son over to Jacob for the circumcision, she smiled into her husband's face, and he kissed her hands.

CHAPTER THREE

Rachel grew quiet. She stopped attending Inna and did not rise from her blanket until Leah shook her and insisted she help the rest of the women in their work. Only then would Rachel spin or weave or work the garden, but wordlessly and without a smile. Jacob could not rouse her from her sadness. Rebuffed by her unbending silence, he stopped calling her to him at night. Her sorrow became a presence so bleak, even the babies began to avoid their pretty auntie. Rachel was alone in her own black night.

Bilhah saw Rachel's despair and went to her where she huddled on her blanket. The little sister lay down beside Rachel and held her as gently as a mother. "Let me go to Jacob on your behalf," said Bilhah, in a whisper. "Let me bear a son on your knees. Let me be your womb and your breasts. Let me bleed your blood and shed your tears. Let me become your vessel until your time comes, for your time will yet arrive. Let me be your hope, Rachel. I will not disappoint you."

Rachel made no reply. She said nothing for a long

time. Bilhah wondered if her sister had slept through her words, or whether her offer had offended. Bilhah said she waited so long for a reply that she began to wonder whether the words that had been gathering in her heart had not even passed her lips.

Bilhah was accustomed to silence and waited. Finally, Rachel turned and kissed her, gathering the small woman close to her body, taking comfort from her warmth. "And the tears she shed were not bitter or even salty," said Bilhah, "but sweet as rainwater."

Bilhah knew that even though her offer to Rachel was made out of love, it also served her own heart's desire. She understood Rachel's longing because it was her own. She was well into her childbearing years. The sounds of lovemaking in the close world of our tents had roused her at night, leaving her shaken and sleepless. Attending her sister's births made her wish to become part of the great mother-mystery, which is bought with pain and repaid with an infant's sparkling smile and silken skin. Her breasts ached to give suck.

Honest Bilhah revealed every corner of her heart to Rachel, who knew the emptiness her sister described. They wept together and slept in each other's arms. The next morning, Rachel sought out Jacob and asked that he sire a child upon Bilhah, in her name. This was not a request, for it was Rachel's right to have a child of Jacob.

There was no other permission to seek or get. Jacob agreed. (Why would he not? Leah nursed her latest son and Rachel's back had been turned to him for long months.) So that night, on the full moon of a chill month, Bilhah went to Jacob, and left him the next morning, no longer a maiden, though not a bride.

There was no henna for Bilhah's hands, no feast, no gifts. There were no seven days to learn the secrets of Jacob's body or the meaning of his words. When the sun rose the next day, Jacob returned to oversee the flocks, and Bilhah went to Rachel, and recounted every detail of her night to her sister. Years later, she told it to me.

She wept when she entered Jacob's tent, and she was surprised by her own tears. She had wanted to be initiated into the mystery of sex, to open her legs and learn the ancient ways of men and women. But she was lonely walking into her husband's tent alone, without sisters or ceremony or celebration. She had no right to the rituals of a dowered bride, and yet she missed them.

"Jacob was kind," Bilhah remembered. "He thought my tears were a sign of fear, so he held me like a child and gave me a woolen bracelet." It was nothing. No precious metal, or ivory, or anything of value. Just a woven braid made from leavings, the kind of thing shepherd boys make absentmindedly, sitting under a tree in the heat of the day, out of tufts of wool caught on brambles or blown to the ground. Jacob had twirled the brown, black, and cream-colored strands against his thigh until he had enough to plait into a braid.

He took the simple thing from his arm and cut it to fit hers. Such a sad little nothing of a bride price, but she wore it throughout her first year as Jacob's third wife, until it fell apart one day and she lost it without even knowing where. Thinking of her bracelet, Bilhah smiled and with her forefinger traced the place where a bit of string had tied her to Jacob.

"He comforted me with that poor gift without a word, and I stopped crying. I smiled into his face. And then, oh, I was so bold, I could hardly believe it was me. I put my hand upon his sex and laid his hand upon mine. He lifted my skirt and massaged my belly and my breasts. He buried his face between my thighs, and I almost laughed out loud at the shock of pleasure. When he entered me, it was as though I had fallen into a pool of water, it was as though the moon were singing my name. It was all I had hoped for.

"I slept in Jacob's long arms, cradled like a child for the first time since my mother held me, may her name be set in the stars. For that night alone, I loved Jacob."

Bilhah told all of this to Rachel. It was not easy for my beautiful aunt to hear it, but she insisted that Bilhah leave nothing out. And the younger sister repeated her story as often as Rachel asked to hear it, until the memory of Bilhah's consummation became Rachel's own memory and her sister's pleasure and gratitude became part of her own feelings for Jacob.

The day after Jacob knew Bilhah for the first time, he was called away to do business with a trader in Carchemish, a journey of two days. Bilhah suffered in his absence, for she was eager to lie with him again. Rachel suffered in the knowledge that Jacob had found happiness with Bilhah. Leah suffered because she felt so distant from her sisters' lives. Zilpah watched it all, said little, and sighed much.

Upon Jacob's return, he brought Rachel a beaded necklace and spent his first night with her. Leah was still nursing, so he called Bilhah to him again often during the next months, especially when Rachel was away attending a birth.

Jacob and his third wife spoke very little when they were together, but their bodies joined in straightforward postures, which yielded them both pleasure and release. "Jacob said I gave him peace," said Bilhah, with great satisfaction.

Bilhah conceived. Rachel greeted the news with kisses and rejoiced with her sister. As the months passed and her belly grew, Rachel coddled her and asked her to name every sensation, every twinge, every mood. Did Bilhah know at what moment life had taken root? Was the tiredness of pregnancy felt in her knees or in her eyes? Did she crave salt or sweet?

The two of them shared a blanket during Bilhah's pregnancy. The barren woman felt the slow swell of her sister's belly and the gathering heaviness of her breasts. She watched the flesh stretch in tan bands across the brown belly and thighs, and noticed the changing color of her nipples. As the child grew in Bilhah, draining her of color and energy, Rachel bloomed. She grew soft and round along with Bilhah, and the hollows that sadness had carved in her cheeks disappeared. She laughed and played with her nephews and the other children of the camp. She baked bread and made cheese without being asked. She lived so deeply inside Bilhah's pregnancy that during the ninth month, Rachel's ankles grew swollen, and when the time came for the baby to enter the world, Rachel called Inna to be midwife so that she alone could stand behind Bilhah during her travail and hold her and suffer with her.

Happily for Bilhah, the birth was as simple and quick as the pregnancy had been difficult. After a morning's worth of panting and groaning, she stood on the bricks while Rachel crouched around her. Bilhah's elbows rested on Rachel's splayed knees, and it was as if the two women shared a womb for the awful hour when the baby pushed his way out. Their faces strained and reddened together, and they cried out with a single voice when his head appeared. Inna said it was as though a two-headed woman had given birth and declared it one of the strangest things she had seen.

When the boy was delivered and the cord severed, Rachel held him first, her eyes streaming, for a very long time. Or so it seemed to Bilhah, who bit her tongue and waited for the moment she would embrace the first issue of her womb. Bilhah's eyes followed Rachel's every move as she wiped the blood from the baby's body and checked to see that he was whole and unblemished. Bilhah barely breathed as the moments passed and her arms remained empty, but she said nothing. By law, this son belonged to Rachel.

Years attending so many births had made Rachel's heart tender, and with a great sigh she placed the boy in Bilhah's arms, where he lifted his eyes to his mother's face and smiled into her eyes before he took her breast.

At that instant, Rachel woke from her dream, and saw that the baby was not her child. Her smile faded and her shoulders sagged and her hands clawed at her girlish breasts. Inna had told Rachel that if she let the baby suck there long enough, he would find milk within her and she could become his milk-mother. But Rachel had no faith in her body's ability to sustain life. Putting a child to nurse on an empty breast would cause suffering to her son, who was not hers at all but Bilhah's. Besides, Bilhah might sicken and even die if she did not empty her breasts, for she had seen that happen. And Rachel loved her sister. She hoped the baby at Bilhah's breast would be as good a man as his mother was a woman.

Rachel left Bilhah with her son and went to find Jacob. She told her husband that the baby's name was Dan, which means "judgment." To the woman who bore him, Dan sounded sweet, but to her in whose name he was borne, it had a bitter ring.

The sight of the baby in Bilhah's arms, day after day, shattered Rachel's confidence again. She was only the aunt, the bystander, the barren one. But now she did not rail against heaven or plague her sisters with temper. She sat, too unhappy to weep, under the acacia tree, sacred to Innana, where the birds gathered at dawn. She went to the asherah and prostrated herself before the wide-mouthed grinning goddess, and whispered, "Give me children or I will die."

Jacob saw her suffering and gathered her to him with the greatest tenderness. And after all the years, all the nights, all the miscarriages and broken hopes, Rachel found delight in his arms. "I really had no idea why Leah and Bilhah sought out Jacob's bed before those days," Rachel said. "I had always gone to his bed willingly enough, but mostly out of duty.

"But after Dan opened Bilhah's womb, somehow my

own passion finally matched Jacob's and I understood my sisters' willingness to lie with him. And then I was newly jealous for all the years that I had missed of the wild sweetness between lovers."

Rachel and Jacob spent many nights together exploring the new heat between them, and Rachel hoped again. Some midwives said that pleasure overheated the seed and killed it. But others claimed that babies only come when women smile. This was the tale she told Jacob to inspire his caresses.

During the last months of Bilhah's pregnancy, Zilpah went to Jacob's bed for the first time. She did not offer herself as Bilhah had, though she was at least five years older, as old as Leah, who had borne five live sons by that time.

Zilpah knew it would happen someday, and she was resigned to it. But unlike Bilhah, Zilpah would never ask. Leah would have to command it. Finally, she did.

"One night, when I was walking in the light of a full moon, she appeared before me," Zilpah said. "At first, I thought I was dreaming. My sister slept as heavily as Laban and never rose at night. Even her own babies had trouble rousing her. But there she was, in the stillness. We walked in the bright white light of the lady moon, hand in hand, for a long time. And again I wondered if this was really my sister or a ghost, because the woman beside me was silent, whereas Leah always had something to say.

"Finally, she spoke with careful words about the moon. She told me how much she loved the white light, and how she spoke to the moon and called to her by name every month. Leah said the moon was the only face of the goddess that seemed open to her because of the way the moon called forth the filling and emptying of her body.

"My sister was wise," said Zilpah. "She stopped and faced me and took both my hands in hers and asked, 'Are you ready to swallow the moon at last?'

"What could I say? It was my time."

Indeed, it was possible that she had waited too long, and Zilpah half hoped she was too old, at five and twenty, to bear. Age alone was no good augury. Rachel had been barren from her youth, despite all her efforts. And Leah, fertile as a watered plain, showed no sign of giving off. The only way to discover what the mother of life had in store for Zilpah was for her to go in to Jacob and become the least of his wives.

The next morning, Leah spoke to Jacob. Bilhah offered to put henna on Zilpah's hands, but she set her mouth and refused. That night she walked slowly to Jacob's tent, where he lay with her and knew her. Zilpah took no pleasure from Jacob's touch. "I did what was required of me," she said, with such a tone that no one dared ask her to say more.

She never complained of Jacob's attentions. He did his best to calm her fears, just as he had with his other wives. He called for her many times, trying to win her. He asked her to sing songs of the goddesses and brushed her hair. But nothing he did moved Zilpah. "I never understood my sisters' eagerness to lie with Jacob," she said, with a weary wave of her long hand. "It was a duty, like grinding grain—something that wears away at the body but is necessary so that life can go on.

"Mind you, I was not disappointed," she said. "It was nothing I expected to enjoy."

Zilpah conceived during Bilhah's pregnancy. And soon after Bilhah's Dan was born, it truly did appear as though Zilpah had swallowed the moon. On her slender frame, the belly looked huge and perfectly round. Her sisters teased her, but Zilpah only smiled. She was glad to be free from Jacob's attentions, for men did not lie with pregnant women. She gloried in her new body, and dreamed wonderful dreams of power and flight.

She dreamed of giving birth to a daughter, not a human child but a changeling of some kind, a spirit woman. Full-grown, full-breasted. She wore nothing but a girdle of string, in front and in back. She strode the earth in great steps, and her moon blood made trees grow everywhere she walked.

"I loved to go to sleep when I was with child," said Zilpah. "I traveled so far in my blankets those months."

But when her time came, the baby was slow to appear and Zilpah suffered. Her hips were too narrow, and labor lasted from sunset to sunset, for three days. Zilpah cried and wailed, sure that her daughter would die, or that she would be dead before she saw her girl, her Ashrat, for she had chosen her name already and told it to her sisters in case she did not survive.

It went hard with Zilpah. On the evening of the third day of her labor, she was all but dead from the pains, which, strong as they were, did not seem to bring the baby any closer to this world. Finally, Inna resorted to an untried potion she had bought from a <u>Canaanite</u> trader. She reached her hand all the way up to the stubborn door of Zilpah's womb and rubbed a strong, aromatic gum that did its work quickly, wrenching a shriek from Zilpah's throat, which by then was so hoarse from her travail that she sounded less like a woman than an animal caught in the fire. Inna whispered a fragment of an incantation in the name of the ancient goddess of healing.

"Gula, quicken the delivery
Gula, I appeal to you, miserable and distraught
Tortured by pain, your servant
Be merciful and hear this prayer."

Soon, Zilpah was up on the bricks, with Leah standing behind her, supporting the birth of the child conceived in her name. Zilpah had no more tears by the time Inna directed her to push. She was ashen and cold. She was half dead, and there was no strength even to scream when the baby finally came, tearing her flesh front and back.

It was not the hoped-for daughter, but a boy, long, thin, and black-haired. Leah hugged her sister and declared her lucky to have such a son, and lucky to be alive. Leah named him Gad for luck, and said, "May he bring you the moon and the stars and keep you safe in your old age."

But the rejoicing in the red tent was cut short because Zilpah cried out again. The pain had returned. "I am dying. I am dying," she sobbed, weeping for the son who would never know his mother. "He will live as I did," she wailed, "the orphan of a concubine, haunted by dreams of a cold, dead mother.

"Unlucky one," she whimpered. "Unlucky son of an unlucky mother."

Inna and Rachel crouched on either side of the despairing mother seeking the source of this new pain. Inna took Rachel's hand and placed it on Zilpah's belly, showing her a second child in the womb. "Don't give up yet, little mother," Inna said to Zilpah. "You will bear twins tonight. Didn't you dream of that? Not much of a priestess, is she?" She grinned.

The second baby came quickly, since Gad had opened the way. He fell out of his mother's womb like ripe fruit, another boy, also dark but much smaller than the first.

But his mother did not see him. A river of blood followed in his wake, and the light in Zilpah's eyes went out. Time and again Inna and Rachel packed her womb with wool and herbs to staunch the bleeding. They wet her lips with water and strong, honeyed brews. They sang healing hymns and burned incense to keep her spirit from flying out of the tent. But Zilpah lay on the blanket, not dead but not alive either, for eight days and more. She was not aware of the circumcision of Gad or her second son, whom Leah named Asher, for the goddess Zilpah loved. Leah nursed the boys, and so did Bilhah and one of the bondswomen.

After ten days Zilpah moaned and lifted her hands. "I dreamed two sons," she croaked. "Is it so?" They brought the babies to her, dark and thriving. And Zilpah laughed. Zilpah's laughter was a rare sound, but the names made her chuckle. "Gad and Asher. Luck and the goddess. It sounded like the name of a myth from the old days," she said. "And I was Ninmah, the exalted lady, who birthed it all."

Zilpah ate and drank and healed, though she could not nurse her sons. Her breasts had gone dry in her illness. But this was a sorrow she could bear. She had two sons, both fine and strong, and she did not regret her dream daughter. When they grew to boyhood and left her side, Zilpah sorrowed over the fact that she had no girl to teach. But when she held them in her arms, she tasted only the joy of mothers, the sweetest tears.

Inna told her that she should take care not to bear for at least two years, but Zilpah had no intention of going through such pain again. She had given her family two sons. She sought out Jacob one morning before he left for the pasture, and told him that another pregnancy would surely kill her. She asked that he remember this when he called a wife to his bed, and she never slept with Jacob again.

Indeed, Jacob had trembled when he learned that he had gotten twins upon her. He was one of two himself, and it had caused him nothing but grief. "Forget that they shared their mother's womb," he ordered. It was so, not because Jacob commanded it but because the two were so different. Gad, long and lean, with his flutes and drum; Asher, the short, wiry husbandman with his father's talent with animals.

Leah's next pregnancy also brought twin boys—Naphtali and Issachar. Unlike Zilpah's, though, these twins looked so much alike that, as children, not even their mother could always tell them apart. Only Bilhah, who could see every leaf on a tree in its own light, was never fooled by those two, who loved each other with a kind of quiet harmony that none of my other brothers knew.

Poor Bilhah. After Dan, all her babies—a boy and two girls—died before weaning. But she never let her sorrow poison her heart, and she loved the rest of us instead.

Jacob was now a man with four wives and ten sons, and his name was known among the men of the countryside. He was a good father and took his boys with him into the hills as soon as they were able to carry their own water, and he taught them the ways of sheep and goats, the secrets of good pasturage, the habits of long walking, the skills of sling and spear. There, too, far from the tents of their mothers, he told them the terrible story of his father, Isaac.

When Jacob and his sons stayed in the far pastures keeping watch where a jackal had been seen or simply to enjoy the cool night air of a summer month, he would tell his sons the story of how his grandfather, Abram, bound Isaac hand and foot, and then raised a knife above the boy's throat, to give El the sacrifice of his favorite son. El was the only god to whom Jacob bowed down—a jealous, mysterious god, too fearsome (he said) to be fashioned as an idol by human hands, too big to be contained by any place—even a place as big as the sky. El was the god of Abram, Isaac, and Jacob, and it was Jacob's wish that his sons accept this El as their god, too.

Jacob was a weaver of words, and he would catch his eager audience in the threads of his tale, telling of the glinting knife, Isaac's eyes wide with fright. The rescue came at the last possible moment, when the knife was at Isaac's throat, and a drop of blood trickled down his neck, just like the tears falling from Abram's brimming eyes. But then a fiery spirit stayed the old man's hand and brought a pure white ram to be sacrificed in Isaac's stead. Reuben and Simon, Levi and Judah would stare at their father's arm, stretched out against the starry night, and shudder to think of themselves on the altar.

"The god of my fathers is a merciful god," Jacob said. But when Zilpah heard the story from her sons, she said, "What kind of mercy is that, to scare the spit dry in poor Isaac's mouth? Your father's god may be great, but he is cruel."

Years later, when his grandsons finally met the boy of the story, by then an old man, they were appalled to hear how Isaac stuttered, still frightened by his father's knife.

Jacob's sons adored their father, and his neighbors respected his success. But he was uneasy. Laban owned everything he had attained—the flocks, the bondsmen and their families, the fruit of the garden, the wool for trade. Nor was Jacob alone in his resentment of Laban. Leah and Rachel, Bilhah and Zilpah chafed under the rule of their father, who seemed to grow more crude and arrogant as the years passed. He treated his own daughters like slaves, and cuffed their sons. He profited from the labor of their looms without a word of thanks. He leered at the bondswomen and took their beer as a bribe against his lust. He mistreated Ruti every day.

The four sisters spoke of these things in the red tent, which they always entered a day before the rest of the women in the camp. Perhaps their early years together when they were the only women in camp created a habit in their bodies that brought on the flow of blood some hours before the bondswomen. Or perhaps it was simply the need of their hearts to spend a day among themselves. In any event, the bondswomen did not complain, nor was it their place to say anything. Besides, Jacob's wives would always greet them with sweets as they entered to celebrate the new moon and rest on the straw.

Ruti said nothing, but her blackened eyes and her bruises reproached them. No older than Leah, Ruti had grown haggard in their midst. After the birth of her sons, Laban had treated her well—the tight-fisted goat had even brought her bangles to brighten her wrists and ankles. But then she gave off bearing and he began to hit her and call her names so ugly my mothers would not repeat them to me. Ruti's shoulders stooped with despair, and several of her teeth were broken from the force of Laban's fists. Even so, he continued to use her body for his own pleasure, a thought that made my mothers shudder.

For all their pity, Jacob's wives did not embrace Ruti. She was the mother of their sons' rivals, their material enemy. The bondswomen saw how the sisters kept themselves apart from her, and they followed suit. Even her own sons laughed at her and treated her like a dog.

Ruti, already alone, kept to herself. She became such a ragged, battered misery to look at that no one saw her. When she came to Rachel, desperate for help, she seemed more a ghost than a woman.

"Lady, I beg you. Give me the herbs to cast out the baby I carry," she whispered in a cold, flat hiss. "I would rather die than give him another son, and if it is a girl, I will drown her before she is old enough to suffer at his hands.

"Help me for the sake of your husband's sons," said Ruti, in a voice from the other side of the grave. "I know you will not do it for me. You hate me, all of you."

Rachel brought Ruti's words to her sisters, who listened in silence and were ashamed.

"Do you know how to do that?" asked Leah.

Rachel waved a hand, dismissing the question as beneath consideration. It was not a difficult matter, especially since Ruti was in the first month.

Bilhah's eyes blazed. "We are no better than he is to have let her suffer alone, to have given her no comfort, no help."

Zilpah turned to Rachel and asked, "When will you do it?"

"We must wait for the next new moon, when all the women come to us," Rachel answered. "Laban is too stupid to suspect anything. I don't think even the subtlest among them realizes what we know and do among ourselves, but it is better to be careful."

The sisters did not change in their apparent treatment of Ruti. They did not speak to her or show her any special kindness. But at night, when Laban snored, one of the four would find her, huddled on her filthy blanket in a far corner of the tent, and feed her broth or honeyed bread. Zilpah took on Ruti's suffering as her own. She could not bear the emptiness in her eyes, or the despair that hung about her like a fog from the world of the dead. She took to visiting her every night to whisper words of encouragement into Ruti's ears, but she only lay there, deaf to any hope.

Finally, the moon waned and all the women entered the red tent. Leah stood before the bondswomen and lied with a pure heart, "Ruti is unwell. Her courses are overdue, but her belly is hot and we fear a miscarriage tonight. Rachel will do everything she can, with herbs and incantations, to save the child. Let us care for our sister, Ruti."

But within a few minutes, it was clear to most of them that Rachel's ministrations were intended not to save the baby but to cast it out. They watched, from the far side of the red tent, where cakes and wine sat untouched, as Rachel mixed a black herbal brew, which Ruti drank in silence.

She lay still, her eyes closed. Zilpah muttered the names of Anath the healer and the ancient Gula, who attends women at childbirth, while Rachel whispered words of praise to Ruti, whose courage unfolded as the night wore on.

When the herbs began to work, causing great ripping cramps, Ruti made no sound. When the blood began to flow, clotted and dark, Ruti's lips did not part. As the hours passed, the blood ran and did not stop, and still she said nothing. Rachel packed Ruti's womb with wool many times, until finally it was over.

No man knew what happened that night. No child

blurted the secret, because none of the women ever spoke of it, not a word, until Zilpah told me the story. By then it was nothing but an echo from the grave.

My mother told me that after the birth of her twin sons, she decided to finish with childbearing. Her breasts were those of an old woman, her belly was slack, and her back ached every morning. The thought of another pregnancy filled her with dread, and so she took to drinking fennel to keep Jacob's seed from taking root again.

But then it happened that the supply of seeds ran low while Inna was far away in the north. Months passed and still she did not return with her pouches of herbs. Leah tried an old remedy—soaking a lock of wool in old olive oil and placing it at the mouth of her womb before lying with Jacob. But her efforts failed, and for the first time, the knowledge of life within her brought her low.

Leah did not wish to take this trouble to Rachel, whose hunger for her own baby had not diminished. The fertile wife had tried to spare her barren sister's feelings by keeping a respectful distance from her. They divided the duties of a chief wife. Leah had charge of the weaving and cooking, the garden and the children. Rachel—still lovely and slim-waisted—served her husband and waited upon traders who came to the camp. She looked after Jacob's needs and, her skills as a healer growing, saw to the pains and illnesses of men, women, and even beasts.

Births and the new moon brought the two women together inside the red tent. But Leah slept facing the western wall while Rachel hugged the east, and they spoke to each other only by way of their sisters: Leah through Zilpah, Rachel through Bilhah.

Now, Leah had no choice. Inna had not returned and Rachel was the only one who knew the herbs, the prayers, the proper massage. There was no one else to ask.

As Rachel left to attend a birth in a nearby camp, Leah made some excuse about fetching water and rushed her steps until she was at Rachel's side. Leah's cheeks burned and she cast her eyes downward as she asked her sister to help her as she had helped Ruti. Rachel surprised her with the gentleness of her answer.

"Do not do away with your daughter," she said. "You are carrying a girl."

"Then she will die," Leah answered, thinking of Rachel's miscarriages. (Inna had pronounced them all girls.) "And even if she lives, she will not know her mother, because I am nearly dead from bearing."

But Rachel argued for all of the sisters, who had long saved their treasures for a daughter. "We will do everything for you as you carry their girl. Leah," she said, using her sister's name for the first time in either woman's memory. "Please," she asked.

"Do as I say before I tell Zilpah," Rachel threatened mischievously. "She will make your life a misery of scorned goddesses if she discovers your plans."

Leah laughed and relented, for her wish for a daughter was still strong.

While I slept in my mother's womb, I appeared to her and to each of my aunties in vivid dreams.

Bilhah dreamed of me one night while she lay in Jacob's arms. "I saw you in a white gown of fine linen, covered with a long vest of blue and green beads. Your hair was braided and you carried a fine basket through a pasture greener than any I have ever seen. You walked among queens, but you were alone."

Rachel dreamed of my birth. "You appeared at your mother's womb with your eyes open and your mouth full of perfect little teeth. You spoke as you slithered out from between her legs, saying, 'Hello, mothers. I am here at last. Is there nothing to eat?' That made us laugh. There were hundreds of women attending your birth, some of them dressed in outlandish clothing, shocking colors, shorn heads. We all laughed and laughed. I woke in the middle of the night laughing."

My mother, Leah, said she dreamed of me every night. "You and I whispered to each other like old friends. You were very wise, telling me what to eat to calm my upset stomach, how to settle a quarrel between Reuben and Simon. I told you all about Jacob, your father, and about your aunties. You told me about the other side of the universe, where darkness and light are not separated. You were such good company, I hated to wake up.

"One thing bothered me about those dreams," said my mother. "I could never see your face. You were always behind me, just beyond my left shoulder. And every time I turned to catch a glimpse of you, you disappeared."

Zilpah's dream was not filled with laughter or companionship. She said she saw me weeping a river of blood that gave rise to flat green monsters that opened mouths filled with rows of sharp teeth. "Even so, you were unafraid," said Zilpah. "You walked upon their backs and tamed their ugliness, and disappeared into the sun."

I was born during a full moon in a springtime remembered for a plenitude of lambs. Zilpah stood on my mother's left side, while Bilhah supported her on the right. Inna was there, to be on hand for the celebration and to catch the afterbirth in her ancient bucket. But Leah had asked Rachel to be midwife and catch me.

It was an easy birth. After all the boys before me, I came quickly and as painlessly as birth can be. I was big—as big as Judah, who had been the biggest. Inna pronounced me "Leah's daughter," in a voice full of satisfaction. As with all of her babies, my mother looked into my eyes first and smiled to see that they were both brown, like Jacob's and those of all her sons.

After Rachel wiped me clean, she handed me to Zilpah, who embraced me, and then to Bilhah, who kissed me as well. I took my mother's breast with an eager mouth, and all the women of the camp clapped their hands for my mother and for me. Bilhah fed my mother honeyed milk and cake. She washed Leah's hair with perfumed water, and she massaged her feet.

While Leah slept, Rachel, Zilpah, and Bilhah took me out into the moonlight and put henna on my feet and hands, as though I were a bride. They spoke a hundred blessings around me, north, south, east, and west, to protect me against Lamashtu and the other baby-stealing demons. They gave me a thousand kisses.

In the morning, my mother began to count out two moon cycles in the red tent. After the birth of a boy, mothers rested from one moon to the next, but the birth of a birth-giver required a longer period of separation from the world of men. "The second month was such a delight," my mother told me. "My sisters treated us both like queens. You were never left lying upon a blanket for a moment. There were always arms to hold you, cuddle you, embrace you. We oiled your skin morning and night. We sang songs into your ears, but we did not coo or babble. We spoke to you with all our words, as though you were a grown sister and not a baby girl. And before you were a year old, you answered us without a trace of a baby's lisp."

As I was passed from my mother to one aunt after another, they debated my name. This conversation never ceased, and each woman argued for a favorite she had long hoped to give to a daughter of her own womb.

Bilhah offered Adahni, in memory of my grandmother Adah, who had loved them all. This led to a long session of sighing and remembering Adah, who would have been so delighted by all of her grandchildren. But Zilpah worried that such a name would confuse the demons, who might think Adah had escaped from the underworld and come after me.

Zilpah liked the name Ishara—which gave homage to the goddess and was easy to rhyme. She had plans for many songs in my honor. But Bilhah didn't like the sound of it. "It sounds like a sneeze," she said.

Rachel suggested Bentresh, a Hittite name she had heard from a trader's wife. "It sounds like music," she said.

Leah listened to them all, and when her sisters got too heated in their arguments about *her* daughter, threatened to call me Lillu, a name they all hated.

In the second full moon after my birth, Leah rejoined her husband and told Jacob my name. She told me that I picked it myself. "During my sixty days, I whispered every name my sisters suggested into your little ear. Every name I had ever heard, and even some I invented myself. But when I said 'Dinah,' you let the nipple fall from your mouth and looked up at me. So you are Dinah, my last-born. My daughter. My memory."

Joseph was conceived in the days following my birth. Rachel had gone to Jacob with the news that he had finally sired a healthy girl. Her eyes shone as she told him, and Jacob smiled to see how his barren wife took pleasure in Leah's baby. That night, after they had enjoyed each other in the gentle fashion of familiar couples, Rachel dreamed of her first son and woke up smiling.

She told no one when her moon blood failed to come. The many false starts and early losses haunted her, and she guarded her secret closely. She went to the red tent at the new moon and changed the straw as though she had soiled it. She was so slender that the slight thickening of her waist went unnoticed by everyone but Bilhah, who kept her own counsel.

At the fourth month, Rachel went to Inna, who told her that the signs looked good for this boy, and Rachel began to hope. She showed her swelling belly to her sisters, who danced in a circle around her. She put Jacob's hand on the hillock of her womb. The father of ten sons wept.

Rachel grew swaybacked. Her little breasts grew full and painful. Her perfect ankles swelled. But she found nothing but delight in the complaints of breeding women. She began to sing as she tended the cooking fires and took up her spindle. Her family was surprised at the sweetness of her voice, which they had never heard raised in song. Jacob slept with Rachel every night of her pregnancy, a shocking breach of manners and an incitement to demons. But he would not listen to warning, and Rachel basked in his attentions as she grew large.

In her eighth month, Rachel began to sicken. Her skin paled and her hair fell out. She could barely stand without falling into a faint. Fear swallowed her hope, and she called for Inna, who prescribed strong broths made from the bones of rams and bulls. She told Rachel to rest, and came to visit her friend as often as she could.

Inna came to deliver Rachel. The baby's feet were down and there was bleeding long before he appeared. Inna's efforts to turn the child caused Rachel terrible pain, and she cried out so pitifully that all the children of the camp burst into tears at the sound. Jacob sat on the bamah, staring at the face of the goddess, wondering whether he ought to make some offering to her, even though he had promised to worship his father's god only. He tore at the grass and held his head until he could stand the sounds of her screams no longer, and he went off to the high pasture until Rachel was delivered.

It was two days before Reuben was sent to bring him back. Two terrible days in which Leah and Zilpah and

Bilhah each bade Rachel goodbye, it seemed so certain that she would die.

But Inna did not give up. She gave Rachel every herb and every medicine in her pouches. She tried combinations that no herb weaver had used. She muttered secret prayers, though she was not initiated into the mysteries of magic words and incantations.

Rachel did not give up, but fought for a heart's desire denied for fifteen years. She battled like an animal, her eyes rolling, sweat pouring from her. Even after three days and three nights, she did not call for death to release her from the torment. "She was mighty to behold," said Zilpah.

Finally, Inna got the baby to turn. But the effort seemed to break something within Rachel, whose body was seized by a shudder that would not let go. Her eyes rolled up into her head and her neck tightened so that she faced backward. It was as though demons had taken possession of her body. Even Inna gasped.

Then it was over. Rachel's body was released from death's grasp, the baby's head appeared, and Rachel found the last of her strength to push him out.

He was small, with a big thatch of hair. A baby like all babies, wrinkled, homely, and perfect. Best of all, he was Rachel's. The tent fell silent as every woman wept grateful tears. Without a word, Inna cut the cord, and Bilhah caught the afterbirth. Leah cleaned Rachel, and Zilpah washed the baby. They sighed and wiped their eyes. Rachel would live to see her baby grow.

Rachel recovered slowly, but she could not give suck. Three days after Joseph's birth, her breasts grew hard and hot. Warm compresses eased her pain, but the milk

dried up. Leah, who was nursing me at the time, took
Joseph to her breast as well. Rachel's old anger at Leah
flared at that, but it vanished when she discovered that
Joseph was a fretful baby who screamed and squirmed
until he lay in his own mother's arms.

PART TWO

MY STORY

CHAPTER ONE

I am not certain whether my earliest memories are truly mine, because when I bring them to mind, I feel my mothers' breath on every word. But I do remember the taste of the water from our well, bright and cold against my milk teeth. And I'm sure that I was caught up by strong arms every time I stumbled, for I do not recall a time in my early life when I was alone or afraid.

Like every beloved child, I knew that I was the most important person in my mother's world. And most important not only to my mother, Leah, but to my mother-aunties as well. Although they adored their sons, I was the one they dressed up and dandled when the boys were wrestling in the dirt. I was the one who continued going to the red tent with them, long after I was weaned.

As a baby, Joseph was my constant companion, first my milk-brother and later my truest friend. At eight months he stood up and walked over to me in my favorite spot at the front of my mother's tent.

Though many months older, I was still unsteady on my feet, probably because my aunties liked to carry me. Joseph held out both his hands to me, and I stood up. My mother said that in return for showing me how to walk, I taught him to speak. Joseph liked to tell people that his first word was "Dinah," though Rachel assured me it was the word for *Mamma*, "Ema."

No one thought Rachel would bear another child after the awful time she had had with Joseph, so he and I received the treatment given to the final fruit of a chief wife. According to the custom of the old days, the youngest child inherited a mother's blessing, and one way or another, fathers usually followed suit. But Joseph and I were petted and spoiled also because we were the babies—our mothers' last-born, and our father's joy. We were also our older brothers' victims.

Age made two separate tribes among the children of Jacob. Reuben, Simon, Levi, and Judah were nearly men by the time I knew their names. They were often gone, tending to the herds with our father, and as a group, they had little use for us small ones. Reuben was, by nature, kind to children, but we avoided Simon and Levi, who laughed at us and teased Tali and Issa, the twins. "How do you know which of you is which?" Levi taunted. Simon was even worse: "If one of you dies, our mother won't mourn since she'll have one exactly the same." That always made Tali cry.

I thought I saw longing in the way Judah watched our games. He was far too old to play with us, but as the youngest of the older brothers he was the least among them and suffered for it. Judah often carried me on

his back and called me Ahatti, little sister. I thought of
him as my champion among the big boys.

At first, Zebulun was the leader of us younger ones,
and he might have been a bully had we not adored him
and obeyed him willingly. Dan was his lieutenant—
loyal and sweet as you'd expect of Bilhah's child. Gad
and Asher were wild, headstrong, and difficult playmates, but they were such wonderful mimics—mocking
Laban's lumbering walk and drink-slurred speech with
such wicked accuracy—we forgave them anything in
exchange for a performance. Naphtali, who was never
called anything but Tali, and Issachar, or Issa, tried to
lord it over me and Joseph because they were nearly two
years older. They would call us babies, but a minute
later they would join us on the ground, tossing a pebble
into the air to see how many other stones we could pick
up with the same hand. It was our favorite game until I
could pick up ten stones to their five. Then my brothers
declared it a game fit only for girls and never played
again.

By our sixth year, Joseph and I had taken charge of
the younger band, because we were the best at making up stories. Our brothers carried us from the well
to my mother's tent and bowed low before me, their
queen. They would pretend to die when Joseph, their
king, pointed a finger at them. We sent them out to do
battle with demons, and to bring us great riches. They
crowned our heads with garlands of weeds and kissed
our hands.

I remember the day that game ended. Tali and Issa
were doing my bidding, piling up little stones as an

altar in my honor. Dan and Zebulun were fanning us with leaves. Gad and Asher were dancing before us.

Then our older brothers happened by. Reuben and Judah smiled and walked on, but Simon and Levi stopped and laughed. "Look at how the babes lead the bigger boys by the nose! Wait until we tell our father that Zebulun and Dan are donkeys for the bare-behinds. He'll make them wait another two years before letting them come up to the high pasture with us." They did not stop mocking until Joseph and I were alone, abandoned by our playmates, who suddenly saw themselves with their brothers' cold eyes.

After that, Zebulun and Dan refused to do any more spinning for our mothers, and after much begging they were permitted to follow their older brothers into the hills. The two sets of twins—when they weren't pulling weeds from the garden or helping at the loom—played by themselves, and the four of them became a tribe of their own, dedicated to hunting games and wrestling matches.

Joseph and I turned more and more to each other, but it wasn't as much fun with just the two of us. Neither of us bent a knee to the other for the sake of a story, and Joseph had to contend with the taunts of our brothers, who abused him for playing with me at all. There were very few girls in our camp—the women joked that Jacob had poisoned the well against them. I tried to make friends with the few daughters of bondswomen, but I was either too old or too young for their games, and so by the time I could carry a water jar from the well, I started to think of myself as a member of my mother's circle.

Not that children were often left to their games. As soon as we were old enough to carry a few sticks of wood, we were put to work pulling weeds and insects from the garden, carrying water, carding wool, and spinning. I do not remember a time before my hand held a spindle. I remember being scolded for my clumsiness, for getting burrs in my wool, and for the unevenness of my string.

Leah was the best mother but she was not the best teacher. Skills came to her so easily that she could not understand how even a small child could fail to grasp something so simple as the turning of string. She lost patience with me often. "How is it that a daughter of Leah could have such unlucky fingers?" she said one day, looking at the tangle I had made of my work.

I hated her for those words. For the first time in my life, I hated my mother. My face grew hot as tears came to my eyes, and I threw a whole day's spinning into the dirt. It was a terrible act of waste and disrespect, and I think neither of us could believe that I had done it. In an instant, the sharp slap of her palm against my cheek cracked the air. I was far more shocked than hurt. Although my mother cuffed my brothers from time to time, it was the first time she had ever struck me.

I stood there for a long moment watching her face twist in pain over what she had done. Without a word I turned and ran to find Bilhah's lap, where I wept and moaned about the terrible wrong that had been done to me. I told my aunt everything that lay heavy upon my heart. I wept over my useless fingers, which would never get the wool to twist evenly or the spindle to drop

and turn smoothly. I was afraid that I had shamed my
mother by being so awkward. And I was ashamed of
the hatred I suddenly felt toward the one I loved so completely.

Bilhah stroked my hair until I stopped crying and fed
me a piece of bread dipped in sweet wine. "Now I will
show you the secret of the spindle," she said, putting a
finger to my lips. "This is something your grandmother
taught me, and now it is my turn to show you."

Bilhah put me on her lap, for which I was nearly
too large. Her arms were barely long enough to reach
around me, but there I sat, a baby once again, embraced
in safety while Bilhah whispered the story of Uttu into
my ear.

"Once, before women knew how to turn wool into
string and string into cloth, people roamed the
earth naked. They burned by day and shivered
by night, and their babies perished.

"But Uttu heard the weeping mothers, and took
pity on them. Uttu was the daughter of Nanna,
god of the moon, and of Ninhursag, the mother
of the plains. Uttu asked her father if she might
teach the women how to spin and weave so their
babies would live.

"Nanna scoffed and said that women were
too stupid to remember the order of cutting,
washing, and combing of wool, the building of
looms, the setting of woof and warp. And their
fingers were too thick to master the art of spinning. But because Nanna loved his daughter
he let her go.

"Uttu went first to the east, to the land of the Green River, but the women there would not put aside their drums and flutes to listen to the goddess.

"Uttu went to the south, but she arrived in the middle of a terrible drought, when the sun had robbed the women of their memories. 'We need nothing but rain,' they said, forgetting the months when their children had died of cold. 'Give us rain or go away.'

"Uttu traveled north, where the fur-clad women were so fierce they tore off a breast to ready themselves for the endless hunt. Those women were too hotheaded for the slow arts of string and loom.

"Uttu went to the east, where the sun rises, but found the men had stolen the women's tongues and they could not answer for themselves.

"Since Uttu did not know how to speak to men, she came to Ur, which is the womb of the world, where she met the woman called Enhenduanna, who wished to learn.

"Uttu took Enhenduanna on her lap and wrapped her great arms around Enhenduanna's small arms, and laid her golden hands around Enhenduanna's clay hands, and guided her left hand and guided her right hand.

"Uttu dropped a spindle made of lapis lazuli, which turned like a great blue ball floating in the golden sky, and spun string made of sunlight. Enhenduanna fell asleep in Uttu's lap.

"As Enhenduanna slept, she spun without

seeing or knowing, without effort or fatigue. She spun until there was enough string to fill the entire storehouse of the great god Nanna. He was so pleased that he permitted Uttu to teach Enhenduanna's daughters how to make pottery and bronze, music and wine.

"After that, the people could stop eating grass and drinking water and ate bread and drank beer instead. And their babies, swaddled in wool blankets, no longer died of the cold but grew up to offer up sacrifice to the gods."

While Bilhah told me the story of Uttu, she put her nimble hands around my clumsy ones. I smelled the soft, loamy musk that clung to my youngest auntie and listened to her sweet, liquid voice and forgot all about the ache in my heart. And when her story was over, she showed me that the string on my spindle was as evenly made and strong as Leah's own handiwork.

I kissed Bilhah a hundred kisses and ran to show my mother what I had done. She embraced me as though I had returned from the dead. There was no more slapping after that. I even came to enjoy the task of twisting clouds of unruly wool into the fine, strong threads that became my family's clothing and blankets and trade goods. I learned to love the way that my mind wandered where it would while my hands followed their own course. Even when I was old and my spinning was of linen rather than wool, I recalled my auntie's perfume and the way she pronounced the name of the goddess, Uttu.

* * *

I told Joseph the story of Uttu the weaver. I told him the tale of the great goddess Innana's journey to the land of the dead, and of her marriage to the shepherd king, Dumuzi, whose love ensured an abundance of dates and wine and rain. These were stories I heard in the red tent, told and retold by my mothers and the occasional trader's wife who called the gods and goddesses by unfamiliar names and sometimes supplied different endings to ancient tales.

Joseph, in turn, told me the story of Isaac's binding and the miracle of his release, and of our great-grandfather Abram's meetings with messengers from the gods. He told me that our father, Jacob, spoke with the El of his fathers, morning and evening, even when he made no sacrifice. Our father said that the formless, faceless god with no other name than god came to him by night, in his dreams, and by day, in solitude only, and that Jacob was sure that the future of his sons would be blessed by this One.

Joseph described to me the wondrous grove of terebinth trees in Mamre, where our great-grandmother spoke to her gods every evening, and where someday our father would take us to pour a libation in the name of Sarai. Those were the stories Joseph heard from Jacob, sitting among our brothers while the sheep and goats grazed. I thought the women's stories were prettier, but Joseph preferred our father's tales.

Our talk was not usually so lofty. We shared the secret of sex and begetting, and laughed, aghast, to think of our parents behaving like the dogs in the dust. We gossiped endlessly about our brothers, keeping close watch on the rivalry between Simon and

Levi, which could flare into blows over something as trivial as the placement of a staff against a tree. There was an ongoing contest, too, between Judah and Zebulun—the two oxen among the brothers—but theirs was a good-natured battle to see which was the stronger, and each would applaud his brother's ability to lift great rocks and carry full-grown ewes across a meadow.

Joseph and I watched as Zilpah's sons became my mother's champions, for Gad and Asher were embarrassed by their own mother's eccentricities. Her inability to make decent bread sent them to Leah's tent. They did not understand or value Zilpah's skill at the loom, and of course they had no way of knowing her talent for storytelling. So they carried their little trophies—flowers, brightly colored stones, the remains of a bird's nest—to my mother's lap. She would tousle their hair and feed them and they would strut like little heroes.

On the other hand, Tali and Issa, the twins of Leah's own womb, were not so fond of her. They hated looking so much alike and blamed their mother for it. They did everything they could to distinguish themselves from each other and were almost never seen together. Issa attached himself to Rachel, who seemed charmed by his attentions and let him carry and fetch for her. Tali became fast friends with Bilhah's Dan, and the two of them liked to sleep side by side in Bilhah's tent, hanging on the words of their big brother Reuben, who was also drawn to the peace and stillness that enveloped my aunt.

Leah tried to bribe Issa and Tali back to her with

sweets and extra bread, but she was far too busy with the work of her family to pine for attentions from two of her many sons. And she did not suffer for lack of love. When I caught her watching one of her boys walking toward another mother's tent at nightfall, I would pull at her hand. Then she would lift me up so that our eyes could meet, and kiss me on one cheek and then on the other, and then on the tip of my nose. This always made me laugh, which would in turn always bring a warm smile to my mother's face. One of my great secrets was knowing I had the power to make her smile.

My world was filled with mothers and brothers, work and games, new moons and good food. The hills in the distance held my life in a bowl filled with everything I could possibly want.

I was a child when my father led us away from the land of the two rivers, south to the country of his birth. Young as I was, I knew why we were going. I could feel the hot wall of anger between my father and my grandfather. I could almost see the heat between them on the rare occasions they sat together.

Laban resented my father for his accomplishments with the herds, and for his sons who were so plentiful and so much more skillful than his own two boys. Laban hated the fact that he owed his success to the husband of his daughters. His mouth turned sour whenever Jacob's name was mentioned.

As for my father, although he was the one who caused the flocks to multiply, the camp to fill with bondsmen, and the traders to make their way to our tents, he was never more than Laban's servant. His wages were meager, but he was thrifty and clever with his little store of goods, and he had been careful with the breeding of his own small flock of brindled goats and gray sheep.

Jacob hated Laban's sloth and the way he and his sons squandered his own good work. When the older boy, Kemuel, left his post guarding the rutting goats one spring, the best of them died from the battle between the strongest males. When Beor drank too much wine and slept, a hawk made off with a newborn kid Jacob had marked for sacrifice.

The worst was when Laban lost Jacob's two best dogs—his smartest and his best loved. The old man had gone for a three-day trading journey to Carchemish and, without asking, had taken the dogs to tend a herd so small a boy could have managed on his own. While Laban was in town, he sold them both for a pittance, which he then lost in a game of chance.

The loss of his dogs put my father in a rage. The night Laban returned to camp, I heard their shouts and curses even as I fell asleep. Afterward, my father's scowl was impenetrable. His fists did not unclench until he had sought out Leah and poured out the details of this latest grievance.

My mother and aunts had nothing but sympathy for Jacob. Their loyalty to Laban had never been strong, and as the years passed, they piled up reasons to despise him—laziness, deceitfulness, the arrogance of his thick-headed sons, and his treatment of Ruti, which only worsened as the years passed.

A few days after the fight about the dogs, Ruti came to my mother and threw herself on the ground.

"I am lost," she cried, a sad puddle of a woman in the dust. Her hair was loose and covered with ashes as though she had just buried her own mother.

Laban had lost more than his coins in that Carchemish game. He had gambled away Ruti as well, and now a trader had arrived to claim her as his slave. Laban sat in his tent and refused to come out and acknowledge what he had done to the mother of his sons, but the trader had his walking staff as a bond, and his overseer as a witness. Ruti put her forehead to the ground and begged Leah for help.

Leah listened and then turned to spit on her father's name. "The backside of a donkey has more merit than Laban," she said. "My father is a snake. He is the putrefied offal of a snake."

She put down the jug of milk she was working into curd, and with heavy steps marched to the near pasture where my father was still brooding about his dogs. My mother was so deep in her thoughts she did not seem to notice that I followed her.

Leah's cheeks turned red as she approached her husband. And then she did something extraordinary. Leah got down on her knees and, taking Jacob's hand, kissed his fingers. Watching my mother submit like this was like seeing a sheep hunting a jackal or a man nursing a baby. My mother, who never wanted for words, nearly stuttered as she spoke.

"Husband, father of my children, beloved friend," she said. "I come to plead a case without merit, for pure pity's sake. Husband," she said, "Jacob," she whispered, "you know I place my life in your keeping only and that my father's name is an abomination to me.

"Even so, I come to ask that you redeem my father's woman from the slavery into which he has sold her. A man from Carchemish has come to claim Ruti, whom Laban staked in his game of chance as though she were an animal from the flock or a stranger among us, and not the mother of his sons.

"I ask you to treat her better than her own husband. I ask you to act as the father."

Jacob frowned at his wife's request, although in his heart he must have been pleased that she addressed him not only as her husband but as leader of her family as well. He stood above Leah, whose head was bowed, and looked down on her tenderly. "Wife," he said, and took her hands to raise her up. "Leah." Their eyes met and she smiled.

I was shocked. I had come to watch Ruti's story unfold, but I discovered something else altogether. I saw the heat between my mother and her husband. I saw that Jacob could cause the glow of assent and happiness that I thought only I could summon from Leah.

My eyes opened for the first time upon the fact that my father was a man. I saw that he was not only tall but also broad-shouldered and narrow in the waist. Although by then he must have passed his fortieth summer, his back was straight and he still had most of his teeth and a clear eye. My father was handsome, I realized. My father was worthy of my mother.

Yet I found no consolation in this discovery. As they moved back to the tents, Leah and Jacob walked side by side, their heads nearly touching as she whispered the ransom that Jacob could collect from among his wives to redeem Ruti: honey and herbs, a stack of copper bangles, a bolt of linen and three of wool. He listened silently, nodding from time to time. There was no room for me between them, no need for me. My mother's eyes were full of Jacob. I did not matter to her the way she mattered to me. I wanted to cry, but I realized that I was too old for that. I would be a woman soon and I would have to learn how to live with a divided heart.

Miserable, I followed as my parents entered the circle of tents. Leah fell silent and resumed her place behind her husband. She fetched a jug of her strongest beer to help Jacob soften the trader's resolve. But the man had seen that though she was worn out and homely, Laban's woman was neither harelipped nor lame, as her price had led him to believe. And he was shrewd enough to notice that his presence had caused a stir. He smelled his advantage, which meant it took all of the women's treasures and one of Jacob's pups before the trader forgave the debt and left without Ruti. Soon, all the women of the camp knew what had happened, and for weeks afterward, Jacob ate like a prince.

Laban never spoke of how Jacob ransomed his wife. He only became fouler in his use of Ruti, whose eyes seemed permanently blackened after that. Her sons, following their father's pattern, showed their mother no respect. They carried no water for her cooking pot and brought her no game from their hunts. She crept around her men in silent service.

Among the women, Ruti spoke only of my mother's kindness. She became Leah's shadow, kissing her hands and her hem, sitting as close to her savior as she could. The ragged woman's presence did not please

Leah, who occasionally lost patience with her. "Go to your tent," she said when Ruti got underfoot. But Leah always regretted rebuking Ruti, who cringed at a single cross word from my mother. After she sent her away, Leah sought her out and sat down beside the poor, wasted soul and let herself be kissed and thanked, again and again.

CHAPTER TWO

In the days following Ruti's redemption, Jacob began to plan our departure in earnest. During his nights with Leah and during his nights with Rachel, he spoke of his longing to leave Laban's tents and return to the land of his father. Jacob told Bilhah that his restlessness consumed his peace and that he slept badly. Jacob found Zilpah on a night when sleeplessness chased them both, separately, to the whispering comfort of the great terebinth that stood by the altar. Even on still, airless nights, breezes hid among the broad flat leaves of Zilpah's tree. Jacob told his fourth wife that his god had appeared to him and said that it was time to leave the land of the two rivers. It was time to take his wives and his sons and the wealth that he had built up with his hands.

Jacob told Zilpah that his dreams had become ferocious. Night after night, fiery voices called him back to Canaan, to the land of his father. Fierce as his dreams were, they were joyful, too. Rebecca shone like the sun and Isaac smiled a blessing. Even his brother no longer threatened, but appeared as a huge, ruddy bull that welcomed Jacob to ride upon his wide back. And it seemed Jacob had no need to fear his brother anymore, for traders from Canaan had brought news that Esau had become a prosperous herdsman with many sons of his own, and a reputation for generosity.

In their day alone in the red tent, Jacob's wives spoke among themselves about their husband's dreams and plans. Rachel's eyes shone at the prospect of moving to the south. She was the most traveled among them, having attended at births throughout the hills, to Carchemish and once to the city of Haran itself. "Oh, to see great mountains, and a real city," she said. "Marketplaces filled with fine goods and fruits whose names we do not even know! We will meet faces from the four corners. We will hear the music of silver timbrels and golden flutes."

Leah was not so eager to discover the new worlds beyond the valley that had given her life. "I am content with the faces I see around me here," she said, "but I would dearly love to be free of Laban's stench. We will go, of course. But I will leave with regret."

Bilhah nodded. "I will grieve to leave Adah's bones. I will miss seeing the sun rise on the place where I gave birth to my son. I will mourn the passing of our youth. But I am ready. And our sons are wild to be gone from here."

Bilhah gave voice to a truth that had gone unspoken. There was not enough room for so many sons to make their way in Haran, where every hillock had been claimed for many generations. There was no land in the country of their mothers. If the family did not leave together, the women would soon break their hearts watching as their sons turned against each other or disappeared in search of their own paths.

Zilpah's breath grew louder and more uneven as her sisters turned their faces to the future. "I cannot go," she burst out. "I cannot leave the holy tree, which is the source of my power. Or the bamah, which is soaked in my offerings. How will the gods know where I am if I am not here to serve them? Who will protect me? Sisters, we will be beset by demons."

She was wide-eyed. "This tree, this place, this is where *she* is, my little goddess, Nanshe." The sisters sat up to hear Zilpah speak the name of her own deity, something done only on a deathbed. Their sister felt herself at the end of hope, and her voice was choked with tears as she said, "You too, sisters. All of your named gods abide here. This is the place where we are known, where we know how to serve. It will be death to leave. I know it."

There was silence as the others stared. Bilhah spoke first. "Every place has its holy names, its trees and high places," she said, in the calm voice a mother takes to a frightened child. "There will be gods where we go." But Zilpah would not meet Bilhah's eyes, and only shook her head from side to side. "No," she whispered.

Leah spoke next. "Zilpah, we are your protection. Your family, your sisters, are the only surety against hunger, against cold, against madness. Sometimes I wonder if the gods are dreams and stories to while away cold nights and dark thoughts." Leah grabbed her sister by the shoulders. "Better to put your trust in my hands and Jacob's than in stories made out of wind and fear."

Zilpah shrank under her sister's hands and turned away. "No," she said.

Rachel listened to Leah's sensible blasphemy in wonder and spoke, picking words for thoughts she discovered only as she gave them voice. "We can never answer your fear with proof, Zilpah. The gods are always silent. I know that women in travail find strength and comfort in the names of their gods. I have seen them struggle beyond all hope at the sound of an incantation. I have seen life spared at the last moment, for no other reason than that hope.

"But I know too that gods do not protect even the kindest, most pious women from heartbreak or death. So Bilhah is right. We will take Nanshe with us," she said, naming Zilpah's beloved goddess of dreams and singers. "We will take Gula, too," naming the goddess of healing, to whom Rachel made offerings. And then, as the idea grew in her mind, Rachel blurted, "We will take all of the teraphim from our tents and carry them into Canaan with our husband and our children.

"They will do us no harm, surely," said Rachel, speaking faster and faster as the plan formed in her mind. "If they are in our keeping, they will do Laban no good," she added slyly. Bilhah and Leah laughed nervously at the idea of Laban stripped of his sacred figures. The old man consulted the statues when he had any choice to make, stroking his favorites absentmindedly, for hours at a time. Leah said they soothed him the way a full breast soothed a cranky baby.

To leave with the teraphim was to incite Laban's

wrath. Even so, Rachel had some claim to them. In the old days, when the family had lived in the city of Ur, it was the unquestioned right of the youngest daughter to inherit all the holy things. Those ways were no longer held in universal respect, and Kemuel could claim the teraphim as part of an older son's birthright with just as much authority.

The sisters sat in silence, considering Rachel's bold idea. Finally Rachel spoke. "I will take the teraphim and they will be a source of power for us. They will be a sign of our birthright. Our father will suffer as he has made others suffer. I will not speak of this again."

Zilpah wiped her eyes. Leah cleared her throat. Bilhah stood up. It had been decided.

I barely took a breath. I was afraid that if they remembered me, I would be sent out of the tent. I sat still between my mother's right hand and Bilhah's left hand, amazed at what I had heard.

Rachel was loyal to Gula, the healer. Bilhah's grain offerings were made to Uttu, the weaver. Leah had a special feeling for Ninkasi, the brewer of beer, who used a brewing vat made of clear lapis lazuli and a ladle made of silver and gold. I thought of the gods and goddesses as aunts and uncles who were bigger than my parents and able to live inside the ground or above the earth as they liked. I imagined them deathless, odorless, forever happy, strong, and interested in everything that happened to me. I was frightened to hear Leah, the wisest of women, wondering if these powerful friends might be nothing but stories told to calm the nightmares of children.

I shuddered. My mother put her hand on my cheek

to feel for fever, but I was cool to her touch. Later that night I awoke screaming and sweating in a terror of falling, but she came to me and lay down beside me, and the warmth of her body comforted me. Secure in the knowledge of her love, I began to cross over into sleep, then I roused for a moment thinking I heard Rachel's voice saying, "Remember this moment, when your mother's body heals every trouble of your soul." I looked around but my auntie was nowhere nearby.

It must have been a dream.

Three days later, Leah walked to the rocky pasture in the west to tell Jacob that his wives were ready to go with him to the land of his birth. I followed after her, carrying some bread and beer for my father. I was not entirely pleased at being pressed into service on such a warm day.

As I came over the rise that separated our camp from the grazing, I was stopped by a scene of perfect wonder. Many of the ewes were heavy with lambs and barely moved in the gathering heat. The rising sun summoned the clover's scent. Only the bees made a sound under the brazen blue banner of sky.

I stopped as my mother walked ahead. The world seemed so perfect, so complete, and yet so impermanent that I nearly wept. I would have to tell Zilpah about this feeling, and ask if she knew a song for it. But then I realized that something in the universe had shifted. Something important had changed. I searched the horizon; the sky was still clear, the clover still pungent, the bees buzzed.

I noticed that my mother and my father were not

alone. Leah stood facing her husband. By her side was Rachel.

The two women had made a kind of peace years earlier. They did not work together or consult with each other. They did not sit next to each other in the red tent, or address each other directly. And they were never in their husband's presence at the same time. Yet now the three stood, in plain sight, talking like old friends. The women had their backs to me.

The conversation ended as I approached. My mother and aunt turned away from Jacob and, upon seeing me, replaced their solemn expressions with the false smiles that adults show children from whom they wish to hide something. I did not return their smiles. I knew they had been talking of leaving. I placed my father's food and drink at his feet and had turned to follow Leah and Rachel back to the tents when Jacob my father spoke.

"Dinah," he said. It was the first time I remember hearing my name in his mouth. "Thank you, girl. May you always be a comfort to your mothers." I looked into his face, and he smiled a real smile at me. But I did not know how to smile at my father or answer him, so I turned to run after my mother and Rachel, who had already begun the walk back to the tents. I slipped my hand into Leah's and peeked back to look at Jacob once more, but he had already turned away from me.

Jacob began to negotiate for our departure that evening. As night fell, and for many nights afterward, the women lay down on their beds with the sounds of men's voices loud in their ears. Laban was perfectly willing to see Jacob gone with his daughters and the grandsons who ate too much and respected him too little. But the old man hated to think that Jacob might leave a rich man.

During the long nights of shouting, Laban sat between his sons, Kemuel and Beor. The three of them drank beer and wine and yawned into Jacob's face, and ended their conversations before anything could be settled.

Jacob sat between his oldest sons, Reuben and Simon, and touched no drink stronger than barley beer. Behind him stood Levi and Judah. The seven younger boys stood outside the tent, straining to hear what was said. Joseph told me what he overheard, and I repeated everything to my mothers. But I did not tell Joseph about the whispered conversations among the women. I did not report their hoarding of hard bread, or how they had taken to sewing herbs into the hems of their garments. I knew better than to breathe of Rachel's plan to carry off the teraphim.

Night after night, Laban argued that he owed Jacob nothing more than the meager dowries he'd bestowed upon Leah and Rachel, which would have left my father without so much as the tents over our heads. Then, in a great show of generosity, he offered twenty head of sheep, and twenty goats—one of each kind for every year of Jacob's service, which had enriched Laban beyond his dreams.

Jacob, for his part, claimed the right of any overseer, which would have given him a tenth of the herds, and the pick of them, too. He demanded his wives' personal

property, which amounted to a good pile of grindstones
and spindles, looms and jugs, jewelry and cheeses. He
reminded Laban that his tents, his flocks, and the bondsmen in his debt had come to him through the work of
Jacob's hands. He threatened to seek justice from the
tribunal at Haran, but that only made Laban sneer. He
had gambled and drunk deeply with the town fathers
for many years and had no doubt whose side they
would take.

Late one night, after weeks of fruitless talk, Jacob
found the words that moved Laban's heart. The husband
of Leah and Rachel, the father of the sons of Zilpah and
Bilhah, fixed Laban with his eye and threatened that the
god of his fathers would not look kindly on one who
swindled the anointed of his tribe. Jacob said that his
god had come to him in a dream and spoken to him and
told him to go with his wives and his sons and his flocks
in abundance. Jacob's god had said that anyone who
tried to thwart him would suffer in his body, in his
flocks, and in his sons.

This troubled the old man, who shivered before the
power of any god. When Jacob invoked the god of his
fathers, the smirk dropped from Laban's lips. Jacob's
success with the flocks, the health of his eleven sons, the
loyalty of the bondsmen to him, and even the prowess
of his dogs—all this signaled that Jacob was blessed
by heaven. Laban remembered all the years of excellent
sacrifice that Jacob had made to his god, and the old
man reckoned that El must be well pleased by so much
devotion.

The next day, Laban shut himself up with his
household gods and was not seen until evening, when

he called for Jacob. From the moment Jacob faced his father-in-law, he could see that the advantage had shifted. He began to bargain in earnest.

"My father," he said, false honey on his tongue, "because you have been good to me, I wish to take only the animals that are brindled and spotted—the ones whose wool and hides will bring me less at market. You will maintain the purebloods of the herds. I will go out from your house poor but grateful."

Laban sensed a trick in Jacob's offer but he couldn't divine the benefit. Everyone knew that the darker animals did not produce wool that spun white, or skins that tanned evenly. What Laban did not know was that the "poorer" beasts were hardier and healthier than the animals that yielded the fancy wool and the pretty skins. The brindled ewes dropped twins more often than not, and most of their offspring were females, which meant more cheese. The hair of his mottled goats was especially oily, which made for a stronger rope. But these were Jacob's secrets, which he had learned during his years with the herds. This was knowledge that Laban's laziness had cost him.

Laban said, "So be it," and the men drank wine to seal the agreement. Jacob would go with his wives and his sons, and with the brindled and spotted flocks, which numbered no more than sixty goats and sixty sheep. There would have been more livestock, but Jacob traded for two of the bondsmen and their women. In exchange for a donkey and an ancient ox, Jacob agreed to leave two of his dogs, including the best of the herders.

All of the household goods of Leah and Rachel were

Jacob's to take, as well as the clothing and jewelry worn by Zilpah and Bilhah. Jacob claimed his sons' cloaks and spears, two looms and twenty-four minas of wool, six baskets of grain, twelve jugs of oil, ten skins of wine, and water skins, one for each person. But that was only the official reckoning, which did not take into account my mothers' cleverness.

They decided upon a date for our departure, in three months' time. While that seemed an eternity when it was first announced, the weeks passed quickly. My mothers set about collecting, discarding, packing, sorting, trading, washing. They devised sandals for the journey and baked loaves of hard bread. They hid their best jewelry deep inside the grain baskets, in case thieves accosted us on the road. They scoured the hills for herbs to fill up their pouches.

Had they chosen to, my mothers could have stripped the garden bare. They could have taken every onion bulb, dug up every buried store of grain, and emptied every beehive within walking distance. But they took only what they considered rightly theirs and nothing more. They did this not out of respect for Laban, but for the bondswomen and their children who would be left behind.

Sent to fetch and carry, I worked hard too. No one petted me or fussed over my hair. No one smiled into my face or praised my spinning. I felt misused and ignored, but no one noticed when I brooded, so I stopped feeling sorry for myself and did as I was told.

It might have been a joyous time had it not been for Ruti, who, in the last weeks of our preparations, lost all heart. She took to sitting in the dust before Leah's tent, a graven image of despair forcing everyone to step around her. Leah crouched down and tried to persuade Ruti to move, to come inside her tent and eat something, to take comfort. But Ruti was past comfort. Leah suffered for the poor woman, who was no older than she, yet whose teeth were gone and who shuffled like a crone. But there was nothing to be done, and after several attempts at coaxing her out of her misery, my mother stood up and moved on.

On the night before the last new moon we spent in the land of the two rivers, the wives of Jacob gathered quietly in the red tent. The sisters sat, letting the three-cornered cakes sit untouched in the basket before them. Bilhah said, "Ruti will die now." Her words hung in the air, unchallenged and true. "One day, Laban will hit her too hard or she will simply waste away from sorrow."

Zilpah sighed into the silence and Leah wiped her eyes. Rachel stared at her hands. My mother pulled me onto her lap, a place that I had outgrown. But I sat there and let her baby me, and enjoyed her thoughtless caresses.

The women burned a portion of their lunar cake in offering as they did for every new moon, as they did every seventh day. But they sang no songs of thanksgiving, nor did they dance.

The next day, the bondswomen joined Jacob's wives for the moon days, but it was more like a funeral than a feast. No one asked the pregnant woman to recount her symptoms. No one spoke of the exploits of her son. The women did not braid one another's hair or rub one another's feet with oil. The sweet cakes went untouched except by babies who wandered in and out, seeking their mothers' breasts and laps.

Of all the bondswomen, only Zibatu and Uzna would be going to Canaan with my mothers. The others would stay behind with their husbands. It was the end of a long sisterhood. They had held one another's legs in childbirth and suckled one another's babies. They had laughed in the garden and sung harmonies for the new moon. But those days were ending and each woman sat with her own memories, her own loss. For the first time, the red tent became a sad place, and I sat outside until I was tired enough to sleep.

Ruti did not appear in the tent. Morning came, and evening, and still she did not come. As the sun rose on the second day, my mother sent me to look for her. I asked Joseph if our grandfather's wife had made bread that morning. I asked Judah if Ruti was anywhere to be found. I asked my brothers and the daughters of the bondswomen, but no one could remember seeing Ruti. No one could recall. By then misery had made her nearly invisible.

I went to the top of the hill where I had been so happy a few months ago, but now the sky was dull and the land appeared gray. I scanned the horizon and saw no one. I walked to the well but I was alone. I climbed the low branches of a tree at the far edge of the near pasture, but I did not see Ruti.

On the way back to tell my mother that she was nowhere to be found, I came upon her. She was lying in the side of a dry wadi, a desolate place where stray lambs sometimes wandered and broke their legs. At first I thought Ruti was asleep on her back, lying against the steep slope. As I walked closer I could see that her eyes were open, so I called out to her, but she made no move to answer me.

That was when I saw that her mouth was slack and that there were flies at the corners of her eyes and on her wrist, which was black with blood. Carrion birds circled above.

I had never seen a corpse before. My eyes filled with Ruti's face, which was no longer Ruti's face but a piece of blue slate bearing traces of a face I remembered. She did not look sad. She did not look pained. She looked nothing but empty. I stared, trying to understand where Ruti had gone. And although I didn't realize it, I was holding my breath.

I might never have moved from that spot had Joseph not appeared behind me. Rachel had sent him out looking for Ruti, too. He walked past me and crouched down beside the body. He blew gently into her fixed eyes, touched her cheek with his finger, and then placed his right hand upon her eyes to close them. I was amazed at my brother's courage and calm.

But then Joseph shuddered and jumped back as though he'd been bitten by a snake. He ran to the bottom of the wadi, down to where water had once flowed and where flowers must have blossomed. Falling to his knees, Joseph retched into the dry bed. With great sobs, he knelt and heaved and coughed. When I walked over to him, he lurched to his feet and motioned me to keep away.

"Go back and tell them," I whispered. "I'll stay here and keep the vultures away." I regretted my words the moment they were out of my mouth. Joseph didn't bother to answer, but bolted as though a wolf were pursuing him.

I turned away from the body, but I could not shut out the sound of the flies at her wrist and the bloody knife that lay by her side. The vultures flapped and squawked. The wind cut through my tunic, and I shivered.

I walked to the top of the wadi and tried to think kind thoughts about Ruti. But all I could remember was the fear in her eyes, the dirt in her hair, the sour smell of her body, the defeated crouch. She had been a woman just as my mother was a woman, and yet she was a creature totally unlike my mother. I did not understand Leah's kindness to Ruti. In my heart, I shared her sons' disdain for her. Why did she submit to Laban? Why did she not demand her sons' respect? How could she find the courage to kill herself when she had no courage for life? I was ashamed of my heart's coldness, for I knew that Bilhah would have cried to see Ruti lying here, and that Leah would pour ashes on her own hair when she learned what had happened.

But the longer I stood there, the more I hated Ruti for her weakness and for making me keep watch. It seemed no one would come for me, and I began to tremble. Perhaps Ruti would rise up and take her knife to me as punishment for my cruel thoughts. Perhaps the gods of the underworld would come for her and take me as well. I started to weep for my mother to come and rescue me. I called the name of each aunt. I called Joseph and Reuben and Judah. But it seemed they had forgotten me.

By the time I saw the shape of two people moving across the meadow, I was sick with worry. But there was no one to comfort me. The women had remained in the tent. Only Ruti's horrible sons had come. They threw a blanket over their mother's face without so much as a sigh. Beor threw the little bundle that was Ruti over his shoulders, as if he were carrying a stray kid. I followed him alone. Kemuel paid no attention to his poor dead mother and hunted a rabbit on the way back. "Ha ha!" he shouted, when his arrow found its mark.

Only when I saw the red tent on the edge of the camp did the tears begin to run down my cheeks again, and I ran to my mothers. Leah searched my face and covered it with kisses. Rachel hugged me close, and laid me down on her fragrant bed. Zilpah sang me a lullaby about abundant rains and luxuriant harvests while Bilhah rubbed my feet until I fell asleep. I did not wake up until the next evening, and by then Ruti was under the ground. We left a few days later.

My father and older brothers, all the bondsmen, and Laban's sons went off to the far pastures to separate the brindled and spotted livestock that now belonged to Jacob. Of all the men, only Laban remained in camp, counting up jugs as they were filled, making messes of neatly piled woolens to check that we took nothing he had not agreed to. "It is my right," he barked without apology.

Eventually Laban grew tired of spying on his daughters' labors and decided to go to Haran "on business." Leah sneered at the announcement. "The old man is going to gamble and drink and boast to the other lazy clods that he is finally rid of his greedy son-in-law and his ungrateful daughters," she told me as we cooked a meal for him to take on his journey. Beor accompanied Laban, who made a great show of leaving Kemuel in command.

"He has my authority in all things," said Laban to the wives and younger sons of Jacob, whom he assembled for his departure. No sooner had Laban disappeared over the hill than Kemuel demanded that Rachel herself bring him strong wine. "Send me no ugly serving girls," he bellowed. "I want my sister."

Rachel made no objection to serving him, as it gave her the opportunity to pour an herb that hastens sleep into his cup. "Drink well, brother," she said sweetly as he swallowed the first cup. "Have another."

He was snoring within an hour of Laban's departure. Every time he roused, Rachel went to his tent with her brew and sat with him, feigning interest in his crude attempts at seduction and filling his cup so full and so often that he lost the whole day and the next one, too.

While Kemuel snored, the men returned, bringing the flocks into the near pasture just over the rise from the tents, so the final hours of our preparation were filled with bleating, dust, and animal smells. They were filled too with the unaccustomed noise and tension of so many men in our midst.

On ordinary days, the tents were populated only by women and children. A sick or feeble man might lie on his bed or sit in the sun while the work of wool and bread and beer progressed about him, but such a man knew enough to be embarrassed and kept to himself.

We had a whole crowd of healthy men with little

to do. "What a nuisance," said my mother, of the relentless presence of her sons.

"They're always hungry," grumbled Bilhah, who never grumbled, after sending Reuben away for the second time that morning with a bowl of lentils and onions. Every few minutes, Bilhah or Leah had to stop what they were doing to heat the bread stones.

The presence of the men presented a more subtle difficulty, as well. The tents were Leah's domain, and although she was the one who knew what needed to be done, she would not give orders with her husband by her side. So she stood behind Jacob and softly asked, "Is my husband ready to dismantle the big loom and lay it into the cart?" and he would direct his sons to do what was needed. And so it went, until everything was ready.

Throughout the weeks of preparation, and especially after Laban departed for Haran, I kept close to my aunt Rachel. I found reasons to follow her from one task to the next, offering to carry for her, asking her for advice on my duties. I stayed by her side until nightfall, even falling asleep upon her blankets, and woke in the morning to find myself covered by her sweet-scented cloak. I tried to be careful, but she knew that I was watching her.

On the night before we left, Rachel caught my eye, which was fixed upon her every move. At first she glared, but then she stared back in a way that told me I had triumphed: I could follow her. We went to the bamah, where Zilpah was lying facedown beside the altar, whispering to the gods and goddesses we were about to abandon. She looked up as we sat down among the roots of the great tree there, but I'm not even sure that Zilpah saw me sitting between Rachel's knees. As we waited, my aunt braided my hair and told me about the healing properties of common herbs (coriander seeds for bellyache, cumin for wounds). She had long ago decided that I should learn what Inna had taught her.

We stayed there, in the lap of the tree, until Zilpah rose, sighed, and left. We sat until the sounds from the tents quieted and the last lamps were extinguished. We stayed until the moon, halfway to fullness, was high in the branches above us, and the only sound was the occasional bleating of a sheep.

Then Rachel rose and I followed as she walked softly to Laban's tent. My aunt made no acknowledgment of my presence, and I was not sure she knew I was behind her until she held the tent flap open for me, to a place I had never been nor wished to go.

It was dark as a dry well in my grandfather's tent, and the air was fetid and stale. Rachel, who had been here to ply Kemuel with drink, walked past his snoring body directly to the corner of the tent where a rough wooden bench served as Laban's altar. The teraphim were arrayed in two rows. Rachel reached out for them without hesitation and dropped them, one by one, into the cloth tied around her waist, as though she were harvesting onions. When the last of the idols fell into her apron, she turned, walked across the tent without a glance at Kemuel, who moaned in his sleep as she passed him, and soundlessly held the tent flap open for me.

We walked out into stillness. My heart pounded in

my ears and I drew a breath to rid myself of the tent's stink, but Rachel did not pause. She walked quickly to her tent, where Bilhah slept. I heard my aunt rustling among the blankets, but it was too dark to see where she hid the idols. Then Rachel lay down and I heard nothing more.

I wanted to shake her and demand that she show me the treasures. I wanted her to hug me and tell me how well I had done in keeping still. But I remained quiet. I lay down to the pounding of my heart, thinking that Kemuel would rush into the tent and kill us all. I wondered if the teraphim would come to life and cast terrible spells on us for disturbing them. I was sure that morning would never come, and I shivered into my blanket, though the night was not cold. Finally, my eyes closed to a dreamless sleep.

I awoke to a great noise of voices outside the tent. Rachel and Bilhah were already gone, and I was alone with two piles of neatly folded blankets. She had taken them with her, I realized. Rachel had moved the idols without me. After all my careful watching and following, I had missed it. I rushed outside to see my brothers rolling up the goatskins that had been my father's tent. All around me, tents were on the ground, the poles collected, the ropes coiled. My home had been dismantled. We were going.

Jacob had risen at dawn and made a sacrifice of grain and wine and oil for the journey. The herds, sensing a change, were bleating and kicking up dust. The dogs would not stop barking. Half of the tents were down, leaving the camp looking lopsided and desolate, as though a great wind had blown away half the world.

We ate a morning meal salted by the tears of those who would not accompany us. The women put away the last of the bowls and stood with empty hands. There was nothing left for us to do, but Jacob gave no sign for us to leave. Laban had not returned from Haran as he had promised.

The sun began to rise higher, and we should have been long gone, but Jacob stood alone at the top of the ridge that faced the road to Haran, squinting for a sign of Laban. Jacob's sons muttered among themselves. Zilpah walked to the bamah, where she ripped her tunic and placed ashes on her hair. It grew hot and still, and even the herds quieted down.

Then Rachel walked past Reuben and Simon, Levi and Judah, who stood at the bottom of the hill where Jacob watched, and she approached her husband and said, "Let us go. Kemuel told me his father will return with spears and riders and prevent us from leaving. He is gone to tell the judges in Haran that you are a thief. We must not wait."

Jacob listened and then replied, "Your father fears my god too much to act so boldly. And Kemuel is a fool."

Rachel bowed her head and said, "My husband may know better, but the herds are ready and the goods are packed. Our feet are shod and we stand with nothing to do. We do not steal away in the dark of night. We take nothing but what is our own. The season is right. If we wait much longer the moon will begin to wane, and a darkening moon is no time to embark upon a journey."

Rachel spoke nothing but the truth, and Jacob had

no wish to see Laban again. Indeed, he was furious with the old man for making him wait, for making him leave like a thief, without giving proper farewell to the grandfather of his sons.

Rachel's words spoke to Jacob's own purpose, and after she left him, he gave the order to go. Impatient to be underway, the sons of Jacob shouted with happiness, but a wail went up from the women who were staying behind.

My father signaled us to follow him. He led us first to the bamah, where each of us placed a pebble by the altar. The men picked up any small rock that lay at their feet to leave in farewell. Leah and Rachel sought out stones from around the foot of the nearby terebinth, which had given them years of shade and comfort.

No words were spoken. The stones would testify for us, though Bilhah kissed hers before laying it on top of the others.

Zilpah and I alone were prepared for this moment. Weeks earlier, my grieving aunt had taken me to the wadi where Ruti had died and showed me a place at the bottom of the ravine filled with smooth, oval-shaped stones. She chose a tiny white one, the size of her thumbnail. I took a red one, streaked with black, nearly as big as my fist. She kept it for me and placed it in my palm as we walked for the last time to the holy place of my family.

Then Jacob led his family over the hill, to where the bondsmen waited with the herd. My mothers did not look back, not even Zilpah, whose eyes were red but dry.

CHAPTER THREE

My father arranged his family, his flocks, and all of his household for the journey. Jacob led, holding a great olive staff in his hand, flanked by Levi and Simon, who strutted with importance. Behind them walked the women and children too young to be tending the herds, so Uzna's little son and daughter stayed near their mother's legs, and Zibatu carried her baby girl in a hip sling. I started out near Zilpah, hoping to lighten the sadness that clung to her, but her sorrow finally chased me to my mother and Bilhah, who were engrossed in planning meals and paid no attention to me. So I found my way to Rachel, whose smile did not fade even as the sun began to beat down on us in earnest. The bundle on her back was more than large enough for the teraphim, and I was sure that was where they were hidden.

Joseph, Tali, and Issa were told to stay with the pack animals, near the women, which made them sulk and kick at the dirt and mutter about how they were old enough to be trusted with more important work than tending a tame donkey and the ox who drew the heavy cart.

Directly behind us and the beasts of burden, Reuben had charge of the herd and the shepherds, who included Zebulun and Dan, Gad and Asher, and the bondsmen, Nomir, husband of Zibatu, and Zimri, father of Uzna's children. The four dogs ran around the perimeter of the flocks, their ears flattened to their heads as they worked. They lifted their brown eyes from the goats and sheep only when Jacob approached, and bounded to their master's side to bask for a moment in the touch of his hand and the sound of his voice.

Judah, our rear guard, walked behind the herds, watching out for stragglers. I would have been lonely there with no one to talk to, but my brother seemed to enjoy his solitude.

I was in awe of our numbers and what seemed our great wealth. Joseph told me that we were a small party by any measure, with only two pack animals to carry our belongings, but I remained proud of my father's holdings and I thought my mother carried herself like a queen.

We had walked for only a little while when Levi pointed out a figure ahead, sitting by the side of the path. As we came closer, Rachel shouted, "Inna!" and ran ahead to greet her friend and teacher. The midwife was arrayed for travel, a donkey laden with blankets and baskets by her side. The caravan did not stop at the unexpected sight of the lone woman; it would have been pointless to bring the herd to a halt in the absence of water. Instead, Inna approached Jacob, leading her donkey and falling in a step behind him. Inna did not address my father but spoke to Rachel so that he would overhear her words.

The midwife presented her case with fancy phrases that sounded odd coming from a mouth that usually spoke in the plainest and sometimes the coarsest of terms. "Oh, my friend," she said, "I cannot bear to see you part. My life would be desolate in your absence, and I am too old to take another apprentice. I wish only to join with your family and be among you for the rest of my days. I would give your husband all of my possessions in exchange for his protection and a place among the women of his tents. I would accompany you as your bondswoman or as your maidservant, to practice my craft in the south, and learn what they have to teach there. I would minister to your family, setting the bricks for your women, healing the wounds of your men, offering service to Gula, the healer, in Jacob's name," Inna said.

She flattered my father, whom she called wise as well as kind. She declared herself his servant.

I was one of many witnesses to Inna's speech. Levi and Simon stayed close, curious to learn what the midwife wanted. Leah and Bilhah had quickened their pace to discover why their friend had appeared among them. Even Zilpah roused herself and drew near.

Rachel turned her face to Jacob, her eyebrows posing the question, her hands clasped at her chest. Her husband smiled into her face. "Your friend is welcome. She will be your maidservant in my eyes. She is yours, as though she were part of your dowry. There is nothing more to say."

Rachel kissed Jacob's hand and placed it for a

moment upon her heart. Then she led Inna and her donkey back to our animals, where the women could talk more freely.

"Sister!" Rachel said to the midwife. "What is this about?"

Inna dropped her voice and began by telling a sorry tale about a deformed stillbirth—a tiny head, twisted limbs—born to a girl made pregnant at her first blood. "Too young," said Inna, with an angry mouth. "Far too young." The father was a stranger, a wild-haired man of many years, who wore only a loincloth and brought his wife to Inna's hut. When the baby and mother both died, he accused the midwife of causing his misfortune by casting spells upon them.

Inna, who had spent three terrible days working to save the mother, could not hold her tongue. Exhausted and sorrowful, she called the man a monster and accused him of being the girl's father as well as her husband. Then she spit in his face.

Enraged, the stranger reached for her throat and would have killed her had it not been for neighbors who were drawn by her screams and pulled him away. Inna showed us the black bruises on her throat. The man demanded restitution from Inna's father, but Inna had no father, nor had she brother or husband. She had lived alone after her mother's death.

Having kept her family's hut, she did not want for shelter, and midwifery kept her in grain and oil and even wool for trade. Since she was a burden to no one, none had troubled about her. But now the angry stranger demanded to know why the townspeople tolerated such an "abomination."

"A woman alone is a danger," he screamed into the faces of Inna's neighbors. "Where are your judges?" he hissed. "Who are your elders?"

At that Inna grew frightened. The most powerful man of her mud village had hated her since she had turned down a marriage offer on behalf of his half-wit son. She feared that he would incite the men against her, and perhaps even enslave her. "Idiots. All of them," she said, and spat into the dust.

"My thoughts turned to you for refuge," she said, addressing all the women of my family, who walked nearby, listening to her every word. "Rachel knows I have always wanted to see more of the world than these dusty hills, and since Jacob treats his wives better than most, I came to see your departure as a gift from the gods," she continued. "And sisters, I must tell you, I am tired of eating my evening meal alone. I wish to see a baby I delivered as he grows into manhood. I wish to celebrate the new moon among friends. I want to know that my bones will be planted well after my death." Looking around at us, she smiled broadly. "So here I am."

The women smiled back at her, happy to have such a healer among them. Although Rachel was skilled, Inna was famous for her golden hands, and beloved for her stories.

Zilpah saw Inna's appearance as a good omen. The midwife's presence lifted her spirits so much that later my aunt began to sing. It was nothing exalted, only a children's song about a fly who bothered a rabbit, who ate the insect but was eaten by a dog, who was in turn eaten by a jackal, who was hunted by a lion, who was killed by a boastful man, who was snatched by An and Enlil, the sky gods, and placed in the heavens to teach him a lesson.

It was a simple song known to every child and thus to every adult who had been a child. By the last verse, all of my mothers and the bondswomen and their children were singing. Even my brothers had joined in, with Simon and Levi making a contest of it, outshouting each other. When the song ended everyone clapped hands and laughed. It was sweet to be free of Laban's shadow. It was sweet to be at the beginning of a new life.

That was the first time I heard women's voices and men's voices raised in song together, and throughout the journey the boundaries between the men's lives and the women's relaxed. We joined the men in the work of watering the herd, they helped us unpack for the evening meal. We listened to them sing herding songs, addressed to the night sky and filled with tales of the constellations. They heard our spinning songs, which we sang as we walked and worked wool with small spindles. We applauded one another and laughed together. It was time out of life. It was like a dream.

Most of the singing took place just before sleep or early in the morning while we were still fresh. By afternoon, everyone was hungry and footsore. It took the women several days to get accustomed to wearing sandals from sunup to sunset—at home we stayed barefoot in and around the tents. Inna relieved our blisters and soothed our aches by massaging our feet with oil perfumed with thyme.

There was nothing wrong with our appetites, though. The long days left everyone ferociously hungry, and it was good that my brothers could supplement the simple bread and porridge of the road with birds and hares they hunted along the way. The meat tasted strange but wonderful the way Inna prepared it, with a bright yellow spice she got in trade.

There was little conversation during the evening meal. The men were in their circle, the women among themselves. By the time the moon rose, everyone was asleep—the women and babies crowded inside one large tent, the men and boys on blankets under the stars. At dawn, after a hurried meal of cold bread, olives, and cheese, we began again. After a few days of this, I could barely remember my old life, rooted in one place.

Every morning brought a new wonder. The first day, Inna joined us. The second day, late in the afternoon, we came upon a great river.

My father had said we would cross the great water, but I had given no thought to the meaning of his words. When we came to the top of a hill overlooking the river valley, I was amazed. I had never seen so much water in one place, nor had any of us except Jacob and Inna. The river was not very wide where we forded it, or "him" as Zilpah would have me say. Even so, it was twenty times wider than the streams I had known. He lay across the valley like a sparkling path, the setting sun catching fire on the way.

We came to a crossing where the bottom was packed with pebbles and the ford was wide. The ground on either bank had been beaten smooth by many caravans, and my father decided we would stop there until morning. The animals were led to water, and we made camp, but before the meal, my father and my mothers gathered by the banks of the Euphrates and poured a libation of wine into the great river.

We were not the only ones at the ford. Up and down the banks, traders had stopped to eat and sleep. My brothers wandered and stared at the new faces and strange clothes. "A camel," Joseph shouted, and our brothers chased after him to get a closer look at the spindly-legged beast. I could not go with them, but I did not regret being left behind. It gave me a chance to go down to the river, which drew me like a storyteller.

I stood by the water's edge until the last trace of daylight had drained from the sky, and later, after the evening meal, I returned to savor the smell of the river, which was as heady to me as incense, heavy and dark and utterly different from the sweet, thin aroma of well water. My mother, Leah, would have said I smelled the rotting grasses of the marsh and the mingled presence of so many animals and men, but I recognized the scent of this water the way I knew the perfume of my mother's body.

I sat by the river even after the others went to sleep. I dangled my feet in the water until they were wrinkled and soft and whiter than I had ever seen them. In the moonlight, I watched as leaves made their way slowly downstream and out of sight. I was lulled by the slow rush of the water against the shallow banks, and was nearly asleep when voices roused me. Turning to look upstream, I saw two shapes moving about in the middle of the river. For a moment I thought they might be river demons or water beasts come to drag me to a watery grave. I had no idea that people could move through the water iike that—I had never seen swim-

ming. But soon I realized they were merely men, the
Egyptians who owned the camel, speaking to one another in their strange, purring language. Though their
laughter was quiet, the water carried the sound as
though they were whispering directly in my ears. I
did not go to my blanket until they had left the water
and returned the river to continue his peaceful journey
through the night, undisturbed.

In the morning, my father and my brothers walked
into the river without even pausing, lifting their robes
to keep dry. My mothers hung their sandals upon their
girdles and giggled about showing so much of their legs.
Zilpah hummed a river song as we crossed. The twins
rushed ahead, splashing each other thoughtlessly.

But I was afraid. Even though I had fallen in love
with the river, I could see that at his deepest point, the
water lapped against my father's waist. That meant
I would be submerged to my neck and I would be swallowed. I thought about taking my mother's hand, like
a baby, but she was balancing a bundle on her head. All
of my mothers' hands were busy, and I was too proud
to ask Joseph for his.

I had no time to be afraid. The pack animals were
at my back, forcing me ahead, so I entered the river and
felt the water rise to my ankles and calves. The current felt like a caress on my knees and thighs. In an
instant, my belly and chest were covered, and I giggled. There was nothing to fear! The water held no
threat, only an embrace I had no wish to break. I stood
to one side as the ox passed, and then the rest of the
animals. I moved my arms through the water, feeling
them float on the surface, watching the waves and

wake that followed my gesture. Here was magic, I thought. Here was something holy.

I watched the sheep craning their necks high out of the water, the goats, wide-eyed, barely touching the bottom with their hooves. And then came the dogs, who somehow possessed the trick of running through the water—pumping their legs and moving along, snorting, but not suffering. Here was more magic; our dogs could swim as well as Egyptians.

Finally Judah came up alongside me, looking as dubious of the water as I had felt just a few moments earlier. "Sister," he said. "Wake up and walk with me. Here is my hand," he offered. But as I reached out to take it, I lost my footing and fell backward. Judah grabbed me and dragged me. I was on my back, the sky above me, and I felt the water holding me up. Aiee. A little shriek escaped from my mouth. A river demon, I thought. A river demon has hold of me. But Judah pulled me out onto the pebbles of the far bank, and I lost the wild lightness in my body.

Later that night, when I lay down to sleep among the women, I told my mothers what I had seen and felt by the side of the river and then in the water, during my crossing. Zilpah pronounced me bewitched by the river god. Leah reached out and squeezed my hand, reassuring us both. But Inna told me, "You are a child of water. Your spirit answered the spirit of the river. You must live by a river someday, Dinah. Only by a river will you be happy."

I loved every moment of the journey to Canaan. As long as I kept my spindle busy, my mothers didn't mind what

I did or where I went, so I wandered from the front of the caravan to the back, trying to be everywhere and see everything. I remember little of the land or sky, which must have changed as we traveled. Once, Rachel and Inna brought me with them to gather herbs and flowers up a hill that grew steeper and more rugged as we headed south. I was amazed to see trees growing so thickly that women as slender as Rachel and Inna had to walk in single file to pass among them. I recall their curious needles that left my fingers smelling green all day.

Best of all I liked the sights of the road. There were caravans heading back to Egypt loaded with cedar, lines of slaves headed for Damascus, and traders from Shechem heading for Carchemish, near our old home. So many strange people passed by: men who were clean-shaven as boys and huge, black, bare-chested men. Although there were fewer women on the road, I glimpsed mothers shrouded in black veils, naked slave girls, and a dancer who wore a breastplate made of copper coins.

Joseph was as fascinated by the people as I, and he would sometimes run over to get a closer look at a particularly strange animal or costume. I was too shy to go with him, and my mothers would not have permitted it. My brother described what he saw and we marveled over it all.

I did not share my observations of my own family with Joseph, though. I felt like a thief, spying upon my parents and brothers, but I burned to know more about them—especially my father. Since Jacob walked with us for a little while every day, I watched him and noticed how he treated my mothers. He spoke to Leah about provisions and plans and to Rachel about memories of his trip north to Haran. He was careful not to slight either woman in his attentions.

Zilpah bowed her head when my father approached, and he responded in kind, but they rarely spoke. Jacob smiled at Bilhah as though she were his child. She was the only one he touched, running his hand over her soft black hair whenever he passed. It was an act of familiarity that seemed to express his fondness, but also proved her powerlessness as the least of his wives. Bilhah said nothing, but blushed deeply at these caresses.

I noticed that Reuben's devotion to Bilhah had not faded over time. Most of my brothers, as they grew into their height and sprouted beards, loosened their childhood ties to mothers and aunties. All except Reuben, who liked to linger near the women, especially Bilhah. During the trip, he seemed to know where she was at every moment. When he called for her, she replied, "Yes, brother," even though he was her nephew. She never spoke of him to anyone and I don't think I ever heard her give voice to his name, but I could see their abiding affection, and it made me glad.

Reuben was easy to know, but Judah was restless. He had chosen his position behind the herd, but sometimes he pressed one of the younger brothers to take his post so he could wander. He would climb to the top of a rocky hill and shout down to us, then disappear until nightfall. "He's young for it, but that one's already hungry for a woman," Inna muttered to my mother one evening, when Judah came to the fire later that night, looking for his supper.

I turned to Judah and realized that my brother's body had begun to take the shape of a man, his arms well muscled, his legs showing hair. He was the handsomest of all my brothers. His teeth were perfect, white and small; I remember this because he smiled so rarely they were always a surprise. Years later when I saw pearls for the first time, I thought of Judah's teeth.

Looking at Judah as a man, I had the thought that Reuben was certainly of an age to marry and father children. Indeed, he was not much younger than Nomir, whose daughter was almost ready to walk. Simon and Levi were old enough to have wives, too. And then I understood another reason why we had left Haran—to get my brothers bride-prices without Laban's sticky fingers getting in the way. When I asked my mother about this, she said, "Well, of course," but I was impressed with my own worldliness and insight.

No one spoke of Laban anymore. As the days passed and the moon began to wane, it seemed we were free of my grandfather's grasp. Jacob had all but stopped visiting Judah at the rear of the herd, looking over his shoulder to see whether his father-in-law was coming. Instead, his thoughts turned toward Edom and his meeting with Esau, the brother whom he had not seen for twenty years, since the day he had stolen his father's blessing and fled. The farther we walked from Haran the more Jacob spoke of Esau.

On the day before the new moon, we stopped early in the afternoon to give us time to prepare the red tent and cook for the three days given to the women. Since we would stay in this place for more than one night, my father raised his tent as well. We were near a pretty little stream where wild garlic grew in profusion. The smell of bread soon filled the camp, and great pots of stew were prepared so that the men would have plenty to eat while my mothers retired from their service.

My mothers and Uzna entered the women's tent before the sun set. I stayed outside to help serve the men. I never worked harder in my life. It was no small task feeding fourteen men and boys, and two young children, not to mention the women inside. Much of the serving fell to me, since Zibatu was often nursing her baby. Inna had no patience for my brothers.

I was proud to be feeding my family, doing the work of a grown woman. When we finally joined my mothers in the tent after dark, I was never so grateful for rest. I slept well and dreamed of wearing a crown and pouring water. Zilpah said these were sure signs that my womanhood was not far off. It was a sweet dream, but it ended the next morning in a nightmare haunted by Laban's voice.

But it was no dream. My grandfather had arrived, demanding justice. "Give me the thief who took my idols," he bellowed. "Where are my teraphim?"

I ran out of the tent just in time to see my father, the olive staff in his hand, stride up to meet Laban. Beor and Kemuel stood behind my grandfather, along with three bondsmen from Haran, who kept their eyes on the ground rather than look into the face of Jacob, whom they loved.

"Whom do you call a thief?" my father demanded.

"Whom do you accuse, you old fool? I served you for twenty years without pay, without honor. There was no thief in this place until you broke its peace."

Laban was struck dumb by his son-in-law's tone. "I am the reason for your comfortable old age," Jacob said. "I have been an honest servant. I took nothing that was not mine. I have nothing here except that which you agreed was mine, and it was not fair payment for what I have given you.

"Your daughters are my wives and want none of you. Your grandsons are my sons, and owe you nothing. While I stood on your land, I gave you honor you did not deserve, but now I am not bound by the obligations of guests and hosts."

By then, all my brothers had gathered behind Jacob, and together they looked like an army. Even Joseph held a staff in his hands. The air was brittle with hatred.

Laban took a step back. "My son! Why do you rebuke me?" he wheedled, his voice suddenly old and soft. "I am here only to say farewell to my beloved family, my daughters and my grandsons. We are kinsmen, you and I. You are my nephew, and I love you as a son. You misunderstood my words. I wish only to kiss my family and give you my blessing," he said, stretching his fingers wide, bowing his head like a dog showing submission. "Is not the god of Abram also the god of my fathers? He is great, to be sure. But my son," Laban said, looking up into Jacob's face, "what of my other gods? What have you done with them?"

"What do you mean?" my father said.

Laban narrowed his eyes and answered, "My household gods have been stolen, and they disappeared upon your departure. I come to claim them for me and for my sons.

"Why do you wish to strip me of their protection? Do you fear their wrath, even though you worship the face-less one only?"

My father spat at Laban's feet. "I took nothing. There is nothing in my household that belongs to you. There is no place for thieves under my tents."

But Laban stood firm. "My teraphim are precious to me, nephew. I do not leave this place without them."

At this, Jacob shrugged. "They are not here," he said. "See for yourself." And with that he turned his back on Laban and walked away, into the woods and out of sight.

Laban began his search. My brothers stood, their arms crossed against their chests, and watched as the old man untied every bundle, unfurled every rolled-up tent, sifted his fingers through every sack of grain, squeezed every wineskin. When he moved toward Jacob's tent, Simon and Levi tried to block his way, but Reuben motioned them aside. They followed Laban and watched as he rummaged through our father's blankets and even lifted the floor mat to kick at the earth, in case a hole had been dug.

The day wore on, and still Laban searched. I ran back and forth from where my grandfather hunted to the red tent, reporting what I saw to my mothers. Their faces stayed blank, but I knew they were worried. I had never seen women's hands working during the new moon, yet here every one of them was busy with her spindle.

After Laban had ransacked my father's tent, there was nowhere left for him to search except the red tent. His eyes fixed upon the women's tent on the edge of the camp. It was unthinkable that a healthy man would walk of his own will inside that place during the head of the month. The men and boys stared to see if he would place himself among bleeding women—even worse, his own daughters.

Laban muttered to himself as he approached the women's tent. At the door, he stopped and looked over his shoulder. He glared at his sons and grandsons, and then Laban opened the flap and walked in.

Laban's hoarse breath was the only sound. He glanced around the tent nervously, not meeting any of the women's eyes. No one moved or spoke. Finally and with great contempt he said, "Bah," and moved toward a pile of blankets.

Rachel stood up from her place on the straw. She did not drop her eyes as she addressed her father. Indeed, she stared straight into his face, and without anger or fear or any apparent emotion she said, "I took them, Father. I have all of the teraphim. All of your gods. They are here.

"I sit upon them. The teraphim of our family now bathe in my monthly blood, by which your household gods are polluted beyond redemption. You can have them if you wish," Rachel continued calmly, as though she were speaking of trifling things. "I will dig them out and even wipe them off for you if you like, father.

But their magic has been turned against you. You are without their protection from this time forward."

No one drew breath as Rachel spoke. Laban's eyes widened, and he began to tremble. He stared at his beautiful daughter, who seemed to glow in the rosy light that filtered through the tent. It was a long and terrible moment that ended when Laban turned and shuffled out of our sight. Outside in the light, he found himself facing Jacob, who had returned.

"You found nothing," my father said, with supreme confidence. When Laban made no reply, Jacob continued, "There are no thieves in my tents. This will be our last meeting, old man. We are finished."

Laban said nothing, but opened his palms wide and bowed his head in acquiescence. "Come," he said. "We will settle our case." My grandfather motioned for Jacob to follow him up the hill to his camp. My brothers followed to give witness.

Laban and Jacob each selected ten stones and layered them one upon another until they had created a cairn to mark the boundaries between them. Laban poured wine over it. Jacob poured oil upon it. Each man swore peace to the other, touching the other's thigh. Then Jacob turned and walked down the hill. It was the last time any of us saw Laban, which we counted as a blessing.

Jacob was eager to be gone from the place, so the red tent was dismantled the next morning and we continued our journey toward the land my father called home.

My father was consumed with memories of Esau. Though it had been twenty years, Jacob could still see his brother's face when Esau finally understood the full meaning of what had befallen him. Not only had Jacob betrayed him by stealing his beloved father's blessing, it was clear that Rebecca had been behind it—the last of many proofs of her preference for her younger son.

Jacob had watched his brother's face as Esau pieced together the family treason, and my father was ashamed. Jacob understood the pain in Esau's belly and knew if he had been in his brother's place, he, too, would have given chase with a drawn dagger.

Jacob dwelt upon a vision of his terrible avenging brother, describing him daily to his sons, and to Leah, Rachel, and Bilhah during his nights with them, for now he raised his own tent so he could be comforted by a woman until morning. Jacob's fear was so great that it had erased all memory of his brother's love, which had always been stronger than his short-lived rages. He forgot the times Esau had fed him and protected him, laughed with him, and praised him.

My father's fear made Esau into a demon of revenge, whom I imagined red as a fox with arms like tree trunks. This uncle haunted my dreams and turned the journey that I had loved into a forced march toward certain death.

I was not the only one who walked in fear. There was no more singing on the road or in camp after my father began to tell his Esau stories. The journey was quiet in the days after we took final leave of Laban, and even Judah no longer wished to walk alone at the back of the herd.

Soon there was another river to be crossed, and Esau

was banished from my thoughts. I rejoiced to see flowing water again and ran up to the riverbank to put my face near the delicious smell and sound.

My father, too, seemed refreshed by the sight of the river and by the task at hand. He declared we would make camp on the far side that night and gathered his oldest sons around him to assign them their duties.

Although the water was nowhere near as wide as it had been at the great river to the north, this river was deeper in the center and much faster. Leaves did not meander downstream, but rushed away as though chasing after swift prey. Our crossing had to be quick, as the sun was already beginning its descent.

Inna and Zilpah poured an offering to the river god as the first of the animals were herded into the water and guided across. The smaller animals had to be taken two by two and by the scruff of the neck, with a man on either side. The dogs worked until they were exhausted. We nearly lost one of them in the current, but Joseph grabbed him and became a momentary hero among his brothers.

All of the men grew weary. Even Judah staggered from the effort of guiding frightened animals while withstanding a current that dragged at him. The river was generous, and none of the animals was lost. By the time the sun was resting on the tops of the trees, only the ox, donkeys, women, and babies remained.

Reuben and Judah struggled with the terrified ox, who bellowed like an animal headed for slaughter. It took a long while for them to drag the beast across, and by then it was dusk. My mother and I were the last to be taken across, my hand in hers this time so that I would not be stolen by the current. When we reached the far shore, it was dark and only my father was left behind.

Jacob called across the water. "Reuben," he said.

And my brother replied, "I am here."

"See to the animals," my father said. "Don't bother with a tent. The night is warm enough. I will cross with the first light. Be ready to leave."

My mother was not pleased by Jacob's plan and told Reuben to call back to our father and offer to cross the river and spend the night with him. He would not permit it. "Tell your mother to sit on her fears. I am neither a child nor a doddering elder. I will sleep by myself under the sky, as I did in my youth when I traveled north. Be ready to leave in the morning," said Jacob, and spoke no more.

The moon was still new, so the night was dark. The water would have sweetened the air had not the wet coats of the animals muddied its perfume with musk. They bleated in their sleep, unused to being wet in the chill of the night. I tried to stay awake to listen to the music of the rushing water, but this time the splashing lulled me into a deep sleep. Everyone slept heavily. If my father cried out, no one heard him.

Reuben was at the riverbank with Leah before sunrise to greet Jacob, but my father did not appear. The birds' greeting of the day had stilled and the sun had begun to dry the dew, but there was no sign of him. At Leah's signal, Reuben, Simon, and Judah plunged into the water to seek their father. They found him beaten and naked in the middle of a brushy clearing where the grass and bushes had been crushed and broken in a wide circle around him. Reuben ran back to us shouting for a robe to cover our father, and then he carried him back across the stream.

Uproar gave way to silence when Jacob was brought, senseless, lying in his son's arms, his left leg hanging at an awkward angle as though it were no longer attached to his body. Inna rushed forward and ordered my father's tent raised. Bilhah built a fire. The men stood by with empty hands. Reuben had no answers to their questions, and they fell silent.

Inna walked out of the tent and said, "Fever." Rachel ran for her herb kit. Inna gestured for Reuben to follow her back inside, and a few moments later we heard the terrible, animal scream as he guided our father's leg back into its place. The whimpering that followed was even worse.

Unnoticed and unneeded, I sat outside the tent, watching Inna's resolute face and Rachel's flushed cheeks as they walked in and out. I saw my mother's lips press into a thin line as she bent her head to hear their reports. I listened through the walls of the tent while my father screamed at a blue river demon and marshaled an army of angels to fight against a mighty enemy that rose from the waters. Zilpah muttered incantations to Gula, and Inna sang of ancient gods whose names I had never heard, Nintinugga, Ninisinna, Baba.

I heard my father weep and beg for mercy from his brother. I heard Jacob, the father of eleven sons, call out for his mother, "Ema, Ema," like a lost child. I heard Inna hush him and encourage him to drink, as though he were a swaddling baby.

On that endless day, no one ate or worked. In the evening, I fell asleep in my place by the tent, my dreams shaped by my father's cries and my mothers' murmurs.

At dawn, I started awake and was greeted by the stillness. I jumped to my feet in terror, certain that my father was dead. Surely we would be captured by Esau and made into slaves. But as I began crying, Bilhah found me and held me.

"No, little one," she said, stroking my matted hair. "He is well. He has recovered his sense, and he sleeps calmly now. Your mothers are sleeping, too, they are so weary from their labors."

By dusk of the second night after his ordeal, my father was well enough to sit by the door of his tent for the evening meal. His leg was still painful and he could barely walk, but his eyes were clear and his hands were steady. I slept without fear again.

We stayed for two months by the river Jabbok, so that Jacob could heal. The women's tents were set up, and the bondsmen's too. Days took on an orderliness, with the men tending the herds while the women cooked. We built an oven with clay from the river, and it was good to have fresh bread again, moist and warm, instead of the dried stuff we had eaten on the road, which always tasted of dust. During the first days of Jacob's illness, two sheep were slaughtered to make strengthening broths from their bones, so there was meat for a while. The rare treat made it seem like a festival.

But as my father recovered his health, his fear returned even greater than before and changed him. Jacob could speak of nothing else but his brother's revenge, and he saw the nighttime attack and his struggle with the army of angels as portents of the battle to come. He grew suspicious of any attempt to calm him and sent gentle Reuben away. Instead, he came to depend upon Levi, who let Jacob number his worries endlessly and nodded grimly at our father's direst predictions.

Among themselves, my mothers pondered the meaning of Jacob's latest dream, so powerful that it had crossed over into this world. They debated Jacob's worries and plans. Should he attack? Was it a mistake to send a messenger to Esau? Would it not have been wiser to appeal to his father, Isaac, for help? Perhaps the women should send a messenger to Rebecca, who was not only their mother-in-law, but their aunt as well? But they made no mention of the change in their husband's manner. The confident man had become tentative and cautious. The affectionate father had turned demanding and even cold. Perhaps they thought it a symptom of his illness, or perhaps they simply did not see what I saw.

I grew to hate every mention of Esau, though after a time my fear gave way to boredom. My mothers did not even notice when I started avoiding their tents. They were too caught up in my father's unfolding story and speculations about what lay ahead, and there was little for me to do. All our wool was spun, and the looms would not be unpacked, so my hands were often idle. No one called for me to fetch water or carry wool, and there was no garden to weed. I was near the end of childhood, and I was freer than I had ever been or would be again.

Joseph and I took to exploring the river. We walked its banks and watched the tiny fish that swarmed in its eddies. We hunted frogs, vivid green ones unlike any we'd ever seen. I picked wild herbs and salads. Joseph trapped grasshoppers to dip in honey. We bathed our feet in the cool, swift waters, and splashed each other until we were dripping. We dried ourselves in the sun, and our clothes smelled like the breeze and the water of the Jabbok.

One day we walked upstream and discovered a natural bridge over the river—a path of flat stones that made for an easy crossing. With no one to forbid it, we crossed to the far side, and we soon realized that we had found the very place where our father had been wounded. We recognized the clearing he had described—the circle of eighteen trees, the beaten-down grass, and the broken and bent bushes. We found a scorched place on the ground where a great fire had burned.

The hairs on my neck stood on end, and Joseph took my hand in his, which was damp with fear. Looking up, we heard nothing—no birdsong or whispering of leaves in the wind. The charred place gave off no smell, and even the sunlight seemed muted around us. The air seemed as dead as Ruti lying in the wadi.

I wanted to leave, but I could not move. Joseph told me later that he would have fled, too. But his feet were rooted in the earth. We lifted our eyes to the sky, wondering if our father's fearful angels would return, but the heavens remained empty. We stood like stones, waiting for something to happen.

A loud crash from the circle of trees broke like thunder, and we shrieked, or at least we tried to cry out, but no sounds issued from our open mouths as a black boar ran out of the forest. He ran straight for us across the battered meadow. We screamed our silent scream again, nor was there any noise from the hooves of the beast, which moved at us with the speed of a gazelle. I thought we were about to die, and my eyes filled with pity for our mothers and I heard Leah sobbing behind me.

When I turned to find her, she was not there. Still, the spell had broken. My feet were free and I ran back toward the river, pulling Joseph with a strength greater than my own. Perhaps there were angels on my side, too, I thought as I reached the foot stones and found my way over. Joseph slipped off the first rock and cut his foot. This time his voice rang out in pain. The sound of his cry seemed to stop the boar in his tracks, and the animal fell, as though struck by a spear.

Joseph recovered his footing and scrambled back to the far shore, where I held out my hands to him, and we embraced, trembling, amid the sounds of the water, the rustling of leaves, and the terrified beating of our own hearts.

"What was that place?" my brother asked, but I could only shake my head. We looked back to the boar and the clearing and the ring of trees, but the beast had vanished and the scene now seemed ordinary and even beautiful: a bird flew across the horizon, chirping, and the trees swayed with the wind. I shuddered, and Joseph squeezed my hand. Without a word, we swore the day to secrecy.

But my brother was never the same. From that night

forward, he began to dream with the power of our father's dreams. At first, he spoke of his wondrous encounters with angels and demons, with dancing stars and talking beasts, to me only. Soon, his dreams were too big for my ears alone.

CHAPTER FOUR

Joseph and I returned to camp, afraid we would be questioned about our absence and worried about trying to keep what had happened from our keen-eyed mothers. But no one saw us come. All eyes were fixed upon a stranger who stood before Jacob. The man spoke in the clipped accents of the south, and the first words I heard from his mouth were "my father." As I crept around to see the face of the messenger, I saw someone who could only be a kinsman.

It was Eliphaz, Esau's oldest son and my cousin, who looked so much like Judah that I clapped my hand over my mouth to keep from blurting it out loud. He was as ruddy and handsome as Judah, though taller—as tall as Reuben, in fact. He spoke with Reuben's gestures, his head tilted to one side, his left arm wrapped around his waist, his right hand clenching and unclenching, as he brought us the news we had dreaded for so long.

"My father arrives before dusk," said Eliphaz. "He comes with my brothers and with bondsmen and slaves, forty in all, including the women. My mother is among them," he added, nodding toward my mothers, who smiled at the courtesy, in spite of themselves.

While Eliphaz spoke, my father's face was a mask—unchanging and impassive. In his heart, however, he railed and wept. Shattered now were his careful plans for dividing our numbers so Esau could not destroy us in one attack. Useless, all those evenings spent directing my brothers as to which animals would be given as a peace offering and which animals should be hidden from Esau's grasp. My mothers had not even begun to separate and prepare the goods my father wanted to present to his older brother in hopes of appeasing his terrible anger.

But now he was trapped, and he cursed himself for occupying his thoughts for too long with demons and angels, and clouding his purpose, for now our tents were in an indefensible position, with the river blocking escape behind us.

Jacob betrayed none of this to his nephew, however. He greeted Eliphaz with equal courtesy and thanked him for his message. He led him to his own tent, bade him rest, and called for food and drink. Leah went to prepare the meal. Rachel brought him barley beer, but the women did not rush so that Jacob could have time to think.

While Eliphaz rested, Jacob found my mother and told her to get the women dressed in their finest robes and to prepare offerings. He had Reuben gather his brothers, also in their finest attire, but he directed that they gird themselves with hidden daggers so that Esau could not massacre them without some cost to himself.

All of this was done swiftly, so that when Eliphaz arose from his meal, we were all arrayed and ready to leave.

"It is not necessary, uncle," Eliphaz said. "My father comes to you. Why not receive him here in comfort?"

But Jacob said no. "I must greet my brother in a manner fit for a man of his station. We go out to give him welcome."

Leaving only the bondsmen and their wives behind, Jacob led us. Eliphaz walked at his side, followed by the animal offering—twelve strong goats and eighteen healthy sheep—shepherded by my brothers. I saw Leah look back over her shoulder, and sadness and fear crossed her face like clouds across the sun, but she put away her sorrow quickly, and remade her countenance into a picture of serenity.

We walked for only a short time—not even long enough for our long robes to grow dusty—before my father put down his staff. Esau was in sight on the far side of a gently sloping valley. Jacob walked out alone to greet his brother, and Esau did the same, as their retinues of grown sons followed at a little distance. From the hillside, I watched in terror as the two men came face to face. In an instant, my father was on the ground before his brother. For one awful moment I thought he had been felled by an unseen arrow or spear. But then he rose to his knees and bowed low, prostrating himself in the dust, again and again, seven times in all. It was the greeting of a slave to a master. My mother looked away in shame.

Apparently my uncle was also distressed by his brother's display, for he leaned down and took Jacob by the arm, shaking his head from side to side. I was too far away to hear words, but we could see the two men talking to each other, first crouching near the ground, then standing.

And then the unthinkable happened. Esau threw his arms around my father. My brothers immediately put their hands on the daggers hidden in their girdles. But Esau had moved not to harm his brother but to kiss him. He gathered our father to his bosom in a long embrace, and when at last they let go of each other, Esau pushed Jacob on the shoulder, a gesture of boys at play. Then he ran his hand through our father's hair, and at that, both men laughed the same hearty laugh that proved they had shared their mother's womb, even though one was dark and one was fair, one was slender and one was stocky.

My father said something to his brother, and again Esau held him to his chest, but this time when they parted, there was no laughter. Reuben later said that their cheeks were wet with tears as they turned to walk back toward us, their arms hung around each other's shoulders.

I was amazed. Esau, the red-faced bloodthirsty avenger, weeping in my father's arms? How could this man be the monster who haunted my dreams and chased the song from my brothers' lips?

My mothers exchanged glances of disbelief, but Inna's shoulders shook with silent laughter. "Your father was such a fool," she said weeks later in Succoth as we retold the story of that day. "To fear such a baby-faced sweetling? To give us all nightmares over such a lamb as that?"

My father led Esau back to where we stood, and

Jacob presented gifts to his brother. Our uncle dutifully declined them three times, and then dutifully accepted his brother's offerings, praising each one in the most flattering terms. The ceremony of the gifts took a long time, and I wanted only to get a closer look at the cousins who stood behind Esau, especially at the women, who wore necklaces and dozens of bracelets on their arms and ankles.

After he had accepted the animals, the wool, the foodstuffs, and Jacob's second-best herding dog, Esau turned to his brother and asked, in what sounded like my father's own voice, "Who are these fine men?"

So Jacob presented his sons, who bowed low before their uncle, as they had been instructed. "Here is Reuben, my firstborn, son of Leah, who stands there." My mother bowed her head very low, less to show respect I think than to keep Esau from noticing her mismatched eyes before he had counted all of her sons.

"And here are more of Leah's children: Simon and Levi. This is Judah," my father said, clapping his fourth son on the shoulder. "You can see how your image was never far from my mind." Judah and Esau smiled at each other with the same smile.

"Zebulun is also Leah's son, and there are her twins Naphtali and Issachar."

Esau bowed to my mother and said, "Leah is the mother of myriads." And Leah blushed with pride.

Next, my father presented Joseph. "This is the youngest, the only son of my Rachel," he said, flaunting his fondness for my aunt. Esau nodded and looked at the favorite son and stared at Rachel's undiminished beauty.

She stared back at him, still thunderstruck by the events of the day.

Next Jacob called out the name of Dan. "This is the son of Rachel's handmaid Bilhah. And here are Gad and Asher, borne to me by Leah's girl, Zilpah."

It was the first time I had heard the distinctions between my brothers, or my aunties, made so clear or public. I saw the sons of the lesser wives whom the world called "handmaids," and I saw how their heads dropped to be so named.

But Esau knew what it was to be second, and he approached the lesser sons just as he had my other brothers, going to Dan, Gad, and Asher, taking their hands in greeting. The sons of Bilhah and Zilpah stood taller, and I was proud to have such an uncle.

Now it was my father's turn to ask about the sons of Esau, who named them each with pride: "You have met Eliphaz already, my firstborn by Adath, who stands there," he said, pointing to a small, plump woman who wore a head covering made of hammered copper disks.

"And here is Reuel," said Esau, putting his arm around a thin, dark man with a full beard. "He is the son of Basemath," nodding at a sweet-faced woman who held a baby on her hip.

"My little boys are Jeush, Jalam, and Korah. They stand with Basemath there, but they are the sons of Oholibama, my youngest wife," Esau said. "She died last spring, in childbirth."

There was much craning of necks as introductions were made, but soon we were able to get a closer look as everyone began the short walk back to Jacob's riverside camp. My older brothers eyed their grown cousins, but did not speak. The women drew together and began the slow process of acquaintance. We found Esau's daughters among them, including Adath's two youngest. Indeed, Adath had borne many girls, some of whom were grown and mothers themselves, but Libbe and Amat were still with her. They were not much older than I, but they ignored me because I still wore a child's dress, and they were women.

Basemath was a kind stepmother to all of Oholibama's children, and especially to the baby girl, Iti, who had cost Oholibama her life. Basemath had lost so many babies, both boys and girls, she could barely number them. She had only the one son, Reuel, and one living daughter, Tabea, who was just my height. Tabea and I fell into step beside each other but kept quiet, not daring to disturb the solemn silence that fell upon the procession.

It was late in the afternoon when we reached our tents. A messenger had been sent to tell the bondswomen to begin the evening meal, and we were greeted by the smell of baking bread and cooking meat. Still, there was much to be done before we could have the kind of feast called for by an occasion as great as the reconciliation of the sons of Isaac.

The women fell to work, and Tabea was sent to help me collect wild onions along the river. We nodded our heads like dutiful daughters, but as soon as we faced away from our elders, I nearly laughed out loud. A wish had been granted. We could be alone.

Tabea and I walked with great purpose toward the onion patch that I had picked bare the first day we had come to the Jabbok, and we found enough new shoots to fill her basket. But we decided that our mothers did not need to know how quickly we had finished, and we took advantage of our freedom, putting our feet into the water and pouring out the handful of stories that compose the memory of childhood.

When I admired the copper bangles on her wrist, she told me her mother's life story. How Esau had been smitten by the lovely young Basemath when he saw her in the marketplace near Mamre, where our grandmother Rebecca lived. For a bride-price, he had offered Basemath's father, in addition to the usual number of sheep and goats, no fewer than forty copper bangles, "so that her wrists and ankles should announce her beauty," he said. Esau loved Basemath, but she suffered at the hands of his first wife, Adath, who was jealous. Not even the stillbirths of Basemath's babies had softened Adath's heart. When I asked how they could celebrate the new moon together with so much anger in the house, Tabea said the women of her family did not mark the moon's death and rebirth together. "That's another thing the Grandmother hates about the wives of Esau," Tabea said.

"You know our grandmother?" I asked. "You know Rebecca?"

"Yes," said my cousin. "I saw her twice, at barley harvests. The Grandmother smiles at me, though she does not speak to my mother, nor Adath, nor did she take notice of Oholibama when she was alive.

"The Grandmother says hateful things about my mother, and that is wrong." My cousin knit her brow and her eyes filled with tears. "But I love the Grandmother's tent. It is so beautiful there, and even though she is the oldest woman I ever saw, her beauty is not erased." Tabea giggled and said, "The Grandmother tells me that I look like her, even though it is clear that I resemble my mother in every way."

Tabea did seem a copy of Basemath, with her thin nose and glossy, dark hair, her fragile wrists and ankles. But when I met Rebecca, I remembered my cousin's words and saw what the Grandmother meant. It was Tabea's eyes that Rebecca could claim as her own, for my cousin's eyes were black and direct as arrows, where Basemath's were brown and always downcast.

I told Tabea about the red tent and how my mothers celebrated the new moon with cakes and songs and stories, leaving ill will outside for the duration of the darkness. And how I, the only daughter, had been permitted inside with them throughout my childhood, although it was against custom for anyone past weaning and not yet a woman to enter. At this, we both looked down upon our chests and pulled our tunics tight to compare what was happening to our bodies. Although neither of us was ready to suckle, it seemed that I would reach womanhood first. Tabea sighed and I shrugged and then we laughed until our eyes filled with tears, which made us laugh even more until we were rolling on the ground.

When we caught our breath, we spoke of our brothers. Tabea said she did not know Eliphaz well, but that Reuel was kind. Of the little boys, she hated Jeush, who pulled her hair at every turn and kicked her shins whenever he was sent to help her in the garden. I told her how Simon and Levi made Joseph and my other brothers abandon our games, and how they treated me like their personal servant whose only duty it was to keep their wine cups filled. I even told her how I spit into their cups when I had the chance. I spoke of Reuben's kindness, and Judah's beauty, and how Joseph and I had been nursed together.

I was shocked when Tabea said she wanted no children. "I have seen my mother cradle too many dead babes," she said. "And I heard Oholibama scream for three days before she gave up her life for Iti. I am not willing to suffer like that." Tabea said she wanted no part of marriage but would rather serve at Mamre and change her name to Deborah. Or else, she said, she would sing at the altar of a great temple like the one in Shechem. "There I would become one of the consecrated women who weave for the gods and wear clean robes always. Then I will sleep alone unless I choose to take a consort at the barley festival."

I did not understand her desires. Indeed, I did not fully understand her words, since I knew nothing about temples or the women who serve there. For my part, I told Tabea I hoped for ten strong children like those my mother had borne, though I wanted five girls at least. It was the first time I had said these things aloud, and perhaps the first time I had even given them thought. But I spoke from my heart.

"You have no fear of childbirth?" asked my cousin. "What of the pain? What if the baby dies?"

I shook my head. "Midwives do not fear life," I said, and I realized that I had come to think of myself as Rachel's apprentice and Inna's granddaughter.

Tabea and I stared into the water and our words ebbed. We pondered the difference between us and wondered if our hopes would be fulfilled, and whether we would ever learn what happened to the other after our fathers took their leave. My thoughts flew back and forth, like the shuttle on a great loom, so that when I finally heard my name in my mother's mouth, there was some anger in it. We had tarried too long. Tabea and I walked quickly, hand in hand, back to the cooking fires.

My cousin and I did our best to stay together after that, watching our mothers circle one another with thinly veiled curiosity. They studied one another's clothes and recipes, politely asking one another to repeat their names, just one more time, if you please, to get the pronunciation right. I could see my mother's eyebrows rise at the Canaanite women's use of salt, and I noticed Adath stiffen at the sight of Bilhah adding a handful of fresh onions to her dried-goat stew. But all judgments were masked under thin smiles amid the rush to prepare the feast.

While the women readied the meal, Esau and Jacob disappeared within my father's tent. After the sons of Esau put up their tents for the night, they gathered near my father's door, where my brothers also stood. Reuben and Eliphaz exchanged pleasantries about their fathers' flocks, subtly comparing the number and health of each herd, sizing up each other's approach to pasturage and skills with dogs. Eliphaz seemed surprised that neither Reuben nor any of his brothers had yet married or sired children, but this was not a subject that Reuben would discuss with the son of Esau. There were long lulls in the conversation between the cousins, who kicked at the dirt and clenched and unclenched their fists in boredom.

Finally, the flap to the tent opened and my father and Esau walked out, rubbing their eyes at the lingering brightness of the day, calling for wine and for the meal to begin. The two brothers sat on a blanket that Jacob himself spread. Their sons arranged themselves in self-conscious order of rank, Eliphaz and Reuben standing behind their fathers, Joseph and Korah sitting at their sides. As I ran back and forth, keeping the wine cups filled, I noticed how my brothers outnumbered Tabea's, and that they were much more handsome than the sons of Esau. Tabea served bread, while our mothers and their servants filled the men's plates until they could eat no more.

Every woman noticed who had taken the most of her stew, her bread, her beer, and each man took pains to compliment the food served by his brother's wives. Esau drank deeply of my mother's beer and favored Bilhah's oniony goat dish. Jacob ate little, but did his best to honor the food brought him by Basemath and Adath.

When the men were done, the women and girls sat down, but as happens with great meals, there was little appetite after the hours of stirring and tasting. The mothers were served by the slaves of Esau—two strong girls wearing small silver rings through holes in their upper ears. One of them was pregnant; Tabea whispered that it was Esau's seed, and if she bore a son, the girl would remove the upper earring and become a lesser wife. I stared at the strapping slave girl, her ankles as thick as Judah's, and then glanced at the slender Basemath, and told Tabea that Esau's taste in wives was as generous as his other appetites. She started to giggle, but a glare from Adath stifled us.

The light was starting to fade when Jacob and Esau began to tell stories. Our bondswomen brought lamps and Esau's slaves kept them filled with oil, so the light from the flames danced upon the faces of my family, suddenly grown numerous. Tabea and I sat knee to knee, listening to the story of our great-grandfather Abram, who had left the ancient home in Ur where the moon was worshiped in the name of Nanna and Ningal, and gone to Haran where the voice of El had come to him and directed him to Canaan. In the south, Abram had done great deeds—killing a thousand men with a single blow because El-Abram had given him the power of ten thousand.

Jacob spoke of the beauty of Sarai, Abram's wife and a servant of Innana, the daughter of Nanna and Ningal. Innana loved Sarai so well that the goddess came to her in the terebinth grove at Mamre and gave her a healthy son in the extremity of her life. That son was our grandfather Isaac, the husband of Rebecca, who was the niece of Sarai the priestess. It was Rebecca, my grandmother, who divined for the people now at Sarai's holy grove in Mamre.

Having recalled the family history in the proper fashion, my father and my uncle moved on to childhood stories, slapping each other on the back as they recalled the times they had slipped away from their mother's garden to play with the baby lambs, helping one another remember the names of their favorite dogs—the Black, the Dappled, and especially the Three-Legged

Wonder, a miraculous bitch that survived a jackal's attack and still herded with the best.

It was wonderful to see my father's face as these stories spilled out. I could see him as a boy again—carefree, strong, willful. His reserve melted as Esau reminded him of a day they had fallen into a wadi and entered their mother's tent covered in thick gray mud. He laughed at the story about a time the brothers stole a whole day's worth of baking, ate themselves sick, and suffered a beating for it.

After many stories, a satisfied hush fell over the company. We listened to the rustling of the herds and the Jabbok's whispers. And then Esau began a song. My father broke into a wide grin and joined in, giving loud and lusty voice to the words of an unfamiliar herding song all about the power of a certain ram. The women pinched their lips together as the verses continued, each one randier and bolder than the last. To my amazement, my brothers and our cousins knew every word and joined in, making a great shout of their voices, and finishing with a whoop and then laughter.

When the men were finished, Esau nodded to his first wife, who gave a sign that opened the mouths of his wives and daughters, his bondswomen and slave girls. It was a hymn to Anat, a name the Canaanite women used for Innana, and it praised the goddess's prowess in war and her power in love.

Their song was unlike anything I'd ever heard, and the hair on the back of my neck stood on end, as though Joseph were tickling me with a stalk of grass. But when I turned to rebuke him, I saw that he sat by our father's side, his eyes shining and fixed upon the singers. They

sang the words in unison, yet somehow created a web
of sound with their voices. It was like hearing a piece of
fabric woven with all the colors of a rainbow. I did not
know that such beauty could be formed by the human
mouth. I had never heard harmony before.

When they finished, I discovered tears in my eyes
and saw that Zilpah's cheeks were wet, too. Bilhah's lips
were parted in admiration, and Rachel's eyes were
closed to listen with perfect attention.

The men applauded and asked for more, so Basemath began anew with a song about the harvest and
the fullness of the earth. Tabea joined with them,
and I was dazzled to think that my friend could perform such a miracle with her mothers. I closed my
eyes. The women sang like birds, only more sweetly.
They sounded like the wind in the trees, but louder.
Their voices were like the rush of the river's water,
but with meaning. Then their words ceased and they
began to sing with sound that meant nothing at all;
yet gave new voice to joy, to pleasure, to longing, to
peace. "Lu, lu, lu," they sang.

When they finished, Reuben applauded the music
of our kinswomen and bowed low to them. Joseph and
Judah and Dan also rose and bowed in thanks, and I
thought, "These four are my favorites, and the best of
my brothers."

There were more songs and a few more stories, and
we sat by the light of the lamps. Only when the moon
began to set did the women clear the last of the cups.
With sleeping children in their arms, the young mothers moved toward their own beds, and the men began
taking their leave too. Finally, only Jacob and Esau

sat, staring silently at the sputtering wick of the last lamp.

Tabea and I slipped away and walked down to the river, our arms around each other's waists. I was perfectly happy. I could have stood there until dawn, but my mother came to find me, and though she smiled at Tabea, she took my hand and pulled me away from my friend.

I woke the next morning to the sounds of Esau's tribe making ready to leave. During their late-night conversation, my father told his brother that he would not follow him back to Seir. As fondly as the brothers had met, their fortunes could not be married. My uncle's lands were vast and his position secure. Had we joined him, Jacob's worth would be judged puny in comparison. My brothers, too, would have been at a disadvantage, since Esau's sons already had flocks and lands of their own. And for all the fellowship of the night before, the sons of Isaac were not entirely reconciled, nor could they ever be. The scars they had borne for twenty years could not be erased with a single meeting, and the habits of those years, lived in such different worlds, were bound to come between them.

Nevertheless, the brothers embraced with declarations of love and promises to visit. Reuben and Eliphaz clasped each other by the shoulder, the women nodded goodbye. Tabea showed her boldness by running from her mother's side to hug me, and we tasted each other's tears. While we held each other she whispered, "Take heart. We will be together again soon at the Grandmother's tent. I heard my mother say we would surely meet you there at the barley festival. Remember everything that happens from now until then, so you can tell me." With that, she kissed me and ran back to her mother's side. She waved her hand until she was out of my sight. As soon as they departed, my father instructed Reuben and my mother to prepare for our own leave-taking.

I did my part with a happy heart, glad to take up our travels free of the fear of Esau, eager to see my friend again and to meet the Grandmother, who had already begun to live in my imagination. I was certain that Rebecca would love my mothers; after all, they were her nieces as well as her daughters-in-law. And I imagined myself her pet, her favorite. Why shouldn't I be, I thought. After all, I was the female heir of her favored son.

The next morning we departed, but we did not travel far. On the second day, my father plunged his staff into the earth near a small stream beneath a young oak tree and announced his intention to stay. We were near a village called Succoth, he said, a place that had been kind to him on his journey north. My brothers had scouted the land before and secured a site for us, and within a few days there were pens and stalls for the animals and a fine clay oven, large enough to bake both bread and cakes. We dwelt there for two years.

The journey from the house of Laban had given me a taste for change, and the daily routines of settled life in Succoth bored me at first. But my days were filled from sunrise to dusk, and soon I learned to enjoy the alchemy of turning flour into bread, meat into stew, water into beer. I also moved from spinning to weaving, which was far more difficult than I had ever imagined, and a skill I never mastered like Zilpah and Bilhah, for whom the warp never broke.

As the oldest girl, I was often given charge of the bondswomen's children, and learned both to love and resent the runny-nosed monsters. I was needed so much within the world of women that I barely noticed how little I had to do with my brothers or how things changed among them. For those were the days when Levi and Simon replaced Reuben at my father's right hand, and became his closest advisers.

Succoth was a fertile place for my family. Zibatu had a new baby, and so did Uzna—both of them sons whom my father took to his altar under the oak tree. He circumcised them and declared them free of their fathers' indenture, full members of the tribe of El-Abram, and the tribe of Jacob grew.

Bilhah conceived in Succoth, but she miscarried before the baby moved in her womb. Rachel was bereaved in this manner as well, and for nearly a month after would not let Joseph out of her sight. My mother, too, lost a child, who came from the womb months too soon. The women looked away from the tiny doomed girl, but I saw only her perfect beauty. Her eyelids were veined like a butterfly's wing, her toes curled like the petals of a flower.

I held my sister, who was never given a name, and who never opened her eyes, and who died in my arms.

I was not afraid to hold that small death. Her face was peaceful, her hands perfectly clean. It seemed she would wake at any moment. The tears from my eyes fell upon her alabaster cheek, and it appeared that she mourned the passing of her own life. My mother came to take my sister from me, but seeing my sorrow, permitted me to carry her to burial. She was shrouded in a scrap of fine cloth and laid beneath the strongest, oldest tree within sight of my mother's tent. No offerings were made, but as the bundle was covered with earth the sighs that poured from my mothers' mouths were as eloquent as any psalm.

As we walked away from the baby's death, Zilpah muttered that the gods of the place were arrayed against life, but as usual, my auntie misread the signs. For the bondswomen grew great with child as quickly as their babies were weaned. Every ewe and goat bore twins, and all of them survived. The flocks grew quickly and made my father a prosperous man, which meant my brothers could wed.

Three of them married in Succoth. Judah married Shua, the daughter of a trader. She conceived during their nuptial week and bore him Er, the first of his sons and the first of my father's grandsons. I liked Shua, who was plump and good-natured. She brought the Canaanite gift of song into our tents and taught us harmonies. Simon and Levi took two sisters to wife—Ialutu and Inbu, daughters of a potter.

It fell to me to stay with the babies and mind the fires while the wives of Jacob attended the festivities. I was furious about being left behind, but in the weeks after the nuptials, I heard my mothers talk over every detail of the weddings so much that I felt I had been there myself.

"Surely you must admit the singing was wonderful,"

said Zilpah, who returned from each one humming a new melody, slapping the rhythm with her hand against a bony thigh.

"Well, of course," said my mother, in an offhand way. "They learn this from their mothers and grandmothers."

Rachel grinned, and leaned over to Leah: "Too bad their grandmothers could not cook, eh?"

Leah smirked in agreement. "When it is Dinah's turn to enter the bridal tent, I will show them all how a wedding feast should be arrayed," she said, running her hand over my head.

Only Bilhah seemed to enjoy her nephews' weddings. "Oh, sister," she said to Leah, "didn't you think the veil was pretty, shot through with golden threads and hung with the dowry coins? I thought she was arrayed like a goddess."

Leah would have none of it. "Are you going to tell me that your belly was full after the meal?" she said.

But Leah was not unhappy in the brides her sons brought her. They were all healthy and respectful, though Shua quickly became the favorite. The two sisters never fully entered my mothers' circle, and they lived with their husbands at a short distance from the rest of us, closer to the herds, my brothers said. I think Simon and Levi moved because Ialutu and Inbu wanted to keep their distance. I did not miss their company at all. They treated me with the same disdain as their husbands, and besides, my mother was right; neither of them could cook.

Of Jacob's older sons, only Reuben remained unmarried. My eldest brother seemed content to serve his mother and to do kindness to Bilhah, whose only son was still too young to hunt.

Early one morning while everyone slept, a woman's voice called, "Where are the daughters of Sarai? Where are the wives of Jacob?"

It was a soft voice, and yet it woke me from a deep sleep where I lay at my mother's feet. Like me, Leah sat up at the sound and hurried outside, arriving at the same moment as Rachel. Within a heartbeat, Bilhah and Zilpah were there as well, the five of us staring at the messenger from Mamre, whose dress shimmered silver in the blue glow that heralds the dawn.

Her speech was formal, in the manner of all messengers. "Rebecca, the oracle at Mamre, the mother of Jacob and Esau, the grandmother of hundreds of myriads, calls you to the canopy of terebinths for the barley festival.

"Let Jacob be told and know."

Silence greeted the declaration of this visitor, who spoke in strange accents that bent every word in three places. It was as though we were all sharing a dream, for none of us had ever seen red hair before, nor had we ever seen a woman carry the messenger's striped bag. And yet it was no dream, as the morning chill made us shiver.

Finally Leah caught her breath and gave welcome, offering the stranger a place to sit and bread to eat. But as soon as we were assembled around our guest, my aunties and I again fell still and stared in plain amazement. The messenger looked around her and broke into a smile that showed a row of small, yellow teeth between a pair of oddly dappled lips. Speaking now in an ordinary voice and with a lightness that set everyone at ease, she said, "I see you number few redheads among you. Where I come from, it is said that redheaded women are begotten during their mother's periods. Such is the ignorance of the lands to the north."

Bilhah laughed out loud to hear such boldness from a stranger. This seemed to please our guest, who turned to my aunt and presented herself. "My name is Werenro and I serve the Grandmother." At that, she pulled her hair back to show her ear, pierced high with the plain bronze stud, and added, "I am the world's happiest slave." Again, Bilhah laughed aloud at such plainspokenness. I giggled, too.

As soon as the men were fed, Leah sent for Jacob and presented the messenger, who by then had covered the fire of her hair and lowered her eyes. "She comes from your mother," Leah said. "Rebecca bids us attend her barley festival. The messenger awaits your reply."

Jacob seemed startled by the newcomer's presence but composed himself quickly and told Leah that they would obey Rebecca in everything, and that he would come to her at harvest time, he and his wives, with his sons and his daughters.

Werenro then withdrew to my mother's tent and slept. I worked nearby all day, hoping to catch a glimpse of her. I tried to think of some reason to enter the tent. I wanted to see that hair again, and my fingers longed to touch the robes that moved like weeds in flowing water. Inna told me Werenro's clothes were made of silk, a kind of cloth that was woven by worms on their own tiny looms. I raised my eyebrow—doing my best to copy my mother's most disdainful gesture—to show that I was too old to be taken in by such nonsense. Inna laughed at me and wasted no further breath on my disbelief.

Werenro rested undisturbed late into the evening, until after the men had eaten and the bowls of the women's evening meal were cleared. My mothers had gathered by their fire, hoping the stranger would appear in time to give us a story.

The messenger walked out of the tent, and seeing us arrayed around her, she bowed deeply, with her fingers stretched wide, in an unfamiliar gesture of obeisance. Then she straightened her back, looked into our faces one by one, and grinned like a little child who has stolen a fig. Werenro was unlike anyone or anything else in the world. I was enchanted.

She bowed her head at my mothers in thanks for the bowl of olives, cheese, and fresh bread that had been left for her. Before eating, she recited a short prayer in a language that sounded like a buzzard's cry. I laughed at the noise, thinking she was making another joke, but the redheaded stranger shot me a look of withering anger. I felt as though my face had been slapped, and my cheeks grew hot and as crimson as her hair, which was once again visible and as improbably red as I remembered. But in the next moment, she smiled forgiveness at me, and patting the ground by her side, welcomed me to a place of honor.

After she put aside the last of her meal, with compliments for the bread and extravagant praise for the beer, Werenro began a chant. There were many strange names in her story, and a melody that was sadder than anything I'd ever heard. She held us all rapt, like a baby on a lap.

It was a story of the beginning of the world, of Tree and Hawk, who gave birth to Red Wolf, who populated the world with a womb that gave birth to all red-blooded life, save woman and man. It was a very long story, mysterious and filled with names of unfamiliar trees and animals. It was set in a place of terrible cold, where the wind screamed in pain. It was frightening and thrilling, and lonely.

When Werenro stopped, the fire was out and only one lamp sputtered a dim light. The little ones were asleep in their mothers' laps and even a few of the women dozed, their heads dropping on their chests.

I looked into the face of the messenger, but she did not see me. Her eyes were closed above smiling lips. She was far away in the land of her story, a cold land of strange myths, where her own mother was buried. I felt the messenger's loneliness, so far from home. I understood Werenro's heart the way I understood the sun when it warmed my face. I reached out my hand and placed it on her shoulder, and Werenro turned to me, opened eyes that glistened with tears, and kissed me on the lips. "Thank you," she said, and stood.

She walked into my mother's tent and left before dawn without telling me how the red wolf in her story gave rise to man and woman. But this did not worry me, for I knew that I would hear the rest of it at Mamre, when we went to see the Grandmother at last.

CHAPTER FIVE

Preparations for the journey began a month before the barley harvest. My father decided that he would bring all of his wives to Mamre and most of his sons. Simon and Levi were told to remain behind with the flocks, and since both of their wives were pregnant for the first time, they did not object. Although Shua was not with child, Judah asked to be left back as well, and the women all knew why; the whooping sounds of their nightly pleasure were a source of jokes and smirking.

My brothers and I were summoned to our mothers, who examined our best clothes and found them wanting. A flurry of washing, mending, and sewing followed. Rachel decided to make a new tunic for her only son. Joseph's robe, decorated with bands of red and yellow, earned him some awful teasing from his brothers. He ignored their taunts and swore he preferred the garment his mother had made for him over the dull stuff that men were given to wear. I couldn't tell if he was putting on a brave front or really liked his finery.

I was given bracelets for my wrists—my first jewelry.

They were only copper, but I loved them, especially the womanly sound they made. Indeed, I spent so much time admiring the way the three bands gathered on my wrists that I paid no attention to my feet and, on the first day I wore them, tripped and scraped my chin raw. I was horrified at the thought that I would meet the Grandmother looking like a scabby child. Every day until we left I studied my face in Rachel's mirror, begged Inna for salve, and picked at the enormous red crust.

The day we left for Mamre, I was beside myself with excitement and ignored every request made of me. My mother, who was everywhere at once, making sure that the oil and wine jars were securely sealed, that the brothers had combed their beards, that everything was ready, finally lost patience with me. It was one of the few times she ever raised her voice to me. "Either you help me, or I will leave you behind to wait upon your brothers' wives," she said. She didn't have to say another word.

The journey took only a few days, and it was a joyful trip. We sang as we walked, preening in our finery and proud of our beautiful flock, for only the best of the animals had been culled for gifts to the Grandmother.

Jacob walked beside Rachel early in the morning, inhaling her perfume, smiling, saying little. Then he took his place beside Leah to discuss the animals, the crops, and the proper etiquette for greeting his parents. Late in the afternoon, Jacob found his way to Bilhah, displacing Reuben, her shadow. My father walked with his hand upon her little shoulder, as though he needed her support.

I was perfectly happy. Joseph stayed beside me and even forgot himself enough to hold my hand from time to time. At night, I settled in beside Zilpah, who fed my awe of the Grandmother with tales about Rebecca's reputation as a diviner, healer, and prophet, so that I could barely fall asleep. I could barely keep myself from running, for I was going to see Tabea again. Werenro would smile at me and tell more of her story. And I would meet the Grandmother, who I imagined would understand me instantly and adore me above any of my brothers.

Midmorning on the third day, we caught sight of Rebecca's tent. Even from a distance it was a marvel, though at first I didn't really understand what shimmered on the far side of the valley before me. It was enormous—far bigger than any tent I had ever seen, and utterly unlike our dull goat-hair dwellings. This was an earthbound rainbow—red, yellow, and blue—billowing upon the high ground under a stand of great old trees whose branches implored a cloudless heaven.

As we came closer, it became clear that this was less a home than a canopy, open on all sides to welcome travelers from every direction. Inside, we caught glimpses of vivid hangings in patterns that were both delicate and bold, with scenes of dancing women and flying fish, stars, crescents, suns, birds. It was more beautiful than any handmade thing I had seen.

When we could almost feel the shade of the sacred

grove, the Grandmother came into view. She did not come out to meet us, nor did she send any of her women out, but waited in the shade of the wonderful tent, arms crossed, watching. I could not take my eyes off her.

I do not remember my father's formal greeting or the ceremony to present my brothers, one by one, and then the gifts, and finally my mothers and me. I saw only her. The Grandmother—my grandmother. She was the oldest person I had ever seen. Her years proclaimed themselves in the deep furrows on her brow and around her mouth, but the beauty of youth still clung to her. She stood as erect as Reuben and nearly as tall. Her black eyes were clear and sharp, painted in the Egyptian style—a pattern of heavy black kohl that made her appear all-seeing. Her robes were purple—the color of royalty and holiness and wealth. Her head covering was long and black, shot through with gold threads, providing the illusion of luxurious hair, where in fact only a few gray strands were left to her.

Rebecca did not notice while I stared. The eyes of the Grandmother were fixed upon the son she had not seen since he was a smooth-cheeked boy, now a man with grown sons and a grandfather. She showed no emotion as Jacob presented his children, his wives, and the gifts he had brought. She nodded, accepting everything, saying nothing.

I thought she was magnificent—aloof as a queen. But I saw my mother's mouth purse in displeasure. She had anticipated a show of maternal love for the favored son. I could not see my father's face to measure his reaction.

After the official welcome, the Grandmother turned away from us and we were taken to the west side of the hill, to set up our tents and prepare for the evening meal. That's where I learned that Tabea had not yet arrived and that Werenro had been sent to Tyre, to trade for the rare purple dye that the Grandmother favored.

No men lived at the grove. Rebecca was attended by ten women, who also saw to the pilgrims who came seeking advice and prophecy from her they called "Oracle." When I asked about my father's father, one of the Grandmother's attendants told me that Isaac dwelt a short distance away, in the village of Arba in a snug hut that was kinder than an open tent to his old bones. "He will come for the meal tonight," said the woman, whose only name was Deborah. The Grandmother called all of her acolytes Deborah, in honor of the woman who had been her childhood nurse and lifelong retainer, and whose bones lay buried beneath the trees of Mamre.

The Grandmother's women spoke in shy whispers and dressed in the same plain white tunic. They were uniformly kind but distant, and I quickly stopped trying to see them as individuals and began to think of them all as the Deborahs.

The afternoon passed quickly in preparation for the evening meal. Just as the first bread was coming off the fire, word came that Isaac had arrived. I raced around to watch as my grandfather approached the grove. Rebecca came to watch, too, and she raised her hand in a brief greeting. My father walked out to greet him, his step growing faster and faster until he was actually running toward his father.

Isaac did not respond to his wife's salute or his son's excitement. He continued, seemingly serene in his cushioned seat upon a donkey being led by a woman wearing the white robes of my grandmother's entourage—though this one wore a veil that covered everything but her eyes. It was only when he came close that I saw that my grandfather was blind, his eyes closed in a tight squint that soured the whole of his face into a permanent scowl. He was small-boned and thin, and would have seemed frail except that his hair was as thick and dark as a younger man's.

The Grandmother watched as the serving woman helped Isaac descend and walked him to his blanket on the east side of Mamre. But before the servant released his elbow, Isaac took her hand in his and brought it to his lips. He kissed her palm and placed it upon his cheek. Isaac's face relaxed into a smile so that anyone who cared to see would know that the veiled one was the companion of my grandfather's heart.

My father stood before Isaac and said, "Father?" in a voice overflowing with tears. Isaac turned his face toward Jacob and opened his arms. My father embraced the old man, and both of them wept. They spoke in whispers as my brothers stood and waited to be introduced. My mothers held back, exchanging glances of concern over the food, which would be dry and tasteless if it wasn't served soon.

But the men would not be rushed. Isaac pulled his son to a seat by his side as Jacob introduced each of his sons. Isaac ran his hands over the faces of my brothers

Reuben and Zebulun, Dan, Gad, and Asher, Naphtali and Issachar. When Joseph was finally named as the youngest son, the Grandfather pulled him down into his lap, as though he were a baby and not a boy nearing manhood. Isaac tenderly ran his fingers over the contours of Joseph's face and over the sinews of his arms. A breeze rose up and lifted the silken tent high above them, embracing the Grandfather and his grandson in its wonderful rainbow. It was a grand sight and it took my breath away. And that is precisely when Rebecca, who had kept her distance until then, finally broke her majestic silence.

"You must be hungry and thirsty, Isaac," she said, offering hospitality in an ungracious voice. "Your children are parched from their journey. Let your Deborah bring you inside. Let your daughters-in-law show me whether they can cook."

A flurry of white garments laid out the meal, and the feast began. My grandfather ate well, taking his mouthfuls from the fingers of the veiled woman. He asked whether his grandsons had eaten enough and reached out from time to time to find his son—placing a doting hand on his shoulder or his cheek, leaving smears of oil that my father did not wipe away. I watched this from behind a tree, for with all those servants there was no need of my carrying food or drink.

My brothers were hungry and finished quickly, and soon Zilpah fetched me back to our side of the great tent, where the women were gathered. The Grandmother sat down, and we watched as she had a single taste of everything before her. She said nothing about the stews or the breads or the sweets. She did not praise the cheese or the giant olives my mothers had collected. She did not acknowledge my mother's beer.

But already, I was not surprised by Rebecca's silence. I had stopped thinking of her as a woman like my mothers, or like any other woman for that matter. In the space of an afternoon, she had become a force of the gods, like a rainstorm or a brushfire.

Because the Grandmother ate little and said nothing, our meal was more somber than festive. There was no passing of bowls for a second taste, no compliments, no questions, no conversation at all. The great feast was done in a few minutes, and the Deborahs cleared the last cups before there was time to think of refilling them.

The Grandmother rose to her feet and walked to the western edge of her tent, where the sun was setting in a blaze of orange and gold. Her attendants followed. Rebecca reached her hands to the sun, as if to touch its last rays.

When she dropped her hands, the attendants began singing a song inviting the barley-harvest moon. The verses repeated an ancient prophecy. When every stalk of every barley field numbered twenty-seven seeds, the end of days would arrive and there would be rest for the weary and evil would vanish from the earth like starlight at sunrise. The last chorus ended just as darkness swallowed the camp.

Lamps were lit among the men and lamps were lit among the women. The Grandmother came with us, and I feared we would sit in silent attendance for the whole of the evening, but my fear was ungrounded, for as soon as the lights were kindled, she began to speak.

"This is the story of the day I came to the tent of Mamre, to the grove of sacred trees, to the navel of the world," said the Grandmother, Rebecca, in tones that could have been heard by the men, had they been listening.

"It was in the weeks after the death of Sarai the Prophet, beloved of Abram, mother of Isaac. She who gave birth when she was too old to carry water, much less carry a child. Sarai, cherished mother.

"On the morning I entered this grove, a cloud descended over the tent of Sarai. A golden cloud that bore no rain, nor did it cover the sun. It was a cloud that is seen only upon great rivers and upon the sea, but never before in a place so high. And yet the cloud hovered above the tent of Sarai while Isaac knew me and I became his wife. We spent our first seven days as husband and wife under that cloud, in which the gods were surely present.

"And there was never a harvest richer in wine and grain and oil than that spring, my daughters," she said, in a whisper that was at once proud and defeated. "Ah, but for me, so many daughters born dead. So many sons, dead in the womb. Only two survive. Who can explain this mystery?"

The Grandmother fell silent, and her dark mood covered her listeners and our shoulders sagged. Even I, who had lost no children, felt a mother's bereavement. After a moment, my grandmother rose and pointed to Leah, that she should follow her into an inner chamber of the great tent, where the lamps were lit with scented oil and the tapestries glowed. The rest of us sat for a while before we realized that we had been dismissed.

My mother's interview with the Grandmother went on late into the night. First, Rebecca took a long look at her daughter-in-law, betraying her shortsightedness by getting very close and peering into her face. Then she began the close interrogation into every detail of Leah's life.

"Why did they not put you out to die at birth, with eyes such as yours? What is your mother's burial place? How do you prepare wool for dying? Where did you learn to make that beer? What kind of father is Jacob, my son? Which of your sons is your favorite? Which of your sons do you fear? How many lambs does my son sacrifice to El at the spring festival? What is your practice at the new moon? How many babies have you lost in childbearing? What plans do you make for your daughter's coming-of-age? How many epahs of barley do you grow in Succoth, and how many of wheat?"

My mother could not even remember all of the questions put to her that night, but she answered them fully and without taking her eyes from the Grandmother's face. This startled the older woman, who was used to unnerving people, but Leah was not cowed. The two of them glared at each other.

Finally, when the Grandmother could think of nothing else to ask, she nodded and made a wordless sound, a grunt of grudging approval. "Very well, Leah, mother of many sons. Very well." With a wave of her hand, my mother was sent away. She found her way to her blanket and fell asleep, exhausted.

Over the next two days, my aunties were called to the Grandmother's inner chamber, one by one.

Rachel was greeted with kisses and caresses. Girlish laughter rang out as the two of them passed an afternoon together. The Grandmother patted my lovely aunt's cheeks and gently pinched her arms. Rebecca, who had been the beauty of her generation, took out her makeup box—a large, black, lacquered thing with many compartments, each one filled with a potion or unguent, perfume or paint. Rachel left the Grandmother's presence smiling and smelling of lotus oil, her eyelids green and her eyes ringed with a shiny black kohl that made her look formidable instead of merely beautiful.

When Zilpah was sent for, my auntie fell upon her face before the Grandmother, and was rewarded with a short poem about the great Asherah, consort of El and goddess of the sea. The Grandmother looked briefly into Zilpah's face, closed her black eyes, and foretold the time and place of my auntie's death. This news, which she never revealed to a soul, did not disturb Zilpah. If anything, it gave her a kind of peace that lasted the rest of her life. From that day forward, Zilpah smiled while she worked at the loom—not a wistful little grin at all, but a big, tooth-showing smile, as though she were remembering a good joke.

Bilhah dreaded her interview with the Grandmother and stumbled as she approached the old woman. The Grandmother frowned and sighed while Bilhah kept her eyes on her hands. The silence grew heavy, and after a short time, Rebecca turned and walked out, leaving Bil-hah alone with the beautiful tapestries that seemed to mock her.

These meetings meant little to me. For three days my eyes were on the horizon, watching for Tabea. She finally arrived on the day of the festival itself, with Esau and his first wife, Adath. The sight of my best friend was more than I could stand, and I ran to her. She threw her arms around me.

When we stood apart, I saw how much she had changed in the few months we had been apart. She was taller than I by a good half head, and there was no need to pull her garments tightly against her chest to see her breasts. But when I saw the belt that declared her a woman, my mouth dropped. She had entered the red tent! She was no longer a child but a woman. I felt my cheeks grow warm with envy as hers grew pink with pride. I had a thousand questions to ask her about what it was like and about her ceremony, and whether the world was a different place now that her place in it was different.

But I had no time to ask my cousin anything. The Grandmother had already taken note of Tabea's apron and approached my coin-covered aunt. Within a few moments, she was screaming at Adath with a fury I thought reserved for gods who had thunder and light-ning at their disposal.

Rebecca's anger was terrible. "You mean to tell me that her blood was wasted? You shut her up alone, like some animal?"

Adath cringed and made as if to answer when the Grandmother raised her fists. "Don't dare to defend

yourself, you ignorant nothing," she hissed. "You ba-
boon! I told you what to do and you disobeyed me, and
now there is nothing to be done. The best of his girls,
the only one of his seed with even a trace of intelligence
or feeling, and you treated her like a . . . like a . . . Pah!"
Rebecca spit at her daughter-in-law's feet. "I have no
words for this abomination."

Her voice grew icy and hushed. "Enough. You are
not fit to be in my tent. Get out of here. Be cursed and
leave this place and never let me see you again."

The Grandmother drew herself up to her full height
and slapped Adath with all her strength. The poor
woman crumpled to the ground, whimpering in fear
that a spell had been cast on her. The men, who had
rushed over to discover the reason for the Grandmother's displeasure, recoiled at the sight of the Oracle's
curse and quickly turned away from what was clearly
women's business.

Adath crawled away, but now Tabea was on the
ground at Rebecca's feet, sobbing, "No, no, no." My
cousin's face had turned ashen and her eyes were
wide with terror. "Take my name and call me Deborah, too. Make me the least of your servants, but do
not banish me. Oh please, Grandmother. Please. I beg
you, I beg you."

But Rebecca did not look at the creature suffering
at her feet. She did not see Tabea tear at her face until
there were bloody streaks down her cheeks. She did not
see her rip her robe into shreds or swallow handfuls of
dust. The Grandmother turned and walked away from
the death throes of Tabea's hope, wrapping her cloak
tightly around her body, as if to protect herself against

the misery before her. Finally, Tabea was lifted from the ground by the Grandmother's followers and carried back to the tents of Esau's wives.

I did not really understand what had happened, but I knew that my dear friend had suffered an injustice. My ears rang and my heart pounded. I could not believe the Grandmother's cruelty. My beloved cousin, who cared more for Rebecca than for her own mother, had been treated worse than the lepers who came seeking miracle cures. I hated Rebecca as I had never hated anyone.

My mother took my hand, led me to her tent, and gave me a cup of sweet wine. Stroking my hair, she answered my question even before I asked. Leah, my mother, said:

"The girl will suffer for the rest of her days, and your compassion is well placed. But your hatred is undeserved, daughter.

"It was not her intention to harm Tabea. I think she loved her well enough, but she had no choice. She was defending her mother and herself, me and your aunties, you and your daughters after you. She was defending the ways of our mothers and their mothers, and the great mother, who goes by many names, but who is in danger of being forgotten.

"This is not easy to explain, but I will tell you. Because you are my only daughter and because we lived for so long in such isolation, you already know much more than you should. You have spent time with us in the red tent. You have even attended a birth, which is something you must never tell the Grandmother. I know that you will not reveal what I tell you now."

I nodded my promise, and my mother sighed from her heart. She looked down at her hands, brown from the sun, wise with use, and rarely in repose as they were now. She placed her palms face up upon her knees and closed her eyes. Half singing, half whispering, Leah said:

"The great mother whom we call Innana is a fierce warrior and Death's bridesmaid. The great mother whom we call Innana is the center of pleasure, the one who makes women and men turn to one another in the night. The great mother whom we call Innana is the queen of the ocean and the patron of the rain.

"This is known to all—to the women and to the men. To the suckling babes and to the failing grandfathers."

Here she stopped and broke into a big, girlish grin. "Zilpah would be so amused at the sight of me speaking legend," she said, looking straight at me for a moment, and I smiled back at her, sharing the joke. But after a moment my mother resumed her formal pose and continued:

"The great mother whom we call Innana gave a gift to woman that is not known among men, and this is the secret of blood. The flow at the dark of the moon, the healing blood of the moon's birth—to men, this is flux and distemper, bother and pain. They imagine we suffer and consider themselves lucky. We do not disabuse them.

"In the red tent, the truth is known. In the red tent, where days pass like a gentle stream, as the gift of Innana courses through us, cleansing the body of last month's death, preparing the body to receive the new month's life, women give thanks—for repose and restoration, for the knowledge that life comes from between our legs, and that life costs blood."

Then she took my hand and told me, "I say this before the proper time, daughter mine, though it will not be long before you enter the tent to celebrate with me and your aunties. You will become a woman surrounded by loving hands to carry you and to catch your first blood and to make sure it goes back to the womb of Innana, to the dust that formed the first man and the first woman. The dust that was mixed with her moon blood.

"Alas, many of her daughters have forgotten the secret of Innana's gift, and turned their backs on the red tent. Esau's wives, the daughters of Edom, whom Rebecca despises, give no lesson or welcome to their young women when they come of age. They treat them like beasts––setting them out, alone and afraid, shut up in the dark days of the new moon, without wine and without the counsel of their mothers. They do not celebrate the first blood of those who will bear life, nor do they return it to the earth. They have set aside the Opening, which is the sacred business of women, and permit men to display their daughters' bloody sheets, as though even the pettiest baal would require such a degradation in tribute."

My mother saw my confusion. "You cannot understand all of this yet, Dinah," she said. "But soon you will know, and I will make sure that you are welcomed into the woman's life with ceremony and tenderness. Fear not."

It was dark when my mother uttered the last of these words. The songs of the barley festival reached our ears, and my mother rose, offering me her hand. We walked out into the night, to watch the offerings, burnt on an altar beside the tallest tree. Wonderful music was sung, harmonies of many parts. The Deborahs danced in a circle to the sound of their own clapping. They spun and crouched, leaped and swayed as though sharing a single mind, a single body, and I understood Tabea's wish to join their dance.

Adath disappeared during the night, taking my friend with her, strapped onto the back of a donkey, like an offering not yet dead, with a rag stuffed in her mouth to muffle the cries.

In the few days before our departure, I avoided the Grandmother and stayed near my mothers. I wished only to leave the place, but as we prepared to return to Succoth, Leah came to me with a grim face. "The Grandmother says that you are to stay here at Mamre for three months," she said. "Rebecca spoke to your father, and it has been arranged without my . . ." She stopped at the sight of my stricken face. "I wish I could stay or leave Zilpah with you, but the Grandmother will have none of it. She wants you only."

There was a long pause before she said, "It is an honor." She cupped my chin between her two hands and added tenderly, "We will be together again when the wheat is ripe."

I did not cry. I was frightened and angry, but I was determined not to weep, so I kept my mouth closed, breathed through my nose, and kept my eyes from blinking. That was how I survived as I watched my mother's form grow smaller and smaller and then disappear into the horizon. I had never imagined the loneliness of being without her or my aunts or even one of my brothers. I felt like a baby left outside to die, but I did not cry. I turned back to the Deborahs who watched me anxiously, but I did not cry.

Only at night, alone on my blanket, I turned my face to the ground and wept until I choked. Every morning I arose, groggy and confused until I remembered that I was alone in my grandmother's tent.

My memories from those months in Mamre seem pale and scattered. When I returned to my mothers, they were disappointed that I could not say more of wonders I had seen or secrets I had learned. It was as though I had walked through a cave filled with jewels and picked up only a handful of gray pebbles.

This is what I do remember.

I recall that once in every seven days, the Grandmother made a great show of baking. The rest of the week she did not soil her hands with the work of women, much less the kneading and handing of dough. But on the seventh day, she took flour and water and honey, turned them and shaped them, and sacrificed a corner from a three-sided cake, "for the Queen of Heaven," she whispered to the dough before consigning it to flame.

I doubted that the Queen would much care for the dry, tasteless things Rebecca offered. "Aren't they good?" she demanded when they came out of the oven. I nodded dutifully, washing my portion down with water, which was all I was given to drink. Luckily, her servants were far better bakers, and their cakes were sweet and moist enough for any queen. Still, when my grandmother whispered over her small domestic offering, it was the only time I saw her smile with her eyes.

It was my job to go to Rebecca early in the morning to assist her morning ablutions in preparation for the pilgrims who arrived at the grove daily. I carried her elaborate cosmetic box, which contained different scents for forehead, wrists, armpits, and ankles, a potion for the skin beneath the eyes, and a sour-smelling concoction for the throat. After the perfumes and creams, she began the careful application of color to lips, eyes, and cheeks. She said that the most important beauty treatment of all was to smell sweet, and her breath was always scented with mint, which she chewed morning and night.

The Grandmother seemed to burn with some kind of fire. She ate little and rarely sat down. She looked down upon anyone who required rest. Indeed, she criticized everyone except her sons, and although she favored Jacob, praising his good looks and his fine sons, it was clear that she depended on my uncle for everything. Messengers came and went from Seir every other day. Esau was called upon to deliver an extra epah of barley or to find meat worthy of the Grandmother's table. I saw him every fortnight at least, his arms full of gifts.

My uncle was a good man and a fine son. He made sure that wealthy pilgrims visited the grove and brought rich offerings. He found Isaac the stone hut that afforded Rebecca the luxury of living like a priestess, without a man to serve. The Grandmother patted Esau's cheek whenever he left her tent, and he would glow as though she had praised him to heaven. Which she never did.

My grandmother never spoke ill of Esau, nor did she say anything good about him. His wives, however, she detested in detail. Although they were dutiful women who, at one time, sent fine gifts in hopes of winning her approval, she dismissed them all as slovenly idiots. For years she had sneered at them openly, so they visited only when Esau insisted.

She was not much kinder about my mothers. She considered Rachel lazy—beautiful, but lazy. She called Bilhah ugly and Zilpah a superstitious stick. She grudgingly admitted that Leah was a good worker and clearly blessed to have delivered so many healthy sons. But even Leah was not good enough for Jacob, who deserved a perfect mate. Not a giantess with mismatched eyes.

She actually said such things in my presence! As though I were not my mother's daughter, as if my aunts were not my beloved mothers, too. But I did not defend them. When the Oracle spoke, no contradictions were permitted. I was not as bold as Leah, and my nighttime tears often tasted of shame as well as loneliness.

Rebecca saved the worst of her tongue for her husband, though. Isaac had grown foolish with old age, she said, and he smelled—something she could not abide. He had forgotten what he owed her, for hadn't she been right to make him give the blessing to Jacob? She spoke incessantly about Isaac's ingratitude, and her suffering at his hands. But it was not clear to me what my grandfather had done. He seemed gentle and harmless when he came on hot days, to enjoy the breezes beneath the great terebinths. I was glad that Isaac had no need of Rebecca's care. He was well served by his veiled Deborah. It was rumored that her covering hid a harelip, though it was unthinkable that such a one would not have been killed in infancy.

When Esau came to Mamre, he visited his mother first and saw to her needs. He was polite and even fond, but as soon as he could, he turned to the Grandfather and accompanied him back to Arba, where the two men enjoyed their evening wine. They stayed up very late, talking and laughing, served by the veiled Deborah.

I learned this from the other ones who wore white. They were kind to me. They patted my shoulder when they gave me my dinner, brushed my hair, and let me work with their beautiful ivory spindles. But they did not tell stories in the evenings, and I never learned the names their own mothers had given them, or how they had come to Mamre, or if they missed the company of men. They seemed mild and content, but as colorless as their robes. I did not envy them their life with the Oracle.

At the new moon, Rebecca did not permit me to enter the red tent with the women who bled; she was strict about this observance. She who was past child-bearing did not enter, nor could I, who was still un-ripe. One of the other Deborahs stayed outside with us as well. She explained that her periods had never come, but did not complain about her lack of rest. She and I cooked and served the celebrants, whose quiet laughter made me long for my mothers' tent.

When the women emerged, rested and smiling, on the morning after the third day, I was permitted to follow them as they stood at the highest point of the hill to watch the sun rise. The Grandmother herself poured out a libation of wine, while the women sang a wordless song of quiet rejoicing. In the deep silence that followed, it seemed to me that the Queen of Heaven was in the trees above us. That memory returns to me at every new moon.

I never learned to love my grandmother. I could not forget or forgive what she had done to Tabea. Nevertheless, the day came when I honored her.

The doors to the Oracle's tent were always open, and from every direction the stranger was made welcome. This had been the decree of Sarai and Abram, who, it was said, gave an equal welcome to princes and beggars. And so, every morning, Rebecca would receive pilgrims inside the beautiful tent. She saw all who came—wretched or resplendent—nor did she hurry with the poor.

I stood with her women as she greeted the guests. First, a childless woman approached and begged for a son. The Oracle gave her a red cord to tie around one of the trees at Mamre, whispered a blessing in the barren one's ear, and bid her go with the Deborah skilled in herbs.

Next there was a trader seeking a charm for his caravan. "It has been a bad season for me," he began. "I am nearly destitute, but I have heard of your powers," he said, with a bit of a dare creeping into his voice. "I've come to see for myself."

The Grandmother moved close to him and looked

into his face until he turned away from her gaze. "*You* must make restitution," she said in a way that sounded like a warning.

His shoulders sagged and his swaggering manner melted. "I don't have the goods to make restitution, Grandmother," he said.

"There is no other way," said the Oracle, in a loud, formal voice. She dismissed him with a wave of her hand, and he backed meekly out of her presence and ran down the hillside as though an army were chasing him.

Rebecca saw my open mouth and explained with a shrug, "Only thieves come looking for business miracles."

The last pilgrim that morning was a mother carrying a child who was old enough to walk—three years, maybe four. But when the woman unwrapped him, we could see why he was still in her arms. His legs were withered and his feet were covered with sores, raw and oozing, and painful to see. From the look in his eyes, it was clear that he was nearly dead with suffering. The Grandmother took the boy from his mother's arms. She carried him to her cushion, her lips pressed against his forehead, and sat with him in her lap. She called for an unguent used for burns, something that soothes but cannot heal. Then, with her own hands, without flinching or drawing back, she rubbed the stuff into his wounds. When Rebecca was done, she wrapped her perfumed hands around his diseased feet, and held them as though they were precious, delicate, and clean. The mother gaped, but the little boy had no awe of his healer. With the pain eased for the moment, he rested his head upon her shallow breast and fell asleep.

No one moved or spoke. I don't know how long we stood as he dozed, but my back ached before the child opened his eyes. He wrapped his arms around the Grandmother's neck and kissed her. She embraced him in return, and then carried him back to his mother, who wept to see the smile on her boy's face, and who wept again to see the sadness upon the Oracle's face, which showed there was nothing she could do to keep this one alive.

I could not hate Rebecca after that. Although I never saw her show such tenderness to anyone else, I could not forget the way she took that little boy's pain into her own hands and gave comfort to him and peace to his mother.

I never spoke about Tabea to my grandmother. I did not dare. In silence, I mourned the loss of my best friend as sorrowfully as if I had wrapped her in a shroud.

But it was Werenro we put into the ground.

I had been anxious to see the messenger again, as were the others at Mamre. She was a favorite among the Deborahs, who smiled when I asked about her return. "Surely she will come soon," said the one who liked to brush my hair. "And then we will have stories in the evening and you will not be so sad."

But word came with a trader on his way from Tyre that Werenro, messenger to Rebecca of Mamre, had been murdered. The remains of her body were found on the edge of the city, the tongue cut out, red hair scattered all around. A trader who had visited the shrine years before remembered the strange-looking woman who served the Oracle and recognized her bag. He gathered what was left of her, to bring her bones back to the Grandmother, who betrayed no emotion at the terrible news.

The sack he carried was pitifully small, and we buried it deep in the earth in a plain earthenware jar. I heard the Deborahs weep that night, and added another layer of salt to my own blanket. But when I dreamed of Werenro, she was smiling her dappled smile from a seat in a great tree, a large bird perched on her shoulder.

The day after Werenro was buried, I went to Rebecca in the morning as usual, but she was already dressed, scented, and painted for the day. She sat on her cushions, silent and withdrawn. I was not even certain she noticed that I had entered. I coughed. She did not look up at me, but after a time she spoke, and I knew why pilgrims came to Mamre.

"I know you are here, Dinah," she said.

"I know that you hate me on behalf of Esau's girl. It was a pity. She was the best of them, and of course it was not her fault. It was the poor stupid mother, who did not do what I told her but what her own stupid mother taught her. I should have taken her as a baby. The girl had no chance."

My grandmother said this without looking at me, as though she were airing her own thoughts. But then she turned her eyes upon me and fixed me in her gaze.

"You are safe from that fate," she said. "Your mother will not let them turn your maidenhood into a prize. She will not permit your blood to be anything but an offering into the womb of the great mother. You are safe in that way.

"Some other unhappiness awaits you, though," she said, peering at me intently, trying to discern my future. "Something I cannot fathom. Just as I could not foresee the end of Werenro. Perhaps your sorrow will be nothing worse than a lost baby or two, or maybe an early widowhood, for your life will be very long. But there's no use in frightening children with the price of life."

There was silence for a time, and when Rebecca next spoke, although her words were about me, it was as though I were no longer there. "Dinah is not the heir, either. I see now that there will be none. Mamre will be forgotten. The tent will not stand after me." She shrugged, as though it was of no great matter.

"The great ones need nothing from us, truly. Our libations and prayers are of no more importance than birdsong or bee song. At least their praises are assured."

She rose and walked toward me, until our noses nearly touched. "I forgive you for hating me," she said, and waved me out of the tent.

Reuben came a few days later, and I left Mamre without so much as a nod from the Grandmother. Glad as I was to be returning to my mother's tent, my eyes stung with tears as we walked away. I returned empty-handed. I had merited little of Rebecca's attention. I had failed to please her.

CHAPTER SIX

Although I had longed for home every moment of my absence, I was shocked by it when I arrived. Nothing was as I remembered it. My brothers, my father, and all of the other men had become impossibly crude and brutish. They grunted rather than spoke, scratched themselves and picked their noses, and even relieved themselves in plain sight of the women. And the stink!

The noise of the camp was overwhelming, too. Barking dogs, bleating sheep, crying babies, and screaming women. How was it that I had never noticed the way they all shrieked at each other and at the children? Even my own mother was changed. Every word out of her mouth was critical, demanding, and imperious. Everything had to be done her way, and nothing I did was good enough. I heard only scorn and anger in her voice when she told me to fetch water, or mind one of the babies, or help Zilpah with the weaving.

Whenever she spoke to me, my eyes stung with tears, my throat closed in shame and anger, and I kicked at the dirt. "What is the matter?" she asked, three times a day. "What is wrong with you?"

There was nothing wrong with me, I thought. It was Leah who had become short-tempered and sour and impossible. Somehow she had aged years in the months I had been gone. The deep lines of her forehead were often caked with dust, and the grime under her fingernails disgusted me.

Of course, I could never voice such disrespect, so I avoided my mother and escaped to the calm of Zilpah's loom and the gentleness of Bilhah's voice. I even took to sleeping in Rachel's tent, which must have caused Leah some pain. Inna, who I now realized was at least as old as the Grandmother herself, scolded me for causing my mother such sorrow. But I was too young to understand that the changes were mine, not my mother's.

After a few weeks, I grew accustomed once more to the daily sound and smell of men again, and found myself fascinated by them. I stared at the tiny buds on the baby boys who ran about naked, and I spied upon mating dogs. I tossed and turned on my blanket and let my hands wander over my chest and between my legs, and wondered.

One night, Inna caught me by the side of Judah's tent, where he and Shua were making another baby. The midwife grabbed my ear and led me away. "It won't be long now, my girl," she told me, with a leer. "Your time is coming." I was mortified and horrified to think that Inna might tell my mother where she had found me. Even so, I could not stop thinking about the mystery of men and women.

* * *

On the nights I was consumed with curiosity and longing, my father and his sons were deep in conversation. The herds would soon be too numerous for the lands at our disposal, and my brothers wanted greater prospects for themselves, and their sons. Jacob had begun to dream again, this time about a walled city and a familiar valley in the shoulder between two mountains. In his dreams, we were already in Shechem, where his grandfather had poured wine over a pile of stones and called it a holy altar. My brothers liked this dream. They did business in the city and returned to the tents full of stories about the marketplace, where wool and livestock got good prices. Shechem's king, Hamor, was peaceful and welcomed tribes who wished to make the land blossom. Simon and Levi spoke to Hamor's vizier in my father's name and returned to Jacob, all puffed up with themselves over their agreement for a good-sized parcel of land with a well on it.

So the tents were taken down and the herds gathered and we traveled the short distance to the place that the king said could be ours. My mothers declared themselves pleased with the valley.

"Mountains are where heaven meets earth," said Zilpah, satisfied that she would find inspiration.

"The mountains will protect us against bad winds," said Leah, with reason.

"I must find a local herb-woman to show us what these hills have to offer," Rachel said to Inna.

Only Bilhah seemed unhappy in the shadow of Ebal, which was the name of the mountain on whose side we raised our tents. "It is so big here," she sighed. "I feel lost."

We built ovens and planted seed. The herds multiplied, and three more of my brothers took wives, young girls who provoked no objections from my mothers. They were of Canaan and knew nothing of the customs of Haran, where mothers are honored for strength as well as beauty. And while my new sisters entered the red tent to please Leah, they never laughed with us. They watched our sacrifice to the Queen of Heaven without interest and refused to learn what to do. "Sacrifices are for men," they said, and ate their sweets. Still, my brothers' brides were hard workers and fertile. I acquired many nieces and nephews in Shechem, and the family of Jacob prospered.

There was peace in our tents except for Simon and Levi, who dwelt in the ever-widening margins of their own discontent. The well, which had made the land seem such a prize, turned out to be an ancient, crumbling pile of stones that dried out soon after we arrived. My brothers dug another, a backbreaking job that failed in the first place they tried. Simon and Levi were certain that Hamor had purposefully swindled them, and they fed on each other's anger about what they called their humiliation. By the time the second well was giving water, their resentment was as much a part of them as their own names. I was grateful that my path rarely brought me in contact with them. They frightened me with their black looks and the long knives that always hung from their belts.

* * *

When the air was sweet with spring and the ewes heavy with lambs, my month arrived. As evening gathered on the first night of darkness, I was squatting to relieve myself when I noticed the smear on my thigh. It took me several moments before I understood what I saw. It was brown rather than red. Wasn't it supposed to be red? Shouldn't I feel some ache in my belly? Perhaps I was mistaken and bled from my leg, yet I could find no scrape or scratch.

It seemed I had been waiting forever for womanhood, and yet I did not jump up to tell my mothers. I stayed where I was, on my haunches, hidden by branches, thinking: My childhood is over. I will wear an apron and cover my head. I will not have to carry and fetch during the new moon anymore, but will sit with the rest of the women until I am pregnant. I will idle with my mothers and my sisters in the ruddy shade of the red tent for three days and three nights, until first sight of the crescent goddess. My blood will flow into the fresh straw, filling the air with the salt smell of women.

For a moment I weighed the idea of keeping my secret and remaining a girl, but the thought passed quickly. I could only be what I was. And I was a woman.

I raised myself up, my fingers stained with the first signs of my maturity, and realized that there was indeed a dull ache in my bowels. With new pride, I carried myself into the tent, knowing that my swelling breasts would no longer be a joke among the women. Now I would be welcome inside any tent when Rachel and

Inna attended at a birth. Now I could pour out the wine and make bread offerings at the new moon, and soon I would learn the secrets that pass between men and women.

I walked into the red tent without the water I'd been sent for. But before my mother could open her mouth to scold me, I held up my soiled fingers. "I am not permitted to carry anything either, Mother."

"Oh, oh, oh!" said Leah, who for once had no words. She kissed me on both cheeks, and my aunts gathered around and took turns greeting me with more kisses. My sisters-in-law clapped their hands and everyone began talking at once. Inna ran in to find out what the noise was about, and I was surrounded by smiling faces.

It was nearly dark, and my ceremony began almost before I realized what was happening. Inna brought a polished metal cup filled with fortified wine, so dark and sweet I barely tasted its power. But my head soon floated while my mothers prepared me with henna on the bottoms of my feet and on my palms. Unlike a bride, they painted a line of red from my feet up to my sex, and from my hands they made a pattern of spots that led to my navel.

They put kohl on my eyes ("So you will be far-seeing," said Leah) and perfumed my forehead and my armpits ("So you will walk among flowers," said Rachel). They removed my bracelets and took my robe from me. It must have been the wine that prevented me from asking why they took such care with paint and scent yet dressed me in the rough homespun gown used for women in childbirth and as a shroud for the after-birth after the baby came.

They were so kind to me, so funny, so sweet. They would not let me feed myself but used their fingers to fill my mouth with the choicest morsels. They massaged my neck and back until I was as supple as a cat. They sang every song known among us. My mother kept my wine cup filled and brought it to my lips so often that soon I found it difficult to speak, and the voices around me melted into a loud happy hum.

Zebulun's wife, Ahavah, danced with her pregnant belly to the clapping of hands. I laughed until my sides ached. I smiled until my face hurt. It was good to be a woman!

Then Rachel brought out the teraphim, and everyone fell silent. The household gods had remained hidden until that moment. Although I had been a little girl when I'd seen them last, I remembered them like old friends: the pregnant mother, the goddess wearing snakes in her hair, the one that was both male and female, the stern little ram. Rachel laid them out carefully and chose the goddess wearing the shape of a grinning frog. Her wide mouth held her own eggs for safekeeping, while her legs were splayed in a dagger-shaped triangle, ready to lay a thousand more. Rachel rubbed the obsidian figure with oil until the creature gleamed and dripped in the light of the lamps. I stared at the frog's silly face and giggled, but no one laughed with me.

In the next moment, I found myself outside with my mother and my aunts. We were in the wheat patch in the heart of the garden—a hidden place where grain dedicated to sacrifice was grown. The soil had been tilled in preparation for planting after the moon's return, and I was naked, lying facedown on the cool soil. I shivered. My mother put my cheek to the ground and loosened my hair around me. She arranged my arms wide, "to embrace the earth," she whispered. She bent my knees and pulled the soles of my feet together until they touched, "to give the first blood back to the land," said Leah. I could feel the night air on my sex, and it was strange and wonderful to be so open under the sky.

My mothers gathered around: Leah above me, Bilhah at my left hand, Zilpah's hand on the back of my legs. I was grinning like the frog, half asleep, in love with them all. Rachel's voice behind me broke the silence. "Mother! Innana! Queen of the Night! Accept the blood offering of your daughter, in her mother's name, in your name. In her blood may she live, in her blood may she give life."

It did not hurt. The oil eased the entry, and the narrow triangle fit perfectly as it entered me. I faced the west while the little goddess faced east as she broke the lock on my womb. When I cried out, it was not so much pain but surprise and perhaps even pleasure, for it seemed to me that the Queen herself was lying on top of me, with Dumuzi her consort beneath me. I was like a slip of cloth, caught between their lovemaking, warmed by the great passion.

My mothers moaned softly in sympathy. If I could have spoken I would have reassured them that I was perfectly happy. For all the stars of the night sky had entered my womb behind the legs of the smiling little frog goddess. On the softest, wildest night since the separation of land and water, earth and sky, I lay panting like a dog and felt myself spinning through the heavens. And when I began to fall, I had no fear.

The sky was pink when I opened my eyes. Inna was crouched beside me, watching my face. I was lying on my back, my arms and legs wide like the spokes of the wheel, my nakedness covered by my mother's best blanket. The midwife helped me to my feet and led me back to a soft corner in the red tent, where the other women still slept. "Did you dream?" she asked me. When I nodded that I had, she drew close and said, "What shape did she take?"

Oddly, I knew what she wanted to know, but I didn't know what to call the creature that had smiled at me. I had never seen anything like her—huge, black, a toothy grin, skin like leather. I tried to describe the animal to Inna, who seemed puzzled. Then she asked, "Was she in the water?"

I said yes and Inna smiled. "I told you that water was your destiny. That is a very old one, Taweret, an Egyptian goddess who lives in the river and laughs with a great mouth. She gives mothers their milk and protects all children." My old friend kissed my cheeks and then pinched them gently. "That is all I know of Taweret, but in all my years, I never knew a woman who dreamed of her. It must be a sign of luck, little one. Now sleep."

My eyes did not open until evening, and I dreamed all day about a golden moon growing between my legs. And in the morning, I was given the honor of being the first one outside, to greet the first daylight of the new moon.

* * *

When Leah went to tell Jacob that his daughter had come of age, she found that he already knew. Inbu had spoken of it to Levi, who whispered to his father of "abominations."

The Canaanite woman had been shocked by the ritual that had brought me into the ancient covenant of earth, blood, and the sky. Inbu's family knew nothing of the ceremony for opening the womb. Indeed, when she married my brother, her mother had run into the tent to snatch the bloodstained blanket of her wedding night, just in case Jacob—who had paid the full bride-price—wanted proof of her virginity. As though my father would wish to look upon a woman's blood.

But now Inbu had told Levi of the sacrifice in the garden—or at least what she guessed of it—and he went to our father, Jacob. Men knew nothing of the red tent or its ceremonies and sacrifices. Jacob was not pleased to learn of them. His wives fulfilled their obligations to him and to his god; he had no quarrels with them or their goddesses. But he could no longer pretend that Laban's teraphim were not in his house, and he could not abide the presence of gods he had forsworn.

So Jacob called Rachel before him and ordered her to bring the household gods she had taken from Laban. He took them all to an unknown place and shattered them, one by one, with a rock. Then he buried them in secret, so no one could pour libations over them.

Ahavah miscarried the next week, which Zilpah called a punishment and a portent of worse to come. Leah was not so concerned about the teraphim. "They were hidden in a basket for years and that did us no harm. The problem is with the wives of my sons, who do not follow our ways. We must teach them better. We must make them our own daughters." And so my mother took Ahavah into her heart, and Judah's Shua. In the following years, she also tried to teach Issachar's bride, Hesia, and Gad's Oreet. But they could not abandon their own mothers' ways.

Inbu's treason left a deep breach in its wake, and a division that never healed. The wives of Levi and Simon never came to the red tent again, but stayed under their own roofs at the new moon and kept their daughters with them. And Jacob began to frown at the red tent.

With every new moon, I took my place in the red tent and learned from my mothers how to keep my feet from touching the bare earth and how to sit comfortably on a rag over straw. My days took shape in relation to the waxing and waning of the moon. Time wrapped itself around the gathering within my body, the swelling of my breasts, the aching anticipation of release, the three quiet days of separation and pause.

Although I had stopped worshiping my mothers as perfect creatures, I looked forward to those days with them and the other women who bled. Once, when it happened that only my mothers and I sat in the tent, Rachel remarked that it was like the old days in Haran. But Leah said, "It is not the same at all. Now there are many to serve us and my daughter sits on the straw with us." Bilhah saw that my mother's words bruised Rachel's heart, for she still longed for a daughter and had not given up hope. My gentle aunt said, "Ah, but

Leah, it truly is pleasant with the five of us again. How Adah would have smiled." My grandmother's name worked its usual charm, and the sisters relaxed in memory of her. But the damage had been done, and the old chill between Leah and Rachel returned to the women's quarters.

Not long after we settled in the shadow of Ebal, Inna and Rachel delivered a large breech baby boy to one of our bondswomen. The mother lived, something rarely seen with foot-first babies in that place. Soon women from the hillsides and even from far down in the valley began to send for them at the first sign of a difficult birth. It was rumored that Inna and Rachel— but especially Rachel, who was blood kin to the line of Mamre—possessed powers to appease Lamashtu and Lillake, ancient demons said to thirst after newborn blood, and much feared by the local people.

Many times I walked out with my aunt and the old midwife, who found it easier to lean on her walking staff without a bag on her shoulder. The hill folk were shocked that they took an unwed girl like me to visit birthing women. But in the valley they did not seem to care, and the first-time mothers, some younger than I, asked that I be the one to hold their hands and look into their eyes when the pains bore down hard.

Though I was certain my teachers knew everything about delivering babies, Rachel and Inna tried to learn what they might from women wherever they went. They were pleased to discover an especially sweet mint that grew in the hills. It settled the stomach quickly and was a blessing for those who suffered from bloating and vomiting during pregnancy. But when Inna saw how some of the hill women painted the mother's body with yellow spirals "to fool the demons," she curled her lip and muttered that it did nothing but irritate the skin.

There was one great gift that my teachers learned from the women of Shechem's valley. It was not an herb or a tool, but a birth song, and the most soothing balm that Inna or Rachel had ever used. It made laboring women breathe easier and caused the skin to stretch rather than tear. It eased the worst pains. Those who died—for even with a midwife as skillful as Inna some of them died—even they smiled as they closed their eyes forever, unafraid.

We sang:

"Fear not, the time is coming
Fear not, your bones are strong
Fear not, help is nearby
Fear not, Gula is near
Fear not, the baby is at the door
Fear not, he will live to bring you honor
Fear not, the hands of the midwife are clever
Fear not, the earth is beneath you
Fear not, we have water and salt
Fear not, little mother
Fear not, mother of us all"

Inna loved that song, especially when the women of the house could add harmonies and make the magic even greater. She was delighted to have learned something so powerful so late in her life. "Even the oldest of us," she said, shaking a bony finger at me, "even we crones can pick up new tricks here and there."

Our beloved friend was aging, and the time came when Inna was too stiff to walk out in the night or to manage steep paths, so Rachel took me with her and I began to learn with my hands as well as with my eyes.

Once when we were called to help a young mother deliver her second son—an easy birth from a sweet woman who smiled even as she labored—my aunt let me place the bricks and tie the cord. On the way home Rachel patted my shoulder and told me I would be a good midwife. When she added that my voice suited the song of the fearless mother, I was never so proud.

CHAPTER SEVEN

Sometimes we were called to assist a laboring mother who lived within sight of the city. Those trips were my special delight. The walls of Shechem awed me more than the misty mountains that inspired sacrifices from Jacob and Zilpah. The minds that had conceived such a great project made me feel wise, and the force of the sinews that had built the fortress made me feel strong. Whenever I caught sight of the walls, I could not look away.

I longed to go inside, to see the temple square and the narrow streets and crowded houses. I knew a little about the shape of the place from Joseph, who had been to Shechem with our brothers. Joseph said that the palace where Hamor the king lived in splendor with his Egyptian wife and fifteen concubines contained more rooms than I had brothers. Joseph said that Hamor had more servants than we had sheep. Not that a dusty shepherd like my brother could even hope for a peek inside such a grand house. Still, I liked his tall stories. Even lies about the place thrilled me, and I fancied that I could smell the perfume of courtesans on my brother's tunic when he returned from the market.

My mother decided she wanted to see the place for herself. Leah was certain that she could drive a better bargain for our wool than Reuben, who was too generous to be trusted with such transactions. I nearly kissed her hands when she said I would go to help her. Reuben settled us into a good spot just outside the gate, but he stood at a distance from us when our mother began calling out to every passing stranger and haggled like a camel trader with those who approached.

There was little for me to do but watch, which I did happily. That day at the eastern gate was a marvel. I saw my first jugglers. I ate my first pomegranate. I saw black faces and brown faces, goats with impossibly curly coats, women covered in black robes and slave girls who wore nothing at all. It was like being on the highway again, but without sore feet. I saw a dwarf hobbling alongside a donkey as white as the moon, and watched a caftaned high priest buy olives. Then I saw Tabea.

Or at least I thought I saw her. A girl of her height and coloring walked toward our display. She was dressed in the white robes of the temple, head shaven, both ears pierced. I stood and called out to her, but she turned on her heels and rushed away. Without thinking and before my mother could stop me, I ran after her, as though I were a child and not a young woman. "Tabea!" I called out. "Cousin!" But she did not hear me, or if she did, she did not stop, and the white robes disappeared through a doorway.

Reuben caught up with me. "What were you doing?" he asked.

"I thought it was Tabea," I said, near tears. "But I was mistaken."

"Tabea?" he asked.

"A cousin from Esau. You do not know her," I said. "I'm sorry I made you chase me. Is Mother angry?"

He laughed at the foolishness of my question, and I laughed too. She was furious, and I had to sit facing the wall the rest of the afternoon. But by then, my light heart had gone out of me, and I was content just listening to the sounds of the marketplace, nursing memories of my lost friend.

After our return from that trip, a messenger arrived from the city. She wore a linen robe and beautiful sandals and would speak only to Rachel. "One of the women in the king's household is about to deliver," she said to my aunt. "Hamor's queen calls for the midwives from Jacob's house to attend her."

Leah was not pleased when I began to prepare my kit for the journey. She went to Rachel and asked, "Why not take Inna to the queen with you? Why do you insist on taking Dinah away from me, just when there are olives to harvest?"

My aunt shrugged. "You know that Inna cannot walk as far as the city any longer. If you wish me to take a slave, I will. But the queen expects two of us, and she will not be so disposed to buy your woolens if I walk into the palace without skilled assistance."

Leah glared at her sister's smooth words, and I dropped my eyes to the ground so that my mother could not see how much I longed to go. I held my breath as my mother decided. "Pah," she said, throwing up her hands and walking away. I clapped my hands over my mouth to keep from crowing, and Rachel grinned at me like a child who had outfoxed her elders.

We finished our preparations and dressed in festival robes, but Rachel stopped me before we walked out, and braided my hair into smooth ropes. "Egyptian-style," she whispered. Bilhah and Zilpah waved us off, but Leah was nowhere to be seen as we headed into the valley with the messenger.

Walking through the gates of the city that first time, I was sorely disappointed. The streets were smaller and dustier than I had imagined. The smell was an awful mixture of rotten fruit and human waste. We moved too quickly to see inside the dark hovels, but I could hear and smell that the goats lived with their owners, and I finally understood my father's disdain for city dwelling.

Once we crossed the threshold of the palace, we entered a different world. The walls were thick enough to block out the sounds and smells of the street, and the courtyard in which we stood was spacious and bright.

A naked slave approached and motioned for us to follow her through one of the doorways into the women's quarters, and then into the room where the mother-to-be panted on the floor. She was about my age and by the look of her, early in her labor. Rachel touched her belly and examined the womb and rolled her eyes at me. We had been summoned for the most straightforward of births. Not that either of us minded; a trip to the palace was an adventure for which we were grateful.

Soon after we met the mother, Hamor's queen walked into the room, curious to see the hill-bred midwives. The queen, who was called Re-nefer, wore a gossamer linen sheath covered by a tunic of turquoise beads— the most elegant clothing I had ever seen. Even so, my aunt was not outshone by the lady. Old as Rachel was, lined by sun and work, crouched on the floor with her hand between the legs of a woman in travail—even so, my aunt glowed her golden light. Her hair was still lustrous and her black eyes sparkled. The women looked each other over with approval and nodded their greeting.

Re-nefer raised her gown above her knees and squatted on the other side of Ashnan, for that was the name of the young mother who huffed and moaned more in fear than pain. The two older women began to talk about oils that might ease the baby's head, and I was impressed both at how much the noblewoman knew of birthing and at Rachel's ease in conversing with a queen.

Ashnan, it turned out, was the daughter of the queen's nursemaid. The woman on the bricks had been a playmate of her own son's infancy and his milk-sister— just like Joseph and me. The nursemaid had died when the children were still babies, and Re-nefer had been tender toward the girl ever since and was even more so now that she was pregnant by Hamor. Ashnan was his newest concubine.

All this we learned from Re-nefer, who stayed beside

Ashnan from noon until nearly sunset. The mother was strong and all the signs were good, but the birth went slowly. Strong pangs were followed by long pauses, and when Ashnan fell asleep late in the afternoon, exhausted by her labors, Re-nefer took Rachel to her own chamber for refreshment and I was left to watch the mother.

I was nearly asleep myself when I heard a man's voice in the antechamber. I should have sent word through the slave girl, but I didn't think of it. I was bored and stiff from sitting so many hours, so I rose and went myself.

His name was Shalem. He was a firstborn son, the handsomest and quickest of the king's children, well liked by the people of Shechem. He was golden and beautiful as a sunset.

I dropped my eyes to the ground to keep from staring—as though he were a two-headed goat or something else that defied the order of things. And yet, he did defy nature. He was perfect.

To avoid looking up into his face, I noticed that his fingernails were clean and that his hands were smooth. His arms were not black from the sun like my brothers', though neither were they sickly. He wore only a skirt, and his chest was naked, hairless, well muscled.

He was looking at me, too, and I shuddered at the stains on my apron. Even my festival tunic seemed shabby and drab compared to the gleaming homespun of the simple garment he wore at home. My hair was awry and uncovered. My feet were dirty. I began to hear the sound of breathing, without knowing if it was my own or his.

Finally, I could not help myself and lifted my eyes to his. He stood taller than me by a handbreadth. His hair was black and shining, his teeth straight and white. His eyes were golden or green or brown. In truth, I did not look there long enough to discern their color because I had never been greeted with such a look. His mouth smiled politely, but his eyes sought the answer to a question I did not fully understand.

My ears rang. I wanted to run, and yet I did not wish to end this strange agony of confusion and need that came upon me. I said nothing.

He was disconcerted, too. He coughed into his fist, glanced toward the doorway where Ashnan lay, and stared at me. Finally, he stuttered a question about his milk-sister. I must have said something, though I have no memory of my words. All I remember is the ache in the moment when we met in that bare little hallway.

It amazes me to think of all that happened in the space of a silent breath or two. All the while I scolded myself, thinking, Foolish! Childish! Foolish! Mother will laugh when I tell her.

But I knew I would not be telling this to my mother. And that thought made me blush. Not the warmth of my feeling for this Shalem, whose name I had not even learned, whose presence made me dumb and weak. What caused my cheeks to color was the understanding that I would not speak of the fullness and fire in my heart to Leah.

He saw me color and his smile widened. My awkwardness vanished and I smiled back. And it was as though the bride-price had been paid and the dowry agreed to. It was as though we were alone in our bridal tent. The question had been answered.

It sounds comical to me now, and if a child of mine confessed such things to me, I would laugh out loud or scold her. But on that day I was a girl who was ready for a man.

As we grinned at each other, I remembered the sounds from Judah's tent and I understood my own fevered nights. Shalem, who was a few years older than I, recognized his own longing and yet he felt more than the simple stirring of desire, or that is what he said after we had redeemed our promise and lay in each other's arms. He said he was smitten and shy in the antechamber of the women's quarters. He said he had been enchanted, struck dumb, and thrilled. Like me.

I do not think we spoke another word before Rachel and the queen swept into the room and pulled me back into the birth chamber. I did not have time to think of Shalem then, for Ashnan's water broke and she delivered a big healthy boy who barely ripped her flesh. "You will heal in a week," Rachel told the girl, who sobbed with relief that it was done.

We slept in the palace that night, though I hardly closed my eyes with excitement. Leaving the next morning was like dying. I thought I might never see him again. I thought perhaps it had been a mistake on my part—the fantasy of a raw country girl in the presence of a prince. But my heart rebelled at the idea and I twisted my neck looking back as we departed, thinking he might come to claim me. But Shalem did not appear, and I bit my lips to keep from weeping as we climbed the hills back to my father's tents.

* * *

Nobody knew! I thought they would all see it in me. I thought that Rachel would guess at my secret and pry the story from me as we walked home. But my aunt wanted only to talk about Re-nefer, who had praised her skills and given her a necklace of onyx beads.

When we returned to camp, my mother hugged me without sensing the new heat in my body and sent me to the olive grove, where the harvest was busy. Zilpah was there overseeing the press and barely answered my greeting. Even Bilhah of the discerning heart was preoccupied with a batch of oil jars that had cracked, and she saw nothing.

Their inattention was a revelation to me. Before my trip to Shechem, I had supposed that my mothers could see my thoughts and look directly into my heart. But now I discovered that I was separate, opaque, and drawn into an orbit of which they had no knowledge.

I delighted in the discovery of my solitude and protected it, keeping myself busy at the far end of the orchard and even sleeping in the makeshift tent near the edge of the harvest with my brothers' wives. I was happy to be alone, thinking only of my beloved, numbering his qualities, imagining his virtues. I stared at my hands and wondered what it would be like to touch his gleaming shoulders, his beautiful arms. In my dreams I saw sunlight sparkling on water and I awoke smiling.

After three days of drunken happiness, my hopes began to sour. Would he come for me? Were these callused hands too rough to delight a prince? I chewed on my fingernails and forgot to eat. At night, I lay sleepless on my blanket, turning our meeting over and over in my mind. I could think of nothing but him, yet I began to doubt my memories. Perhaps his smile had been one of indulgence rather than of recognition. Perhaps I was a fool.

But just as I began to fear that I would betray myself to my mothers in a flood of tears, I was saved. The king himself sent for me. Hamor would deny his young consort nothing, and when Ashnan asked if Jacob's kind young daughter could be brought to distract her during her confinement, a messenger was dispatched. The king's man even brought a slave to take my place in the harvest. My mother found the gesture thoughtful and generous. "Let her go," she said to my father. Jacob did not object, and sent Levi to accompany me to the door of the women's quarters in Hamor's palace.

Waving to my mothers, I could see Bilhah and Rachel peering after me. Either my haste or my pleasure at the king's bidding alerted them to something, but by then it was too late to ask. They waved back as I descended into the valley, but I could feel their questions at my back. A hawk circled high above us all the way down into the valley. Levi said it was a good sign, but the messenger spit on the ground every time the bird's shadow crossed our path.

My brother left me at the door of Hamor's palace, charging me in a loud, pompous voice for the benefit of the messenger "to behave as befits one of the daughters of Jacob." Since I was Jacob's only surviving daughter, I smiled. I had been told to behave as myself, and I had every intention of doing that.

In the next three weeks, I met the daughters of Shechem. The wives of all the important men came to visit Ashnan and her little boy, who would not be publicly named until he reached three months, according to the custom of Egypt. "So the demons will not know how to find him," Ashnan whispered, fearing the presence of evil even within the safety of her comfortable rooms.

Ashnan was rather a silly girl with fine teeth and big breasts, which regained their shape and beauty quickly after the baby was given to a nurse. I had never heard of a healthy woman giving an infant to another woman's breast; in my world, a wet nurse was used only when the mother was dead or dying. But then, what did I know of the lives of royal women? Indeed, I was amazed by almost everything I saw at first.

I did not much care for being Ashnan's servant, for that is how she treated me. I brought her food and fed it to her. I bathed her feet and her face. She wanted massage, and so I learned the art from an old woman of the house. She wanted paints as well, and chattered away as she taught me how to apply kohl around my own eyes, and a ground green powder to my lids. "Not only does it make you look beautiful," said Ashnan, "it keeps the gnats away."

Ashnan also taught me boredom, which is a dreadful calamity visited upon women in palaces. There was one afternoon I actually shed tears at the monotony of having to sit still as Ashnan slept. All I had to occupy myself with was worry over whether Shalem was aware of my presence under his father's roof. I began to doubt that he remembered the unkempt assistant to his milk-sister's midwife. I was trapped without answers, for the walls between the women's world and men's quarters were thick, and in the world of the palace there was no work to create a crossing of paths.

After many days, Re-nefer looked in upon Ashnan and I tried to find the courage to speak to her about her son. But all I could do was stammer in her presence and blush. "Do you miss your mother, child?" she kindly asked. I shook my head, but looked so miserable that the queen took my hand and said, "You need some distraction, I think. A girl like you who lives under the sun must feel like a trapped bird within these walls."

I smiled at Re-nefer and she squeezed my fingers. "You will go out into the marketplace with my maid," she said. "Help her pick the best of the pomegranates, and see if you can hunt up some fine figs for my son. Shalem likes figs."

The next morning I walked out of the palace and into the babble of the city, where I stared to my heart's content. The servant by my side seemed in no hurry and let me wander where I would. I stopped at almost every stall and blanket, wonder-struck at the variety and quantity of lamps, fruits, woven goods, cheeses, dyes, tools, livestock, baskets, jewelry, flutes, herbs, everything.

But there were no figs to be had that day. We searched for them until I was nearly dizzy from heat and thirst, but I hated to return to the palace without satisfying the queen's request, without bringing fruit to my beloved. Finally, when we had looked in every corner, there was nothing to do but turn back.

At the moment we set our path for the palace, I spied the oldest face I had ever seen—an herb seller whose black skin was lined deep as a dry wadi. I stood by her blanket and listened to her rattle on about some liniment "good for the backache." But when I leaned down to finger a root I had never seen, she grabbed my wrist and stared up into my face. "Ah, the young lady wants something for her lover! Something magic that will bring her young man to bed, so she may be rid of her tiresome virginity."

I pulled my arm away, horrified that the conjurer had seen so far into my heart. It was probably only a speech she made to every young girl who approached, but Re-nefer's maid saw my confusion and laughed. I was mortified, and rushed away from the old one.

I did not see Shalem approach, but he stood before me, the afternoon sunlight filling the sky around his head like a glowing crown. I looked into his face and gasped. "Are you well, my lady?" he asked, in the sweet, reedy voice that I remembered. I was mute.

He looked at me with the same hunger I felt, and put a warm hand on my elbow to squire me back to the palace, the queen's woman following us, wearing a big grin. Her mistress had been right; there was a light between the prince and the granddaughter of Mamre.

Unlike me, Re-nefer's son had not been able to hide his heart from his mother. Re-nefer had despised the women of the city since she arrived in Shechem as a young bride. "Stupid and empty," she branded them all. "They spin badly, weave atrociously, dress like men, and know nothing of herbs. They will bear you stupid children," Re-nefer had told her son. "We will do better for you."

Re-nefer had been impressed by the bearing of the midwife from the hills, and she had liked the looks of the girl carrying her bag, too. She approved of my height and the strength of my arms, my coloring and the way I carried my head. The fact that one as young as I was already walking in a midwife's path told her I was no fool. When Rachel had gone with the queen for refreshment during Ashnan's labor, Re-nefer had gotten more information about me so discreetly that Rachel did not suspect her purpose as she was quizzed about my age, my mother's status, my skill at hearth and loom.

When Re-nefer and Rachel surprised me and Shalem in the anteroom, she discerned at once that the seed of her idea had already sprouted on its own. She did what she could to nurture its growth.

Re-nefer told Ashnan to send for me from my father's house, and she told her son to go out to seek me in the market that morning. "I'm afraid that the little girl from the hills will be lost," she said to Shalem. "You know that my servant is fool enough to let her out of her sight. But maybe you do not remember the looks of the one called Dinah?" she asked her son. "She was the dark-eyed girl with the curly hair and the fine hands who came with the midwife. You spoke to her in the antechamber when Ashnan was in travail." Shalem agreed to do his mother's bidding with such speed that Re-nefer had trouble stifling a laugh.

When the prince and I returned to the palace, we found the courtyard deserted, as Re-nefer had instructed. The servant disappeared. We stood in silence for only a moment and then Shalem drew me into the shadow of a corner and put his hands on my shoulders and covered my mouth with his mouth and pressed his body against mine. And I, who had never been touched or kissed by any man, was unafraid. He did not hurry or push, and I put my hands on his back and pressed into his chest and melted into his hands and his mouth.

When his lips found my throat, I groaned and Shalem stopped. He looked into my face to discover my meaning, and seeing only yes, he took my hand and led me down an unfamiliar corridor into a room with a polished floor and a bed that stood on legs carved like the claws of a hawk. We lay down upon sweet-smelling black fleece and found one another.

I did not cry out when he took me, because, though he was young, my lover did not rush. Afterward, when Shalem lay still at last and discovered that my cheeks were wet, he said, "Oh, little wife. Do not let me hurt you again." But I told him that my tears had nothing of pain in them. They were the first tears of happiness in my life. "Taste them," I said to my beloved, and he found they were sweet. And he wept as well. We clung to each other until Shalem's desire was renewed, and I did not hold my breath when he entered me, so I began to feel what was happening to my body, and to understand the pleasures of love.

No one disturbed us. Night fell and food was left at the doorway—wonderful fruit and golden wine, fresh bread and olives and cakes dripping in honey. We ate every morsel like famished dogs.

After we ate, he washed me in a large tub of warm

water that appeared as mysteriously as the food. He told me of Egypt and of the great river where he would take me to bask and swim.

"I cannot swim," I told Shalem.

"Good," he replied. "Then I can be the one to teach you."

He put his hands into my hair until they were tangled in knots and it took us long moments to free him. "I love these shackles," he said, when he could not free himself, and he grew large and our coupling was exquisitely slow. His hands caressed my face, and we cried out in pleasure together.

Whenever we were not kissing or coupling or sleeping, Shalem and I traded stories. I told him of my father and my mothers and described my brothers, one by one. He was delighted by their names and learned each one, in the order of his birth, and knew which one came from the womb of which mother. I'm not sure my own father could have listed them so well.

He told me of his tutor, a cripple with a wonderful voice, who taught him to sing and to read. Shalem told me of his mother's devotion and his five half brothers, none of whom had learned the arts of Egypt. He told me of his trip to the priestess, who initiated him in the art of love in the name of heaven. "I never saw her face," he said. "The rites take place in the innermost chamber, where there is no light. It was like a dream locked inside a dream." He told me of three times he had slept with a slave girl, who giggled in his embrace and asked for payment afterward.

But by the end of our second day together, our embraces outnumbered his experiences with other women. "I have forgotten them all," he said.

"Then I will forgive you them all," I said.

We made love again and again. We slept and awoke with our hands on each other. We kissed each other everywhere, and I learned the flavor of my lover's toes, the smell of his sex before and after coupling, the dampness of his neck.

We were together as bride and groom for three days before I began to wonder why I had not been fetched to go and wash Ashnan's feet or rub her back. Shalem, too, forgot his obligatory evening meals with his father. But Re-nefer took care that we should know nothing of the world and that the world should give us peace. She sent choice foods at all hours of the day and night and instructed the servants to fill Shalem's bath with fresh scented water whenever we slept.

I had no worries for the future. Shalem said our love-making sealed our marriage. He teased me about the bride-price he would bring to my father: buckets of gold coins, camels laden with lapis and linen, a caravan of slaves, a herd of sheep so fine their wool never needed washing. "You deserve a queen's ransom," he whispered, as we drifted back to our shared dreams.

"I will build you a tomb of surpassing beauty," Shalem said. "The world will never forget the name of Dinah, who judged my heart worthy."

I wish I had been as bold with my words. Not that I was shy. Shalem knew of my delight in him, my gratitude for him, my lust for him. I gave him everything. I abandoned myself to him and in him. It was only that I could not find a voice for the flood of my happiness.

While I lay in Shalem's first embrace, Levi was storming out of Hamor's palace, furious that he had not been given the audience with the king that he considered his due. My brother had been dispatched to see when I would be sent home, and had he been given a fine meal and a bed for the night, my life might have had a different telling.

Later, I wondered what might have happened had Reuben or Judah come for me. Hamor was not eager to meet with that particular son of Jacob, the quarrelsome one who had accused him of swindling the family. Why should the king suffer through another round of accusations by some whining son of a shepherd?

If it had been Reuben, Hamor would have welcomed him to dine and spend the night. Indeed, if it had been any of the others, even Joseph, he would have received a fine welcome. Hamor approved of Jacob nearly as much as his queen liked Jacob's wives. The king knew that my father tended his flocks with such skill that he had quickly become the richest shepherd in the valley. Jacob's wool was the softest, his wives skilled, and his sons loyal. He caused no feuds among neighbors. He had enriched the valley, and Hamor was eager for good relations with him. Marriages between their two houses were much to be desired, so Hamor was pleased when Re-nefer whispered that his son favored Jacob's daughter. Indeed, as soon as the king heard that Shalem was lying with me, he began to count out a handsome bride-price.

When Hamor heard from the servants that the young

couple were well matched, adoring, and busy producing his grandson, the news aroused him so much that
he called Ashnan to his bed a full week before her confinement was due to end. When Re-nefer discovered
them, she barely scolded her husband and the girl, so
great was her joy at her son's match.

On the fourth day of our happiness, Shalem arose
from our bath, dressed, and told me he was going to
speak to his father. "It is time for Hamor to arrange
for the bride-price." He looked so handsome in his
tunic and sandals that my eyes filled with tears again.
"No more weeping, not even for happiness," he said,
and lifted me, still wet from the water, and kissed my
nose and my mouth and put me on the bed and said,
"Wait for me, beloved. Do not dress. Only lie here so
I may think of you like this. I won't be long."

I covered his face with kisses and told him to
hurry back. I was asleep when he slipped beside me,
smelling of the world beyond our bed for the first
time in days.

Hamor departed for Jacob's camp early the next
morning, a laden wagon behind him. He did not bring
a tent or servants for a night's stay. He did not expect
to stay or to haggle. How could he have imagined any
objection to his good news and generous gift?

The news about Shalem and Jacob's daughter was wide-
spread in the city, but unknown in Jacob's tents. When
he heard that I had been taken as wife by the prince of
the city, he said nothing and made no reply to Ham-
or's offer. He stood like a stone, staring at the man of
whom his sons Levi and Simon had spoken with

such venom—a man of his own years, it turned out, but richly dressed, smooth spoken, and fat. The king waved at a cart laden with goods and trailing sheep and goats. He declared them kin, soon to share a grandchild.

Jacob hooded his eyes and covered his mouth with his hand so Hamor would not see his discomfort or surprise. He nodded as Hamor praised his daughter's beauty. Jacob had given no thought to a marriage for his daughter, although his wife had begun to speak of it. She was of age, to be sure. But Jacob was uneasy about this match, although he could not say why, and he felt his neck stiffen at Hamor's expectation that he would do as he was told.

He searched his mind for a way to postpone a decision, a way to regain the upper hand. "I will discuss this with my sons," he told the king, with more force than he meant.

Hamor was stung. "Your daughter is no virgin, Jacob," the king pressed. "Yet here is a bride-price fit for a virgin princess of Egypt—more than my own father gave for my wife. Not that your daughter is unworthy of this and more. Name what you wish and it is yours, for my son loves the girl. And I hear she is willing, too," and here Hamor smiled a bit too broadly for Jacob's taste. He did not like to hear his daughter spoken of so crudely, even though he could not quite conjure up the image of Dinah's face. All he could recall clearly was the sight of hair, unruly and wild, as she chased after Joseph. The memory came from long ago.

"I will wait for my sons," said Jacob, and he turned

away from the king, as though the lord of Shechem were no more than a shepherd, and left it to his wives to welcome the king with drink and food. But Hamor saw no reason to stay and headed back to his palace, trailing his gifts behind him.

Jacob called for Leah and spoke to her in the hardest words he had ever used with a wife. "Your daughter is no longer a girl," he said. "You were insolent to keep this from me. You have overreached before, but never to shame me. And now this."

My mother was as surprised as her husband and pressed Jacob for news of her daughter. "The prince of Shechem has claimed her. His father comes to pay the full bride-price of a virgin. And so I assume that she was until she went within the walls of that dung heap of a city." Jacob was bitter. "She is of Shechem now, I suppose, and of no use to me."

Leah was furious. "Go seek out your wife, my sister," she said. "It was Rachel who took her there. Rachel is the one with eyes for the city, not me, husband. Ask your wife." And the smell of bile rose from my mother's words.

I wonder if she thought of me at all then, if she suffered over whether I had consented or cried out, if her heart reached out to discover whether I wept or rejoiced. But her words spoke only of the loss of a daughter, gone to the city where she would reside with foreign women, learn their ways, and forget her mother.

My father called for Rachel next. "Husband!" cried Rachel, smiling as she approached him. "I hear there are happy tidings."

But Jacob did not smile. "I do not like the city or its king," he said. "But I like even less an untrustworthy daughter and a lying wife."

"Say nothing you will regret," replied Rachel. "My sister sets you against me and against your only daughter, who is beloved of your mother at Mamre. This is a good match. The king says they are fond, does he not? Have you forgotten your own fire, husband? Have you grown so old that you do not remember that longing?"

Jacob's face betrayed nothing. He looked long at Rachel, and she returned his gaze. "Give them your blessing, husband," Rachel said. "Take the wagons laden with silver and linen and give Hamor the welcome due a king. You are the master here. There is no need to wait."

But Jacob stiffened at Rachel's insistence. "When my sons return from their travels, I will decide."

Hamor could not recall ever being treated so badly. Even so, he was well disposed toward Jacob. "A good ally, I think," he told Shalem the next day. "But an enemy to avoid. He is a proud man," Hamor said. "He does not like to lose control of his family's fate. Odd that he should not yet know how children stop serving their parents once they are grown. Even daughters."

But Shalem pressed his father to return as soon as possible. "I love the girl," he said.

Hamor grinned. "Fear not. The girl is yours. No father would want her back as she is now. Go back to your wife, and let me worry about the father."

Another week passed, and my husband and I grew to love each other in subtler ways, with caresses and endearments. My feet did not touch ground. My face ached from smiling.

And then I received a special wedding gift: Bilhah came to see me. My aunt appeared at the palace gate asking for Dinah, wife of Shalem. She was taken first to Re-nefer, who plied her with questions about Jacob's hesitancy over her husband's offer. The queen asked about Leah and Rachel as well, and told Bilhah not to leave the palace without gifts for her daughter-in-law's family. And then Re-nefer herself brought my aunt to me.

My hug lifted my little aunt off the ground, and I covered her dark face with a dozen kisses. "You are glowing," she said, when she stood back, holding my hands in hers. "You are happy." She smiled. "It is wonderful that you should find such happiness. I will tell Leah and she will be reconciled."

"Is my mother angry?" I asked, bewildered.

"Leah believes Rachel sold you into the hands of evil. She is like your father in her distrust of the city, and she is not pleased that you will make your bed within walls. Mostly, I think, she misses you. But I will tell her of the light in your eyes, of the smile on your lips, and of your womanly bearing now that you are a wife.

"He is good to you, yes?" Bilhah asked, giving me the chance to praise my Shalem. I found myself bursting to tell someone the details of my happiness, and I spilled everything into Bilhah's willing ear. She clapped her hands to hear me speak like a bride. "Oh, to love and be loved like this," she sighed.

Bilhah ate with me and peeked at Shalem. She agreed that he was beautiful but refused to meet him. "I cannot speak to him before my husband does," she demurred. "But I have seen enough to bring back a good report of our daughter."

In the morning, she embraced me and left with Reuben, who had brought her. She carried the word of my happiness into my father's tents, but her voice was drowned out by the shouts of my brothers, who called me harlot. And Jacob did nothing to stop their foul mouths.

Simon and Levi had returned to our father after several days, defeated in a secret purpose. They had been in Ashkelon seeking trade not merely for the family's goats and sheep, wool, and oil, but to speak with slave traders, whose business could yield far greater wealth than any hard-earned harvest of the earth. Simon and Levi wanted wealth and the power it would bring them, but they had no hope of inheriting those from Jacob. It was clear that Reuben would get their father's birthright and the blessing would go to Joseph, so they were determined to carve out their own glory, however they could.

But Levi and Simon discovered that the slavers wanted nothing but children. Business was bad. Too many traders had weakened the market, and now they were assured of a good price only for healthy youngsters. My brothers could get nothing at all in trade for the two old serving women they had from their wives' dowries. They returned home thwarted and bitter.

When they heard that Hamor had offered my father

a king's bride-price for me, they raised their voices against the marriage, sensing that their own positions would be diminished by such an alliance. Jacob's house would be swallowed up in the dynasties of Shechem, and while Reuben might expect to become a prince, they and their sons would remain shepherds, poor cousins, nobodies. "We will be lower than Esau," they muttered to each other and to the brothers over whom they still held sway: Zebulun, Issachar, and Naphtali, of Leah's womb, and Zilpah's Gad and Asher.

When Jacob called all his sons to his tent to consider Hamor's offer, Simon raised his fist and cried, "Revenge! My sister has been ravaged by an Egyptian dog!"

Reuben spoke on behalf of Shalem. "Our sister did not cry out," he said, "nor does the prince cast her aside."

Judah agreed. "The size of the bride-price is a compliment to our sister, to our father, and to all the house of Jacob. We will become princes ourselves. We would be fools not to take the gifts that the gods give us. What kind of idiot mistakes a blessing for a curse?"

But Levi ripped his clothing as though mourning my death, and Simon warned, "This is a trap for the sons of Jacob. If we permit this marriage, the fleshpots of the city will consume my sons and my brothers' sons. This marriage displeases the god of our father," he said, challenging Jacob to disagree.

Their voices grew loud and my brothers glared at one another across the lamps, but Jacob did not let his own thoughts be known. "The uncircumcised dog rapes my sister every day," Simon thundered. "Am I to permit this desecration of our only sister, my own mother's daughter?"

At this, Joseph pulled a skeptical face and half-whispered to Reuben, "If my brother is so concerned about the shape of our brother-in-law's penis, let our father demand his foreskin for a bride-price. Indeed, let all the men of Shechem become like us. Let them pile up their membranes as high as my father's tent pole, so that their sons and ours will piss the same, and rut the same, and none will be able to tell us apart. And thus will the tribe of Jacob grow not merely in generations to come, but even tomorrow."

Jacob seized upon Joseph's words, which had been spoken only in mockery of the brothers who had tortured him since infancy. But Jacob did not hear the edge in his son's words. He said, "Abram took up the knife for those of his household who were not of his covenant. If the men of Shechem agree to this, none could say that our daughter was injured. If the men of the city make such sacrifice to the god of my fathers, we shall be remembered as makers of souls, as gatherers of men. Like the stars in the heavens, as it was told to our father Abram. Like the sands of the sea, was it foretold by my mother Rebecca. And now I will make it come to pass. I will do what Joseph says, for he has my heart." Jacob spoke with such passion that there was no use in further speech.

Levi's face twisted in anger at Jacob's decision, but Simon placed a hand on his brother's arm and pulled him away into the night, far from the light of lamps and the ears of their brothers.

* * *

When Hamor journeyed to Jacob's tent the second time, Shalem accompanied him. Determined not to return to the city without my father's blessing, he brought two donkeys laden with still more gifts. My beloved was confident as he left, but when he reached my father's tent, the king's party was again met with crossed arms, and not so much as a ladle of water was offered before the men began discussing terms.

My father spoke first, and without ceremony. "You come for our daughter," he said. "We will agree to the marriage, but I doubt if our terms will suit you, for they are severe."

Hamor replied, his earlier warmth for the man blasted by the insulting lack of hospitality. "My son loves the girl," the king said. "He will do anything for her, and I will do what my son wishes. Name your terms, Jacob. Shechem will fulfill them so that your children and my children will bring forth new generations upon the land."

But when Jacob named the price for his daughter, Hamor paled. "What form of barbarity is this?" he asked. "Who do you think you are, shepherd, to demand the blood of my son's manhood, and mine, and that of my kinsmen and subjects? You are mad from too much sun, too many years in the wilderness. Do you want the girl back, such as she is? You must think very little of this daughter to make such sport of her future."

But Shalem stepped forward and put his hand on his father's arm. "I agree to the demands," he said to Jacob's face. "Here and now, if you like. I will honor the custom of my wife's family, and I will order my slaves and their sons to follow me. I know my father speaks out of fear for me and in loyalty to his men, who would suffer. But for me, there is no question. I hear and obey."

Hamor would have argued against his son's offer, and Levi and Simon were poised to spit in his face. The air smelled like lightning, and daggers might have been drawn had Bilhah not appeared, with water and wine. Women with bread and oil followed, and Jacob nodded for them to serve. They ate a few mouthfuls in silence.

The terms were agreed to that evening. Jacob accepted four laden donkeys for a bride-price. Shalem and Hamor would go under the knife in three days, as would the men of Shechem, noble and slave alike. All of the healthy men found within the walls of the city on that same morning would also accept the mark of Jacob upon them, and Hamor promised that every son born within the city from that time forth would be circumcised on the eighth day, as was the custom among the sons of Abram. Hamor also pledged that the god of Jacob would be worshiped in his temple, and the king went so far as to call him Elohim, the one god of the many gods.

My father made me a handsome dowry. Eighteen sheep and eighteen goats, all of my clothing and jewelry, my spindle and grindstone, ten jars of new oil and six great bolts of wool. Jacob agreed to permit marriages between his children and those of Shechem, from that time forth.

Hamor put his hand under Jacob's thigh and Jacob

touched the king as well, and my betrothal was sealed without a smile or satisfaction.

That same night, Shalem slipped away from his father's tent and back into our bed with the news. "You are a married woman now and not merely a ruined girl," he whispered, waking me before the first light of morning.

I kissed him and pushed him away. "Well then, now that I am wed and you may not put me aside, I may tell you that my head aches and I cannot receive my lord at this moment," I said, gathering my robe about my shoulders, and feigning a great yawn even as I slipped my hand between my husband's legs. "You know, my lord, that women only submit to the caresses of their husbands—they do not enjoy the rough use of their bodies."

Shalem laughed and pulled me down on the bed, and we made love with great tenderness that morning. It was a reunion after what had been our longest parting since that day he found me in the market and led me to his bed, which we had made ours.

We slept late into the day, and only after we had eaten did he tell me my father's demand. I grew cold and my stomach turned. In my mind's eye, I saw my beloved in agonies of pain, saw the knife cut too deep, the wound fester, and Shalem dying in my arms. I burst into tears like a little child.

Shalem made light of it all. "It is nothing," he said. "A flesh wound. And I hear that afterward, my pleasure of you will be even greater than it is now. So prepare yourself, woman. I will be upon you night and day."

But I did not smile. I shivered with a cold that entered my bones and would not leave.

Re-nefer tried to reassure me, too. She was not displeased at the bargain her husband had struck. "In Egypt," she said, "they take boys for circumcision when their voices change. It is a merry enough time— they chase the boys and catch them, and afterward, they are petted and fed on every sweet and savory thing they ask for. Rest assured, they all survive.

"We will have my guard do the deed," she said. "Nehesi has dispatched many a foreskin. I can care for the pain, and you will help me, little midwife." She rattled on and on about how easy it would be, and then whispered, with a knowing leer, "Do you not find the male member more attractive without its hood?" But I found nothing amusing about Shalem's test, and I did not return my mother-in-law's smile.

The three days passed. I clung to my husband like a wild thing those nights, and tears ran down my face even as I reached greater pleasures than before. My husband licked the water from my cheeks and ran his salty tongue the length of my body. "I will tease you about this when our first son is born," he whispered, as I lay on his chest, still shaking with cold.

The appointed hour arrived. Shalem left me at dawn. I stayed in bed, pretending to sleep, watching him wash and dress through closed eyes. He leaned down to kiss me, but I did not turn my face up to meet his lips.

I lay there alone, counting my hatred. I hated my father for asking such a terrible price. I hated my husband and his father for agreeing to pay it. I hated my mother-in-law for smoothing the way. I hated myself most for being the cause of it all.

I lay on the bed, huddled beneath blankets, shivering with anger and fear and unrecognized foreboding, until he was brought back to me.

It was done in the king's antechamber. Shalem was first, and then his father, Hamor. Nehesi said that neither king nor prince cried out. Ashnan's little son followed, and wailed, but the little one did not suffer long, since he had a full breast to console him. The men of the household and the few poor souls who had not disappeared to the countryside outside the walls were not so lucky. They felt the knife keenly, and many screamed as though they were murdered. Their cries pierced the air throughout the morning, but ceased by noon.

It turned into an unmercifully hot day. There was no breeze or cloud, and even within the thick walls of the palace the air was damp and heavy. The recovering men sweated through their clothing and soaked the beds where they slept.

Hamor, who uttered no sound when he was cut, fainted in pain, and when he woke put a knife between his teeth to keep from screaming. My Shalem suffered too, though not as badly. He was younger and the salves seemed to ease him, but for him too, the only complete remedy was sleep. I dosed him with a sleeping draft, and whenever he roused, he was thick-headed and weary, slack-jawed and dazed. I bathed my beloved's face as he slept his drugged sleep and washed his sweating back with the softest touch I could muster. I did my best not to weep so my face would be fresh when he awoke, but as the day wore on the tears came in spite of my efforts. By nightfall, I was exhausted, and I slept by my husband's side swathed in blankets against the icy winds of my fears, even as Shalem slept naked in the heat.

In the night, I woke once to feel Shalem caressing my cheek. When he saw my eyes open, he managed a wincing smile and said, "Soon this will be nothing but a dream and our embraces will be sweeter than ever." His eyes closed again, and I heard him snore for the first time. As I drifted into sleep, I thought how I would tease him about the noise he made in his sleep—like an old dog in the sun. To this day I am not sure that Shalem spoke those words to me, or if it was a dream to comfort me.

The rest I know to be true.

First, there was the sound of a woman screaming. Something terrible must have happened to that poor soul, I thought, trying to turn away from the keening, shrieking, shrilling cry, too dreadful for the real world, the noise of a nightmare.

The wild, terrified scream came from a great distance, but its distress was so insistent and disturbing that I could not push it aside, and sought to awaken from my heavy sleep and escape the cries. They grew more and more frightening until I realized that my eyes were open and that the tormented soul I pitied was not dreamed or even distant. The screams were my own screams, the unearthly sound was coming from my twisted mouth.

I was covered in blood. My arms were coated with

the thick, warm blood that ran from Shalem's throat and coursed like a river down the bed and onto the floor. His blood coated my cheeks and stung my eyes and salted my lips. His blood soaked through the blankets and burned my breasts, streamed down my legs, coated my toes. I was drowning in my lover's blood. I was screaming loud enough to summon the dead, and yet no one seemed to hear. No guards burst through the door. No servants rushed in. It seemed that I was the last person alive in the world.

I heard no footsteps and had no warning before strong arms seized me, prying me loose from my beloved. They carried me off the bed trailing blood, screaming into the blackness of the night. It was Simon who lifted me and Levi who stopped up my mouth, and the two of them trussed me hand and foot like a sacrificial goat, loaded me on the back of donkey, and packed me off to my father's tent before I could alarm any poor soul still left alive in the doomed city. My brothers' knives worked until the dawn revealed the abomination wrought by the sons of Jacob. They murdered every man they found alive.

But I knew nothing of that. I knew only that I wanted to die. Nothing but death could stop my horror. Nothing but death could give me peace from the vision of Shalem slashed, bleeding, dead in his startled sleep. Had someone not loosened the gag when I vomited, I would have had my wish. All the way back up the hillside to the tents of Jacob I screamed in silence. Oh gods. Oh heaven. Oh Mother. Why do I still live?

CHAPTER EIGHT

I was the first they knew of it. My own mother saw me and shrieked at the sight of my bloodied body. She fell to the ground, keening over her murdered child, and the tents emptied to learn the cause of Leah's grief. But Bilhah unbound me and helped me to stand, while Leah stared—first horrified, then relieved, and finally thunderstruck. She reached out her hands toward me but my face stopped her.

I turned, intending to walk back to Shechem. But my mothers lifted me off my feet, and I was too weak to resist. They stripped off my blankets and robes, black and stiff with the blood of Shalem. They washed me and anointed me with oil and brushed my hair. They put food to my lips, but I would not eat. They laid me down on a blanket, but I did not sleep. For the rest of that day, no one dared speak to me, and I had nothing to say.

When night fell again, I listened to my brothers' return and heard the sound of their booty: weeping women, wailing children, bleating animals, carts creaking under the weight of stolen goods. Simon and Levi shouted hoarse orders. Jacob's voice was nowhere to be heard.

I should have been defeated by grief. I should have been exhausted past seeing. But hatred had stiffened my spine. The journey up the mountain, bound like a sacrifice, had jolted me into a rage that fed upon itself as I lay on the blanket, rigid and alert. The sound of my brothers' voices lifted me off of my bed and I walked out to face them.

Fire shot from my eyes. I might have burned them all to a cinder with a word, a breath, a glance. "Jacob," I cried with the voice of a wounded animal. "Jacob," I howled, summoning him by name, as though I were the father and he the wayward child.

Jacob emerged from his tent, trembling. Later he claimed that he had no knowledge of what had been done in his name. He blamed Simon and Levi and turned his back on them. But I saw full understanding in his clouded eyes as he stood before me. I saw his guilt before he had time to deny it.

"Jacob, your sons have done murder," I said, in a voice I did not recognize as my own. "You have lied and connived, and your sons have murdered righteous men, striking them down in weakness of your own invention. You have despoiled the bodies of the dead and plundered their burying places, so their shadows will haunt you forever. You and your sons have raised up a generation of widows and orphans who will never forgive you.

"Jacob," I said, in a voice that echoed like thunder,

"Jacob," I hissed, in the voice of the serpent who sheds life and still lives, "Jacob," I howled, and the moon vanished.

"Jacob shall never know peace again. He will lose what he treasures and repudiate those he should embrace. He will never again find rest, and his prayers will not find the favor of his father's god.

"Jacob knows my words are true. Look at me, for I wear the blood of the righteous men of Shechem. Their blood stains your hands and your head, and you will never be clean again.

"You are unclean and you are cursed," I said, spitting into the face of the man who had been my father. Then I turned my back upon him, and he was dead to me.

I cursed them all. With the smell of my husband's blood still in my nostrils, I named them each and called forth the power of every god and every goddess, every demon and every torment, to destroy and devour them: the sons of my mother Leah, and the son of my mother Rachel, and the sons of my mother Zilpah, and the son of my mother Bilhah. The blood of Shalem was embedded beneath my fingernails, and there was no pity in my heart for any of them.

"The sons of Jacob are vipers," I said to my cowering brothers. "They are putrid as the worms that feed on carrion. The sons of Jacob will each suffer in his turn, and turn the suffering upon their father."

The silence was absolute and solid as a wall when I turned away from them. Barefoot, wearing nothing but a shift, I walked away from my brothers and my father and everything that had been home. I walked away from love as well, never again to see my reflection in my mothers' eyes. But I could not live among them.

I walked into a moonless night, bloodying my feet and battering my knees on the path to the valley, but never stopped until I arrived at the gates of Shechem. I kept a vision before me.

I would bury my husband and be buried with him. I would find his body and wrap him in linen, take the knife that had stolen his life and open my wrists with it so we could sleep together in the dust. We would pass eternity in the quiet, sad, gray world of the dead, eating dust, looking through eyes made of dust upon the false world of men.

I had no other thought. I was alone and empty. I was a grave looking to be filled with the peace of death. I walked until I found myself before the great gate of Shechem, on my knees, unable to move.

If Reuben had found me and carried me back, my life would have ended. I might have walked and wept for many years more, half mad, finishing my days in the doorway of a lesser brother's third wife. But my life would have been finished.

If Reuben had found me, Simon and Levi would surely have killed my baby, leaving it out in the night for the jackals to tear apart. They might have sold me into slavery along with Joseph, ripping my tongue out first, to stop me from cursing their eyes, skin, bones, scrotums. I would never be appeased by their pain and suffering, no matter how ghastly.

Nor would I have been mollified when Jacob cowered and took a new name, Isra'El, so that the people would not remember him as the butcher of Shechem. He fled from the name Jacob, which became another word for "liar," so that "You serve the god of Jacob" was one of the worst insults one man could hurl at another in that land for many generations. Had I been there to see it, I might have smiled when his gift with animals deserted him and even his dogs ran from his side. He deserved no less than the agony of learning that Joseph had been torn by wild beasts.

Had Reuben found me at the gates of Shechem, I would have been there to give Rachel the burial she deserved. Rachel died on the highway, where Jacob had gone to flee the wrath of the valley, which set out to avenge the destruction of Hamor and the peace of Shechem. Rachel perished in agony, giving birth to Jacob's last son. "Son of woe," she named the little boy who cost her a river of black blood. But the name Rachel chose for her son was too much of an accusation, so Jacob defied the wish of his dying wife and pretended that Ben-Oni was Benjamin.

Jacob's fear chased him away from Rachel's poor drained body, which he buried hastily and without ceremony at the side of the road, with nothing but a few pebbles to remember the great love of his life. Perhaps I would have stayed there at Rachel's grave with Inna, who planted herself in that spot and gathered beautiful stones to make an altar to the memory of her only daughter. Inna taught the women of the valley to speak the name of Rachel and tie red cords around her pillar, promising that, in return, their wombs would bear only living fruit, and ensuring that my aunt's name would always live in the mouths of women.

If Reuben had found me, I would have watched my curse wrap itself around his neck, unleashing a lifetime of unspent passion and unspoken declarations of love for Bilhah and of hers for him. When that dam broke, they went breathlessly into each other's arms, embracing in the fields, under the stars, and even inside Bilhah's own tent. They were the truest lovers, the very image of the Queen of the Sea and her Lord-Brother, made for each other yet doomed for it.

When Jacob came upon them, he disinherited the most deserving of his sons and sent him to a distant pasture, where he could not protect Joseph. Jacob struck Bilhah across the face, breaking her teeth. After that, she began to disappear. The sweet one, the little mother, became smaller and thinner, more silent, more watchful. She did not cook anymore but only spun, and her string was finer than any woman had ever spun, as fine as a spider's web.

Then one day, she was gone. Her clothes lay upon her blanket and her few rings were found where her hands might have lain. No footprints led into the distance. She vanished, and Jacob never spoke her name again.

Zilpah died of fever the night that Jacob smashed the last of Rachel's household gods under a sacred tree. He had come across the little frog goddess—the one that had unlocked the wombs of generations of women—and he took an ax to the ancient idol. He urinated on the crushed stone, cursing it as the cause of all his misfortune. Seeing this, Zilpah ripped at her hair and screamed into the sky. She begged for death and spit upon the memory of the mother who left her. She lay on the ground and put handfuls of dirt into her mouth. Three men were needed to tie her down to keep her from doing herself harm. It was an awful death, and as they prepared her for the grave, her body broke into pieces like a brittle old clay lamp.

I am glad I did not see that. I am grateful I was not there as Leah lost the use of her hands and then her arms, nor to see her on the morning she awoke in her own filth, unable to stand. She would have begged me, as she begged her unfeeling daughters-in-law, to give her poison, and I would have done it. I would have taken pity and cooked the deadly drink and killed her and buried her. Better that than to die mortified.

Had Reuben carried me back to the tents of the men who had turned me into the instrument of Shalem's death, I would have done murder in my heart every day. I would have tasted bile and bitterness in my dreams. I would have been a blot upon the earth.

But the gods had other plans for me. Reuben came too late. The sun shone above the walls of the city when he arrived at the eastern gate, and by then other arms had carried me away.

PART THREE

EGYPT

CHAPTER ONE

I lay senseless in the arms of Nehesi, Re-nefer's steward and guard. He carried me to the palace, which swarmed with flies drawn to the blood of fathers and sons. My demon brothers had lifted their knives even against Ashnan's baby, and his poor mother bled to death defending him—her arm severed trying to block the ax's blade.

Of all the men in that house, only Nehesi survived. When the screams began, he ran to the king's chambers in time to protect Re-nefer against Levi and one of his men. The queen had lifted a knife against Levi when Nehesi arrived. He wounded my brother in the thigh and killed his henchman outright. He wrested the blade from the queen to keep her from burying it in her own heart.

Nehesi brought me to Re-nefer, who sat in the dirt of the courtyard, her head against the wall, dust in her hair, fingernails caked with blood. It was years before I understood why she did not leave me to die, why the murder of her loved ones did not fill her with rage against me, who caused it all. But Re-nefer blamed only herself for the death of her husband and son, because she had wished for our marriage and made sacrifices to ensure our union. She had sent Shalem to seek me in the market and arranged for us to fall into each other's arms unhindered. She took the guilt upon herself and never put it aside.

The other reason for Re-nefer's compassion toward me was even stronger than remorse. She had hope of a grandchild—someone to build her tomb and redeem the waste of her life, someone to live for. Which is why, in the moments before she fled Canaan, Re-nefer roused herself and sent Nehesi out into the wailing town to seek me.

Her servant obeyed in silence, but with dread. He knew the queen better than anyone—better than her serving women, better than her husband surely. Nehesi had come to Shechem with Re-nefer when she first arrived, a frightened young bride. And when he found me, he wondered whether he should add to his mistress's grief by carrying still more sorrow into her presence. I lay in his arms like a corpse, and when I did stir, it was to scream and scratch at my throat until I drew blood. They had to tie my hands and bind my mouth so that we could slip out of the city undetected in the dark of that night.

Re-nefer and Nehesi unearthed jars filled with gold and silver and stole away, with me, to the port at Joppa, where they hired a Minoan boat for the journey to Egypt. During the journey, there was a terrible storm that tore the sails and nearly overturned the ship. The sailors who heard me screaming and sobbing thought

I was possessed by a demon who roiled the waters against them. Only Nehesi's sword kept them from laying hands on me and tossing me into the waves.

I knew none of this as I lay in the darkness, swaddled, sweating, trying to follow my husband. Perhaps I was too young to die of grief, or maybe I was too well cared for to perish in sorrow. Re-nefer never left me. She kept my lips moist and spoke to me in the soothing, all-forgiving tone that mothers take with fretful babies.

She found cause to hope. A new moon arrived while I lay in my own darkness and no blood stained the blankets beneath my legs. My belly was soft and my breasts burned and my breath smelled of barley. After a few days, my sleep became less fevered. I gulped at the broths that Re-nefer fed me and squeezed her fingers in mute gratitude.

On the day of our landing, my mother-in-law came to me, placed her fingers firmly on my lips, and spoke with an urgency that had nothing to do with my health. "We return to the land of my mother and father," she said. "Hear what I say and obey.

"I will call you daughter in front of my brother and his wife," she said. "I will tell them that you served in my household and that my son took you, a virgin, with my consent. I will say that you helped me to escape from the barbarians. You will become my daughter-in-law, and I will be your mistress. You will bear your son on my knees, and he will be a prince of Egypt."

Her eyes found mine and demanded understanding. She was kind and I loved her, and yet something seemed wrong. I could not name my fear as she spoke. Later I realized that my new mother had not named her son, my husband, saying nothing of his murder, nor of my brothers and their deception. We never wept or mourned over Shalem, nor did she tell me where my beloved was buried. The horror was to remain unspoken, my grief sealed behind my lips. We never again spoke of our shared history, and I was bound to the emptiness of the story she told.

When I set foot in Egypt, I was pregnant and widowed. I wore the white linen of an Egyptian, and although I was no longer a maiden, I went with uncovered head like the other women of the land. I carried a small basket for Re-nefer, but I brought nothing of my own. I had not so much as a scrap of wool woven by my own mothers, nor even the consolation of memory.

There were many wonders to see on the journey to the great city of the south which was home to Re-nefer's brother. We passed cities and pyramids, birds and hunters, palms and flowers, sandy wastes and cliffs, but I saw nothing of these. My eyes stayed mostly upon the river itself, and I stared into the water, trailing a hand into the darkness, which was, by turn, brown, green, black, gray, and once, as we passed a tannery, the color of blood.

That night, I woke clutching my neck, drowning in blood, screaming for Shalem, for help, for my mother, in a nightmare that would visit me again and again. First, I felt the weight of Shalem against my back, a wonderful heaviness that comforted me completely. But

then came an unnatural heat onto my chest and hands
and then I discovered my mouth was full of Shalem's
blood, my nose clogged with the dusty smell of life ebb-
ing out of him. My eyes were thick with blood and I
struggled to open them. I screamed without drawing
breath, though I heard no sound. Still I kept screaming, in hope that my heart and stomach would rise out
of me in the scream and I could die, too.

On the fourth night of this dream, just as the blood
began to swallow me and my mouth opened to seek
death, I was shocked to my senses by searing pain
that left me gasping. I sat up to find Nehesi above me,
the flat edge of his broad sword laid against the soles
of my feet, where he had struck me. "No more of
this," he hissed. "Re-nefer cannot bear it."

He left me, my hair on end, struggling to catch my
breath. And from that night, I woke myself as soon as
I felt warmth oozing onto my breasts. Panting and
sweating, I lay on my back and tried not to fall asleep
again. I came to dread the sunset the way some men
dread death.

By day, the sun bleached away my fears. In the morning, before the heat bore down, Re-nefer sat with me
and Nehesi and recounted cheerful stories from her
childhood. We saw a duck, and she recalled hunting
expeditions with her father and brothers, the eldest of
whom was to be our refuge. As a little girl she had
been entrusted with the throwing sticks, handing
them to the hunters, anticipating their needs. When we
passed a great house, Re-nefer described her father's
home in Memphis, and the many gardens and pools in

its great courtyard. Her father had been a scribe for the priests of Re, and life had been pleasant for his family.

Re-nefer recalled every servant and slave who had waited upon her as a child. She spoke of her own mother, Nebettany, whom she remembered as lovely but distant—always at her kohl pots, happiest when the servants poured pot after pot of scented water over her back in her beautiful bath. But Nebettany died in childbirth when Re-nefer still wore the forelock of a little girl.

My mother-in-law retraced her days with charming tales and stories from her infancy until the very week that she left Egypt to be married. The preparations were elaborate, and a great dowry was assembled. Re-nefer could recall the very quantities of linen in her chests, the jewels on her fingers and neck, the bargemen who carried her up to the sea.

I leaned forward, hoping to learn some detail about life in Shechem, to hear the story of Shalem's birth or a tale from his boyhood. But she stopped just at the point she arrived in her husband's palace; a blank stare replaced her gaiety. She said nothing of Canaan, nor of her husband, nor of the babies she bore him. She did not speak the name of Hamor even once, and it was as though Shalem had never been born, nor loved me, nor bled to death in my arms.

Re-nefer's silence throbbed with pain, but when I reached out to touch her hand, she resumed a cheerful smile and turned away to chatter about the beauty of palm trees or her brother's great position as chief scribe and overseer to the priests of Re. I returned my gaze to the water and kept my eyes there until we arrived at Thebes.

The great city was dazzling in the setting sun. To the west, purple cliffs held a green valley dotted with brightly painted temples, hung with pennants of green and gold. On the east bank, there were great houses as well as temples and whitewashed warrens of smaller buildings, all glowing shades of rose and gold as the sun began its retreat behind the western bluffs. I saw white tents on the rooftops, and wondered if a separate race of people lived above the city-dwellers.

The streets that led away from the river were noisy and dusty, and we moved through them quickly, seeking our destination before nightfall. The scent of lotus grew stronger as the light faded. Nehesi asked a passerby if he knew the way to the home of the scribe Nakhtre. The man pointed toward a large building that sat beside one of the grand temples of the eastern bank.

A naked little girl opened the large, burnished door and blinked at the three strangers before her. Re-nefer demanded an audience with Nakht-re, her brother. But the child only stared. She saw an Egyptian lady who wore a dusty robe and no makeup or jewelry, a large black guard with a dagger at his waist but no shoes on his feet, and a foreigner in an ill-fitting dress who kept her head so low she might be hiding a harelip.

When the servant did not budge after Re-nefer repeated her request, Nehesi pushed the door open and walked through the vestibule into a great hall. The master of the house was concluding the business of the day, scrolls in his lap and assistants at his feet. He stared at Nehesi, startled and uncomprehending, but when he saw Re-nefer, Nakht-re leaped to his feet, scattering papers as he rushed to embrace her.

As his arms encircled her, Re-nefer began to weep—not tears of relief and happiness from a woman glad to be reunited with her family, but the raw sobs of a mother whose child had been murdered in his bed. Re-nefer howled in her bewildered brother's arms. She dropped to her knees and keened, giving voice to a broken heart.

The terrible sound brought all of Nakht-re's household into the room: cooks and gardeners, bakers and children, and the lady of the house. Nakht-re gathered his sister up and put her on his own chair, where she was fanned and given water. All eyes were fixed on Re-nefer, who took her brother's hands in hers and told him the bare details of her tale, as she had rehearsed it to me. She said that her home had been overrun by barbarians, her possessions stolen, her family butchered, her whole life pillaged. She spoke of her escape and the storm at sea. When Nakht-re asked about her husband, she replied, "Dead. And my son!" and collapsed in tears once more. At this, the women of the house commenced a high-pitched wail of mourning that crept up the flesh of my neck, like a curse.

Again Re-nefer was embraced by her brother, and again she composed herself. "Nehesi is my savior," she said, directing all eyes to where he stood beside me. "I should have died but for his strong arm and his wisdom and comfort. He brought me out of Canaan, with this girl who was my son's consort and who carries my grandson in her womb." All eyes turned to my belly now, and my hands moved, of their own accord, to the place where the baby grew.

This was a dumb show for me. I knew only a handful of words in their language, and these I had learned from my beloved in bed. I knew the words for the parts of the body, for sunset and sunrise, for bread and wine and water. For love.

But Egyptians are expressive people who speak with their hands and show their teeth when they talk, and I followed the story well enough. I watched Re-nefer's face and learned that her father had died, that her younger brother was far away, that a favorite friend—or perhaps a sister—was dead in childbirth, that Nakht-re was as successful as their father had been.

I stood by the door, safely forgotten, until I collapsed. I awoke some time later in the dark, on a sweet-smelling pallet beside a bed where Re-nefer slept softly. The rest of the household seemed asleep as well. The silence was so deep, if I had not walked through the noisy streets of a city that very afternoon, I would have thought myself in the middle of a deserted meadow or on top of a mountain.

A bird broke the hush, and I listened, trying to find the melody in its wild song. Had I ever heard a bird sing at night? I could not remember. For a moment, I forgot everything but the sound of a bird singing to a half-moon, and I nearly smiled.

My pleasure ended the next moment, when I felt a light touch on my fingers. I jumped to my feet but, remembering Nehesi's sword on my feet, stifled my scream. A small shadow moved in a circle around me. The bird still trilled, but now it seemed to mock the joy I had felt a moment earlier.

I watched in horror as the shadow leaped onto Re-nefer's bed and then seemed to disappear. My eyes ached from searching in the dark, and I found myself weeping over the death of my good mistress, for surely the creature had killed her. I wrung my hands and pitied myself, alone and abandoned in a far land. A sob escaped me, and Re-nefer stirred.

"What is it, child?" she murmured, half asleep.

"Danger," I hiccuped.

She sat upright, and the shadow leaped down toward me. I covered my head and shrieked.

Re-nefer laughed softly. "A cat," she explained. "It is only the cat. Bastet rules the heart of the house here. Sleep now," she sighed, and turned back to her pillow.

I lay down, but my eyes did not close again that night. Before long, light began to filter through the windows which lined the walls up near the ceiling. As sunshine filled the room, I studied the white-washed walls, and watched a spider weave a web in the corner. I looked at unfamiliar teraphim tucked into niches around the walls, and reached out to touch the handsome leg of my mistress's bed, carved in the likeness of a giant beast's foot. I inhaled the aroma of my bed—hay sweetened with the scent of an unfamiliar flower. The room seemed crowded with elaborate baskets and plaited mats. A collection of flacons sat on an inlaid box, beside a large stack of folded cloths, which I later learned were bath towels. Every surface was dyed or painted in bright colors.

I had no place among all of these wonderful things, and yet, this was my only home.

I was barely aware of the child within me those first few weeks. My body looked no different, and I was so occupied with my new surroundings that I didn't notice the moon's progress, which Egyptian women marked with little ceremony and no separation. I stayed beside Re-nefer, who spent her first days resting in the garden, and translated when I didn't comprehend the few words addressed to me.

I was not ill-treated. Everyone in the household of Nakht-re was kind, even his wife, Herya, who suddenly had to share her home with a long-forgotten sister and her two alien servants. Nehesi knew how to make himself useful, and Nakht-re soon sent him to carry messages between the house and the temple and the tombs being built in the western valley.

I was not quite a servant and not quite a niece, a foreigner without language or obvious skills. The lady of the house patted me when she saw me, rather like a cat, but turned away before there was any need of speech. The servants did not know what to make of me either. They showed me how to spin linen so that I might help with the work of the house, but my hands were slow to learn, and since I could not gossip with them in the kitchen, I was left alone.

My main occupation was attending Re-nefer, but she preferred solitude, so I found other tasks to occupy my days. I was drawn especially to the stairways of the house and took any excuse to walk up and down, watching how the room changed with every step. I assumed the task of sweeping them in the evening and washing them in the morning, and took a mindless pride in their maintenance.

Whenever I could, I climbed all the way to the roof, where a northern breeze from the river might lift the tent hung for shade. Much of the household slept up there on hot nights, though I never joined them, fearing to bring my nightmare among others.

From the rooftop, I stared at the sun reflecting on the river and at the grace of the sailing boats below. I remembered the first great water I had seen as a girl, when my family had crossed from Haran to the south. I thought of the river where Joseph and I had been charged by an unseen power and saved by our mothers' love. When I remembered Shalem's promise to teach me how to swim, my throat closed in agony. But I fixed my eyes wide, as I had at Mamre, and stared at the horizon to keep from sobbing and to keep from walking off the roof.

The days passed in a blur of new ways and sights, but the nights were always the same. I struggled against the dreams that left me drenched in sweat, soaking the pallet as Shalem's blood had soaked our bed, gasping for air and afraid to make a sound. In the morning, my eyes ached and my head throbbed. Re-nefer fretted over me and consulted with her sister-in-law. They ordered me to rest in the afternoon. They tied a red cord around my waist. They made me drink goat's milk mixed with a yellow potion that stained my tongue.

As my belly began to swell, the women of the house doted on me. It had been a long time since there had been a baby in Nakht-re's family, and they were hungry for a little one. I was fed amazing foods, as exotic to me as the flowers of the perpetually blooming garden behind the house. I ate melons with orange flesh and melons with pink flesh, and there were always dates in abundance. On the many feast days dedicated to gods or family holidays, there was goose made with garlic or fish in honey sauce.

But best of all were the cucumbers, the most delicious food I could imagine, green and sweet. Even in the heat of the sun, a cucumber kissed the tongue with the cool of the moon. I could eat them endlessly and never get full or sick. My mother would love this fruit, I thought the first time I bit into its watery heart. It was my first thought of Leah in more than a month. My mother did not know I was pregnant. My aunts did not even know that I was alive. I shuddered with loneliness.

Herya saw my shoulders tremble and, taking me by the hand, walked me to the vestibule at the front door. We stopped at the wall niche, and she gestured for me to remove the little goddess. It was a water horse standing on her hind legs, with an enormous belly and a huge, smiling mouth. "Taweret," she said, touching the clay figure and then moving her hand to my belly. I frowned. She squatted down, like a woman in labor, and placed the figure between her legs, and in pantomime, showed me that Taweret would ensure an easy labor.

The lady of the house thought I was afraid of giving birth. I nodded and smiled. She said, "Boy," and patted my belly again.

I nodded. I knew I was carrying a son. "Boy," I said, in the language of the house.

Herya closed my hands around the statue, indicating that I should keep it, and kissed my cheeks. For a moment the hoarse rattle of Inna's laughter sounded so loud in my ears I thought the old midwife was in the room with me chortling over her prophecy that Taweret would take me for her own.

In the next week, I felt a flutter like a bird's wing beneath my heart. I was thunderstruck at my love for the life I carried. I began to whisper to my unborn son as I lay on my pallet, and hummed the songs of my childhood to him as I swept and spun. I thought of my baby as I combed my hair and as I ate, morning and evening.

The bloody dreams about Shalem were replaced by a joyful dream of his son, whom I called Bar-Shalem. In the dream, my son was not a baby but a tiny copy of his father, nestled in my arms, telling me stories about his childhood in the palace, about the wonders of the river, about life on the other side of this life. In this dream, my beloved protected me and fought off a hungry crocodile that had come for me and the boy.

I hated to wake up and took to sleeping later and later only to remain inside this dream. Re-nefer permitted me my bed and everything else. Before we slept, she and I would watch my belly roll and shake. "He is strong," she rejoiced.

"May he be strong," I prayed.

I was not prepared when my time came. Confident of everything I had learned from Rachel and Inna, I had no concerns about giving birth. I had witnessed the arrival of many healthy babies and the courage of many capable mothers. I imagined I had nothing to fear.

When the first real pain grabbed my belly and robbed me of breath, I remembered the women who had fainted, the women who had screamed and wept and begged to die. I remembered a woman who died with her eyes wide open in terror, and a woman who died in a torrent of blood, her eyes sunken in exhaustion.

A sob broke from my mouth when my water broke and washed down my legs. "Mother," I cried, feeling the absence of four beloved faces, four pairs of tender hands. How far away they were. How alone I was. How I longed to hear their voices speaking comfort in my own tongue.

Why had no one told me that my body would become a battlefield, a sacrifice, a test? Why did I not know that birth is the pinnacle where women discover the courage to become mothers? But of course, there is no way to tell this or to hear it. Until you are the woman on the bricks, you have no idea how death stands in the corner, ready to play his part. Until you are the woman on the bricks, you do not know the power that rises from other women—even strangers speaking an unknown tongue, invoking the names of unfamiliar goddesses.

Re-nefer stood behind me, my weight on her knees, praising my courage. Herya, the lady of the house, held my right arm, muttering prayers to Taweret, Isis, and Bes, the ugly dwarf god who loved babies. The cook, on my left side, waved a bent stick carved with birth

scenes over my head to ease the pain. Crouching before me to catch the baby was a midwife named Meryt.
She was unknown to me, but her hands were as sure
and gentle as I imagine Inna's must have been. She blew
into my face so that I could not hold my breath when
the pains came, and even made me laugh a little and
blow back at her.

The four women chatted over my head when the
pangs subsided, and cooed encouragement when the
pains returned. They put fruit juice in my mouth, and
wiped me down with sweetly scented towels. Meryt
massaged my legs. Re-nefer's eyes shone with tears.

I wept and I yelled. I gave up all hope and I prayed.
I vomited and my knees buckled. But even though their
brows furrowed in response to my pains, none of them
appeared worried or anxious. So I fought on, reassured.

Then I began to push because there was nothing
else I could do.

I pushed and I pushed until I thought I would faint.
I pushed and still the baby did not come. Time passed.
More pushing. No progress.

Meryt looked up at Re-nefer, and I saw them exchange a glance that I had seen pass between Rachel
and Inna at moments such as this, when the ordinary
passage of life into life became a struggle between
life and death, and I felt the shadow in the corner lean
toward me and my son.

"No," I screamed, first in my mother tongue. "No,"
I said, in the language of the women around me.

"Mother," I said to Re-nefer, "bring me a mirror so
that I can see for myself." I was brought a mirror and
a lamp that showed me the tautness of my own skin.

"Reach in," I said to Meryt, remembering Inna's practice. "I fear he is turned away. Reach in and turn his face, his shoulder."

Meryt tried to do as I asked, but her hands were too large. My skin was too tight. My son was too big. "Bring a knife," I said, almost screaming. "He needs a bigger doorway."

Re-nefer translated, and Herya answered her in a grave whisper. "There is no surgeon in the house, daughter," Re-nefer explained to me, in turn. "We will send for one now, but . . ."

The words came to me from far away. All I wanted to do was to empty myself of this boulder, to expel the agony, and sleep, or even die. My body cried out to push, but when the shadow in the corner nodded approval, I refused to obey.

"You do it," I said to Meryt. "Take a knife and open the way for him. Please," I begged, and she looked at me in uncomprehending pity.

"A knife! Mother!" I screamed, desperate. "Rachel, where are you? Inna, what shall I do?"

Re-nefer called out, and a knife was brought. Meryt took it fearfully. As I screamed and struggled to keep from pushing, she put the blade up to my skin and opened the door, front to back, as I had seen it done before. She reached up to move the baby's shoulder. The pain was blinding, as though I had sat upon the sun itself. In an instant, the baby was out. But instead of a joyful shout, he was greeted by silence; the cord was at his neck, his lips were blue.

Meryt hurried. She cut the cord from his throat and took up her reeds, sucking death from his mouth, blowing life into his nostrils. I was screaming, sobbing, shaking. Herya held me as we all watched the midwife work.

The shadowy dog's head of death moved forward, but then the baby coughed and with an angry cry banished all doubts. The dark corner brightened. Death does not linger where he is defeated. The voices of four women echoed around me, chattering, laughing, loud. I fell back on the pallet, and knew nothing more.

I woke in the darkness. A single lamp flickered beside me. The floor had been washed, and even my hair smelled clean. The girl set to watch me saw my eyes open and ran to fetch Meryt, who carried a linen bundle. "Your son," she said.

"My son," I answered, dumbfounded, taking him in my arms.

Just as there is no warning for childbirth, there is no preparation for the sight of a first child. I studied his face, fingers, the folds in his boneless little legs, the whorls of his ears, the tiny nipples on his chest. I held my breath as he sighed, laughed when he yawned, wondered at his grasp on my thumb. I could not get my fill of looking.

There should be a song for women to sing at this moment, or a prayer to recite. But perhaps there is none because there are no words strong enough to name that moment. Like every mother since the first mother, I was overcome and bereft, exalted and ravaged. I had crossed over from girlhood. I beheld myself as an infant in my mother's arms, and caught a glimpse of my own death. I wept without knowing whether I rejoiced or mourned.

My mothers and their mothers were with me as I held my baby.

"Bar-Shalem," I whispered. He took my breast and fed in his sleep. "Lucky one," I said, overcome. "Two pleasures at once."

We both slept under the watchful eye of the Egyptian midwife, whom I knew I would love forever even if I never saw her face again. In my dream that night, Rachel handed me a pair of golden bricks and Inna presented me with a silver reed. I accepted their gifts solemnly, proudly, with Meryt by my side.

When I woke up, my son was gone. Frightened, I tried to stand, but the pain kept me pinned to my bed. I cried out, and Meryt arrived with soft packing and unguents for my wounds. "My son," I said, in her language.

She looked at me tenderly and replied, "The baby is with his mother." I thought I misunderstood her. Perhaps I had not used the right words. I asked again, speaking slowly, but she touched me with pity and shook her head, no. "The baby is with his mother, the lady."

Still confused, I cried out, "Re-nefer. Re-nefer. They have taken my baby boy. Mother, help me."

She came, carrying the baby, who was swaddled in a fine white linen blanket, bordered in gold thread. "My child," said Re-nefer, standing above me, "you did well. Indeed, you were magnificent, and all the women of Thebes will know of your courage. As for me, I will be forever grateful. The son you bore on my knees will be a prince of Egypt. He will be raised as the nephew of the great scribe Nakht-re, and the grandson of Paser, scribe of the two kingdoms, keeper of the king's own ledger."

She looked into my confused and stricken face and tried to reassure me even as she laid me low. "I am his mother in Egypt. You will be his nurse and he will know that you gave him life. His care will be your blessing, but he will call us both Ma and stay here until he is ready for school, and for this, you can be grateful.

"For this is my son, Re-mose, child of Re, that you have borne for me and my family. He will build my tomb and write your name upon it. He will be a prince of Egypt."

She handed me the baby, who had begun to cry, and turned to leave us. "Bar-Shalem," I whispered in his ear. Re-nefer heard and stopped. Without turning to look at me she said, "If you call him by that name again, I will have you thrown out of this house and into the street. If you do not heed my instructions in this, and in all matters regarding the education of our son, you will lose him. You must understand this completely."

Then she turned, and I saw that her cheeks were wet. "My only life is here, by the river," she said, her voice heavy with tears. "The bad fortune, the evil thing that stole my *ka* and cast it down amid beasts in the western wilderness, is over at last. I am restored to my family, to humankind, to the service of Re. I have consulted with the priests my brother serves, and it seems to them that your *ka*, your spirit, must belong here as

well, or else you could not have survived your illness, or the journey, or this birth."

Re-nefer looked upon the baby at my breast and with
infinite tenderness said, "He will be protected against
ill winds, evildoers, and naysayers. He will be a prince
of Egypt." And then, in a whisper that hid nothing of
her resolve, "You will do as I say."

At first, Re-nefer's words held little meaning for me. I
was careful never to call my son Bar-Shalem when
anyone else was in the room, but otherwise I was his
mother. Re-mose stayed with me day and night so that
I could nurse him whenever he cried. He slept by my
side, and I held him and played with him and memo-
rized his every mood and feature.

For three months we lived in Re-nefer's room. My
son grew from hour to hour, becoming fat, and sleek,
and the finest baby ever born. Under Meryt's good care
I healed completely, and in the heat of the afternoon,
Re-nefer watched him so that I might bathe and sleep.

The days passed without shape or work, without
memory. The baby at my breast was the center of the
universe. I was the entire source of his happiness,
and for a few weeks, the goddess and I were one and
the same.

At the start of his fourth month, the family gathered in the great room where Nakht-re sat among his
assistants. The women assembled along the walls as the
men clustered around the baby and placed the tools
of the scribe into his little hands. His fingers curled
around new reed brushes, and he grasped a circular

dish upon which his inks were mixed. He waved a scrap of papyrus in both hands like a fan, which delighted Nakht-re, who declared him born to the profession. So was my son welcomed into the world of men.

Only then did I remember the eighth day, when newborn boys of my family were circumcised and first-time mothers cowered in the red tent while the older women reassured them. My heart broke in two pieces, half mourning that the god of my father would not recognize this boy, nor would my brother Joseph or even his grandmothers. And yet I was fiercely proud that my son's sex would remain whole, for why should he bear a scar that recalled the death of his own father? Why should he sacrifice his foreskin to a god in whose name I was widowed and my son orphaned?

That night there was a feast. I sat on the floor beside Re-nefer, who held the baby on her lap and plied his lips with mashed melon and tickled him with feathers and dandled him so that he laughed and smiled into the faces of the guests who came to celebrate the arrival to Nakht-re's house of a new son.

Food and drink were brought in quantities I could not fathom: fish and game, fruit and sweets so rich they set the teeth on edge, wine and beer in abundance. Musicians played pipes and sistrums, instruments with jingling hammers that sound like nothing so much as falling water. There were silly songs, love songs, and songs to the gods. When the sistrums appeared, dancing girls ran to the floor, whirling and leaping, able to touch the tops of their heads to the ground behind them.

The headpieces given to every guest at the door were cones of perfumed wax, which melted as the eve-

ning waned in streams of lotus and lily. My baby was
sticky with perfume when I lifted him, sound asleep,
from Re-nefer's lap, and the aroma clung to his dark
hair for days.

Among the many wonders of my first banquet was
the way women ate together with men. Husbands and
wives sat side by side throughout the meal, and spoke
to one another. I saw one woman place a hand upon her
husband's arm, and a man who kissed the fingers of his
companion's bejeweled hands. It was impossible to
think of my own parents eating a meal in each other's
company, much less touching before others. But this
was Egypt, and I was the stranger.

That night marked the end of my seclusion. My
wound had healed and the child was healthy, so we were
sent into the garden, where his mess did not soil the
floors and where his prattle would not disturb the work
of the scribes. So my days were spent outdoors. While
my son napped in the flower beds, I weeded and gathered whatever the cook called for and learned the flowers and fruits of the land. When he woke, he was greeted
by the songs of Egyptian birds, and his eyes widened in
delight as they took flight.

The garden became my home and my son's tutor. Re-
mose took his first steps by the side of a large pond
stocked with fish and fowl, which he watched in open-
mouthed wonder. His first words—after "Ma"—were
"duck" and "lotus."

His grandmother brought him fine toys. Almost
every day, she would surprise him with a ball or top or
miniature hunting stick. Once, she presented him
with a wooden cat whose mouth opened and closed

by working a string. This marvel delighted me no less than the baby. My son loved Re-nefer, and when he saw her approach he would toddle to greet her with a hug.

I was not unhappy in the garden. Re-mose, who was healthy and sunny, gave me purpose and status, since everyone in the household adored him and credited me with his nice manner and pleasant temper.

Every day, I kissed my fingers and touched the statue of Isis, offering thanks to distribute among the multitude of Egypt's goddesses and gods whose stories I did not know, in gratitude for the gift of my son. I gave thanks every time my son hugged me, and every seventh day I broke a piece of bread and fed it to the ducks and fish, in memory of my mothers' sacrifice to the Queen of Heaven, and in prayer for the continued health of my Re-mose.

The days passed sweetly, and turned into months, consumed by the endless tasks of loving a child. I had no leisure for looking backward and no need of the future.

I would have stayed forever within the garden of Re-mose's childhood, but time is a mother's enemy. My baby was gone before I knew it, and then the hand-holding toddler was replaced by a running boy. He was weaned, and I lost the modesty of Canaan and wore a sheer linen shift like other Egyptian women. Re-mose had his hair shaved and shaped into the braided sidelock worn by all Egyptian children.

My son grew strong and sinewy, playing rough-and-tumble with Nakht-re, his uncle, whom he called Ba. They adored each other, and Re-mose accompa-

nied him on duck-hunting parties. He could swim like
a fish, according to Re-nefer. Though I never left the
house and gardens, she went on the barge to watch.
When he was only seven, my son could beat his uncle at
senet and even twenty-squares, elaborate board games
that required strategy and logic to win. From the time
he could hold a stick, Nakht-re showed my son how to
make images on bits of broken stone, first as a game and
then as teacher to student.

As he grew, Re-mose spent more time inside the
house, observing Nakht-re at work, practicing his let-
ters, eating the evening meal with his grandmother.
One morning when he took breakfast with me in the
kitchen, I saw him stiffen and blush when I split a fig
with my teeth and handed him half. My son said nothing
to cause me pain—but Re-mose stopped eating with
me after that and began to sleep on the roof of the house,
leaving me alone on my pallet in the garden, wondering
where eight years had gone.

At nine, Re-mose came of the age when boys tied
their first girdle, putting an end to his naked days. It was
time for him to go to school and become a scribe. Nakht-re decided that the local teachers were not accomplished enough for his nephew, and he would attend
the great academy in Memphis, where the sons of the
most powerful scribes received their training and
commissions, and where Nakht-re himself had been
taught. He explained all of this to me in the garden
one morning. He spoke gently and with compassion,
for he knew how much it would grieve me to see Re-
mose go.

Re-nefer scoured the markets for the right baskets for

his clothing, for sandals that would last, for a perfect box in which to put his brushes. She commissioned a sculptor to carve a slate for mixing ink. Nakht-re planned a great banquet in honor of Re-mose's departure and made him a gift of an exquisite set of brushes. Re-mose's eyes were large with excitement at the prospect of going out into the world, and he spoke about his journey whenever we were together.

I watched the preparations from the bottom of a dark well. If I tried to speak to my son, my eyes overflowed and my throat closed. He did his best to comfort me. "I am not dying, Ma," he told me, with a serious sweetness that made me sadder still. "I will return with gifts for you, and when I am a great scribe like Ba, I will build you a house with the biggest garden in all of the Southern Lands." He hugged me and held my hand many times in the days before his departure. He kept his chin high so that I would not think him afraid or unhappy, though of course he was just a little boy, leaving his mothers and his home for the first time. I kissed him for the last time in the garden near the pond where he had marveled at the fish and laughed at the ducks, and then Nakht-re took his hand.

I watched them leave the house from the rooftop, a cloth stuffed in my mouth so that I could finally weep until I was empty. That night, the old dream returned in all its force, and I was alone in Egypt once more.

CHAPTER TWO

From the moment of his birth, my life revolved around my son. My thoughts did not stray from his happiness and my heart beat with his. His delights were my delight, and because he was such a golden child, my days were filled with purpose and pleasantness.

When he left, I was even lonelier than I had been when I first found myself in Egypt. Shalem was my husband for a few short weeks and his memory had dwindled to a sad shadow who haunted my sleep, but Re-mose had been with me for the whole of my adult life. In the space of his years, my body had taken its full shape and my heart had grown in wisdom, for I understood what it was to be a mother.

When I glimpsed myself in the pond, I saw a woman with thin lips, curling hair, and small, round, foreign eyes. How little I resembled my dark, handsome son, who looked more like his uncle than anyone else and who was becoming what Re-nefer had prophesied: a prince of Egypt.

I had little time to brood about my loneliness, for I

had to earn my place in the great house of Nakht-re. Although Re-nefer was never unkind, with Re-mose gone we had less to say to each other, and I felt the silence grow ominous between us. I rarely went into the house.

I made myself a place in the corner of a garden shed used to store scythes and hoes—a spot where Re-mose used to hide his treasures: smooth stones, feathers, bits of papyrus gleaned from Nakht-re's hall. He left these things behind without a backward glance, but I kept them wrapped in a scrap of fine linen, as though they were ivory teraphim and not merely a child's discarded toys.

The men who tended the garden did not object to having a woman among them. I worked hard, and they appreciated my knack with the flowers and fruit, which I supplied to the cooks. I did not want company and rebuffed the attentions of men so often that they stopped seeking me out. When I saw my son's family enjoying the shade of the garden, we nodded and exchanged nothing more than polite greetings.

When there was word of Re-mose from Memphis, Nakht-re himself brought me the news sent by Kar, the master teacher who had been his own instructor. Thus I learned that Re-mose had mastered something called *keymt* in only two years—a feat of memorization that proved my son would rise high, and perhaps even serve the king himself.

There was never any word of his coming home. Re-mose was invited to go hunting with the governor's sons, and it would not do to reject such an auspicious offer. Then my son was chosen as an apprentice and aid to Kar when the master was called to rule upon a case of law, which took up the weeks during which other boys visited their families.

Once, Nakht-re and Re-nefer visited Re-mose in Memphis, making pilgrimage to their father's tomb there. They returned with fond greetings to me and news of his growth; after four years away he was taller than Nakht-re, well spoken and self-assured. They also brought proofs of his education—shards of pottery that were covered with writing. "Look," said Nakht-re, pointing a finger at the image of a falcon. "See how strong he makes the shoulders of Horus." They made me a gift of this treasure from my son's hand. I marveled over it and showed it to Meryt, who was duly impressed at the regularity and beauty of his images. I was awed by the fact that my son could discern meaning from scratchings on broken clay bits, and took comfort in the knowledge that he would be a great man someday. He could be scribe to the priests of Amun or perhaps even vizier to a governor. Had Nakht-re himself not said that Re-mose might even aspire to the king's service? But of course, none of these dreams filled my arms or comforted my eyes. I knew my son was growing to manhood and feared that the next time I saw him, we would be strangers.

I might have vanished during those long years without anyone taking more than passing notice except for Meryt. But Meryt was always there, unfailing in kindness even when I turned away from her and gave her no reason to love me.

The midwife had come to see me every day in the

weeks after Re-mose's birth. She tended my bandages and brought broth made of ox bones for strength, and sweet beer for my milk. She rubbed my shoulders where they were stiff from cradling the baby, and she helped me to my feet for my first real bath as a mother, pouring cool, scented water over my back, wrapping me in a fresh towel.

Long after my confinement was over, Meryt continued her visits. She fussed over my health and delighted in the baby; she examined him closely and gave him slow, sensuous massages that helped him sleep for hours. On the day he was weaned, Meryt even brought me a gift—a small obsidian statue of a nursing mother. I was confused by her generosity, but when I tried to refuse any of her attentions or gifts, she insisted. "The midwife's life is not easy, but that is no reason for it to be unlovely," she said.

Meryt always spoke to me as one midwife to another. No matter that I had not seen the inside of a birthing room since my own son was born; she continued to honor the skill I had shown at Re-mose's birth. When she returned to her own house after my son was born, she asked her mistress to learn what she could about me; her lady, Ruddedit, had sought out the story from Re-nefer, who provided only a few details. Meryt took these and wove them into a fabulous tale.

As Meryt told it, I was the daughter and granddaughter of midwives who knew the ways of herbs and barks even better than the necromancers of On, where the healing arts of Egypt are taught. She believed me a princess of Canaan, the descendant of a great queen who had been overthrown by an evil king.

I did not correct her, fearing that if I named my mothers or Inna the whole of my history would come pouring out of me and I would be thrown out of the house and my son cast out for bearing the blood of murderers in his veins. So Meryt embroidered my history, which she repeated to the women that she met, and they were many, as she attended most of the births of the northern precincts, noble and lowborn alike. She told the tale of how I had saved my son's life with my own hands, always leaving out her own part in it. She spoke of my skill with herbs and of the renown I had earned in the western wilderness as a healer. These things she imagined entirely on her own. And when I helped one of Nakht-re's servants deliver her first baby, Meryt spread the news of how I turned it inside the womb in the sixth month. Thanks to Meryt, I became a legend among the local women without once venturing out of Nakht-re's garden.

Meryt had her own story to tell. Though she had been born in Thebes, her mother's blood was mingled with that of the distant south and her skin showed the color of Nubia. But unlike Bilhah, whose face would appear to me while Meryt chattered on, she was tall and stately. "Had I not become a midwife," she said, "I should have liked to be a dancing girl, hired for grand parties in the great houses and even the king's own palace.

"But that life goes too fast," she said, with a mock sigh. "I am already too fat to dance for princes," slapping at the skin beneath her skinny arm, which did not budge, and breaking into a laugh I could not resist.

Meryt could make anyone laugh. Even women

deep in travail forgot their agony to smile at her jokes. When he was little, Re-mose called her "Ma's friend" even before I realized that she was truly my friend, and a blessing.

I knew everything there was to know about Meryt, for she loved to talk. Her mother was a cook married to a baker, and known as a singer, too. She was often called upon to entertain at the parties of her master. Her voice caused audiences to shudder with pleasure at its deep resonance. "Had she not been bare-breasted, they would have doubted she was a woman at all," Meryt said.

But the mother died when her daughter was still a girl and the household had no use for her, so Meryt was sent to the place where she lived even to the days when I knew her. As a child, she carried water for Ruddedit, a daughter of On, where the priests are famous as magicians and healers. The lady looked kindly upon Meryt, and when she saw that Meryt was clever, Ruddedit sent her to learn from the local granny midwife, a woman with uncommonly long fingers who brought luck to her mothers.

Meryt grew to womanhood in that house and, like her mother, married a baker there. He was a good man who treated her well. But Meryt was barren, and nothing could induce her womb to bear fruit. After many years, Meryt and her man adopted two boys whose parents had been felled by river fever. The sons were now grown to manhood and baked bread for the workers in the village of the tomb-makers, on the west bank of the river.

Her husband was long dead, and Meryt, though she saw her sons rarely, often boasted of their skills and health. "My boys have the most beautiful teeth you've ever seen," she would say solemnly, for her own mouth was a pit of decay and she chewed marjoram all day to ease the pain.

For years, Meryt spared me no detail of her life in hope that I would share some hint of mine. Finally, she gave up asking me about myself, but never ceased inviting me to attend upon birthing women with her. She would stop at Nakht-re's house and request of Herya or Re-nefer that I be permitted to accompany her. The ladies deferred to me, but I always declined. I had no wish to stray from Re-mose, nor had I any desire to see the world. I had not stepped outside the grounds since I arrived, and as the months became years, I came to fear the very thought. I was certain I would be lost, or worse, somehow discovered. I imagined that someone would recognize the sin of my family upon my face and I would be torn apart on the spot. My son would discover the truth about his mother and about her brothers, his uncles. He would be exiled from the good life that he seemed destined to inherit, and he would curse my memory.

I was ashamed of these secret fears, which made me turn my back on the lessons taught to me by Rachel and Inna, and thus upon their memory. My worthlessness imprisoned me; still I could not do what I knew I should.

Meryt never gave up. Sometimes, if a birth went badly, she returned afterward, even in the dead of night, waking me from my pallet in the garden shed to tell the story and ask how she might have done better. Often I could reassure her that she had done the best anyone could do, and we would sit silently together. But sometimes I would hear a story and my heart would sink. Once, when a woman had died very suddenly giving birth, Meryt did not think to take up a knife to try to free the baby in the womb, so both of them perished. I did not shield my dismay well enough, and Meryt saw my face.

"Tell me, then," she demanded, grabbing me by the shoulders. "Do not curl your lip when you might have saved the baby. Teach me at least, that I might try."

Shamed by Meryt's tears, I began to speak of Inna's methods, her way with a knife, her tricks at manipulation. I tried to explain her use of herbs, but I lacked the Egyptian names for plants and roots. So Meryt brought her herbal kit, and we began to translate. I described my mothers' ways with nettle, fennel, and coriander, and she scoured the markets searching out leaves and seeds I had not seen since childhood.

Meryt brought me samples of every flower and stem sold at the wharf. Some of it was familiar but some of it stank, especially the local concoctions which depended upon dead things: bits of dried animals, ground rocks and shells, and excrement of every description. Egyptian healers applied the dung of water horses and alligators and the urine of horses and children to various parts of the body in different seasons. There were times that the most odious preparations appeared to help, but I was always amazed that a people so concerned with bodily cleanliness would accept such foul remedies.

Although Egyptian herbal lore was deep and old, I

was pleased to find methods and plants of which they knew little. Meryt found cumin seed in the marketplace, and she was surprised to learn that it aided the healing of wounds. She bought hyssop and mint with their roots still intact, and they flourished in the pungent black soil of Egypt. No one suffered from a sour stomach in the house of Nakhtre again. Thus Meryt became famous for "her" exotic herbal cures, and I had the satisfaction of knowing that my mothers' wisdom was being put to good use.

My quiet life ended during the fourth year after Remose left the house of Nakht-re, when Ruddedit's daughter came to stand upon the bricks.

Her name was Hatnuf, and she was in a bad way. Her first baby had been born dead—full-sized and perfect in every feature, but lifeless. After years of miscarrying, another child had finally taken root, but she faced this labor in terror, and after a full day of travail, the pains had not advanced the baby's progress. Meryt was in attendance, and the lady of the house had sent for a physician-priest, who chanted prayers and hung the room with amulets and set a pile of herbs and goat dung to smoking while Hatnuf crouched over it.

But the smell had caused the mother to faint, and in falling, the girl cut her forehead and bled. After that, Ruddedit banished the doctor from the room and had him wait outside the front door, where he recited incantations in the nasal drone of a priest. Day turned to night again, and night began to brighten to another dawn, and still the pains did not abate, nor did the baby move. Hatnuf, the lady's only daughter, was nearly dead with fear and pain when Meryt suggested I be summoned.

This time, it was not a matter of being asked. Meryt appeared at the doorway of my garden hut with Ruddedit standing in the dawn's light behind her. Weariness barely dimmed the beauty in a face no longer young. "Den-ner," she said, in the accents of Egypt, "you must come and do what you can for my child. We have nothing left to try. The smell of Anubis is in the birth chamber already. Bring your kit and follow me."

Meryt quickly told me the story, and I grabbed a few herbs I'd been drying in the rafters of my shed. The lady was nearly running. I barely had time to realize that I was out of the garden. We walked past the front of Nakht-re's house, and I remembered the day I first saw the place, a lifetime earlier. Sunlight caught the gold-tipped flag-poles in front of the great temple, where banners hung lifeless in the still of the dawn. Ruddedit's house was just on the other side of the temple, so it took no time to reach the antechamber where Hatnuf lay whimpering on the floor, surrounded by the servants of the house, who were nearly as exhausted as the laboring mother.

Death was in the room. I caught sight of him in the shadows beneath a statue of Bes, the friendly-grotesque guardian of children, who seemed to grimace at his own powerlessness here.

Ruddedit introduced me to her daughter, who looked up at me with empty eyes, but did as I asked. She moved to her side so I could reach an oiled hand up to the womb, but I felt no sign of the baby's head. The room was very still as the women waited to see what I would do or ask of them.

The dog-shaped shadow of death stirred, sensing my dismay. But his eagerness only made me angry. I cursed at his bark and his tail and his very mother. I did this in my native tongue, which sounded harsh even to me after so many years of Egyptian words in my ears. Meryt and the others thought I uttered a secret charm, and murmured approval. Even Hatnuf stirred and looked around.

I called for oil and a mortar and mixed the strongest herbs I had at hand: birthwort and an extraction of hemp, both of which sometimes cause the womb to expel its contents early in pregnancy. I did not know if they would work, and worried that the combination might cause damage, but I knew there was nothing else to be tried, for she was dying. The baby was already dead, but there was no reason to give up on the mother.

I applied the mixture, and soon strong pains seized the girl. I had the women help Hatnuf back up to the bricks, where I massaged her belly and tried to push the baby downward. Hatnuf's legs could not hold her, and soon Meryt had to take Ruddedit's place behind her, where she whispered encouragement as I reached in again to feel the baby's head, which was now near the door.

The pains became ceaseless and intolerable to the poor woman on the bricks. Her eyes turned back in her head, and she fell into Meryt's arms, senseless and unable to push.

It was full daylight now, but the shadow in the room

would not let the sun's rays penetrate the gloom. My
cheeks were streaked with tears. I did not know what
to do next. Inna had once told a tale of freeing a baby
from its dead mother's womb, but this mother was not
dead. I had no other tricks to try, no other herbs.

And then I remembered the song in which Inna had
taken such delight, the song which she learned in the
hills above Shechem.

"Fear not," I sang, recalling the melody easily, reaching deep for the words.

> "Fear not, the time is coming
> Fear not, your bones are strong
> Fear not, help is nearby
> Fear not, Gula is near
> Fear not, the baby is at the door
> Fear not, he will live to bring you honor
> Fear not, the hands of the midwife are clever
> Fear not, the earth is beneath you
> Fear not, we have water and salt
> Fear not, little mother
> Fear not, mother of us all"

Meryt joined me in singing the words "Fear not,"
sensing the power of the sounds without knowing
what she was saying. By the third time, all of the women
were singing "Fear not," and Hatnuf was breathing
deeply again.

The baby was delivered soon after, and indeed he
was dead. Hatnuf turned her face to the wall and closed
her eyes, wishing only to join him. But when Meryt
began to pack her poor, battered womb with boiled

linen, Hatnuf cried out again in the voice of a laboring mother. "There is another child," said Meryt. "Come, Den-ner," she said. "Catch the twin."

With just one more push, Hatnuf delivered a baby utterly unlike his brother. Where the first one was fat and perfect and lifeless, this one was puny and wrinkled and bellowed with the lungs of an ox.

Meryt laughed at the sound, and the room erupted in peals and gales and giggles of relief and joy. The bloody, unwashed, squalling baby was passed from hand to hand, kissed and blessed by every woman there. Ruddedit fell to her knees and laughed and wept with her grandson in her arms. But Hatnuf did not hear us. The little one arrived in a torrent of blood that would not cease. No amount of packing stanched the flow, and within moments of her son's birth, Hatnuf died, her head on her mother's lap.

The scene in the room was terrible: the mother dead, one baby dead, a scrawny newborn wailing for the breast that would never feed him. Ruddedit sat, bereaved of her only daughter, a grandmother for the first time. Meryt wept with her mistress, and I crept away, wishing I had never ventured out of my garden.

After the horror of that scene, I thought I would be forbidden to enter another birth chamber. But as Meryt told the story, I alone was responsible for saving the life of the surviving child, who had been born, she said, on a day so hated by Set that it was a miracle he drew a single breath.

Soon messengers from other important houses of Thebes came to the door of Nakht-re's garden with orders not to return home without Den-ner the mid-wife. These were the servants of priests and scribes and others who could not be gainsaid. I consented only if Meryt would accompany me, but since she always agreed, we became the midwives of our neighborhood, which comprised many fine houses where the ladies and their servants enjoyed fertile wombs. We were called at least once every seven days, and for every healthy baby, we were rewarded with jewelry, amulets, fine linen, or jars of oil. Meryt and I divided these goods, and though I offered my share to Re-nefer, she insisted that I keep them.

Within a year my shed was cluttered with a collec-tion of objects I did not use or care for. Meryt looked around one day and declared that I needed a wicker box to contain my belongings. Since I owned more than enough to trade, Meryt selected an auspicious day for us to go to market.

By then I had gone out to attend at many births, still I dreaded this venture out into the larger world. Meryt knew I was afraid and held my hand as we walked out of my garden, chattering all the way to keep me from dwelling upon my fears. I held on to her like a baby in fear of losing her mother but after a time found the courage to look upon the sights of the busy Theban quay. The harvest was still many days off and most of the farmers had little to do but wait for ripen-ing, so the stalls were clogged with country folk who had nothing much to trade except time.

Meryt exchanged a beaded necklace from one of her mothers for some sweet cake, and we ate as we wandered, arm in arm, from one stall to the next. I marveled at the amount of jewelry for sale and wondered who could afford so many baubles. I saw sandal-makers turning out cheap shoes, made to order. A line of men waited for one particular barber, known to have the best gossip. I averted my eyes from a pile of Ca-naanite woolens, which might have been woven by my own aunts. Meryt and I laughed over the antics of a monkey, who held a brace of tall, hungry-looking dogs on leads and made them beg for scraps of food.

After we had taken in the sights, my friend said it was time to start our hunt, but the first basket-maker we came upon had nothing large enough to suit my needs, so we walked on, passing the wine and oil mer-chants, bakers, and men selling live birds. We saw many beautiful things, too: incised Kushite pottery, ham-mered bronze vases, household gods and goddesses, three-legged stools and chairs. My eye fell upon a handsome box with an inlaid cover that bloomed with a garden made of ivory and faience and mother-of-pearl. "Now there's a piece for the master's tomb," said Meryt, in honest admiration.

The carpenter appeared behind his work and be-gan to tell the story of its making: where he pur-chased the acacia wood, and how much difficulty he had in applying the ivory. He spoke thoughtfully and slowly, as though he were telling a story rather than trying to make a sale. I kept my eyes on the box as he spoke, hearing only the warmth of his voice, and staring at his hands as they traced the design upon his handiwork.

Meryt started teasing the fellow. "What do you take us for, knave?" she asked. "Do you think we are rich ladies disguised as midwives? Who but a rich man could afford anything so fine as this? Who could lay claim to such a work of art except the king's own tomb-maker? You are pulling my leg, little man," she said.

He laughed at her words and replied, "If you think me little, you must come from a land of giants, sister. I am Benia," he introduced himself. "And you might be surprised at the bargains available at my stall. It all depends upon the buyer, my dear," he teased back. "Beautiful women always get what they want."

At this, Meryt howled with laughter and poked me in the ribs, but I said nothing, for I knew that his words had been aimed at me. In an instant Meryt, too, understood that the carpenter had been talking to me, and although I had not said a word, the sound of his voice and the gentleness of his words had moved me.

My fingers, almost of their own accord, traced the pattern of a milky-white leaf that was inlaid upon the box. "This comes from the heart of a sea creature that lives far to the north," Benia said, pointing to another part of the design.

I noticed the size of his hands. His fingers were thick as the branches on a young fruit tree, and even longer than his massive palms, which hard work had gnarled into mountains and valleys of muscle. He caught me staring and drew his hand away, as if in shame.

"When I was born, my mother took one look at me and cried out when she saw these," Benia said. "They were far too large for my body, even then. 'A sculptor,' she said to my father, who apprenticed me to the finest stonecutter.

"But I had no talent for stone. The alabaster cracked when I so much as looked at it, and even granite would not permit me to approach. Only wood understood my hands. Supple and warm and alive, wood speaks to me and tells me where to cut, how to shape it. I love my work, lady."

He looked into my eyes, which I had raised to his face as he spoke.

Meryt saw the look pass between us and leaped into the silence like a shrewd fishwife. "This is Denner, tradesman, a widow and the finest midwife in Thebes. We come to the market in search of a simple basket to hold payment from her grateful mothers."

"But a basket will not do for a master," said Benia, turning to bargain with Meryt. "Let me see what you brought to trade, Mother, for I have been sitting here all day without luck." .

Meryt unpacked our collection of trinkets: a carved slate for mixing malachite into green eye shadow, a large carnelian scarab too red for my stomach, and a beautiful beaded head covering, the gift of a pretty young concubine who gave birth to a fine little boy she handed directly to her mistress, without even looking at the baby. (Meryt and I saw many strange things in the birthing rooms of Thebes.)

Benia feigned interest in the scarab. "For your wife?" Meryt asked, without pretense at subtlety.

"No wife," Benia replied, simply. "I live in my sister's house and have these many years, but her husband is impatient of my place at his table. Soon I will be leaving the city to live among the workmen in the Valley of the Kings," he said slowly, speaking again to me.

At this, Meryt grew excited on her own behalf and told him all about her sons, who were bakers employed for the workmen there. "When I go, I will seek them out," Benia promised, and added, "I will be given my own house there, as befits a master craftsman. Four rooms for myself only," he said, as though he could hear his own voice echoing through the empty chambers already.

"What a waste, carpenter," Meryt replied.

As the two of them exchanged these confidences for my benefit, my fingers followed the edges of the pond that Benia had fashioned on the box cover. Before I could draw away, he covered my hand with his own.

I was afraid to look into his face. Perhaps he was leering. Perhaps he thought by making this absurd transaction—trading a pretty bauble for a master-work—I then would owe him the use of my body. But when Meryt jabbed me in the ribs to answer, I saw only kindness on the carpenter's face.

"Bring the box to the garden door at the house of Nakht-re, scribe to the priests of Amun-Re," Meryt said. "Bring it tomorrow." She handed over the scarab.

"Tomorrow in the morning," he said. And we left.

"Now that was a good transaction, girl," said Meryt. "And that scarab was a lucky piece to buy you a trea-sure box and a husband, too."

I shook my head at my friend and smiled as though she were babbling, but I did not say no. I said nothing at all. I was embarrassed and thrilled. I felt an unfa-miliar tightness between my legs and my cheeks were flushed.

And yet, I did not fully understand my own heart, for this was nothing like what I felt when I first saw Shalem. No hot wind blew through Benia and into me. This feeling was much cooler and calmer. Even so, my heart beat faster and I knew my eyes were brighter than they had been earlier in the day.

Benia and I had exchanged a few words and brushed against each other's fingers. And yet, I felt connected to this stranger. I had no doubt that he felt the same.

All the way home, my step beat out the rhythm of my wonder—"How can this be? How can this be?"

As we approached Nakht-re's house, Meryt broke an unaccustomed silence and laughed, saying, "I'll deliver your babies yet. By my count, you are not yet thirty years in this world. I'll see grand-babies through you, daughter of my heart," and she kissed me good-bye.

But once I walked into the garden all thoughts of Benia were banished. The house was in an uproar. Re-mose was back!

He had arrived soon after I had left. The servants had been sent to search for me, and since I never left the grounds without informing Re-nefer first, she had grown alarmed and even sent word to her friend Ruddedit. When my mother-in-law saw me enter the yard carrying a half-eaten cake from the market, she grew angry and turned on her heel without speaking. It was the cook who told me to hurry and see my son, who had come home to recover.

"Recover?" I asked her, suddenly cold with fear. "Has he been ill?"

"Oh, no," she said with a broad grin. "He comes home to heal from the circumcision and to celebrate his manhood in high style. I'll be working from dawn till midnight all this week," she said and pinched my cheek.

I heard nothing past the word "circumcision." My head rang and my heart pounded as I rushed into the great hall where Re-mose was arrayed on a litter near Nakht-re's chair. He looked up at me and smiled easily, without a trace of pain in his face, which was now a different face altogether.

It had been nearly five years since he left me, and the little boy was now a young man. His hair, no longer shaved, had grown in thick and black. His arms showed muscle, his legs were no longer silky smooth, and his chest bespoke his father's beauty. "Ma," said the young man who was my son. "Oh Ma, you look well. Even better than I remembered."

He was merely being polite. He was a prince of Egypt addressing the serving woman who had given him birth. It was just as I feared: we were strangers, and our lives would never permit us to become more than that. He motioned for me to come and sit beside him, and Nakht-re smiled his approval.

I asked if he suffered, and he waved the question away. "I have no pain," he said. "They give you wine laced with the juice of poppies before they draw the knife, and afterward too," he said. "But that all happened a week ago, and I am quite recovered. Now it is time to celebrate, and I am home for the banquet.

"But how are you, Ma?" he said. "I am told you are a famous midwife now, that you are the only one the great ladies of Thebes will trust when called to child-bed."

"I serve as I can," I said quietly and turned his question aside, for what can a woman tell a man about babies and blood? "But you, son, tell me what you learned. Tell me of your years in school and of the friendships and honors you earned, for your uncle says you were the best of your fellows."

A cloud passed over Re-mose's face, and I recognized the little boy who burst into tears when he found a dead baby duck in the garden. But my son did not speak of the taunts of his schoolmates, nor recount for me the mocking cries that followed him everywhere during the first year of his studies: "Where is your father? You have no father."

Re-mose did not speak of his loneliness, which grew as he proved himself the best of his class and the teacher took note of him and made him the favorite. He spoke only of his teacher, Kar, whom he loved and obeyed in all things, and who doted upon him.

Unlike other masters, he never beat his students or berated them for their mistakes. "He is the most noble man I ever met, apart from Uncle," said Re-mose, taking Nakht-re's hand in his. "I am home to celebrate not only my coming of age, but the great gift Kar has given me.

"My teacher asks that I accompany him south to Kush, where the trade in ebony and ivory has been revived, and where the vizier was caught embezzling from the king. The king himself has asked Kar to go and oversee the installation of a new overseer, and to take stock and report upon what he finds there.

"I will go to assist my teacher, and watch when he sits as judge and the people bring their disputes before him." Re-mose paused so I would hear the importance of his next words. "I am instructed to learn the duties of a vizier. After this journey, my training will be complete and I will receive my own commission, and begin to earn honor for my family. My uncle is pleased, Mother. Are you pleased as well?"

The question was sincere, echoing with the longing of a boy who asks his mother to pronounce upon his achievement. "I am pleased, my son. You are a fine man who will do honor to this house. I wish you happiness, a kind wife, and many children. I am proud of you, and proud to be your mother."

That was all I could say. Just as he did not tell me of the pain he suffered at school, I did not speak of how much I missed him, or how empty my heart had been, or how he had taken the light from my life when he left. I looked into his eyes, and he returned my gaze fondly. He patted my hand and lifted it to his lips. My heart beat to the twin drums of happiness and loneliness.

Two nights later, I watched Re-mose from across the room at the feast given in his honor. He sat beside Nakht-re and ate like a boy who has not been fed for a week. He drank of the wine and his eyes glittered with excitement. I drank wine, too, and stared at my son, wondering at the life he would live, amazed that he was a man already, only a few years younger than his father had been when I saw him for the first time, in his father's house.

Poised on the edge of manhood, Re-mose was half

a head taller than Nakht-re, clear-eyed, and straight as a tree. Re-nefer and I sat side by side for the first time in years and admired the man-child who had given us both a reason to live. My hand brushed hers and she did not withdraw from my touch but held my fingers in hers, and for a moment at least we shared our love for our son, and through him for the unnamed son and husband of Shechem.

A pretty serving girl raised her eyes to him, and he flirted back. I laughed to think of the baby whose bottom I had washed now warming to a woman. My face ached from smiling, and yet my sighs were so loud that Re-nefer once turned to ask if I was in any pain.

It was the finest banquet I had ever seen, with much of noble Thebes in attendance. The flowers shone in the light of one hundred lamps. The air was thick with the smells of rich food, fresh lotus, incense, and perfume. Laughter, fed by six kinds of beer and three varieties of wine, pealed through the room, and the dancers leaped and twirled until they glistened with sweat and panted on the floor.

A second troupe of musicians had been hired to supplement the local performers. This company sailed the river, stopping at temples and noble houses to play, but unlike the others, they refused to play with dancers on the floor, insisting that audiences attend to their songs, said to have magical qualities. The mysterious leader was a veiled lady. Blind like many masters of the harp, she was mistress of the sistrum, the hand-held bell-drum.

According to the gossip, the singer had escaped the jaws of Anubis and won a second life, but he had bitten off her face, which is why she wore the veil. The tale was told with a wink and a nudge, for Egyptians knew how a juicy story could be used to drum up business. Still, when the veiled singer was led into the room, an expectant hush fell and the tipsy crowd sat up.

She was dressed in white, covered head to toe in a gauzy stuff that floated in layers to the floor. Re-nefer leaned toward me and whispered, "She looks like a puff of smoke."

Settled on a stool, she freed her hands from her garments to take up the instrument, and the hush released a soft gasp, for her hands were as white as her robes, unearthly pale, as though scarred by a terrible fire. She shook the sistrum four times and produced four entirely different sounds, which sobered the listeners, who quieted to attention.

First the group played a light song of flutes and drums, then a lone trumpet produced a mournful melody that caused the ladies to sigh and the men to stroke their chins. An old children's song made everyone in the room smile with the open faces they once wore as boys and girls.

There was indeed magic to this music, which could transform the blackest sorrow to the brightest joy. The guests clapped their hands high in the direction of the performers and raised their cups in gratitude at Na-kht-re for the wonderful entertainment.

After the applause died down, the sistrum-player began to sing, accompanied by her own instrument and a single drum. It was a long song, with many refrains. The story it told was unremarkable: a tale of love found and lost—the oldest story in the world. The only story.

As the song began, the man returned the girl's love, and they delighted in each other. But then the tale took a sorry turn and the lover spurned his lady, leaving her alone. She wept and prayed to the Golden Lady Hathor, but to no avail. The beloved would not take her back. The girl's sorrow was endless and unbearable. The women wept openly, each remembering her youth. The men wiped their eyes, unashamed, recalling their earliest passion. Even the young ones sighed, feeling the pangs of losses yet to come.

There was a long silence after the song ended. The harpist picked out a quiet air, but the conversation ceased. No more cups were raised. Re-nefer stood and left the room without ceremony, and then, one by one, the rest of the company took their leave. The party ended quietly, and the hall emptied to the sounds of sighs and murmured thanks. The musicians packed up their instruments and led their leader away. Some of the servants slept on the floor, too exhausted to begin cleaning up until morning. The house was completely still.

Dawn was some hours distant when I found my way to where the musicians slept. The veiled one leaned against a wall motionless. I thought she was sleeping as well, but she turned, her hands out-stretched to discover who approached. I put my hands in hers, which were small and cool.

"Werenro," I said.

The sound of my accent startled her. "Canaan," she

said, in a bitter whisper. "That was my name in torment."

"I was a child," I said. "You were the messenger of Rebecca, my grandmother. You told us a story I never forgot. But you were murdered, Werenro. I was there with the Grandmother when they brought you back. I saw them bury your bones. Did you truly return from the dead?"

There was a long silence and her head fell forward beneath the veils. "Yes," she said. And then, after a moment, "No. I did not escape. The truth is, I am dead.

"How strange to find a ghost of that time here in a great house by the river. Tell me," she asked, "are you dead, too?"

"Perhaps I am," I answered, shuddering.

"Perhaps you are, for the living do not ask such questions, nor could they bear the pain of truth without the consolation of music. The dead understand.

"Do you know the face of death?" she asked.

"Yes," I said, remembering the doglike shadows that attend so many births, patient and eager at the same time.

"Ah," she said, and without warning lifted the veil. Her lips were unharmed, but the rest of her face was torn and scarred. Her nose had been broken and ripped open, her cheeks were collapsed and seamed with deep scars, her eyes were milky stones. It seemed impossible that anyone could survive such destruction.

"I was leaving Tyre with a flagon of purple dye for her, for the Grandmother. It was dawn and the sky put all the tents of Mamre to shame. I was looking up when they came upon me. Three of them, Canaanite men like any others, filthy and stupid. They said nothing to me or to each other. They took my pouch and my basket and ripped them open, and then they turned on me."

Werenro began to rock, back and forth, and her voice went flat. "The first one pushed me to the ground right in the middle of the road. The second one tore off my clothes. The third lifted his robe and fell upon me. He emptied himself into me, who had never laid with a man. And then he spit into my face.

"The second one took his turn, but he could not do the deed, and so he began to beat me, cursing me for causing his problem. He broke my nose and knocked several teeth from my mouth, and only when I was bleeding was he aroused enough to do what he wished.

"The third one turned me over and ripped me open from the backside. And laughed." She stopped rocking and sat up straight, hearing that laughter still.

"I lay, facedown on the road, as the three of them stood over me. I thought they would kill me and end my torment.

"But it was not for them. 'Why do you not cry out?' cried the one who laughed. 'Do you have no tongue? Or perhaps you are not really a woman at all, for you are not the color of woman. You are the color of a sick dog's shit. I will hear you cry out, and we will see if you are a woman or a phantom.'

"And that is when they did to me what you can see. I need not speak of that." Werenro lowered her veil and began to rock again.

"At the first sound of footsteps, they left me for dead," she said. "A shepherd's dog found me where I lay, followed by a boy, who cried out at the sight of me. I heard him retch and thought he would flee, but instead he covered me with his robe and brought his mother. She applied poultices to my face, and unguents to my body, and stroked my hands in pity, and kept me alive, and never asked me to explain.

"When it was certain that I would survive, she asked whether she should send word to Mamre, for she had recognized the tatters of my robe. But I said no.

"I was finished being a slave, finished with Rebecca's arrogance, and finished with Canaan. My only desire was to come home and smell the river and the perfume of the lotus in the morning. I told her I wished to be dead in Mamre, and she made it so.

"She cut handfuls of my hair and wrapped it with my clothes and a few sheep's bones inside my bag. She sent her son into town, where he found a merchant headed for Mamre, who brought the Grandmother news of my death.

"The Canaanite woman gave me a veil and a walking stick and led me to Tyre. She searched out a caravan headed for the land of the great river. They took me in exchange for one of her flock, and for the promise that I would entertain them with songs and stories. The traders brought me to On, where a sistrum found its way into my hands, and now I find myself here with you, with Canaan in my mouth again." At this she turned her head away from me and spat. A snake slithered from the spot where her spittle fell, and I shivered in the cold blast of Werenro's anger.

"I would curse the whole nation but for that Canaanite woman's kindness. My eyes were put out, so I never saw her face, but I imagine it shining with light and beauty. Indeed, when I think of her, I see the face of the full moon.

"Perhaps she was atoning for some wrong she had done. Or perhaps she had once been abandoned and someone helped her escape. Or maybe no one had helped her when she was in need. She asked me nothing, not even my name. She saved me for no reason other than the goodness of her heart. Her name was goodness itself, Tamar, the sustaining fruit," said Werenro, and she began rocking again.

We sat together in the hour before dawn, silent for a long while. Finally, she spoke again, to answer a question I would never have thought to ask.

"I am not unhappy," she said. "Nor am I content. There is nothing in my heart. I care for no one, and for nothing. I dream of dogs with bared teeth. I am dead. It is not so bad to be dead."

The sighs and snores of the sleeping musicians interrupted her words. "Good souls," she said of her companions, with tenderness. "We ask nothing of one another.

"But you," said Werenro, "how did you come to speak the language of the river?"

Without hesitation, I told her everything. I leaned my head back, closed my eyes, and gave voice to my life. In all of my years, I had never before spoken so much or so long, and yet the words came effortlessly, as though this were something I had done many times before.

I surprised myself, remembering Tabea, remembering Ruti, remembering my coming of age in the red tent. I spoke of Shalem and our passionate lovemaking without blushing. I spoke of our betrayal and his murder. I told her about Re-nefer's bargain with me, and Meryt's care for me, and I spoke of my son with pride and love.

It was not difficult. Indeed, it was as though I had been parched and there was cool water in my mouth. I said "Shalem" and my breath was clean after years of being foul and bitter. I called my son "Bar-Shalem," and an old tightness in my chest eased.

I recited the names of my mothers, and knew with total certainty that they were dead. I leaned my face into Werenro's shoulder and soaked her robe in memory of Leah and Rachel, Zilpah and Bilhah.

Through it all, Werenro nodded and sighed and held my hand. When at last I was quiet she said, "You are not dead." Her voice betrayed a little sorrow. "You are not like me. Your grief shines from your heart. The flame of love is strong. Your story is not finished, Dinah," she said, in the accents of my mothers. Not "Den-ner" the foreign midwife, but "Dinah," a daughter beloved of four mothers.

Werenro stroked my head, which rested on her shoulder, as the room began to brighten with the first hints of dawn. I fell asleep leaning there, but when I awoke she was gone.

Re-mose left a week later, in the company of Kar, who arrived from Memphis on his way to Kush. Re-mose brought the venerable master into the garden to introduce us, but he barely acknowledged the lowborn mother of his favorite student. After they left I wondered, without pity, whether the old man would survive such a long journey.

CHAPTER THREE

B enia had delivered the box as he had said he would, but I was not there to receive it. When he brought it to the garden gate, he was brusquely told that Denner was sitting in the great hall with her son and could not be called away by a tradesman. The box was placed in a corner of the kitchen, and I did not see it until after Re-mose had left Thebes and the house had returned to normal.

When the cook gave it to me, her curiosity overwhelmed her. How had something so elegant and rare come to be mine? And who was the man who asked after me so eagerly? I said nothing of him or the box to anyone in the house, and the gossip soon died away. I sent no word to Benia either, hoping he would take my silence as a rejection of the indirect offer he had made me in the marketplace. Although I had been moved by his words and by his touch, I could not see myself living like other women. Despite Werenro's words, I was sure that Re-mose would tell the next and final chapters of my story.

Meryt was furious at me for turning Benia down. "A man like that? So accomplished? So kind?" She threatened never to speak to me again, but we both knew that could never happen. I was her daughter, and she would never cut me off.

But Benia's box remained an embarrassment and a reproach to me. It did not belong in a garden shed. It was not made for a foreign-born midwife without status or standing. It was mine only because the carpenter had recognized my loneliness and because I had seen the need in him, too. I filled the box with gifts from my mothers, but covered its gleaming beauty with an old papyrus mat so that it would not remind me of Benia, whom I resigned to the corner of my heart, with other dreams that had died.

The weeks flowed quietly into months, the passage of time marked by the stories of births, most of them healthy. I learned that a tonic made of the red madder growing in my garden eased childbirth for many, and Meryt and I were called to ever more distant neighborhoods. Once, a barque was sent to bring us to the town of On, where a priest's favorite concubine lay dying. We found a girl far too young to be a mother, screaming in terror, alone in a room without the comfort of another woman. Shortly after we arrived, we closed her eyes and I tried to free the baby, but she, too, was dead.

Meryt went to speak to the father, who, far from bereaved, began to curse my friend and me for killing his wife and child. He rushed into the birthing chamber before I had time to cover the poor mother. "The foreigner raised a knife to her?" he shrieked. "Only a surgeon can do such a thing. This woman is a menace, a demon sent from the east to destroy the kingdom of the river." He lunged at me, but Meryt stopped him, and with strength I did not know she possessed, pinned him against a wall and tried to explain that I had cut the mother in hope of saving the child.

But I saw no reason to explain myself. I looked into his eyes and saw an odious and petty soul, and I was filled with rage and pity for the young woman who lay at my feet. "Pervert," I roared, in the language of my mothers. "Foul son of a maggot, may you and others like you wither like wheat in the desert. This was an unloved girl who lies here dead. The stench of her unhappiness clings to her. For this, you will die in agony."

Both Meryt and the priest stared at me as I spewed out my curses, and when I was finished the man began to shudder and in a terrified whisper said, "A foreign sorceress in the House of the Gods!"

The sound of our voices had drawn other priests, who did not meet my eyes and held their brother so we could leave. On the journey back, I watched the shoreline pass and remembered Inna's prophecy that I would find my heart's desire by the banks of a river. I shook my head over the irony of her vision, and returned to my garden shed unsettled and discontented.

For the first time since my childhood, I was restless. I no longer dreamed of Shalem or his death but woke up every morning haunted by visions of deserted landscapes, gaunt sheep, wailing women. I rose from my pallet vainly trying to name my disquiet. Meryt noticed gray hairs on my head and offered to make me a dye of ash and the blood of a black ox. I laughed at the idea, although I knew she used the potion and looked far younger than her years because of it. Her suggestion made me view my restlessness as nothing more than a sign of the passing years. I was nearly of the age when women stop bleeding at the new moon, and I pictured myself passing the twilight of my days in the familiar peace of Nakht-re's garden. I set a statue of Isis over my bed, and prayed for the wisdom and tranquillity of the lady goddess, healer of women and men.

But I neglected to pray for the well-being of my earthly protectors. Late one night, I was awakened by the sound of howling cats, and the next morning Nakht-re came to tell me that Re-nefer had died in her sleep. Her body was collected by priests, who would prepare her body for the next life with elaborate ritual in her father's tomb in Memphis, where a statue had been prepared in her memory. The rites would last for three days.

Nakht-re asked if I would like to attend the ritual with him. I thanked him but said no. He must have been relieved, for we both knew that there was no comfortable place for me among the celebrants.

In the days after Re-nefer's death, I cursed her as much as I wept for her. She had been my savior and my jailer. She had given me Shalem and then stolen his memory. Finally, I did not know the woman at all. I had seen little of her since Re-mose had gone to school and had no idea how she kept busy all those years; if she spun or wove, if she slept the days away, if she wept at night for her son and her husband. If she hated me or pitied me or loved me.

I dreamed in vivid detail in the nights following her death, and Re-nefer visited me in the form of a small bird flying out of the sunrise, screaming "Shechem" in a familiar voice that I could not name. The Re-nefer bird tried to lift people and objects from the ground but had no strength and beat her wings in frustration until she was exhausted and furious. Every night, she disappeared into the sun, shrieking. It seemed her troubled soul would never find peace. After seven nights of that vision, I felt nothing but pity for her.

Nakht-re died the following season, and for him I mourned without reservation. Honest, generous, good-humored, and always kind, he was the model of an Egyptian nobleman. My son was blessed to have had such a father, and I knew Re-mose would weep for the only Ba he had ever known. I assumed that Re-mose went to Memphis for the rites, though I was not told. Only Nakht-re had thought to tell me about my son's travels. With his death, I felt my connection to Re-mose weaken.

After Nakht-re was gone, his wife went to live with her brother, somewhere north in the Delta. The house would be given to a new scribe. Had Re-mose been a little older and more practiced in the politics of the temple, he might have been given the position. Instead, one of Nakht-re's rivals was chosen. Most of the staff would remain, and the cook urged me to stay on, too. But the chill in the eyes of the new mistress who came to survey what was to be her home made me want nothing less.

Meryt, too, was facing a change. Her older son,

Menna, had offered her a place under his roof in the Valley of the Kings. He had been appointed chief baker and given a larger house, where his mother was welcome. Menna made the journey to see his mother and said that though many babies were born to the wives of craftsmen in the valley, there were no skilled midwives and many women had died. Meryt would be an honored citizen if she came to live among them.

My friend was tempted. Since the disastrous journey to On, rumors had begun to circulate about the foreign-born midwife and her companion. The priest I had cursed had lost the use of his voice after I saw him, and then he went lame. There were fewer calls to attend at the births of noblewomen, though their servants and the tradesmen's wives still sought us out.

I knew that my friend relished the thought of honor and a new start, but she worried about living with a daughter-in-law and fretted about giving up the comforts of life in Thebes. She told her son that she would weigh his invitation until the following season, when the new year began. After all, she explained to me, the appearance of the dog star marked the most auspicious time for making changes.

My friend and I weighed our choices, but we often fell silent, keeping our worst fears to ourselves. In truth, I had nowhere to go. Herya had not offered me a place with her. I would simply have to stay where I was and hope for the best. If Meryt left for her son's house, loneliness would swallow me, but I kept still about that and listened as she described life in the valley.

Meryt never considered leaving without me, but she worried about asking her daughter-in-law to put up

with two women in her house. My friend presented
her dilemma to her good mistress, and Ruddedit
begged her to stay and gave her word that I, too, would
always have a place under her roof.

But the lady's husband was nothing like Nakht-re. He
was a narrow-minded tyrant with a temper that sometimes broke upon the backs of his servants, and even
Ruddedit kept her distance from him. My life would
be pinched and furtive if I went to that house.

I might have lost heart except for the consolation I
found in my dreams, where a garden of a thousand
lotuses bloomed, children laughed, and strong arms
held me safe. Meryt put great store in these dreams,
and visited a local oracle who foresaw love and riches
for me in the steaming entrails of a goat.

The new year came and Menna returned to see his
mother. His wife, Shif-re, accompanied him this time
and said, "Mother, come home with us. My sons work
with their father in the bakery all day and I am often
alone in the house. There is plenty of room for you to
sit in the sun and rest. Or if you wish to continue as a
midwife, I will carry your kit and become your assistant. You will be honored in my husband's house, and
after your death we will honor your memory with a fine
stele with your name on the west side."

Meryt was moved by her daughter-in-law's speech.
Shif-re was a few years younger than I, a plain woman
except for her eyes, which were large and ringed with
thick black lashes, and radiated compassion. "Menna
is lucky in you," said Meryt, taking the woman's hands
in hers.

"But I cannot leave Den-ner here. She is my

daughter now, and without me she is alone in the world. In truth, she is the master midwife, and I am her assistant. It is she the women of royal Thebes call for when their time is at hand.

"I cannot ask you to take her in. And yet, if you offer her the same hospitality, I believe you will be well rewarded in this life. She carries the mark of money and luck. She dreams with great power and sees through lies. All of this has rubbed off on me, and it will benefit you and your house, too."

Shif-re went to her husband with Meryt's words. Menna was not pleased at the prospect of yet another aging woman in his house, but the promise of luck struck a chord with him. He came with his mother and wife to my shed to make me welcome, and I accepted his offer with genuine gratitude. I took a turquoise scarab from my box and gave it to Menna. "Hospitality is the gods' own treasure," I said, placing my forehead to the ground before the baker, who was embarrassed to be shown such obeisance.

"Perhaps my brother can give you his garden for your own," he said, helping me to my feet. "His wife has no knack with growing things, and my mother tells me you have Osiris's own touch with the soil." Then it was my turn to be embarrassed at his kindness. How had I come to find so many kind people in my life? What was the purpose of such good fortune?

Menna's work called him home, so we had only a few days to prepare for our journey. First, I went to the marketplace and hired a scribe who wrote on behalf of unlettered people, and through him sent word to Re-mose, assistant to Kar the scribe, residing in Kush, to inform him that his mother Den-ner had moved to the Valley of the Kings, to the house of the chief baker called Menna. I sent him blessings in the name of Isis and her son Horus. And I paid the scribe double his fee to make sure the message would find my son.

I gathered the herbs of my garden, taking cuttings of roots as well as dried plants. As I worked, I remembered how my mothers stripped their garden before leaving one life for another. I ventured into the market by myself and traded most of my trinkets for olive oil and castor oil, for juniper oil and berries, for I heard that few trees thrived in the valley. I scoured the stalls for the finest knife I could find, and the day before we left, Meryt and I went to the river and collected reeds enough to deliver a thousand babies.

I packed what I owned inside Benia's box, which had grown even more beautiful as the wood mellowed with age. Closing the lid, I tasted relief at my escape from an unhappy future.

The night before I left the house of Nakht-re I kept watch in the garden, walking around the pool, running my fingers over every bush and tree, filling my nose with the rich smells of blooming lotus and fresh clover. When the moon began to set, I crept inside the house and wandered past sleeping bodies up to the roof. The cats rubbed up against me, and I smiled, remembering my first fright at seeing the "fur snakes" of the land.

All of my days in Egypt had been spent in that house, and looking back on them in the night air, I recalled little but good: the scent of my infant son and the face of Nakht-re, cucumbers and honeyed fish, Meryt's laughter and the smiles of the new mothers to whom I delivered healthy sons and daughters. The painful things—Werenro's story, Re-nefer's choice, even my own loneliness—seemed like the knots on a beautiful necklace, necessary for keeping the beads in place. My eyes filled as I bade farewell to those days, but I felt no regret.

I was sitting outside the garden door, my box and a small bundle beside me, when the others arrived in the morning. Ruddedit walked with us as far as the ferry and embraced me before I got on the boat. She wept into Meryt's arms for a long while, but she was the only one weeping as the ferry pulled away from shore. I waved at her once, but then I set my eyes to the west.

The journey from the house of the scribe to the house of the baker took only one day, but the passage measured the difference between two worlds. The ferry was crowded with valley residents in a gala mood, on their way home from market. Many of the men had paid for the ministrations of open-air barbers, so their cheeks gleamed and their hair glistened. Mothers chatted about the children at their sides, petting them and scolding them in turn. Strangers struck up conversations with one another, comparing purchases and trying to establish a connection by comparing family names, occupations, and addresses. They seemed always to find a common friend or ancestor, and then clapped one another on the back like long-lost brothers.

They were at ease with themselves and one another like no other people I had ever seen, and I wondered what made it so. Perhaps it was because there were no lords or guards on the boat, not even a scribe. Only craftsmen and their families, heading home.

After the ferry, there was a short, steep climb to the town, which sprawled in the entrance to the valley like a giant wasp nest. My heart fell. It was as ugly a place as I'd ever seen. In the searing heat of the afternoon sun, the trees along the deserted streets looked limp and dirty. Houses crowded together, side by side, by the hundreds, each one as unremarkable and drab as the next. The doorways led down off the narrow pathways into darkness, and I wondered if I would be too tall to stand erect in the largest of them. The streets gave no hint of gardens, or colors, or any of the good things in life.

Somehow, Menna recognized one street from another and led us to the doorway of his brother's house, where a small boy stood watching. When he saw us, he shouted for his father, and Meryt's second son, Hori, rushed into the street, both hands filled with fresh bread. He ran to Meryt and lifted her up by the elbows, swinging her around and around, smiling with Meryt's own smile. His family gathered and clapped their hands as their grandmother laughed into her son's face and kissed him on the nose. Hori still had a house full of children, five in all, ranging from a marriageable daughter to the naked toddler who first spied us.

The family spilled into the street, drawing neighbors to the doorways, where they smiled at the commotion. Then Meryt was led through the antechamber of Hori's house and into his hall, a modest room where high windows let in the afternoon light on brightly colored floor mats and walls painted with a lush garden scene. My friend was seated on the best chair of the house and formally introduced, one by one, to her grandchildren.

I sat on the floor against a wall, watching Meryt bask in the glory of her children. The women brought food in from the back rooms, where I caught sight of a kitchen garden. Meryt praised the food, which was well spiced and plentiful, and declared the beer better than any she had tasted in the city of the nobles. Her daughter-in-law beamed at those words, and her son nodded with pride.

The children stared at me, having never seen a woman quite so tall or a face so obviously foreign. They kept their distance, except for the little sentinel, who clambered up on my lap and stayed there, his thumb in his mouth. The weight of a child on my chest reminded me of the sweetness of the days I held Re-mose so. Forgetting myself, I sighed with such longing the others turned toward me.

"My friend!" cried Meryt, who rushed over to my side. "Forgive me for forgetting you." The child's mother came and took him from me, and Meryt drew me to my feet.

"This is Den-ner," she announced, and turned me around, like a child, so that everyone would see my face. "Menna will tell you that she is a friendless midwife he has taken in out of compassion. But I tell you that I am her friend and her sister, and that I am her student, for I have never seen nor heard tell of a more skilled midwife. She has Isis's hands, and with the goddess's love of children, shows the compassion of heaven for mothers and babies."

Meryt, her cheeks flushed with the attentions of her family, spoke about me like a merchant in the marketplace selling her wares. "And she is an oracle, too, my dears. Her dreams are powerful, and her anger is to be feared, for I have seen her blast an evil man out of the prime of his life for harming a young mother. She sees clearly into the hearts of men, and none fool her with fine words that conceal a lying heart.

"She comes from the east," said Meryt, now intoxicated with the sound of her own voice and her children's attention. "There, women are often as tall as the men of Egypt. And our Den-ner is as clever as she is tall, for she speaks both the language of the east and our tongue. And she gave birth to Re-mose, a scribe, the heir of Nakht-re, who will someday be a power in the land. We are lucky to have his mother among us, and the house of Menna will find itself lucky when she sleeps under his roof."

I was mortified to have so many eyes upon me. "Thanks," was all I could say. "Thank you," I said, bowing to Menna and Shif-re, and then to Hori and his wife, Takharu. "Thank you for your generosity. I am your servant, in gratitude."

I returned to my corner by the wall, content to observe the family as they ate and joked and enjoyed one another. As the light began to fade, I closed my eyes for a moment and saw Rachel holding Joseph on her lap, her cheek pressed against his.

I had not thought of my brother Joseph for years, and

I could not place the memory exactly. But the scene was as vivid as my recollections of Leah's touch, as clear in my mind's eye as the tents of Mamre. Even as a child, I knew that Joseph would be the one to carry the family story into the next generation. He would be the one to change into someone more interesting and complicated than simply a beautiful man born of a beautiful mother.

Meryt's family thought I napped as I sat by the wall, but I was lost in thoughts of Joseph and Rachel, Leah and Jacob, my aunties and Inna and the days before Shechem. I sighed again, the sigh of an orphan, and my breath filled the room with a momentary melancholy that announced the end of the welcoming party.

Night was falling as Menna led Meryt and me through the moonlit streets to his house, which was nearby. Although it was larger and even better appointed than Hori's, it was hot and airless inside, so we carried our pallets up a ladder to the roof, where the canopy of stars seemed only a handbreadth away.

I woke just before sunrise and stood up to see the entire town dreaming. They lay alone or in pairs, or in clusters with children and dogs. A cat walked down the street below, carrying something in her mouth. She placed it on the ground, and I saw it was a kitten, whom she began to lick clean. As I watched, the sun turned the cliffs pink and then gold. Women stirred and stretched, and then climbed down the ladders. Soon, the smell of food filled the air and the day began.

At first, Shif-re would not permit me or Meryt to do anything in her kitchen or garden, so the two of us sat useless, watching her work. Meryt had a horror of becoming a meddling mother-in-law, but her hands ached to be busy. "Only let me press out the beer," she asked. "I could sweep the roof," I proposed. But Shif-re seemed insulted by our offers. After a week of sitting, I could bear it no longer. Picking up a large empty jug, I announced, "I'm going to the fountain," and walked out the door before my hostess could object, surprising myself as well as Meryt. After years of fearing the street in Thebes, I rushed into this one, not entirely sure of where to go. But since there were always other women on their way to and from the fountain, I quickly discovered my route.

As I walked, I peered into doorways and smiled at naked children playing in the dust. I began to see differences between one house and the next; flowers planted here and there, lintels painted red or green, stools set up by the doorways. I felt like a girl again, my eyes open to new scenes, my day empty of work.

Near the fountain, I overtook a pregnant woman waddling in front of me. "This is not your first, is it?" I asked brightly as I reached her side. When she spun around to look at me, I saw Rachel's face as it must have appeared in the long years before Joseph was finally born to her. The woman's face twisted in anger and desperation.

"Oh, my dear," I said, ashamed. "I spoke before I understood what this means to you. Fear not, little mother. This boy will be fine."

Her eyes widened with fear and hope, and her mouth dropped wide. "How dare you speak to me so? This one will die like the others before. I am hated by the gods."

Bitterness and anguish colored her words. "I am a luckless woman."

My answer came out of me with the assurance of the great mother herself, a voice that came through me but not from me. "He will be born whole, and soon. If not tonight, then tomorrow. Call me and I will help you upon the bricks and cut the cord."

Ahouri was her name, and after we filled our jars, she led me back to the baker's house. She lived only a few doorways east of Menna, and when her time came the following night, her husband came seeking the foreign-born midwife.

With Meryt, I attended as easy and straightforward a birth as any I ever saw. Ahouri sobbed with relief as she held the third child of her womb, but the only one born breathing. It was a strapping boy she called Den-ouri, the first to be named in my honor. Her husband, a potter, gave me a beautiful jar in thanks and kissed my hands and would have carried me home in his arms had I permitted it.

Meryt spread the story that I had performed some sort of wonder for Ahouri, and soon we were busier than we had been in Thebes. Most of the men who worked the valley were young, with wives of bearing age, and we attended as many as ten births in a month. Shif-re no longer had idle guests to feed, and indeed, quickly gained more dainties and extra linen than she knew what to do with. Menna was proud to have such respected women under his roof and treated me like his own aunt.

Weeks and months passed quickly, and life in the valley took on its own orderly pace. Mornings were the busiest times, before the great heat descended. The men left early and children played in the streets while the women swept out their homes, cooked the day's meals, and fetched water at the fountains, where news was exchanged and plans laid for the next festival.

While the great river was not visible from the town, it still ruled the ebb and flow of daily life in the arid valley. Its seasons were celebrated in high spirits by the craftsmen, who grew up imbibing the rhythms of farming by the Nile. After so many years in the land of the great river, I finally learned the beautiful names of its seasons. *Akhit*—the inundation; *perit*—the going-out; *shemou*—the harvest. Each had its own holiday and lunar rite, its own festive foods and songs.

Just before my first harvest moon in the valley, a scribe came to Menna's door with a letter from my son. Re-mose wrote to say that he was living in Thebes again, assigned as scribe to a new vizier called Zafe-nat Paneh-ah, the king's choice. He sent greetings in the names of Amun-Re and Isis, and a prayer for my good health. It was a formal note, but I was happy that he thought of me enough to send it. And that shard of limestone, written in his own hand, became my most prized possession and regardless of my protests, be-came proof of my status as a person of importance.

Not long after my son's letter arrived, another man appeared at the door seeking the woman named Den-ner. Shif-re asked him if it was his wife or his daugh-ter who had need of a midwife's bricks, but he said, "Neither." Then she asked if he was a scribe with another letter from Thebes, but he said no. "I am a carpenter."

Shif-re came to the garden with curious news about a bachelor carpenter who sought a midwife. Meryt looked up from her spinning sharply and with a great show of disinterest said, "Den-ner, go and see what the stranger wants." I went without thinking.

His eyes were sadder, but in all other ways he was the same. I stood for only a moment before Benia reached out to me with his right hand. Without hesitation, I placed my left hand in it. I extended my right hand and he took it with his left. We stood like that, hand in hand and smiling like fools without speaking, until Meryt could stand the suspense no longer. "Oh, Den-ner," she called with false concern. "Are you there, or was that a pirate at the door?"

I led him back through the house to where Meryt hopped like a bird from one foot to the other, wearing the wild grin of the god Bes. Shif-re smiled too, having just learned how Meryt had spent the past months seeking out the artist who had offered me his heart along with the luxurious box that accompanied me from Thebes.

They bade him sit and offered beer and bread. But Benia looked only at me. And I returned his gaze.

"Go ahead then," Meryt said, giving me a hug and then a push. "Menna will bring your box to you in the morning and I will follow him with bread and salt. Go, in the name of the lady Isis and her consort Osiris. Go and be content."

Leaving my friend's house to follow a stranger, I was surprised by my own certainty, but I did not hesitate.

We walked through the streets, side by side, for what seemed like a very long time, saying nothing. His house was near the edge of the settlement, close to the path leading up to the tombs, many streets away from Meryt. As we walked, I recalled my mothers' stories about hennaed hands and songs for the groom and bride on their way to the bridal tent. I smiled to think of myself as being in a kind of procession at that moment, walking toward my own marriage bed. I smiled too to think of how Meryt would rush from fountain to fountain the next morning, telling everyone about the love affair between Benia the master carpenter and Den-ner the magical midwife. I nearly laughed at the thought. Benia heard the sound that escaped from my mouth as distress. He put his arm around me, placed his lips to my ear, and whispered, "Fear not."

Magic words. I laid my head on his shoulder and we walked the rest of the way holding hands, like children.

When we arrived at his house, which was nearly as large as Menna's, he took me through the rooms, and with great pride showed me the furniture he had built—two thronelike chairs, an ornately carved bed, boxes in many shapes. I laughed when I saw the easing stool, which was far too beautiful for its foul purpose. "I thought of you when I made these things," he said, shrugging in embarrassment. "I thought of you sitting here, sleeping here, putting things to right in your own way. When Meryt found me I made this for you."

He took an exquisite little box from a niche in the wall. It was unadorned but perfect, made of ebony— wood that was used almost exclusively for the tombs of kings—and it had been burnished until it shone like a black moon. "For your midwife's kit," he said, and held it out to me.

I stared at it for a moment, overwhelmed by his generosity and tenderness. "I have nothing to give you by way of a token," I said. He shrugged with one shoulder, in a gesture I soon came to know as well as I knew my own hands. "You don't have to give me anything. If you take this from my hands freely, your choice will be your token."

Thus I became a married woman in Egypt.

Benia laid out a meal of bread and onions and fruit for us, and we sat in the kitchen and ate and drank in nervous silence. I had been a girl the last time I had lain with a man. Benia had been thinking of me since that day in the market, two years earlier. We were shy as two virgins who had been matched by their parents.

After we ate, he took my hand and led me to the main hall, where the fine bed stood, piled with clean linen. It reminded me of Re-nefer's bed in Nakht-re's house. It reminded me of Shalem's bed, in his father's house. But then Benia turned me toward him and put his hands on my face and I forgot every bed I had ever seen before that moment.

Lying together was a tender surprise. From our very first night, Benia took great care of my pleasure and seemed to discover his own in mine. My shyness vanished in the course of that night, and as the weeks passed, I found wells of desire and passion that I had never suspected in myself. When Benia lay with me, the past vanished and I was a new soul, reborn in the taste of his mouth, the touch of his fingers. His huge hands cupped my body and untied secret knots created by years of loneliness and silence. The sight of his naked legs, thick and ropy with sinew, aroused me so much that Benia would tease me as he left in the morning, lifting his skirt to reveal the top of his thigh, making me blush and laugh.

My husband went to his workshop every morning, but unlike the stonecutters and painters, he did not have to work in the tombs, so he returned to me in the evening, where he and I discovered greater pleasure in each other—and the sorry fact that I did not know how to cook.

During my years in Nakht-re's house, I rarely strayed into the kitchen, much less prepared a meal. I had never learned how to make bread in an Egyptian oven or to gut fish or pluck fowl. We ate unripe fruit from Benia's neglected garden and I begged bread from Menna. Shamefaced, I asked Shif-re for a cooking lesson, which Meryt attended only to tease me.

I tried to recreate my mother's recipes, but I lacked the ingredients and I forgot the proportions. I felt sheepish and ashamed, but Benia only laughed. "We won't starve," he said. "I have kept myself alive for years on borrowed bread and fruit and the occasional feast at the house of my fellows and family. I did not marry you to be my cook."

But while I was a stranger in the kitchen, I found great joy in keeping my own house. There was such sweetness in deciding where to place a chair, and in choosing what to plant in the garden. I relished creating my own order and hummed whenever I swept the floor or folded blankets. I spent hours arranging pots in the kitchen first in order of size, then according to color.

My house was a world of my own possession, a country in which I was ruler and citizen, where I chose and where I served. One night, when I returned home very late, exhausted after attending at the birth of healthy twins, I thought I had lost my way. Standing in the middle of the street in the dead of night, I recognized my home by its smell—a mixture of coriander, clover, and Benia's cedary scent.

A few months after I moved to my own house, Menna prepared a small banquet for me and Benia. My husband's workmen sang songs of their workshop. Meryt's sons sang of bread. And then all the men, together with their wives and children, joined voices for love songs, of which there seemed to be an endless number. I was bashful at the attention showered upon us, the cups raised, the broad smiles and kisses. Even though Benia and I were really too old for such nonsense, we were giddy with delight in each other. When Meryt leaned over and told me to stop grudging people the chance to bask in the light of our shared happiness, I put aside all shyness in gratitude and smiled into the faces of my friends.

I had been right to trust Benia, who was the soul of kindness. One night we lay on our backs staring up at the heavens. There was only a sliver of moon and the stars danced above when he told me his life. His words came slowly, for many of the memories were sad ones.

"I have only one memory of my father," said Benia. "The sight of his back, which I saw as he walked away

from me in a field where I sat behind the plow breaking up clods. I was six years old when he died, leaving
Ma with four children. I was the third son.

"She had no brothers, and my father's people were
not generous. She had to find places for us, so my mother
took me to the city and showed my hands to the stonecutters. They took me on as an apprentice, and taught
me and worked me until my back was strong and my
hands callused. But I became a joke in the workshops.
Marble would crack if I walked into a room and granite would weep if I raised a chisel to it.

"Wandering in the market one day, I watched as a
carpenter repaired an old stool for a poor woman. He
saw my belt and bowed low, for even though I was
only an apprentice, stonecutters who work in immor-
tal materials are considered far greater than wood-
workers, whose greatest achievements decay like a
man's body.

"I told the carpenter that his respect was misplaced
and that mere sandstone defeated me. I confessed that
I was in danger of being turned into the street.

"The woodworker took my hand in his, turning it
this way and that. He handed me a knife and a scrap of
wood and asked me to carve a toy for his grandson.

"The wood seemed warm and alive, and a doll took
shape in my hands without effort. The very grain of
the pine seemed to smile at me.

"The carpenter nodded at the thing I made and
took me to the workshop of his teacher, presenting me
as a likely apprentice. And there I discovered my
life's work."

Here my husband sighed. "There, too, I met my wife,

who was a servant in the house of my master. We were so young," he said softly, and in the silence that followed I understood that he had loved the wife of his youth with his whole heart.

After a long pause he said, "We had two sons." Again he stopped, and in the silence I heard the voices of little boys, Benia's doting laughter, a woman singing a lullaby.

"They died of river fever," Benia said. "I had taken them from the city to see my brother, who had married into a farming family. But when we arrived at the house, we found my brother dying and the rest of his family stricken. My wife cared for them all," he whispered. "We should have left," he said, with self-reproach still raw after many years.

"After that," he said, "I lived only in my work and loved only my work. I visited the prostitutes once," he confessed sheepishly. "But they were too sad.

"Until the day I saw you in the marketplace, I did not bother to hope for anything. When I first recognized you as my beloved, my heart came to life," he said. "But when you disappeared and seemed to scorn me, I grew angry. For the first time in my life, I raged against heaven for stealing my family and then for dangling you before my eyes and snatching you away. I was furious and frightened of my own loneliness.

"So I took a wife."

I had been perfectly still until then, but that announcement made me sit up.

"Yes, yes," he said, embarrassed. "My sister found me a marriageable girl, a servant in the house of a painter, and I brought her here with me. It was a disaster. I was too old for her; she was too silly for me.

"Oh Den-ner," he said, in a misery of apology. "We were so mismatched it could have been funny. We never spoke. We tried sharing my bed, twice, and even that was awful.

"Finally, she was braver than I, poor girl. After two weeks, she left. Walked out of the house while I was at work, down to the ferry and back to the painter's house, where she remains.

"I was resigned to making strong drink my regular companion until Meryt sought me out. She visited me three times before I would agree to see you. I am lucky that your friend does not understand the meaning of 'no.'"

I turned to my husband and said, "And my luck is measured by your kindness, which is boundless."

We made love very slowly that night, as though for the last time, weeping. One of his tears fell in my mouth, where it became a blue sapphire, source of strength and eternal hope.

Benia did not ask for my story in return. His eyes would fill with questions when I mentioned my mother's way of making beer, or my aunt's skill as a midwife, but he stepped back from his need to know. I think he feared that I might vanish if he so much as asked me the meaning of my name or the word for "water" in my native tongue.

On another moonless night, I told him as much of my truth as I could: that Re-mose's father was the son of Re-nefer, sister of Nakht-re, and that I came to Thebes after the murder of my husband, in our own bed. When he heard that, Benia shuddered, took me into his arms as though I was a child, and stroked my hair, and said nothing but "Poor thing." Which was everything I had longed to hear.

Neither of us ever gave voice to the names of our beloved dead ones, and for this act of respect, they permitted us to live in peace with our new mates and never haunted our thoughts by day or visited our dreams at night.

Life was sweet in the Valley of the Kings, on the west bank of the river. Benia and I had everything we needed in each other. Indeed, we were rich in all ways but one, for we lacked children.

I was barren, or perhaps only too old to bear. Although I had already lived a full life—close to twoscore years—my back was strong and my body still obeyed the pull of the moon. I was certain that my womb was cold, but even so I could never root out all hope from my heart, and I grieved with the flux of every new moon.

Still we were not completely childless, for Meryt often sat in our doorstep, trailing her grandchildren, who treated us as uncle and aunt—especially little Kiya, who liked to sleep in our house so much that her mother sometimes sent her to stay with us, to help me in the garden and to brighten our days.

Benia and I shared stories in the evenings. I told him of the babies that I caught and of the mothers who died, though they were blessedly few. He spoke of his commissions—each one a new challenge, based not only upon the desires of the buyer and builders, but also upon the wishes of the wood in his hand.

The days passed peacefully, and the fact that there was little to mark one from the next seemed a great gift to me. I had Benia's hands, Meryt's friendship, the feel of newborn flesh, the smiles of new mothers, a little girl who laughed in my kitchen, a house of my own.

It was more than enough.

CHAPTER FOUR

I knew about Re-mose's message even before the messenger arrived at my house. Kiya ran to the door with the news that a scribe had come to Menna's house seeking Den-ner the midwife and was on his way to Benia's door.

I was delighted at the prospect of another letter from my son. It had been more than a year since the last one, and I imagined myself showing Benia my son's own writing on the limestone tablet when he arrived home that evening.

I stood in the doorway, anxious to discover the contents of this letter. But when the man turned the corner, surrounded by a pack of excited little children, I realized that the messenger brought his own message.

Re-mose and I stared at each other. I saw a man I did not know—the image of Nakht-re except for his eyes, which were set like his father's. I saw nothing of myself in the prince of Egypt who stood before me, dressed in fine linen, with a gold pectoral gleaming on his chest and new sandals on his manicured feet.

I did not know what he saw as he looked at me. I thought I detected disdain in his eye, but perhaps that was only my own fear. I wondered if he could see that I stood taller now that I carried less grief on my back. Whatever he saw or thought, we were strangers.

"Forgive my manners," I said finally. "Come inside the house of Benia, and let me give you some cool beer and fruit. I know the journey from Thebes is dusty."

Re-mose recovered too, and said, "Forgive me, Mother. It is so long since I saw your dear face." His words were cool and his embrace a quick, awkward hug. "I would gladly take a drink," he said, and followed me into the house.

I saw each room through his eyes, which were accustomed to the spacious beauties of palaces and temples. The front room, my room, which I treasured for the colorful wall painting, suddenly looked small and bare, and I was glad when he hurried through it. Benia's hall was larger and furnished with pieces seen only in great houses and tombs. The quality of the chairs and bed found approval in my son's eyes, and I left him there to fetch food and drink. Kiya had followed us in and stared at the beautifully dressed man in my house.

"Is this my sister?" asked Re-mose, pointing to the silent child.

"No," I said. "This is the niece of a friend, and like a niece to me." My answer seemed to relieve him. "The gods seem to have ordained that you remain my only child," I added.

"I am glad to see you healthy and successful. Tell me, are you married yet? Am I a grandmother?"

"No," said Re-mose. "My duties keep me too busy for my own family," he said, with a tight little wave of his hand. "Perhaps someday my situation will improve and I can give you little ones to dandle on your knee."

But this was nothing more than polite conversation, which hung in the air and smelled of falsehood. The gulf between us was far too wide for any such familiarity. If and when I became a grandmother, I would know my grandchildren only through messages sent on limestone slabs meant to be discarded after they are read.

"Ma," he said, after drinking from his cup, "I am here not only for my own pleasure. My master sends me to fetch the finest midwife in Egypt to attend his wife's labor.

"No, it is true," he said, dismissing my shrug. "Say nothing to diminish your repute, for no one has taken your place in Thebes. The lady of my master has miscarried twice and nearly died from a stillbirth. The physicians and necromancers have done her no good, and now the midwives fear to attend a princess who has had so much bad luck in childbed. Her own mother is dead, and she is afraid.

"My master dotes on this wife and wishes nothing more than to have sons by her. As-naat heard of your skills from her servants and asked her husband to search out the foreign-born woman with the golden hands who once served the women of Thebes. My lord depends upon me for all things and called upon me in this matter as well," said Re-mose, his mouth growing smaller and more pursed at every mention of his master.

"Imagine my surprise when I learned that he sought none but my own mother. He was suddenly impressed by my lineage when he learned that you were a countryman of his," Re-mose added ironically. "The vizier charged me to put aside duties of state, to walk into the Valley of the Kings and accompany you to his house. He ordered me not to return without you."

"You do not like this man," I said mildly.

"Zafenat Paneh-ah is vizier in Thebes at the king's pleasure," said my son, in formal but damning tones. "He is said to be a great diviner who sees into the future and reads dreams as easily as a master scribe perusing the glyphs of a schoolboy. But he is illiterate," said Re-mose bitterly. "He cannot cipher or write or read, which is why the king assigned me, the best of Kar's students, to be his right hand. And that is where I am now, wifeless, childless, second to a barbarian."

I stiffened at the word. Re-mose noticed my reaction and colored in shame. "Oh Ma, not you," he said quickly. "You are not like the rest of them, or else my father and grandmother would never have chosen you. You are fine," he said. "There is no mother in Egypt better than you." His flattery made me smile in spite of myself. He embraced me, and for a moment I regained the loving boy who had been my son.

We drank our beer in silence for a moment, then I said, "Of course I will follow you to Thebes. If the king's vizier commands you to bring me, I will come.

But first I must speak with my friend, Meryt, who is my right hand in the birth chamber and should come with me.

"I must talk with my husband, Benia, the master carpenter, so that he knows where I go and when I might return."

Re-mose pursed his lips again. "There is no time for this, Ma. We must leave now, for the lady is in travail and my lord expects me every hour. Send the girl here to inform the others. I cannot tarry."

"I'm afraid you must," I said, and I left the room. Re-mose followed me to the kitchen and grabbed me by the elbow, like a master about to strike a disobedient servant.

I pulled away and looked into his face. "Nakht-re would sooner die than treat a relative—much less a mother—in this fashion. Is this how you honor the memory of the only father you ever knew? I remember him as a noble man to whom you owe everything, and whose name you dishonor."

Re-mose stopped and hung his head. His ambition and his heart were at war, and his face showed the division in his soul. He fell to the ground and bowed low, his brow at my feet.

"I forgive you," I said. "It will only take me a moment to prepare, and we will find my friend and husband on our path to Thebes."

Re-mose raised himself from the ground again and waited outside while I prepared for a journey I hated to make. As I gathered my kit and a few herbs, I smiled at my own brazenness, shaming my powerful son for his rudeness, insisting on my farewells. Where was the meek woman who lived in Nakht-re's house all those years?

Meryt waited for me at her son's door, hungry for the news. Her eyes grew large when I introduced her to Re-mose, whom she had not seen since he was a boy. She covered her mouth in awe at the invitation to wait upon the wife of the king's vizier, but Meryt could not accompany me. Three women in the town were due to give birth at any moment, and one of them was kin, the daughter of Shif-re's brother. We embraced, and she wished me the touch of Isis and the luck of Bes. She stood at her door and waved gaily. "Bring me back some good stories," she shouted, and her laughter followed me down the street.

Benia did not send me away with laughter. He and my son looked at each other coolly; Benia dipped his head in recognition of the scribe's position, and Re-mose nodded at the carpenter's authority over so important a workshop. There was no way for my husband and me to take a proper leave of each other. We exchanged our parting vows with our eyes. I would return. He would not be content until I did.

Re-mose and I walked out of the valley, saying little to each other. Before we began the descent from the valley to the riverbank, I put my hand on his arm, signaling him to stop. Turning to face home, I dropped a twist of rue from my garden and a piece of bread from my oven to ensure a speedy return.

It was dark by the time we reached the river, but we had no need to wait for the morning ferry. The king's barque, lit with a hundred lamps, waited for us. Many oars rowed us, and in no time we were hurrying through the sleeping streets of the city and into the great palace, where Re-mose left me at the door to the women's quarters. I was taken to a chamber where a pale young woman sat perched on her great bed, alone.

"You are Den-ner?" she asked.

"Yes, As-naat," I replied gently, placing my bricks on the floor. "Let me see what the gods have in store for us."

"I fear this one is dead, too," she whispered. "And if it is so, let me die with him."

I put my ear to her belly and touched the womb. "This baby is alive," I said. "Fear not. He is just resting for the journey."

At daylight, her pains began in earnest. As-naat tried to be quiet as befits a royal lady, but nature had made her a screamer, and she soon filled the air with roars at every pang.

I called for fresh water to bathe the mother's face, for fresh straw, for lotus cones to freshen the room, and for five serving women, who gathered around their mistress to offer encouragement. Sometimes it is easier for the poor, I thought. Even those without family live in such close quarters to their neighbors that the cries of a laboring mother bring out other women like geese responding to the call of a leader in flight. But the rich are surrounded by servants too fearful of their mistresses to act as sisters.

As-naat did not have an easy time, but it was nowhere near the worst labor I'd seen. She pushed for long hours, supported by women who became her sisters, at least for that day. Just after sunset, she produced a skinny but healthy son, who roared for the breast as soon as he was held upright.

As-naat kissed my hands, covering them with joyful tears, and sent one of her servants to tell Zafenat Paneh-ah that he was the father of a fine son. I was taken to a quiet room, where I fell into a dark, dreamless sleep.

I awoke the following morning drenched in sweat, my head throbbing, my throat on fire. Lying on the pallet, I squinted at the light pouring through the high windows and tried to remember the last time I had been ill. My head pounded, and I closed my eyes again. When next they opened, the light was draining from the room.

A girl sitting by the wall noticed I was awake and brought me a drink and placed a cool towel on my brow. Two days passed, or maybe it was three, in a blur of fevered sleep and compresses. When my head finally cooled and the pain subsided, I found myself too weak to stand.

By then a woman called Shery had been sent to attend me. I stared with an open mouth when she introduced herself, for her name, which means "little one," sat oddly upon the fattest woman I'd ever seen.

Shery washed the sour smell from my body and brought me broth and fruit and offered to fetch anything else I might wish. I had never been waited upon like that, and while I did not enjoy her hovering over me, I was grateful for her help.

After a few days my strength began to return, and I asked Shery to tell me the news of the baby I had delivered. She was delighted by my question and settled her weight about her on a stool, for Shery loved an audience.

The baby was well, she reported. "He is ravenous, and has nearly worn off his mother's nipples with constant feeding," said Shery with a wicked grin. She had pitied her mistress's childlessness, but found As-naat an arrogant snip of a mistress. "Motherhood will teach her everything," my new friend confided.

"The father has named the boy Menashe, an awful name that must mean something fine in his native tongue. Menashe. It sounds like chewing, does it not? But you are of Canaan as well, are you not?"

I shrugged. "It was so long ago," I said. "Please, continue with the story, Shery. It is almost magical, the way your words make me forget my aches and pains."

She gave me a sharp look to let me know that flattery did not hide my reticence. But she continued anyway.

"Zafenat Paneh-ah is truly an arrogant son of a bitch," she said, proving her trust in me by swearing about the master. "He likes to talk of his lowly beginnings as though this makes his powerful position even greater due to his rise. But this is no great thing in Egypt. Many great men—statesmen and craftsmen, warriors and artisans—are born of the lowly. Such is the case with your own husband, eh, Den-ner?" she asked, letting me know that my history was not entirely closed to her. But I only smiled.

"The Canaanite is handsome, no doubt about that. Women swoon at the sight of him—or at least they did when he was younger. Men are drawn to him as well, and not only the ones who prefer boys.

"Of course, that beauty did not serve him well when he was young. His own brothers hated him so much they sold him to a pack of slavers—can you imagine an Egyptian doing such a thing? Every day I thank the gods that I was born in the valley of the great river."

"No doubt," I said, surveying her girth, for there was no other land that could support such excess. Shery caught my meaning and grabbed at her midsection with both hands. "Ha, ha! I am a creature of amazing proportions, am I not? The king once pinched me and said that only dwarves please him more than the sight of someone as large and round as me. You would not believe how many men find this desirable," Shery said. "In my own youth," she began in a conspiratorial whisper, "I gave pleasure to the old king, until his wife grew jealous and had me packed off to Thebes.

"But that"—she winked—"is another story for another time. You want the history of this house, which is juicy enough," she confided.

"Zafenat Paneh-ah was sold into slavery, as I said, and his new masters were swine, the most Canaanite of the Canaanites. I don't doubt that he was beaten and raped and forced to do the dirtiest work. Of course, his majesty does not speak of that anymore.

"Zafenat Paneh-ah did not acquire that pompous name until recently. 'The God Speaks and He Lives,' indeed! They used to call him Stick, for when he first came to Egypt he was as skinny as his newborn son.

"When his owners came to Thebes, he was sold to Po-ti-far, a palace guard with sticky fingers who lived in a great house on the outskirts of the city. Because Stick was more clever than his master by half, he was put in charge of the garden, and then given oversight of the wine-pressing. Finally, he was set above the other servants in the house, for Po-ti-far loved the Canaanite boy and used him for his own pleasure.

"But Po-ti-far's wife, a great beauty called Nebetper, also looked upon him with longing, and the two of them became lovers right under the master's nose. There is even some gossip about who fathered her last daughter. In any case, Po-ti-far finally discovered them in bed together and he could no longer pretend not to know what was going on. So in a great show of anger and vengeance, he sent Stick to prison."

By that point I had lost interest in Shery's story, which apparently had no end. I wanted to sleep, but there was no stopping the woman, who did not see my hint when I yawned, or even when I closed my eyes.

"The Theban jail is no laughing matter," she said darkly. "A hideous pit where men die of murder and despair as much as fever, full of madmen and cut-throats. But the warden came to pity his handsome inmate, who was neither hateful or insane. Soon he was taking his meals with the Canaanite, who spoke a good Egyptian by then.

"The warden was a bachelor and childless, and he treated Stick like a son. As the years passed he gave Stick responsibility for his fellows, until finally he was the one to determine which man slept near a window and which man was chained close to the latrine, so the inmates did what they could to bribe and please him.

I tell you, Den-ner," Shery said, shaking her head in admiration, "wherever this fellow goes, power seems to move into his hands.

"Meanwhile, the old king died, and the new king had a habit of punishing minor offenses against him by sending people to jail. If he was displeased by the texture of his bread at dinner, he might send the baker to jail for a week or even longer. Cupbearers, wine stewards, sandal-makers, even captains of the guard were sent to languish in that place, where they met Stick.

"Everyone was struck by his princely bearing and by his ability to interpret dreams and divine the future. He told one poor drunkard that he would not live out the week, and when he was found dead—not murdered, mind you, simply done in by years of strong drink—the prisoners proclaimed him an oracle. When a cupbearer returned from prison with a story about a jailer who saw into the future, the king sent for Stick and set him to interpret a series of dreams that had plagued him for months.

"It was not a difficult dream to divine, if you ask me," said Shery. "Fat fish being devoured by bony fish, fat cows being trampled by skinny cows, and then seven fat stalks of wheat which were beaten down, leaving seven dead stalks.

"Any half-wit magician who pulls birds from beneath baskets in the marketplace could have interpreted that one," Shery sniggered. "But the dreams haunted and frightened the idiot king, and it calmed him to hear that he had seven years in which to prepare for the coming famine. And so he elevated the jailer, an unlettered foreign-born conniver, to become his first-in-command.

"I imagine your son has already told you that this so-called Zafenat Paneh-ah is totally dependent upon Re-mose. And now that Zafenat is not only vizier but a father as well, there will be no stopping his pride," Shery fumed, bustling around the room, preparing my bed, for she had talked away the whole afternoon.

"And yesterday," she grumbled, speaking to herself by that point, "this madman demanded that his son be circumcised. Not when he is at manhood's door and able to withstand such a thing. Not like civilized people, but now. Immediately! Can you imagine wanting to do that to a tiny baby? It only goes to prove that a born barbarian does not change. As-naat screamed and carried on like a gutted cat at the order. And I can't blame her there."

"Joseph," I whispered, in horror and disbelief.

Shery peered up at me. "What?" she said. "What did you say, Den-ner?"

But I closed my eyes, suddenly unable to breathe. All at once I understood why I had been summoned to Thebes and why Shery had told me the endless story of the vizier. But surely this could not be. It was fever that weakened my reason. Dizzy and light-headed, I lay down on the bed, panting.

Shery noticed that something was amiss with me. "Den-ner," she said. "Are you unwell? Can I get you something? Maybe you are ready for solid food now.

"But here is something to cheer you up," she said, looking up at the sound of footsteps. "Your son comes to pay respects. Here is Re-mose. I will bring you both some refreshment," she burbled, and left me with my son.

"Mother?" he said, formally with a stiff bow. But when he saw my face he started. "Ma? What is it? They told me you were much improved and that I might see you today," he said doubtfully. "But perhaps this is not the right time."

I turned my face toward the wall and waved him out of the room. I heard Shery go out with him and murmur an explanation. His hurried footsteps fading in the distance were the last thing I knew before I fell asleep.

Shery had told Re-mose of our conversation and repeated the word I had spoken before falling back into a fevered darkness of mind. Thus my son took "Joseph" into his mouth and, unannounced, went into the great hall, where the vizier of Egypt sat alone, whispering comfort to his firstborn son, who had been circumcised earlier that day.

"Joseph," said Re-mose, throwing the name at him like a challenge. And the one known as Zafenat Paneh-ah trembled.

"Do you know a woman called Den-ner?" he demanded.

For a moment Zafenat Paneh-ah said nothing, and then he asked, "Dinah?" The master looked into his scribe's eyes. "I had a sister named Dinah, but she died long ago. How do you come by her name? What do you know of Joseph?" he commanded.

"I will tell you what there is to tell after you describe her death," said Re-mose. "But only then."

The threat in his voice rankled Joseph. But even

though he sat on a throne with a healthy son in his arms and guards ready to do his bidding, he felt bound to answer. It had been a lifetime since he had heard his own name, twenty years since he had spoken his sister's name aloud.

So he began. In a quiet voice that drew Re-mose close to the throne, he told him that Dinah had gone to the palace in Shechem with his mother, Rachel the midwife, to tend to a birth in the house. "A prince of the city claimed her for a bride," said Joseph, and Re-mose heard how Jacob turned away the handsome bride-price, and finally accepted him only on the cruelest of conditions.

Re-mose shuddered to learn his father's name from Joseph's lips, but in the next moment he learned that my brothers, his own uncles, had slaughtered Shalem in his own bed. Re-mose bit his tongue to keep from crying out.

Joseph declared his repugnance for the crime and proclaimed his own innocence. "Two of my brothers bloodied their hands," he said, but admitted that perhaps four of them had had some part in the murder. "All of us were punished.

"She cursed us all. Some of my brothers fell ill, others saw their sons die. My father lost all hope, and I was sold into slavery."

Joseph said, "I used to blame my sister for my misfortunes, but no longer. If I knew where she was buried, I would go and pour libations and build a stele in her memory. At least I survived my brothers' villainy, and with the birth of this son, the god of my fathers shows me that I will not die forgotten. But my sister's name was blotted out, as though she had never drawn breath.

"She was my milk-sister," said Joseph, shaking his head. "It is strange to speak of her now that I am a father. Perhaps I will name the next one in her honor," and he fell silent.

"And what is Joseph?" Re-mose asked.

"Joseph is the name my mother gave me," said Zaf-enat Paneh-ah quietly.

Re-mose turned to leave, but the vizier called him back. "Wait! We have a bargain. Tell me how you came to know my name and the name of my sister."

Re-mose stopped and without facing him said, "She is not dead."

The words hung in the air. "She is here, in your palace. Indeed, you bade her brought here. Den-ner the midwife, the one who delivered your son, is your sister, Dinah. My mother."

Joseph's eyes grew wide in wonder, and he smiled like a happy child. But Re-mose spit at his feet.

"Would you have me call you uncle?" he hissed. "I hated you from the first. You robbed me of a position that is rightly mine, and you advance in the king's eyes because of my skill. Now I see that you blasted my life from birth! You slaughtered my father in the prime of his youth. You and your barbarian brothers murdered my grandfather too, who, though a Ca-naanite, acted honorably.

"You ripped the heart out of my grandmother. You betrayed your sister, widowed my mother, and made me an orphan and an outcast.

"When I was a boy, my grandmother's servant told me that when I finally found my father's murderers, their names would rip my soul into pieces. His words were true.

"You are my uncle. Oh gods, what a nightmare," Re-mose cried. "A murderer and a liar. How dare you claim innocence in this abomination? Perhaps you raised no sword yourself, but you did nothing to stop them. You must have known something of the plot, you and your father and the rest of his seed. I see the blood of my father on your hands. Your guilt is still in your eyes."

Joseph looked away.

"There is nothing left but for me to kill you, or die a coward. If I do not avenge my father, I will be unworthy of this life, much less the next."

Re-mose's voice, raised in hatred, alerted the guards, who subdued him and led him away while Menashe wailed in his father's arms.

When I finally woke, Shery sat beside me, her face stricken.

"What is it?" I asked.

"Oh lady," she said, in a great rush to tell me what she knew, "I have bad news. Your son and the vizier have quarreled, and Re-mose is under guard in his chambers. The master is said to be furious, and they say that the young scribe is in mortal danger. I do not know the cause of their quarrel, not yet at least. But when I learn it, I will tell you immediately."

I got to my feet, wobbling but determined. "Shery," I commanded. "Listen to me now, for I will not argue or repeat myself. I must speak to the master of the house. Go and announce me."

The serving woman bowed from the waist, but in a small voice said, "You cannot go to Zafenat Paneh-ah looking as you do. Let me give you a bath and dress your hair. Put on a clean gown so you can make your case like a lady and not a beggar."

I nodded my assent, suddenly frightened by the scene ahead. What words could I use to a brother I had not seen for a lifetime? I crouched in the bath as Shery poured cool water over me and leaned back as she brushed and arranged my hair. I felt like a slave about to be paraded before a gallery of buyers.

When I was ready, Shery led me to the door of Zafenat Paneh-ah's hall, where he sat with his head in his hands.

"Den-ner, the midwife, requests an audience," she said.

The vizier stood up and waved me in.

"Leave us," he barked. Shery and all of his retainers disappeared. We were alone. Neither of us moved. We kept our places on opposite ends of the room and stared.

Though the years had cost him his smooth cheeks and a few of his teeth, Joseph was still fair of face and strong, still the son of Rachel.

"Dinah," he said. "Ahatti—little sister," he said, in the language of our youth. "The grave has set you free."

"Yes, Joseph," I said. "I am alive, and amazed to be in your presence. But the only reason I come to you is to ask what has become of my son."

"Your son knows the story of his father's death and

he threatens my life," said Joseph stiffly. "He holds me responsible for the sins of my brothers. His threat alone could cause his execution, but because he is your son, I will only send him away.

"He will not come to harm, I promise," said Joseph kindly. "I have recommended that the king give him charge of a prefecture in the north, where he will be second to none. In time, he will fall in love with the sea—they all do—and he will build a life seasoned with salt air and salt water and not wish for any other.

"You must tell him to do as I say and forget this talk of revenge," said Joseph. "You must do this now, tonight. If he raises a hand to me, if he so much as threatens me in the company of my guard, he must die."

"I doubt that my son will listen to my words," I said sadly. "He hates me, for I am the cause of his unhappiness."

"Nonsense," said Joseph, with the supreme self-confidence that made our brothers so jealous. "The men of Egypt honor their mothers like no other men in the world."

"You do not know," I said. "He called his grandmother Ma. I was no more than his wet nurse."

"No, Dinah," said Joseph. "He suffers too much for that to be true. He will listen to you, and he must go."

I looked at my brother and saw a man I did not know. "I will do as you say, master," I said, in the voice of a good servant. "But ask me for nothing else. Let me be free of this place, for it is a tomb to me. Seeing you is like stepping into the past where my sorrow lies. And now because of you, I lose all hope of my son."

Joseph nodded. "I understand, Ahatti, and it will be as you say except in one matter. When my wife comes to the bricks again—and I have already dreamed of a second son—you must come and attend her.

"You may come without seeing me if you like, and you will be well paid. Indeed, you will be paid in land if you wish, you and the carpenter."

I bridled at the suggestion that I was a pauper, and announced, "My husband, Benia, is master craftsman in the Valley of the Kings."

"Benia?" he asked, and Joseph's face crumbled into regret. "That was the baby-name for our brother Benjamin, the last-born of my mother, who died giving him life. I used to hate Benia for killing her, but now I think I would give half of what is mine only to hold his hand."

"I have no desire to see him," I said, surprising both of us with the anger in my voice. "I am no longer of that world. If my mothers are dead, then I am an orphan. My brothers are no more to me than the livestock of our youth. You and I were kin as children, when we knew each other well enough to share our hearts. But that was in another life."

The great room was silent, each of us lost in memories.

"I will go to my son," I said finally. "Then I will be gone."

"Go in peace," said Joseph.

Re-mose lay facedown on the bed in his handsome suite. My son did not move or speak or show me any sign of recognition. I spoke to his back.

His windows overlooked the river, which glittered in the moonlight. "Your father loved the river," I said, fighting tears. "And you will love the sea.

"I will not see you again, Re-mose, and there will be no other opportunity to speak these words again. Listen to your mother, who comes to say goodbye.

"I do not ask you to forgive my brothers. I never did. I never will. I ask only that you forgive me for the bad luck of being their sister.

"Forgive me for never speaking to you of your father. That was your grandmother's command, for she saw secrecy as the only way to keep you from the agony that cuts you low today. She knew that the past could threaten your future, and we must continue to protect you against the accidents of birth. The true story of your parentage is still known only by you, me, and Zafenat Paneh-ah. There is no need to tell anyone else.

"But now that we share this secret, I will tell you something else.

"Re-mose, your father was called Shalem, and he was as beautiful as the sunset for which he was named. We chose each other in love. The name I gave you at my breast was Bar-Shalem, son of the sunset, and your father lived in you.

"Your grandmother called you Re-mose, making you a child of Egypt and the sun god. In either language and in any country, you are blessed by the great power of the heavens. Your future is written on your face, and I pray that you will have the fullness of years denied to your father. May you find contentment.

"I will remember you in the morning and in the

evening, every day until I close my eyes forever. I forgive your every harsh thought of me and the curses you may hurl at my name. And when at last you do forgive me, I forbid you to suffer a moment's guilt in my name. I ask that you remember only my blessing upon you, Bar-Shalem Re-mose."

My son did not move from his couch or say a word, and I took my leave, brokenhearted but free.

CHAPTER FIVE

Returning home was like being reborn. I buried my face in the bed linens and ran my hands over every piece of furniture, every garden plant, delighted to find things where I had left them. Kiya walked in to find me embracing a water jug. I sent her to tell Meryt I was home and then walked as fast as I could to Benia's workshop.

My husband saw me approach and rushed out to greet me. It seemed that we had been parted for years rather than days. "You are so thin, wife," he whispered as he held me in his arms.

"I fell ill in the city," I explained. "But I am healthy again."

We studied each other's faces. "Something else happened," Benia said, drawing his fingers across my forehead and reading something of the past days' shocks. "Are you back to stay, beloved?" he asked, and I understood the cause of the shadows beneath his eyes.

I reassured him with an embrace that earned us a

loud hoot from the men in the workshop. "I will be home as soon as I can," he said, kissing my hands. I nodded, too happy to say more.

Meryt was waiting with warm bread and beer when I returned to my house. But when she saw me, she cried, "What did they do to you, sister? You are skinny as a bone, and your eyes look as though you have wept a river."

I told my friend about the fever and of Re-mose's quarrel with his master. When my friend heard that he was posted to the north, her eyes filled in sympathy.

After we ate what Meryt had brought, she ordered me to the bed and massaged my feet. All the pain of the past weeks melted as she kneaded my toes and cradled my heels. After I was at peace and still, I asked her to sit by my side and I took her hand, still warm and moist with oil, and told her the rest of what had happened to me in Thebes, including how it came to pass that Zafenat Paneh-ah, the king's right hand, was my brother Joseph.

Meryt listened in stillness, watching my face as I recounted my mothers' history, and the story of Shechem and the murder of Shalem. My friend did not move or utter a sound, but her face revealed the workings of her heart, showing me horror, rage, sympathy, compassion.

When I finished, she shook her head. "I see why you did not tell me this before," she said sadly. "I wish I had been able to help you bear this burden from the very first. But now that you entrust your past to my keeping, it is safe. I know you need no oath from me, or else you would not have told me.

"Dear one," she said, putting my hand to her cheek, "I am so honored to be the vessel into which you pour this story of pain and strength. For all these years, no daughter could have made me happier or more proud than you. Now that I know who you are and what life has cost you, I am in awe that I number you among my beloved."

After a comfortable silence, Meryt gathered her things and prepared to leave. "I will go to give you time to prepare for Benia's arrival," she said, taking my two hands in hers. "Blessings of Isis. Blessings of Hathor. Blessings of the mothers of your house."

But before she walked out the door, my friend's face regained its impish grin and with a friendly leer she said, "I will call upon you tomorrow. See if you can't get off your back long enough between now and then to make me something to eat for a change, eh?"

Benia ran in soon after, and we fell upon the unmade bed like youthful lovers, breathless and hurried. Afterward, knotted in each other's clothes, we slept the famished sleep of reunited lovers. I awoke once in the night, startled and smiling, hating to close my eyes upon the joy of being home.

After my return, I never fully lost my reverence for ordinary pleasures. I arose before Benia to study his face and breathed silent prayers of thanks. Walking to the water fountain or pulling weeds in the garden, I was overcome by the understanding that I had spent a whole day without the weight of the past crushing my heart. Birdsong brought me to tears, and every sunrise seemed a gift shaped for my eyes.

When the vizier's messenger arrived at our door, as

I knew he would someday, I froze with dread at the thought of leaving for so much as a day, but to my relief, the letter did not summon me to the great house on the east bank. Joseph's dream had been fulfilled, and a second son was born to him. This one came so fast, however, that As-naat did not have time to send for me before the one called Efraem found his way into the world.

Even though I had rendered him no service, Zafenat Paneh-ah sent a gift of three lengths of snowy linen. When Benia asked me why the gift was so extravagant, I told him everything.

It was the third time I had given voice to the full story; first to Werenro, then to Meryt. But this time my heart did not pound nor my eyes fill as I told it. It was only a story from the distant past. After hearing me out, Benia took me in his arms to comfort me, and I nestled into the sheltering peace between Benia's hands and his beating heart.

Benia was the rock upon which my life stood firm, and Meryt was my wellspring. But my friend was older than I by a generation, and age was taking its toll.

The last of her teeth had fallen from her mouth, for which she claimed herself grateful. "No more pain," she chuckled. "No more meat, either," she said, with a doleful shrug. But her daughter-in-law, Shif-re, chopped and mashed every dish, and my friend remained hearty and enjoyed her beer and her jokes as much as ever. She attended many births with me, taking delight in newborn smiles, weeping over the deaths that came our way. We shared countless meals, and I always left her table chuckling. We knew her days were numbered and kissed each other goodbye at every parting. Nothing between us was left unsaid.

The morning came when Kiya appeared at the door to say that Meryt could not rise from her bed. "I am here, dear one, sister," I said when I arrived at her side, but my old friend could no longer give me greeting. She could not move at all. The right side of her face had collapsed, and her breathing was labored.

She returned the pressure of my fingers in her left hand and blinked at me. "Oh, sister," I said, trying not to weep. She stirred, and I could see that even though she was nearing death, Meryt was trying to comfort me. That would not do. I looked into her eyes and managed a midwife's smile. I knew my task.

"Fear not," I whispered, "the time is coming.

"Fear not, your bones are strong.

"Fear not, good friend, help is nearby.

"Fear not, Anubis is a gentle companion.

"Fear not, the hands of the midwife are clever.

"Fear not, the earth is beneath you.

"Fear not, little mother.

"Fear not, mother of us all."

Meryt relaxed and closed her eyes, surrounded by sons and daughters, grandsons and granddaughters. She sighed one long sigh, the wind through reeds, and left us.

I joined with the women in the high-pitched keening death song that alerted the whole neighborhood to the passing of the beloved midwife, mother, and friend. Children burst into tears at the sound, and men rubbed their eyes with damp fists. I was heartbroken but comforted by one of Meryt's last gifts to me, for at her deathbed I became one of her grieving family.

Indeed, I was treated as the oldest female relative and given the honor of washing her withered arms and legs. I swaddled her in Egypt's finest linen, which was mine to give. I arranged her limbs in the crouch of a baby about to enter the world and sat with her through the night.

At dawn we carried her to rest in a cave on a hill overlooking the tombs of kings and queens. Her sons buried her with her necklaces and rings. Her daughters buried her with her spindle, her alabaster bowl, and other things she loved. But the midwife's kit had no place in the next life, and it passed to the keeping of Shif-re, who held Meryt's tools with reverence, as though they were made of gold.

We buried Meryt with songs and tears, and on the way home laughed in her honor, recalling her delight in surprises, jokes, food, and all the pleasures of the flesh. I hoped that she would continue her enjoyment of these in the life to come, which she believed to be much like this world, only deathless and eternal.

That night, I dreamed of Meryt and woke up laughing at something she said. The following night I dreamed of Bilhah, waking to tears on my cheeks that tasted of the spices my aunt used in her cooking. One night later, Zilpah greeted me and we flew through the night sky, a pair of she-hawks.

When the sun set again, I knew I would meet with Rachel in dreams. She was as beautiful as I remembered. We ran through a warm rain that washed me clean as a baby, and I woke up smelling as though I had bathed in well water.

Eagerly I awaited my dream of Leah, but she did not come the next night or the night after. Only at the dark of the new moon was I visited by the mother of my flesh. It was the first time my body failed to give the moon her due. I was past giving life, and my mother, who had borne so many children, came to comfort me.

"You are the old one now," she said gently. "You are the grandmother, giving voice to wisdom. Honor to you," my mother Leah said, touching her forehead to the ground before me, asking forgiveness. I lifted her up, and she turned into a swaddling baby. Holding her in my arms, I begged her pardon for ever doubting her love, and I felt her pardon in the fullness of my heart. I went to Meryt's tomb the morning after Leah's dream and poured out wine, thanking her for sending my mothers back to me.

With Meryt gone, I was the wise woman, the mother, grandmother, and even great-grandmother of those around me. Shif-re, a new grandmother, and Kiya, about to be married, attended me wherever I went to place the bricks. They learned what I had to teach, and soon went on their own to deliver women from the fear and loneliness of birth. My apprentices became sister and daughter. In them, I found new water in the well I thought would remain forever dry after my Meryt died.

Months passed and years. My days were busy, my nights peaceful. But there is no lasting peace before the grave, and one night, after Benia and I had gone to bed, Joseph appeared inside our door.

* * *

The sight of him there, clad in a long black cloak that turned him into a shadow, was so strange that I thought him part of a dream. But the edge in my husband's voice woke me to the moment, suddenly dark and dangerous.

"Who comes into my house without knocking?" he growled, like a dog sensing danger, for this was clearly no distraught father in search of the midwife.

"It is Joseph," I whispered.

I lit lamps and Benia offered my brother the best chair. But Joseph insisted on following me back to the kitchen, where I poured him a cup of beer, which sat untouched.

The silence was thick and stiff. Benia's hands were clenched, for he was fearful that I was about to be taken from him; his jaw was locked, for he was unsure how to speak to the noble perched on a stool in his kitchen. Joseph sent me glances full of unspoken urgency, for he was unwilling to speak in front of Benia. I looked from one face to the other and realized how old we had grown.

Finally I told Joseph, "Benia is your brother now. Say what it is you came to say."

"It's Daddy," he said, using a baby word that I had not heard since Canaan. "He is dying and we must go to him."

Benia snorted in disgust.

"How dare you?" Joseph said, jumping to his feet and putting his hand on the dagger at his side.

"How dare you?" Benia replied with equal passion, stepping closer. "Why should my wife weep by the bedside of a father who murdered her happiness and his

own honor? A father who sent you to the long knives
of men known for their ruthlessness?"

"You know the story then," said Joseph, suddenly defeated. He sat down and put his head in his hands and
groaned.

"They sent me word from the north where my brothers and their sons tend the flocks of Egypt. Judah says
that our father will not live out the season, and that
Jacob wishes to give my sons his blessing.

"I do not wish to go," Joseph said, looking at me as
though I had some answer for him. "I thought I had
finished with my duty there. I thought I had even forgiven my father, though not without exacting a price.

"When they came to my house starving and seeking refuge, I twisted the knife. I accused them of theft
and forced them to grovel before the mighty Zafenat
Paneh-ah. I watched Levi and Simon put their foreheads
to the ground at my feet and tremble. I gloated and
sent them back to Jacob, demanding Benjamin be
sent. I punished our father for choosing favorites. I
punished my brothers, too, and kept them in fear of
their lives.

"Now the old man wishes to place his hands on the
heads of my boys, to choose them for his blessing. Not
the sons of Reuben or Judah, who have supported him
all these years and borne his moods and whims. Not
even the sons of Benjamin, the last-born.

"I know Jacob's heart. He wishes to atone for the
wrongs of the past by blessing my sons. But I fear for
them with such a birthright. They will inherit tor-
menting memories and strange dreams. They will come
to hate my name."

Joseph railed on as Benia and I listened. The hurts of the past clung to him, caught in the folds of his long dark cloak. He flailed around like a drowning lamb.

As he talked about fat years and lean years, about loneliness and sleepless nights, about how life had treated him so cruelly, I searched for the brother I remembered, the playfellow who listened to the words of women with respect and who once looked at me as his friend. But I saw nothing of that boy in the self-absorbed man before me, whose mood and voice seemed to change from moment to unhappy moment.

"I am a weakling," said Joseph. "My anger has not abated and I have no pity in my heart for Jacob, who has become blind, like his father before him. And yet I cannot say no to him."

"Messages get lost," I said softly. "Messengers are sometimes waylaid."

"No," Joseph said. "That lie would finally kill me. If I do not go, he will haunt me forever. I will go and you will come with me," said Joseph, suddenly shrill, a man accustomed to power.

I did not try to hide my disgust at his tone, and when he saw my contempt he dropped his head in shame. And then my brother bowed down with his forehead on the dirt floor of a carpenter's kitchen and apologized to me, and to Benia, too.

"Forgive me, sister. Forgive me, brother. I do not wish to see my father dying. I do not wish to see him at all. And yet, I cannot disobey. It is true that I can force you to go with me, and for no other reason than to hold my hand. But you will prosper in this, too."

He stood and resumed the demeanor of Zafenat

Paneh-ah. "You will be my guests," he said smoothly. "The master carpenter will do business on behalf of the king. I go to purchase timber in the north, and I require the services of an artist who knows how to select the finest wood. You will go to the marketplace of Memphis and see olive, oak, and pine in abundance, choosing only what belongs in the king's house and tomb. You will bring honor to your profession and to your own name."

His words were seductive, but Benia looked only at me.

Then Joseph brought his face close to mine and gently said, "Ahatti, this is your last chance to see the fruits of your mothers' wombs, their grandsons and granddaughters. For those are not only the children of Jacob; they are also the children of Leah, Rachel, Zilpah, and Bilhah.

"You are the only aunt of their mothers' blood, and our mothers would wish for you to see their grandaughters. After all, you are the only daughter, the one they loved."

My brother could talk the wings off a bird, and he talked until the sun rose and Benia and I were exhausted. Although we never said yes, there was no saying no to Zafenat Paneh-ah, the king's vizier, just as there had been no saying no to Joseph, son of Rachel, grandson of Rebecca.

We left with him in the morning. At the river, we were met by a barque of surpassing luxury, filled with chairs and beds, painted plates and cups, sweet wine and fresh beer. There were flowers and fruit everywhere. Benia was stunned at the riches, and neither of us could look into the faces of the naked slaves who waited upon us with the same servility they showed Zafenat and his two sons and their noble retinue.

The lads were old enough to grow their hair, and they were good boys, curious about their father's guests but polite enough not to ask questions. Benia delighted them by carving little creatures out of wood, and naming each one. He caught me watching him, and his plaintive smile told me that he had done the same for his own sons, dead long ago.

As-naat did not come with us, and Joseph never spoke a word of his wife. My brother was attended by a youthful guard, all of them as beautiful as he had been in his youth, and I often saw him staring at his handsome companions wistfully. He and I barely spoke on the voyage north. We took our meals separately, and no one suspected that the carpenter's wife had anything to say to the powerful vizier. When we did exchange words—to say good morning or to comment about the children—we never spoke in our mother tongue. That might have drawn attention to his foreign birth, which was a sore point among many in the king's service.

Joseph kept to himself at the prow of the barque under a gleaming awning, wrapped in his dark cloak. Had I been alone, I might have sat like him, reliving the journey that had brought me to the house of Nakht-re, where I became a mother, remembering, too, the loss of my son. Had it not been for Benia, I would have thought of the impending meeting with my brothers and opened the old wounds in my heart.

But Benia was always nearby, and my husband was

captivated by the sights of a journey that was, for him, like the gift of an extra life. He directed my eyes at the sails in the wind, or when the air was still, at the harmony of the rowers' oars. Nothing escaped his attention, and he pointed to horizons and trees, birds in flight, men plowing the fields, wildflowers, a stand of papyrus that looked like a field of copper in the setting sun. When we came upon a herd of water horses, his excitement was matched only by that of Joseph's boys, who crowded by his side to watch the children of Taweret splash and roar in the reeds.

On the third day of the journey, I set aside my spinning and sat quietly, watching the water lap against the shore, my mind as calm and wordless as the surface of the river. I inhaled the loamy smell of the river and listened to the sound of the water on the hull, which was like a constant breeze. I trailed my fingers through the water, watching them grow wrinkled and white.

"You are smiling!" said Benia when he came upon me.

"When I was a child, I was told that I would only find contentment beside a river," I told him. "But it was a false prophecy. The water soothes my heart and settles my thoughts, and it is true that I feel at home by the water, but I found my joy in dry hills, where the fountain is distant and the dust is thick." Benia squeezed my hand, and we watched Egypt pass, emerald green, while the sun sparked the water into countless points of light.

In the mornings and at sunset when the barque docked for the night, Menashe and Efraem would jump

into the water. The servants watched for crocodiles
and snakes, but my husband could not resist the boys'
invitation to join them. He removed his loincloth and
jumped in with a roar that was answered by childish
squeals. I laughed to see my husband dive under the
surface and shoot up again, like a heron, like a boy.
When I told Benia of a dream in which I was a fish, he
grinned and promised to make it so.

So one night, under a full moon, Benia put his finger to his lips and led me down to the water's edge.
Silently, he motioned for me to lie back in his arms,
where he held me effortlessly, as though I were as
light as a baby and he as strong as ten men. With his
hands, he coaxed and reassured me until I put my
head back and unclenched my hands and lay as though
on a bed. When I relaxed, my husband released me so
that I felt only his fingertips on my back, while the
river held me and the moonlight turned the water
silver.

Every night I grew bolder. I learned to float without
the support of my husband's hands, and then to move
on my back, facing the waning moon. He showed me
how to stay on the surface and swim like a dog, kicking and kneading the water for dear life. I laughed and
swallowed water. It was the first time I had frolicked
like a child since my son was a baby.

By the end of the journey north, I could duck my
head underwater and even swim side by side with Benia. Whispering on our pallet afterward, I told him
about the first time I ever saw anyone swimming, at the
river on our way out of Haran. "They were Egyptians,"
I said, remembering their voices. "I wonder if they were

comparing the water of that river with this just as I am tonight."

We turned to each other and made love as silently as fishes and slept like children rocking on the bosom of the great river, source and fulfillment.

At Tanis we left the river and began the journey into the hills where the sons of Jacob lived. In Egypt, farmers and even tanners were held in higher esteem than shepherds, whose work was considered the lowest and most odious of occupations. The official purpose of Zafenat Paneh-ah's journey was to conduct a census of the flocks and to select the finest animals for the king's table. In fact, this was a task beneath his station, the sort of thing usually assigned to a middle-ranked scribe. Still, it served my brother as an excuse to visit the relations he had not seen for ten years, since he granted them refuge from the famine in Canaan.

Traveling in Zafenat Paneh-ah's caravan was nothing like the journeys of my childhood. My brother was carried on a litter by his military bearers and his sons rode donkeys behind. Benia and I, who walked, were surrounded by servants who offered cool beer or fruit if we so much as raised a hand to shade our eyes. At night, we rested on thick pallets under pure white tents.

Luxury was not the only difference. This journey was very quiet, almost hushed. Joseph sat alone, his brow knit, his knuckles white on the arms of his chair. I was uneasy too, but there was no way for me to speak to Benia without being overheard.

Only the sons of Joseph were carefree. Menashe and Efraem dubbed their donkeys Huppim and Muppim and invented stories about them. They tossed a ball back and forth between them, and laughed and complained that their backsides were black and blue from riding. Had it not been for them, I might have forgotten how to smile.

After four days, we came upon the camp where the sons of Jacob lived. I was shocked by the size of it. I had imagined a gathering like the one in Shechem, with a dozen tents and half as many cooking fires. But here was a whole village; scores of women with covered hair scurried back and forth, carrying water jugs and firewood. Babies' cries rose up from the murmur of my mother tongue being spoken, shouted, and crooned in accents both familiar and unfamiliar. But it was the smells that brought me to tears: onions frying in olive oil, the musky dust of the herds mixing with the perfume of baking bread. Only Benia's hand kept me from faltering.

A delegation of the tribe's leaders walked forward to meet the vizier, their kinsman. Joseph faced them with his sons at his sides, flanked by his handsome guards. Behind them stood servants, bearers, and slave girls, and off to one side, a carpenter and his wife. Joseph's face was nearly white with anxiety, but he showed his teeth in a large, false smile.

The sons of Jacob stood before us, but I recognized none of these old men. The eldest among them, his face deeply lined and hidden by dirty gray hair, spoke slowly, awkwardly, in the language of Egypt. He delivered formal greetings to Zafenat Paneh-ah, their protector and savior, the one who had brought them to the land in peace and fed them.

It was only when he switched to the speech of his birth that I recognized the speaker. "In the name of our father, Jacob, I welcome you, brother, to our humble tents," said Judah, who had been so beautiful in youth. "Daddy is near the end," he said. "He is not always in his own mind and thrashes on the bed, calling for Rachel and Leah. He wakes out of a dream and curses one son, but in another hour blesses the same man with lavish praise and promises.

"But he has been waiting for you, Joseph. You and your sons."

As Judah spoke, I began to recognize some of the men behind him. There was Dan, with his mother's black, mosslike hair, his skin still unlined and his eyes calm as Bilhah's. It was no longer difficult to distinguish Naphtali from Issachar, for Tali was lame and Issachar stooped. Zebulun still resembled Judah, though he looked far less worn down by life. Several of the younger men, my nephews I guessed, recalled Jacob as he had been in his youth. But I could not guess whose sons they were or which might be Benjamin.

Joseph listened to Judah without once meeting his brother's eyes, which were fixed upon him. Even when Judah was finished speaking, Joseph did not reply or lift his head.

Finally Judah spoke again. "These must be your boys. What names did you give them?"

"Menashe is the older and this is Efraem," Joseph replied, placing his hands upon their heads in turn. Hearing their names, the boys looked up to their father, their faces shining with curiosity about what was being said in the strange-sounding tongue they had never before heard from their father's mouth.

"They barely understand why we are here," Joseph said. "I do not know myself."

Anger flashed across Judah's face, but it quickly changed to defeat. "There is no undoing the wrongs of the past," he said. "Still, it is good of you to give the old man a peaceful death. He lived in torment from the moment we called you dead, and he never recovered even after he learned you were still alive.

"Come," said Judah. "Let us go and see if our father is awake. Or will you eat and drink first?"

"No," Joseph answered. "Better to do it."

Taking his sons by the hand, Joseph followed Judah to the tent where Jacob lay dying. I stood with the rest of Zafenat Paneh-ah's servants and retainers, watching as they disappeared into the dusty village.

I was fixed to the earth, trembling, furious that not one of them knew me. But I was relieved, too. Benia led me gently to where the servants were setting up tents for the evening, and we waited there.

There was barely time to number my feelings before Joseph reappeared, with Menashe and Efraem, their eyes fixed on the ground in fear. My brother strode past me and into his tent without a word.

Benia could not coax me to eat that night, and although I lay down beside him, I did not close my eyes. I stared into darkness and let the past wash over me as it would.

I remembered Reuben's kindness and Judah's beauty. I remembered Dan's voice in song and the way Gad and

Asher mimicked our grandfather until I collapsed in laughter. I remembered how Issa and Tali wept when Levi and Simon tormented them and said they were interchangeable in their mother's eyes. I remembered how Judah once tickled me until I peed, but never told a soul. I remembered how Reuben used to carry me on his shoulders, from where I could touch the clouds.

Finally, I could lie still no longer and walked out into the night, where Joseph waited for me, pacing by the side of my tent. We walked away from the camp slowly, for there was no moon and darkness covered everything. After some distance Joseph flung himself onto the ground and told me what had happened.

"At first, he did not know me," my brother said. "Daddy whimpered like a tired child, crying, 'Joseph. Where is Joseph?'

"I said, 'Here I am.' But still he asked, 'Where is my son Joseph? Why does he not come?'

"I put my mouth to his ear and said, 'Joseph is here with his sons, just as you asked.'

"After many such exchanges he suddenly understood and grabbed at my face, my hands, my robes. Weeping, he repeated my name over and over and begged forgiveness of me and of my mother. He cursed the memory of Levi and Simon and Reuben, too. Then he wailed because he had not forgiven his firstborn.

"He named each of my brothers in turn, blessing them and cursing them, turning them into animals, sighing over their boyhood pranks, calling out to their mothers to wipe their bottoms.

"How horrid to grow old like that," said Joseph, with pity and disgust in his voice. "I pray I die before the day comes when I do not know if my sons are infants or grandfathers.

"Jacob seemed to sleep, but after a moment he called out again, 'Where is Joseph?' as though he had not already kissed me.

" 'Here am I,' I answered.

" 'Let me bless the boys,' said Jacob. 'Let me see them now.'

"My sons trembled at my side. The tent stank with his illness and his ranting had frightened them, but I told them that their grandfather wished to bless them, and I pushed them toward him, one on either side.

"He put his right hand on Efraem's head and his left hand on Menashe's. He blessed them in the name of Abram and Isaac, then sat up and roared, 'Remember me!' They shrank back and hid behind me.

"I told Jacob his grandsons' names, but he did not hear me. He stared, sightless, at the roof of the tent, and spoke to Rachel, apologizing for abandoning her bones at the side of a road. He wept for his beloved, and begged her to let him die in peace.

"He did not notice when I left with my sons."

As Joseph spoke, I felt an old heaviness return to my heart and recognized the weight I had carried during my years in Nakht-re's house. The burden was not made of sorrow as I had thought. It was anger that rose out of me and found its lost voice. "What of me?" I said. "Did he mention me? Did he repent of what he did to me?

"Did he speak of the murder of Shechem? Did he

weep for the innocent blood of Shalem and Hamor? Did he repent for the slaughter of his own honor?"

There was silence from the ground where Joseph lay. "He said nothing of you. Dinah is forgotten in the house of Jacob."

His words should have laid me low, but they did not. I left Joseph on the ground and stumbled back to the camp by myself. I was suddenly exhausted and every step was an effort, but my eyes were dry.

After Joseph arrived, Jacob stopped eating and drinking. His death would come within hours, days at the most. So we waited.

I passed the time sitting at the door of my tent, spinning linen, studying the children of Leah, Rachel, Zilpah, and Bilhah. I saw my mothers' smiles and gestures, and heard their laughter. Some of the connections were as clear as daylight. I recognized an exact copy of Bilhah in what had to be Dan's daughter; another little girl wore my aunt Rachel's hair. Leah's sharp nose was evident everywhere.

On the second day of Jacob's deathwatch, a girl approached, a basket of fresh bread in her hands. She introduced herself in the language of Egypt as Gera, the daughter of Benjamin and his Egyptian wife, Neset. Gera was curious to discover how a woman of my status sat and spun while the others who attended Zafenat Paneh-ah cooked and fetched and cleaned all day.

"I told my sisters that you must be nurse to the sons of the vizier, my uncle," she said. "Is it so? Did I guess well?"

I smiled and said, "You made a good guess," and asked her to sit down and tell me of her sisters and brothers. Gera accepted my invitation with a satisfied grin and began to lay out the warp and weft of her family.

"My sisters are still children," said the girl, herself still a few years away from womanhood. "We have twins, Meuza and Naamah, who are too young even to spin. My father, Benjamin, had sons in Canaan as well by another wife who died. My brothers are called Bela, Becher, Ehi, and Ard, and they are good enough fellows, though I do not know them any better than the sons of my uncles, who are as numerous as our flocks and just as noisy," she said, and winked at me as though we were old friends.

"You have many uncles?" I said.

"Eleven," Gera said. "But the three oldest are dead."

"Ah," I nodded, bidding farewell to Reuben in my heart.

My niece settled in beside me, drawing a spindle from her apron and setting to work as she unraveled the skein of our family's history. "The eldest was Reuben, son of Leah, my grandfather's first wife. The scandal there is that Reuben was found lying with Bilhah, the youngest of Jacob's wives. Jacob never forgave his firstborn, even after Bilhah died, even though Reuben gave him grandsons and more wealth than the rest of the brothers combined. They say my uncle wept for Jacob's forgiveness when he died, but his father would not come to him.

"Simon and Levi, also born of Leah, were murdered in Tanis when I was a baby. No one knows the whole tale there, but among the women there is talk that the two of them tried to get the better of a trader in some small matter. For their victim they chose the most ruthless cutthroat in Egypt, who killed them for their greed."

Gera looked up and saw Judah walking into Jacob's tent. "Uncle Judah, son of Leah, has been clan leader for many years. He is a fair man and bears the burdens of the family well, though some of my cousins think he's grown too cautious in his old age."

Gera went on, teaching me the story of my brothers and their wives, pointing out their children, reciting the names of nieces and nephews, flesh of my flesh, with whom I would never exchange a word.

Reuben had three sons with a wife named Zillah. His second wife, Attar, bore him two girls, Bina and Efrat.

Simon had five sons by the odious Ialutu, whom Gera remembered as an awful scold with bad breath. He had another son by a Shechemite woman, but that one walked into a flooded wadi and drowned. "My mother says he killed himself," said Gera in a whisper.

"That man over there is called Merari," she said. "The miracle in him is that he is a good fellow despite the fact that he was born to Levi and Inbu. His brothers are as bad as their father was."

A slack-jawed man shuffled up to Gera, who handed him a bit of bread and sent him away. "That was Shela," she explained, "Judah's son by Shua. He is feeble-minded, but sweet. My uncle had a second wife named Tamar, who gave him Peretz and Zerach, and my best friend, Dafna. She is the beauty of my family in this generation.

"Over there is Hesia," she said, nodding to a woman nearly my own age. "Wife to Issachar, son of Leah. Hesia is the mother of three sons and Tola, who has taken up the midwife's life. If Dafna is heir to Rachel's beauty, Tola has her golden hands."

"Who is Rachel?" I asked, hoping to hear more of my aunt.

"That is your master's mother," she said, surprised at my ignorance. "Though I suppose there is no reason for you to know her name. Rachel was the second wife, Jacob's beloved, the beauty. She died giving birth to Benjamin, my father."

I nodded, and patted her hand, seeing the shape of Rachel's fingers there. "Go on, dear," I said. "Tell me more. I like the sound of your family's names."

"Dan was the only son of Bilhah," Gera said. "She was Jacob's third wife, Rachel's handmaid and the one who lay with Reuben. Dan has three daughters by Timna, named Edna, Tirza, and Berit. All of them are kindhearted women; they are the ones who tend to Jacob.

"Zilpah was the fourth wife, handmaiden to Leah, and she bore twins. The first was Gad, who loved his wife, Serah Imnah, with a great love. But she died giving birth to her fourth child, her first daughter, Serah, who is gifted with song," said Gera.

"Asher, Gad's twin brother, married Oreet," she continued. "Their eldest was a daughter, Areli, who gave birth to a daughter last week, the newest soul in the family, whose name is Nina.

"Leah's Naphtali fathered six children upon Yedida, whose daughters are Elisheva and Vaniah. And of course, you know the sons of Joseph better than anyone," Gera said. "He has no daughters?" she asked.

"Not yet," I replied.

Gera caught sight of two young women and, pointing at me, nodded her head emphatically. "Those are two of the daughters of Zebulun, son of Leah. Their mother, Ahavah, produced six girls who are their own little tribe. I like it when they include me in their circle. It's a merry group.

"Liora, Mahalat, Giah, Yara, Noadya, and Yael," she said, counting out their names on her fingers. "They have the best gossip. It was they who told me the story of the Shechemite woman's son who killed himself. He went mad," she said, lowering her voice, "when he learned the terrible circumstances of his birth."

"What could have caused him such despair?" I asked.

"It's an ugly tale," she replied coyly, leaning in to whet my interest.

"Those often make for the best stories," I answered.

"Very well," Gera said, setting down her spinning and looking me straight in the eye. "According to Auntie Ahavah's story, Leah had one daughter who lived. She must have been a great beauty, for she was taken in marriage by a Shechemite nobleman, a prince, in fact. The son of King Hamor!

"The king brought Jacob a handsome bride-price with his own hands, but it wasn't enough for Simon and Levi. They claimed that their sister had been kidnapped and raped, and that the family honor was demeaned. They put up such a noise that the king, bowing to his son's great passion for Leah's daughter, doubled the bride-price.

"Still my uncles were not satisfied. They claimed it was a plot of the Canaanites to take what was Jacob's and make it Hamor's. So Levi and Simon tried to undo the marriage by demanding that the Shechemites give up their foreskins and become Jacobites.

"Now comes the part of this story that makes me think it is nothing more than a tale that girls tell each other. The prince submitted to the knife! He and his father and all the men in the city! My cousins say this is impossible, because men are not capable of such love.

"In the story, though, the prince agreed. He and the men of the city were circumcised." Gera lowered her voice, setting a dark tone for the sorrowful ending.

"Two nights after the cutting, while the men of the city groaned in pain, Levi and Simon stole into the city and slaughtered the prince, the king, and all the men they found within its gates.

"They took the livestock and the women of the city too, which is how Simon came to have a Shechemite wife. When their son learned about his father's villainy, he drowned himself."

My eyes had been fixed upon my spindle as she recounted the tale. "And what of the sister?" I asked. "The one who was loved by the prince?"

"That is a mystery," said Gera. "I think she died of grief. Serah made up a song about her being gathered by the Queen of Heaven and turned into a falling star."

"Is her name remembered?" I asked softly.

"Dinah," she said. "I like the sound of it, don't you?

Someday, if I am delivered of a daughter, I will call her Dinah."

Gera said nothing more about Leah's daughter, and prattled on about feuds and love affairs among her cousins. She chatted until late in the afternoon before thinking to ask about me, and by then I could excuse myself, for it was time for the evening meal.

Jacob died that night. I heard one woman sobbing and wondered who among his daughters-in-law wept for the old man. Benia folded me in his arms, but I felt neither grief nor anger.

Gera had given me peace. The story of Dinah was too terrible to be forgotten. As long as the memory of Jacob lived, my name would be remembered. The past had done its worst to me, and I had nothing to fear of the future. I left the house of Jacob better comforted than Joseph.

In the morning, Judah prepared to take Jacob's body to lie with his fathers in Canaan. Joseph watched as they lifted his bones onto his gold-covered litter, which he gave for the funeral voyage.

Before Judah left to put his father into the ground, he and Joseph embraced for the last time. I turned away from the sight, but before I reached my tent I felt a hand on my shoulder and turned to face Judah, whose expression was a map of uncertainty and shame.

He held out a fist to me. "It was our mother's," he said, struggling to speak. "When she died, she called me to her and said to give this to her daughter. I thought she was out of her mind," said Judah. "But she foresaw our meeting. Our mother never forgot you, and although Jacob forbade it, she spoke of you every day until she died.

"Take this from our mother, Leah. And may you know peace," he said, pressing something in my hand before walking away, his head hung low.

I looked down to see Rachel's lapis ring, Jacob's first gift to her. At first I thought to call Judah back and ask him why my mother had sent me the token of Jacob's love for her sister. But of course, he would have no way of knowing.

It was good to see the river again. After the heat of the hills, the embrace of the Nile was sweet and cool. And at night in Benia's arms, I told him all that I had heard from Gera and showed him the ring.

I puzzled over its meaning and prayed for a dream to explain the mystery, but it was Benia who gave me the answer. Holding my hand to the light and peering at it with eyes practiced at seeing beauty, he said, "Perhaps your mother meant it as a token that she had forgiven her sister. Maybe it was a sign that she died with an undivided heart, and wished the same for you."

My husband's words found their mark, and I recalled something that Zilpah had told me when I was a child in the red tent, and far too young to understand her meaning. "We are all born of the same mother," she said. After a lifetime, I knew that to be true.

Although the journey was uneventful and my hands were idle, I was exhausted by the trip home. I longed to return to my own house, to see Shif-re and Kiya's baby, who had been born during my absence.

I was terribly restless during the three days' stop in Memphis, but kept my impatience to myself because of Benia. He returned from the marketplace every evening, overflowing with the beauty he had seen. He exclaimed at the silkiness of the olive wood, the pure black of the ebony, the aromatic cedars. He brought back scraps of pine and taught Joseph's sons to carve. He bought me a gift too, a pitcher in the shape of a grinning Taweret that made me smile every time I looked at her.

The vizier's barque trailed a barge laden with fine timbers when we sailed out of Memphis for the last part of the journey to Thebes. Joseph and I said goodbye in the darkness of the last night. There was no need for sorrow at our parting, he said lightly. "This is only a farewell. If As-naat bears again, we will call for you."

But I knew we would not meet again. "Joseph," I said, "it is out of our hands.

"Be well," I whispered, touching his cheek with a hand that bore his mother's ring. "I will think of you."

"I will think of you, too," he replied softly.

In the morning Benia and I eagerly turned to the west. Once home, we resumed the order of our days. Kiya's new son was good-natured, and he learned to crow happily when his mother handed him to me on nights she went to attend at a birth. I rarely accompanied her past sunset, though, for I was growing old.

My feet ached in the morning and my hands were stiff, but still I counted myself lucky that I was neither feeble nor dull. I had strength enough for my house and to care for Benia. He remained strong and sure, his eye ever clear, his love for his work and his love for me as constant as the sun.

My last years were good ones. Kiya had two more babies, another boy and a girl, who took over my house and my husband's heart. We received countless sweet-breathed kisses every day. "You are the elixir of youth," I said, as I tickled them and laughed with them. "You sustain these old bones. You keep me alive."

But not even the devotion of little children can stave off death forever, and my time arrived. I did not suffer long. I woke in the night to feel a crushing weight on my chest, but after the first shock there was no pain.

Benia held my face between his great, warm hands. Kiya arrived and cradled my feet between her long fingers. They wept, and I could not form the words to comfort them. Then they changed before my eyes, and I had no words to describe what I saw.

My beloved turned into a beacon as bright as the sun, and his light warmed me through and through. Kiya glowed like the moon and sang with the green and solemn voice of the Queen of the Night.

In the darkness surrounding the shining lights of my life, I began to discern the faces of my mothers, each one burning with her own fire. Leah, Rachel, Zilpah, and Bilhah. Inna, Re-nefer, and Meryt. Even poor Ruti and arrogant Rebecca were arrayed to meet me. Although I had never seen them, I recognized Adah and Sarai as well. Strong, brave, wonderstruck, kind, gifted, broken, loyal, foolish, talented, weak: each one welcoming me in her way.

"Oh," I cried, in wonder. Benia held me even tighter

and sobbed. He thought that I suffered, but I felt nothing but excitement at the lessons that death held out to me. In the moment before I crossed over, I knew that the priests and magicians of Egypt were fools and charlatans for promising to prolong the beauties of life beyond the world we are given. Death is no enemy, but the foundation of gratitude, sympathy, and art. Of all life's pleasures, only love owes no debt to death.

"Thank you, beloved," I said to Benia, but he did not hear me.

"Thank you, daughter," I said to Kiya, who had put her ear to my chest, and hearing nothing, started to keen.

I died but I did not leave them. Benia sat beside me, and I stayed in his eye and in his heart. For weeks and months and years, my face lived in the garden, my scent clung to the sheets. For as long as he lived, I walked with him by day and lay down with him at night.

When his eyes closed for the last time, I thought perhaps I would finally leave the world. But even then, I lingered. Shif-re sang the song I taught her and Kiya moved with my motions. Joseph thought of me when his daughter was born. Gera named her baby Dinah. Re-mose married and told his wife about the mother who had sent him away so that he would not die but live. Re-mose's children bore children unto the hundredth generation. Some of them live in the land of my birth and some in the cold and windy places that Werenro described by the light of my mothers' fire.

There is no magic to immortality.

In Egypt, I loved the perfume of the lotus. A flower

would bloom in the pool at dawn, filling the entire garden with a blue musk so powerful it seemed that even the fish and ducks would swoon. By night, the flower might wither but the perfume lasted. Fainter and fainter, but never quite gone. Even many days later, the lotus remained in the garden. Months would pass and a bee would alight near the spot where the lotus had blossomed, and its essence was released again, momentary but undeniable.

Egypt loved the lotus because it never dies. It is the same for people who are loved. Thus can something as insignificant as a name—two syllables, one high, one sweet—summon up the innumerable smiles and tears, sighs and dreams of a human life.

If you sit on the bank of a river, you see only a small part of its surface. And yet, the water before your eyes is proof of unknowable depths. My heart brims with thanks for the kindness you have shown me by sitting on the bank of this river, by visiting the echoes of my name.

Blessings on your eyes and on your children. Blessings on the ground beneath you. Wherever you walk, I go with you.

Selah.

ACKNOWLEDGMENTS

I would like to thank Barbara Haber, curator of books at the Arthur and Elizabeth Schlesinger Library on the History of Women in America at Radcliffe College. At her suggestion I applied for a library fellowship at the Schlesinger, which was kind enough to support a project far afield from its stated mission. Radcliffe College also provided me with help from a wonderful undergraduate research partner, Rebecca Wand.

Thanks to the Women's Studies Department at Brandeis University for my appointment as visiting scholar, and to the Museum of Fine Arts, Boston, for permission to photograph the Statue of the Lady Sennuwy. Ellen Grabiner, Amy Hoffman, Renée Loth, and Marla Zarrow—the members of my writing group—provided three years of encouragement, careful reading, good advice, and friendship that sustained me. Long-distance colleagues Eddy Myers and Valerie Monroe held my hand (mostly via E-mail) before, during, and after.

Thanks to Larry Kushner, who introduced me to Midrash.

For their various contributions, thank you to Iris Bass, Professor Mark Brettler, Jane Devitt Gnojek, Judith Himber, Karen Kushner, Gila Langner at *Kerem* magazine, Barbara Penzner, David Rosenbaum, Janice Sorkow at the Museum of Fine Arts, Boston, and to Diane Weinstein.

Many thanks to my agent, Carolyn Jenks, for her belief in this book and for introducing me to Bob Wyatt, a thoughtful editor and full-fledged mensch.

My husband, Jim Ball, has been infinitely patient. My mother Hélène Diamant, and my daughter, Emilia Diamant, cheered me on. My brother, Harry Diamant, did me the good turn of introducing me to Carolyn Jenks. My father (whose memory is a blessing) always thought I would write a novel someday.